A PRICE TO PAY

Book 3 in the Harry Miller Trilogy

Joe Halliday

Copyright © 2023 Joe Halliday

All rights reserved

The characters and events portrayed in this book are fictitious. Any similarity to real persons, living or dead, is coincidental and not intended by the author.

No part of this book may be reproduced, or stored in a retrieval system, or transmitted in any form or by any means, electronic, mechanical, photocopying, recording, or otherwise, without express written permission of the publisher.

Cover design by Ana Marinovic

PART ONE

CHAPTER ONE

Stretching from the eastern shores of the Mediterranean across thousands of miles of land, Asia forms a vast and complex continent. Seen from space, the undulating landmass progresses gradually through shades of brown through to green.

The Philippines sit separate, the archipelago its own entity amidst several dark blue seas. Its most northerly and populated island, Luzon, is hundreds of miles from the rest of the continent and looks as if a large bite has been taken from its western flank. This forms the bay upon which Manila sprawls low and wide to the north, east, and south.

From high enough above, so that you only make out its main roads, Manila makes sense. Those thoroughfares are arranged logically. Descend further and the city becomes an impossibly intricate network of smaller streets splitting off from the larger ones, like capillaries from arteries. Keep descending, into those endless smaller streets which comprise the world's most densely-populated city, and you lose all sense of the whole.

Moving north along one of those major arteries in Taguig - a separate city of over eight hundred thousand still comprising part of the Manilan whole - was a long line of shining black metallic objects. The line was moving at considerable speed in the leftmost lane of Carlos P. Garcia Avenue, and other, smaller shining objects seemed to flee from its approach.

There were ten vehicles in the line, seven larger and three smaller. The latter were at the front, and Luuk Jansen sat in the passenger seat of the second SUV.

His left arm was upon the rest between himself and his driver. In his right hand he held a large pistol, the safety of which he flicked on and off. His face was set somewhere between a smile and a grimace and the veins in his neck and across his forehead bulged. His eyes moved back and forth between the road and the screen built into the dashboard, upon which a map of the city was centred on the convoy.

The car in front cut diagonally right without slowing, the vehicles in that lane braking suddenly and their drivers beeping as they narrowly avoided a collision. Jansen's driver accelerated into the gap to follow the leading SUV across the lanes then down the exit ramp.

They turned right at the bottom and entered Taguig proper. Jansen lifted his left hand and pushed the button on the small plastic component dangling below his earpiece. "One minute," he said, and nine voices replied in sequence.

After the final response Jansen glanced between the screen and the window. They were moving more slowly now. The road was narrow and layered with light brown dirt and the vehicle bumped over the uneven surface. On either side were small houses pressed together in a seemingly endless line. All were two storeys tall with corrugated iron roofs, and all looked old and tired.

It was midday and hot outside of the air conditioned interior of the car. Few people walked along the ruined sidewalks, but individuals and sometimes whole families could be seen sitting in the shade of their open doorways and staring out.

"Hell of a place to have your regional headquarters," the driver said.

"Hidden in plain sight," said one of the men in the back.

"Not something you could say for ours."

"And look where that got us."

Silence returned to the car as images of the so-called Organisation's attack in Singapore came to each man's mind. Jansen realised the leg on which his pistol rested was bouncing up and down, and stilled it. Between the travel and the equipment and the bribe to keep the police away, the operation was the most expensive he had ever been a part of. The funding had been a significant statement of trust in him from the higher-ups, especially coming so soon after his promotion.

Jansen saw his predecessor lying on the floor of the briefing room with the pool of blood spreading around her and felt the weight of the gun in his hand. Then he pushed the recollection away and cleared his throat.

"Thirty seconds. Everybody get ready," Jansen said, and half-listened to the series of acknowledgements. He checked his pistol and glanced again at the map. The decision to make the hit in broad daylight had also been his. It was a statement of intent, and he hoped it would be a defining one in winning the war.

Looking once more at the map, Jansen saw they were only one street away from their target. He forced himself to remember who he was, felt the nerves and doubts fading away, and found the familiar grin spreading across his face.

He pressed the button near his earpiece. "Lock and load, boys," he said, the car in front slowing for the final turn. "We're finishing these bastards once and for all." His words were met with a chorus of approval and swearing and Jansen felt the adrenaline begin to surge through him as they braked too then turned.

This street looked much like the others but for an unusually lengthy building halfway along and to their left. They were still too far away to see the faded sign, but from the surveillance leading up to the operation Jansen knew the building was supposed to be a garage. No cars ever went in or out, however, and the large sliding doors never opened. Only an innocuous entrance towards the left of the building's front was used, through which people came and went throughout the day and night.

After finishing its turn the car in front had quickly sped up. Jansen's driver put his foot down too and Jansen grabbed the handhold above the window as the engine whirred and the vehicle bounced violently over bumps and potholes. Glancing in the wing mirror he saw the rest of the convoy following behind in a perfectly spaced line, with the rearmost vehicles not yet turned onto the street.

They were flying down the rough road now with the cramped houses and old parked cars blurring past on either side, and were only a couple of hundred metres from the supposed garage, then one hundred. "Here we go," Jansen said, heart hammering and his grin broad. "Remember, the moment we stop, we're-"

He stopped mid-sentence as he saw the movement up ahead and to the right and put his finger to his earpiece once more and shouted, "Rooftop! Two o'cl-", but it was too late.

The man he'd seen had a weapon resting on his shoulder and had already aimed, and the projectile whooshed down trailing smoke on a direct line straight towards the leading SUV and struck the front with exquisite precision. The fuel in the engine ignited and the vehicle exploded, a fireball billowing up towards the cloudless blue sky.

Jansen's driver had begun to slow automatically. "Keep going!" Jansen bellowed at him. "Put us right behind it." The driver put his foot down again then slammed on the brakes when they were within stopping distance of the smoking husk of the lead car which had been destroyed almost directly opposite the far end of the garage.

"Everybody out. Right side." Jansen was already opening his door and the driver scrambled over to follow him. Looking left Jansen saw men streaming out from the small door beside the garage's main entrance. He put a few quick shots in that direction as his team joined him in the cover of their SUV and fired that way too.

Jansen glanced back and saw the rest of the convoy coming to a halt in a long line. More of the Organisation's men were already firing on them from the far side but the Company's operatives were calmly and swiftly exiting their vehicles and taking cover behind them as Jansen and his team had done. The larger trucks were stopping too and a half-dozen of Jansen's more heavily-armed men were jumping from the rear of each.

Crouched behind the bonnet of his car, Jansen looked to where the RPG had been fired from with his gun aimed upwards, and waited. It only took a few moments for the man on the roof to try his luck once more. Jansen squeezed the trigger. The bullet took the bastard straight through his head and he slumped forwards onto the low wall which ran along the edge of the rooftop.

They had expected heavy resistance, despite the street's innocuous appearance, and that was exactly what they had found. Seemingly every window and doorway and rooftop across the entire far side of the road, not only in the garage's two stories but in the houses to either side too, had been filled with impressive quickness by an enemy, and the barrage of gunfire was constant. Jansen's men were in a difficult position, but he trusted that they were better trained and certainly better equipped.

As he looked back along the line of his convoy Jansen saw a man crouched behind the bonnet of the next SUV taking quick and careful aim with a grenade launcher, heard the brief expulsion of air, watched the small object arc across the street and straight through an open window, heard the soft thud and an ensuing pair of screams. A couple of cars further along another operative, under the covering fire of his colleagues, had just set up a machine gun on the bonnet of his SUV. Steadying the weapon with one hand he squeezed the trigger with the other and let forth a torrent of fire which swept along the opposing rooftop, blasting apart the thin, crumbling wall there and ripping through the heads of two enemies who had been attempting to return fire. A rocket from an RPG flew from the far side of the street and struck one of the trucks, killing at least one man, but another of Jansen's machine guns answered immediately and filled the window from which the weapon had been fired with ten millimetre slugs.

The air was heavy with explosions and gunfire, shouts and screams. Even as the bullets thudded into the SUV behind which he was crouched, Jansen breathed in the metallic smell and let the smile spread across his face and the joy of battle fill him. He looked along the line of the dozens of men under his command, fighting and killing with such precision and professionalism, and thought what a beautiful life it was.

Fifteen minutes later the battle was over.

The far side of the street was in ruins and the ground was littered with debris and bodies and parts of bodies. Jansen's men had split into teams, most of which were sweeping the houses one-by-one. The occasional gunshot rang out as a survivor was found. There was no rush; they were still comfortably inside the window of time purchased from the police.

Jansen had sent his two best teams into the headquarters. They had encountered heavy resistance inside, as expected. Jansen was standing by the small door, getting an estimate on their casualties from a subordinate, when the man who had led the final assault emerged.

Jansen held up a hand to shut up the first man then turned to the second. "All clear?"

"Yes, sir."

"Anything left in there?"

"They were doing a good job of smashing the place up. There's still plenty we can look into, though."

Jansen looked around. "Where's the nerd?"

"Here, boss." The tech specialist had been lingering nearby and appeared at Jansen's side immediately.

"Get in there and start sniffing around. Work your geeky magic and bag anything that looks useful."

"Not yet."

Jansen had already been turning back to the operative who'd helped clear the building. He looked around again, not recognising the voice. The tech specialist had stopped in his tracks too. The three of them watched as another man approached.

He was dressed all in black. Unlike the rest of them he wore no bulletproof vest nor did he even seem to be armed. He wore long sleeves but there was no hint of sweat on his brow despite the heat. He was around six feet tall, and by the leanness of his face and the way his shirt hugged him there didn't seem an ounce of fat on his body, but still he looked strong. He had a short, military haircut and was clean-shaven.

Jansen would never have admitted to being intimidated in his life, internally or out loud, and that wasn't about to change. But the man produced a certain feeling in him. It was hard to meet the pale blue eyes set deep in the angular face as the newcomer stood there and stared at him. He noticed the two other men with him were leaning back a little.

"I'm going inside to study the surviving data before your men take it." Jansen guessed the man was British, but his voice was almost devoid of accent as well as inflection.

Recovering himself, Jansen let out a loud, fake bark of laughter. "That's not how it works around here. I give the orders, and you'll get your ass kicked if you try again. Who the hell are you? How did you even get here?"

The man was already reaching into his pocket. Thinking he was going for a gun, the two men beside Jansen both raised their weapons. The man noted their movements but didn't hesitate. He withdrew a phone, opened a simple communications app, and tapped the screen. The call was quickly answered. The screen now showed an anonymous portrait.

"Are you outside?"

"Yes."

"Is Mr Jansen there?"

Jansen recognised the cadence and voice masking software immediately. It was the man who had ordered him to kill his predecessor in Singapore. His throat felt suddenly dry as he realised he was speaking to one of the three people who ran the entire Company.

"I'm here, sir."

"The man in front of you is our single most valuable asset. His codename is Vocitus. Also known simply as the Assassin. You will give him everything he asks for, then stay out of his way. Is that understood?"

"With all due respect, sir, this is my-"

"Is it understood?"

Jansen glanced up. The man's pale blue eyes were fixed on his. He looked away again. "Yes, sir."

The call ended abruptly and the man put the phone away. His

eyes were still upon Jansen's. "I'm going inside to study the data."

Jansen grimaced, then spat on the ground. "Knock yourself out."

The man still stood there, staring. "Afterwards, you'll tell me everything you know about Daniel Miller."

The man finally looked away, and Jansen felt as if a burning spotlight had been taken off him. Unhurried, the man walked into the building.

Jansen watched him go and the door close behind him and found something deep in his stomach which he barely recognised. It was a sensation he hadn't felt in a long time, not even for a moment during the preceding battle. It was the feeling of fear.

CHAPTER TWO

"Tilt the rearview mirror down a moment, would you, Charlie?"

The driver did so, and Rupert Granville studied his reflection with some pleasure. He made a miniscule adjustment to his bow tie, replaced a wisp of hair which had escaped its styling, and nodded at himself.

"That'll do. Thank you."

Rupert settled back into the deep leather seat and looked out as they passed Marble Arch, then Speaker's Corner, without truly seeing any of it. They slowed and turned left, away from Hyde Park and onto Upper Brook Street before circling leafy Grosvenor Square and pulling up on the far side.

Rupert checked his watch. "No need to hang about," he said. "I'll take a cab home."

"Very good, sir."

Rupert gathered his coat around him then stepped out onto the pavement and into the cold night. He gave his driver a short wave and the Rolls Royce pulled away.

Rupert crossed the street towards the seven-storey red brick building. He was just looking over the blue plaque, stating that some important personage or other had lived there in the nineteenth century, when the varnished black door opened to reveal an elderly, liveried servant.

"Good evening. Rupert Granville. I hope I'm expected."

"Of course, Mr Granville." The man lowered his wizened stoop into a momentary bow, then closed the door behind Rupert. "I'll take your coat, sir. Ms Thomas will show you inside."

A younger servant was already approaching. She also bowed then turned for Rupert to follow. Rupert straightened his bow tie again as he was led along the red-carpeted corridor, the strains of a Mozart concerto wafting out to greet him. The corridor ended at a white door with elegant swirls carved into it, which Thomas opened before standing respectfully aside.

"Have a pleasant evening, sir."

The music crescendoed as Rupert entered the ballroom. It came from a grand piano in the far corner, which had been polished so exquisitely that light seemed to emanate from it. Large paintings of British landscapes and wealthy predecessors lined the walls, with elaborate brass light fittings affixed to the white wallpaper in between.

The brightest circle of light fell under an enormous chandelier in the centre of the room, which seemed to serve as the de facto hub for its inhabitants. Even from the doorway Rupert could see the house's owner there. Lord Mowbray was decked out in his finery, his wife and aristocratic acolytes surrounding him. Dozens of people fanned out from this heliocentric point, clustered into small groups of diminishing importance the further they were from their host.

Another man might have been intimidated by such scenes. Rupert had been raised in them. The only challenge, in this case, was to present himself in the correct manner.

Rupert lowered his chin an inch so that he was looking up at the room. He put his hands in his pockets, opened his eyes a little wider, and looked around as if lost. When another servant passed with a tray of champagne flutes he grabbed one immediately, and - in case anybody was watching - downed half in one go. He looked around again, playing the lost sheep to the best of his ability, and took uncertain steps towards the chandelier.

It didn't take long before Rupert was waylaid by Lord Hall, then Lady Chesterton, then one of the Prime Minister's old Eton classmates who Rupert recognised but didn't know. A cabinet colleague - Deborah White, a woman ten years his senior and in charge of a larger department - smiled through gritted teeth during the latter exchange. She had been arguing with the PM's friend when Rupert approached, and he heard the conflict quickly escalating again as he moved on.

The handshakes and smiles and kind words continued, and it became difficult - even for Rupert - to maintain the unprepossessing air, to make his smile shy, to shuffle uncomfortably at all the words of praise which he had craved for so long.

And then, suddenly, he was through the outer clusters and at the centre of it all. Lord Mowbray was engaged in conversation, but he had seen Rupert and his white, bushy eyebrows had briefly raised in recognition.

With practised skill, developed across many decades in such situations, Mowbray continued listening to the man beside him and appearing interested even as he glanced again at Rupert. He made some parting comment suggesting a prompt follow-up, then nodded, smiled, and shook the man's hand before turning towards Rupert.

"Well! If it isn't the man of the hour," Mowbray announced, holding his hand out.

Rupert gave a half-bow and a shy smile as he shook it. "Really, Lord Mowbray, you're far too kind," he said, matching Mowbray's patrician tones while still keeping his voice quiet. "For the invitation in the first place, never mind the compliment."

"Nonsense!" Mowbray blustered. "It might have been a safe seat, but an election's still an election, and winning is still winning. Then there's the real work, of course. I've rarely seen a young minister make waves so swiftly. Especially at one of the, ah… one of the less *heralded* departments. No offence intended, of course."

"None taken. Frankly, I'm shocked that such minor news has reached your ears."

"Oh, these old ears of mine still pick up most things worth hearing," Mowbray beamed. "One of the little privileges of being the party's largest donor, you know, is that people tend to keep you in the loop."

Rupert gave a low chuckle, as if the old man had said something profoundly witty.

"Knew your father, you know. Back at Eton."

"He mentioned you often, Lord Mowbray."

"Kept tabs on you, ever since you entered politics. From a distance, you know. Invariably been impressed with the news which reached me. Regarding your work for the party, and in other areas."

There had been the slightest of pauses before Mowbray said *and other areas*. Rupert met his eye directly then, and gave a firm nod.

"Anything for the cause, Lord Mowbray."

"Anything indeed. Wonderful! That's the kind of youthful, committed spirit we need." Mowbray held out his wrinkled hand again. "My congratulations once more, Mr Granville. You're off to a fine start. I have great expectations for your future."

Rupert shook the man's hand limply, his smile broad, as if the praise and well wishes were almost overwhelming. Then he nodded to Mowbray's wife and shook her hand too before tactfully withdrawing from the limelight.

Rupert looked around, genuinely unsure where to go this time, and met a pair of pale grey eyes across the room which were fixed upon his own. Lord Frost stood apart from the crowd, near to the piano. A woman in her early twenties hovered beside him but the two weren't talking. Frost gave a slight nod, and Rupert made his way over.

Frost was exquisitely dressed in an outfit which looked at least as expensive as Mowbray's. A champagne flute rested in his left hand, although it seemed untouched. He offered his right to Rupert, who gave his usual deferential bow as he shook it.

"A pleasure to find you here, Lord Frost."

"I'm sure. This is my niece, Judith."

"How do you do?"

The young woman bobbed a quick, old fashioned curtsy. She looked friendly and unsure of herself; she bore little resemblance to her uncle. Frost directed a look towards her.

"I'll just pop to the loo," she said quietly. Frost watched her hurry off then turned his eyes back onto Rupert.

"You seem to be enjoying yourself."

Rupert grimaced and shook his head. "I always excelled in drama, back at Harrow. This evening has demanded every ounce of my lingering acting ability. I'm really not one for such events, Lord Frost."

"No?" Frost's penetrating eyes searched Rupert's for a moment. "Well, many of the most prominent politicians feel the same, though you wouldn't guess it to look at them while they're glad-handing. Never was a problem with John, of course. Meeting and greeting, mingling with the high and low alike, was always one of his strengths."

"I'd heard the Prime Minister was attending tonight?"

"I advised him it would not be wise, under the current circumstances. The optics would be... unfavourable, when he's already under such pressure from the public. The common man has turned on John remarkably easily, in fact, with a little clandestine encouragement in that direction. You'd do well to remember how easily such a feat might be managed, by those with the necessary know-how."

Frost's eyes bored into Rupert's again. Rupert masked the genuine discomfort he felt and instead frowned and nodded gravely. "Indeed, Lord Frost. In politics, even the greatest fortresses are built upon beds of sand."

"Quite so." Frost continued to hold his gaze, then finally looked away and took a miniscule sip of his champagne. Rupert's own glass was empty, and he hurriedly exchanged it as a servant passed by.

Frost's eyes appeared to glaze over momentarily as he looked around the room. When he looked back to Rupert his face had softened very slightly. "If I'm hard on you, Granville, it's because I have hopes for your future. It's rare that I take an interest in such a young man. John was the last one, and that worked out rather well for him; although not, I fear, for our country."

"I'm incredibly grateful for the support you've already given, Lord Frost," Rupert said. "I'm sure that putting an unknown forward for the by-election cost you some considerable political capital. Any more help that you happened to provide would only be a bonus."

Frost gave another brief nod of uncaring acknowledgement at Rupert's gratitude. Then he leant forward a little. "I trust my judgement implicitly, Granville, which is why I was so... *perturbed* with your recent missteps," he said, voice lowered. "I speak, of course, of your utter failure to control Miller, and the subsequent destruction of the London operation. Your lack of liaising between the bank and the Company also, which must surely have contributed to our old contact's premature demise."

"All fair, Lord Frost. I can quite understand why your confidence was shaken."

"But," Frost said. "You've redeemed yourself swiftly and ably. You handled your duties in the brief campaign with aplomb, despite it being one of our safest seats."

Rupert fought to keep his face steady. He'd heard some variation of the phrase 'safe seat' in-person or online countless times already in the few days since the by-election, and one more might make him burst.

"Your new policy initiative was also eye-catching, and played well with press and public alike, which is all that truly matters. It made waves rarely seen at such a far-flung posting as the... What is it? The Department for Culture, Media and Sport?"

"'Digital' too, Lord Frost."

The older man gave the briefest of nods before continuing. "The recent interview with our mutual acquaintance, Ms Archer, also played brilliantly. It received a good deal of *traffic* online, or so I was informed. I presume you got back in touch with her after your first meeting?"

"I was only fortunate she hadn't published the results of our turgid first interview, which would have been an opportunity missed. An opportunity which you created, of course."

"It also seems you've made a strong first impression on our new representative from the bank."

"We've got a working relationship up and running, nice and quickly. I won't let this one slip away, Lord Frost."

Frost gave another brief nod then leant away again and surveyed the room. Rupert felt a buzzing in his pocket and took his phone out automatically. The message was from Yuri Tinkov. He was one of the Three, the trio which ran the entire

Company, and one of the most powerful people in the world.

A jolt of panic passed through Rupert. He swiped to the side to dismiss the preview of the message. It took a great deal of self-restraint to avoid looking up immediately to see whether Frost had noticed. Instead Rupert calmly locked his phone, put it away, took a sip of his champagne as he gazed around, then looked back at Frost.

The older man's eyes were piercing his. "Everything all right?"

"Quite all right."

"Nothing I need know about?"

Rupert got the impression that Frost saw straight through him, ignoring the words that he spoke and going instead straight to the source where he might discern the truth for himself.

"Something... personal, Lord Frost."

It was a calculated gamble. But after a couple more uncomfortable moments Frost's frown seemed to lift.

"As long as your own house is in order."

"It certainly is." Feeling the suspicion still radiating over him, Rupert cleared his throat. "Good news, about Manila."

For the very first time, Rupert saw a look of uncertainty flash across Frost's face. It was quickly gone, but there remained an unusual note in his voice when he spoke again. "Taken place already, has it?" Frost asked, looking away into the middle distance.

"My apologies. I was sure you'd have been kept abreast of-"

"No need to apologise, Granville," Frost said curtly. "I have a lot on my plate at any given moment, believe it or not. When I've got my supposed best man on a job, I don't feel the need to get into the weeds myself."

"Quite right too."

"I was aware that the… 'operation' was imminent. I simply hadn't heard of its conclusion."

"Of course. I'm pleased to say that it went swimmingly. Our competitor was dealt a blow which…" Rupert looked around. "Which we believe should be terminal."

"Glad to hear it."

Something caught Frost's eye. Rupert looked around and saw that Judith, Frost's niece, was standing beside a very elderly and wealthy-looking couple and beckoning him over.

"Duty calls." Frost held out his hand once more. "Congratulations on your fine week. Consider my trust in you strengthened once more." Frost leant closer again and spoke very softly. "Don't let it go to your head. You might be everybody's 'rising star' for now. But if gravity chooses to exert itself, that star can be pulled back to Earth very quickly and violently indeed." Frost gave his hand a final squeeze. "It would be such a shame to see you get burned up."

With that, the older man was gone.

Rupert stood and surveyed the room with one hand in his pocket while he worked through the rest of his drink. Then he covertly headed back towards the door, staying close to the wall. He had almost reached his destination when he felt a hand on his arm. Turning, he found himself face to face with his senior colleague in the cabinet.

"Ah," he said. "Deborah."

"Ah indeed." The older woman held an empty flute in her hand. It clearly wasn't the first she'd had. "And what should I call you? Starboy? Heir of Churchill? Lord Granville of Bloomsbury, MP?"

"I was actually just departing. But I'll see you in-"

"I don't want any of your precious time," she said, waving the empty glass. "I wanted to give you some advice."

"Please, enlighten me."

"You're playing with fire, Granville, and you don't have the equipment nor the experience to do so. It was all Frost, wasn't it, who made poor Terry Heath step down, after decades of hard constituency work?"

"Terry's health had deteriorated significantly, to the point where-"

"Oh, old Heath's still as strong as an ox. Frost wanted you elected, and that was the safest seat he could think to rig for you. The old man's attention is a blessing. But if you anger him, or try to go against him in any way, it'll be worse than any curse you could imagine."

Rupert met her eyes for several long moments. Then he nodded, and smiled. "Really must be off. See you at Number 10, Debbie."

Rupert had barely descended the steps back onto Upper Brook Street, and was just buttoning his coat against the chill wind, when his Rolls Royce pulled up. Rupert jumped in and gladly threw his coat off again as they pulled away.

"Charlie! You waited."

"Figured I'd give you an hour, sir, just in case. Save you the trouble of finding a cab."

"You're wonderful. Remind me to give you a raise."

"You just gave me one, sir, when I found the security badge for your office under the back seat."

"Very honest of you, Charlie. And you've had the heated seats on for me already. You're a God-send."

Granville took his phone out as they headed back towards Bloomsbury and opened Tinkov's message. He read through the contents twice, put his phone away, and started to plan.

CHAPTER THREE

Harry Miller ran his hand lightly over the two bright pink holes, one in his left shoulder and the other high in his chest, and felt them burn. He pictured the moment at which each projectile had entered his body and tried to imagine the tips puncturing his skin and driving their way deeper and deeper.

"Very attractive. Perhaps bullet holes can be the new tattoos."

Harry tensed and looked up quickly into the mirror. Unthinkingly, he'd left the bathroom door ajar. Anna had pushed it open and now stood watching him, leaning against the door frame with her arms folded. Harry forced himself to relax, and smiled at her reflection.

He took a fresh bandage from the shelf between the his-and-hers sinks. Anna came to take it from him and began applying it herself. She'd left her long, dark brown, blonde-highlighted hair loose and it fell in front of his face as she worked, the scent filling Harry's nostrils. He tilted his chin upwards and kissed her throat. She paused to kiss him back, then continued. She worked in silence and was done in a minute.

"Very professional."

"Clearly I've found my natural calling as a field nurse. Very much the opposite of what I've been doing thus far with my life."

"It's never too late to change. How are Tasha and Maria?"

"I just got off the phone with them. Maria's exhausted, being back on full-time parent duty at her age, poor cow." Anna's face fell suddenly. "I wish…"

"I know." Harry took her hand and kissed it. "It won't be long now."

"Being here in the Chilterns has changed you, Captain Miller. What's this sudden mania for saying things that sound nice, but which you clearly don't truly believe?"

"It doesn't suit me?"

"It almost makes me long for your wild rampage, when all you did was grunt. No, it doesn't suit you one jot, and I'll kindly remind you that I'm not a weak-willed maiden who needs to be molly-coddled, sugar-coated, and all the rest of it."

"Fine. You'll never leave your life of violence, and I've got no idea whatsoever when you'll see your family again. Happy now?"

"Delighted."

"Hand me those, would you?"

Anna passed the clippers over from where Harry had left them on the side of the enormous bath. He caught the look in her eye.

"Yes?"

"Nothing. Nothing whatsoever, Captain Miller. There's nothing at all strange about a grown man cutting his own hair rather than shelling out a tenner for someone to give him a quick shear."

Harry checked the number two guard was attached and flicked the switch. The clippers buzzed into life and he went to work on the right side of his head.

"You're barely even taking anything off. That's another thing."

"Don't you have somewhere else to be?"

"Absolutely nowhere, actually."

Anna stood beside Harry, watching him in the mirror with a

bemused half-smile on her lips while he tried to concentrate on the task at hand. His eyes kept flicking over to meet hers, and when they did a smile would cross his face too.

"You've got hair on you," Harry said, as he swapped to a four guard and began on the top of his head.

"We can take a shower when you're done," she replied, running a finger along the top of his uninjured right shoulder.

"There's a very important meeting to attend, in case you'd forgotten."

She moved her hand so that it was underneath his arm, then flat on his chest, then trailing downwards. "The fate of the world can wait a few minutes. Don't you think, Captain Miller?"

At that moment, Daniel Miller appeared beside the open door. Harry caught his eye in the mirror, saw the look on his face as he immediately turned to retreat, and burst out laughing. "Wait."

Daniel paused, his enormous frame filling the doorway. "I'll come back later."

"Stay," Anna said. "I'm not wanted here anyway."

"Are you done with the clippers?"

Anna snorted again. "What a family." Briefly she kissed Harry on the cheek, then Daniel stood aside to let her pass.

Harry lopped off a stray strand of hair near his crown. He turned off the clippers, checked himself over briefly, and nodded. "Come on," he said, looking at Daniel in the mirror. Daniel looked back at him. "Come on," he said again. "It's much easier having someone else do it."

Daniel hesitated, then came forward to stand by the sink. Harry took the t-shirt he'd discarded to check his wounds and put it around Daniel's neck and shoulders. He changed the guard, turned the clippers back on, and went to work.

Daniel had been back in Britain several days. But this was the first time they had been alone together longer than a few moments. For the first minute there was silence but for the buzzing which pitched higher and lower.

Daniel had rarely initiated a conversation, even before everything had changed. Harry had previously started the ball rolling without thinking twice, but now he found a mental block. There were a hundred things they could and should and must talk about, but the act of broaching them felt monumental. The slew of regular, everyday topics which he could introduce instead seemed foolish by comparison.

Harry finished the back and sides and changed the guard. He started the clippers again and shook his head briefly at his own pathetic weakness.

"This bathroom is bigger than some people's flats," he said, waving the clippers generally around the expansive, marble-white space. "Interesting to see how the other half live, isn't it?"

"Where does his money come from?"

"The Granville fortune? I never asked. Nowhere good, I'm sure."

"Do you trust him?"

Harry ran the clippers over Daniel's head without answering. "I suppose so," he said at last. "Although I'm as surprised to say that as you must be to hear it."

"Why?"

"He's given me no direct reason not to. And it makes sense he'd feel guilty for being involved in all that stuff for so long." Harry broke off as he remembered who he was talking to. But Daniel was still looking straight ahead and his face remained impassive. "Perhaps he's got his own objectives. He doesn't hide his political ambitions. But as long as they dovetail with our plans, there shouldn't be a problem."

Harry's phone buzzed on the sink. "Talk of the devil," he said, eyes passing swiftly over the message. "Granville's heading over. When he gets here, we can finally figure out how the hell the five of us will take down a multinational criminal enterprise with unlimited resources."

"You'll find a way."

Harry looked at him in the mirror. His brother's voice had been typically devoid of emotion, but for once he met Harry's eyes. Harry smiled, gave a brief nod as a feeling swelled in his chest, then finished up the haircut.

Harry and Daniel descended the main staircase and crossed the central atrium into the vast kitchen. Finding it empty, they went back across the entrance hall and into the even larger living room.

All the vestiges of old British wealth could be found there, from a grand piano in one corner to a sizable drinks cabinet in another. The walls were lined with paintings by contemporary artists, all of them originals. In the centre of the carpeted room four large sofas were arranged in a square with an enormous coffee table between them.

Anna lay on one of the sofas, holding a newspaper above her, while Noy and Sarah Miller sat on another. The three of them were talking and barely looked up as Harry and Daniel entered.

"So this only his second house? Not even live here? Not really?" Noy asked.

"Second, third, fourth," Sarah shrugged. "Who knows?"

"The one where my grandmother and daughter are hiding out is almost as big."

Noy turned to Anna. "This normal, in England?"

"Definitely not."

"How many houses you have, Mrs Miller?"

"Sarah, dear, for the hundredth time. And only the one, you'll be shocked to know. I'm quite the pauper."

"What's a pauper?"

"A poor person. We're all paupers compared to Rupert Granville."

"How he get so many houses?"

"Aristocratic wealth, I suppose. Family money."

"His father give them to him?" Noy screwed up her face. "All my father give me was my name and a job cleaning plates in Chiang Rai. Work twelve, sixteen hours a day, then send the money back home."

Sarah put her hand on Noy's knee. "You can choose your friends, but not your family. Certainly not your parents, for better or worse."

"You can say that again," Anna said, flicking through the pages of her paper. "We'll have a summit one day, Noy, and try to work out whose father was the bigger bastard. But I'll warn you I'm a heavy favourite."

Sarah had looked around at Harry and Daniel when she finished talking, and her eyes lingered on them. Her smile returned as she looked back to Noy. "Some people simply hit the jackpot, and few hit bigger or better than Rupert."

"Still unfair, no? He do nothing to deserve this." Noy held up a hand. "Nice man. I don't say bad things about him, even if I don't understand his accent. But still, doesn't deserve it."

They all heard the heavy front door closing, then Granville appeared at the living room doorway. "Ah!" he beamed, looking around the room. "We're all gathered, then. Wonderful to see a few friendly faces at last, I must say. There were precious few at Downing Street, I can tell you." His expression dropped slightly. "Weren't talking about me, were you?"

"Yes, we were," Noy said.

"Ah, well, I..." Granville blustered, as Anna laughed behind her newspaper. "Nothing *too* nasty, I take it?"

Noy pulled a face, but Sarah held up her hand. "Not at all, Rupert. Noy was just asking about your property portfolio, and how you came by it."

"Ah," he said again, and adjusted his tie slightly. "Well, to cut a very long story short, the nineteenth century was rather kind to the Granville family. The eighteenth century wasn't too shabby either, truth be told. I'd be happy to talk you through it all, if-"

"Another time, Rupert," Harry said. "When there's literally nothing else to talk about. We have more pressing concerns."

"Of course. Quite so. I'll slip into something more comfortable, have a quick bite to eat, then we'll get straight to it. Fix me a drink while I'm gone, would you, old chap? Nothing like a touch of booze to put one's lateral thinking facilities in full flow."

CHAPTER FOUR

Half an hour passed before Granville reappeared. His 'more comfortable' outfit consisted of a different pair of pressed trousers and a collared shirt; the sleeves of which, at least, were rolled up.

Harry had Anna's long legs resting in his lap, while Daniel sat largely silent on the sofa opposite Noy and Sarah. It was only around four o'clock, but the winter sun was already setting through the large windows and double doors at the far end of the room, all of which looked out onto the expansive grounds.

Granville looked around at the company as he entered, eyes lingering on the drinks held by everyone except Daniel. "Delighted to see you've all made yourselves comfortable."

"Firstly, we knew you'd take forever," Anna said. "Secondly, we're not 'the help', I'm afraid, though I can see how easily you might make that mistake."

Granville's mouth opened and closed a couple of times. "Ms Cavill, you're a *guest* here. If I ever made you feel as if-"

"She's joking, Rupert," Harry said. "Now make yourself a drink and let's bloody well get on with it."

Noy stood up as ice tinkled into a glass in the far corner of the room, walked around the coffee table with her drink in hand, and sat down beside Daniel. She took his hand in hers without looking and sipped her drink. Daniel looked down at her hand, then at her, and smiled.

Harry watched his mother. He hadn't seen her talk to Daniel alone since arriving in the Chilterns either, and her eyes only flickered towards him now then away again.

Granville seated himself in the space beside Sarah which Noy had just vacated. He took a sip of his whiskey, smacked his lips, and looked around expectantly. "Who wants to get the ball rolling, then?"

Harry looked towards Sarah. "Are you sure you want to stay for this, Mum? Once you've heard what we discuss here, you'll be-"

"I'll be what? 'Implicated'?" Sarah met his gaze while the glass in her hand trembled slightly. "They took us from our bed during the night, Harry. They killed your father. Not to mention everything else they seemingly get up to, of which I keep hearing hints. I'm perfectly willing to be implicated in any plan which harms these evil men and women."

"Just thought I'd check." Harry gently lifted Anna's legs off him and leant forward with his whiskey glass clasped in both hands. "Let's get to it then. Rupert, lead us off. Tell us who we're up against."

Granville cleared his throat. "Very well. The group is popularly - if I can use that term - known as 'the Company', although it has no formal title. Officially, it doesn't exist. Everyone in this room, however, knows that not to be the case. In reality, the Company is a multinational organisation specialising in people trafficking. Its focus is on Asia, particularly the southeastern region. It's very much present in Africa and South America too, however, with the victims in each case typically transported northwards. In total, this accounts for billions of dollars in profits each year."

"How is that possible? I've never even heard a whisper of it," Sarah said. "Who's in charge?"

"You've never heard a whisper, my dear, because if one ever begins to waft out then it is immediately silenced. As to who's in charge, they're usually referred to as 'the Three' or even 'the

Trinity'. For them, the world is divided into a trio of simple sections. One member of the Three oversees the operations in the Americas, Europe and Africa, and Asia and Oceania respectively."

"And specifically?"

"We only know the identity of one, Yuri Tinkov. And that merely by proximity, since he's headquartered in London. Another man runs the Americas, I believe from New York, but I've no idea who. Nor do I have a clue who's in charge out east."

"It's a woman," Noy said. "I overhear someone mention her once, in the compound. Right, Farang?"

"That's the rumour. The regional headquarters are in Singapore. But she's supposedly based in Hong Kong."

"Well, there you are," Granville beamed. "Information sharing at its finest. Anything to add, Ms Caville?"

"Not a huge amount," Anna said. "The Three are supposed to be completely equal partners, but I did hear that the eastern member holds the most sway. Rumour has it she's the one who really got the whole thing going, back in the nineties."

"I heard the same," Daniel said.

"And what happens to all these billions they make?" Sarah asked the room at large.

"That's where our multifaceted friend comes in," Anna said, nodding towards Granville. "Or should it simply be multi-faced?"

Granville turned to Sarah with a grave face. "I'm afraid I was indeed caught up in that unsavoury side of things," he said. "But I was younger and more unapologetically ambitious then, and I-"

"Nobody asked for your life story, Granville," Anna said. "And nobody ever will, for future reference. Where does the money go?"

"Indeed, yes. Thank you." Granville took a larger sip of his whiskey than usual. "That's where it gets a little more… complicated. People trafficking is as old as time itself. That certainly doesn't make it right, but it's true. Its contemporary illegality, combined with a globalised modern banking system, has given rise to an absolutely enormous secondary industry of money laundering. A significant portion of this takes place with what we'd call 'high street banks' - the big brands, with whom we have our current accounts, mortgages, and so on."

"Surely not," Sarah said. "We'd have heard about it."

"That was my reaction exactly," Harry muttered. "Only one bank has been caught for it, apparently, and even that story isn't widely-known."

Noy was watching the conversation with interest. She turned to Daniel and asked for a translation of 'money laundering'. Sarah's eyebrows briefly raised when her son replied, still not used to him speaking Thai, before she looked back to Granville.

"There's another layer to all this, I'm afraid," he said, frowning into his now-empty glass. Harry stood and went to top him up as Granville continued. "The banking system and the government are inextricably intertwined. Neither can function without the other."

"You're not saying that some members of the government know about all this?" Sarah said.

Anna snorted. "Swap 'some people' for 'everyone who matters', and 'know about' for 'are wrist-deep in', and you've hit the nail on the head."

"Maintaining good relationships with the banks is vital for the government," Granville said, nodding to Harry who passed him a fresh glass of whiskey before settling back on the sofa. "Over eight percent of the country's GDP is generated through financial services. The sector itself is worth some 130% of the nation's entire output."

"Not to mention the kickbacks and all the other perks the politically powerful get from these 'relationships'," Anna said. "No offence, Granville."

"You worked for the banks?"

Granville avoided meeting Sarah's eyes over the top of his glass. "I was appointed as the liaison between the government and one of the nation's biggest banks, in charge of maintaining that... special relationship we've been discussing. A role I still hold, in addition to my cabinet posting and - thus far admittedly lacklustre - constituency work, although not for much longer if all goes to plan."

"And what is this plan?" Noy asked. "Everybody know who the enemy is. Everybody already know how big and powerful they are. Question is, when are we going to stop sitting around on big sofas, drinking cocktails in fancy houses, and stop them." She considered the drink in her hand. "I don't complain about the cocktails. Delicious. But still, we have a job to do, no?"

Harry leant forward again, nodding. "I've thought about it a lot these past few days. We need to cut the head off the snake. We need to go straight for the Three. The unholy Trinity."

Noy was the first to speak. She looked around at the others, then shrugged. "Well I like this plan," she said.

"Yes, it's truly a thing of genius," Anna said. "All we have to do is kill three of the richest, most powerful, most brutal men and women in the entire world. Not that we know where any of them are, nor even know the names of two. That aside, it's the perfect plan."

"I didn't say it would be easy, but I don't see any alternative. We'd never be able to dismantle the entire physical infrastructure of the Company with so little firepower or manpower. Certainly not before they reacted and blew us away. In fact, we need to use our lack of numbers to our advantage."

"Guerilla warfare," Daniel said quietly.

"Exactly."

"That's all well and good," Anna said. "But how will it work on a practical level? If we kill one leader, even part of the very top brass, another will step up to take their place."

"My thoughts exactly, Ms Cavill."

"Thank you, Mr Granville," Anna replied, nodding with mock gravity.

"You might think so, sure," Harry said. "But it doesn't work that way. Look at the most dangerous terrorist organisations in the past couple of decades. At one point it seemed as if each was dominant. Unstoppable. But as the leadership was taken out, one by one, each began to crumble. That's what we're aiming for, but we need to do it quickly. Very quickly. Speed is of the absolute essence. That's why we need to cut the head off the snake, effectively in one go, rather than going about it piece by piece."

Daniel grunted his approval, his eyes fixed on Harry now.

"The Three, still presumably in their original iteration, have been running this operation for a while now. Perhaps over two decades. If one was removed, the other two would surely groom somebody to take their place, but it would take time. They'd be taking over a hell of a job. If we can remove all three, quickly enough, who in the world could step into that void and hold the whole thing together?"

Anna tilted her head from side to side with her bottom lip sticking out. "It's not the worst idea in the world," she said at last.

"That's sweet. Thank you."

Noy's brow was more furrowed than usual. "What is it?" Daniel asked.

"It's a good plan. Not bad at all. Your brother is smart, like me. But this plan only deal with the Company."

"Meaning?"

"Meaning, Farang, even if we stop this group, someone else just start to do the same thing. The Organisation, maybe, your old bosses - not doing so good right now, but maybe they come back. Maybe someone else entirely. You guys want revenge on the Company. Okay. But this plan doesn't stop the big problem. Doesn't stop thousands or millions of people like me being taken, being sold."

Harry considered, frowning and annoyed with himself. Given a specific problem to solve, particularly on an operational level, the solutions had come to him effortlessly. Thinking of the wider issue, or any ensuing consequences - as Anna had once told him in no uncertain terms - was not his strong suit. "Good point," he conceded at last.

"We can't go around blasting away the leader of every criminal enterprise across the globe that might fill the void," Anna said. "Taking out the Company's three overlords in rapid succession is already borderline impossible."

There was silence in the room for a full minute. The light outside the windows had faded entirely now and rain began to patter against the glass.

"You won't need to." To Harry's surprise it was his mother who spoke. "Expose the entire thing publicly, with enough unassailable proof, and surely the system will be brought crumbling down. At the moment, your plan is utterly clandestine. Not that that's a criticism, dear."

"Thanks, Mum."

"But Noy is right. It won't have a wider, longer-lasting impact. To do that, you have to let the whole world know exactly what's going on." Sarah looked around, and caught Granville's expression. "Something wrong, Rupert? If my thoughts are foolish go right ahead and tell me."

"Of course not. What you say is perfectly logical."

"Then what?"

"He dislikes the thought of where that would lead," Anna said. "Namely, straight to the British government, not to mention any others around the world, and I'm positive there are many, who may be complicit."

"My motives aren't for self-preservation."

"You're sure about that?"

"Yes!" Granville's voice was pitched high and his face was growing pink. "Come now. I won't be painted as a villain simply for stating that we must think of the repercussions. The people's trust in their government would be utterly destroyed."

"And justifiably so, if all this is true, wouldn't you say?" Sarah asked.

"Entire sections of the governmental and financial worlds could be brought down."

Noy made a loud scoffing noise. "And?" she asked. "These big systems make guys like you a lot of money, and make a lot of other people suffer. Not good for you, and people like you, if they get blown up. You the ones who lose power and money. Maybe your country lose some money too, who knows. But better overall, for whole planet, right?"

"Definitely," Harry said. "Everybody else? I'd prefer a unanimous agreement, if nobody has a better idea."

"Count me in," Anna said. Sarah, Noy, and Daniel all nodded.

"Rupert?"

"I'm not against the idea at a base level, you understand. Morally, I'm in full support. It's the consequences that I fear."

"Understood, but we have to do something, and this is the best plan we've got. So it's a simple question. Yes or no?"

"Very well. I agree we should take it public, though *preferably* in a way which doesn't destroy the entire economy. This does raise another question, I'm afraid, as to how we're actually planning to release the information."

Silence descended again, but it was soon broken by Anna. "The journalists," she said. "The ones in Thailand."

"Which journalists?"

"The British ones who were investigating the Company, dullard," she said, whacking Harry across his shoulder. "One of them had already... disappeared." Both the pause in her speech and the look she directed towards Daniel were brief, but they were there. Harry's gaze went automatically to his mother to see if she'd caught them. She had followed Anna's glance and her own eyes now rested on her younger son. "But the other was still in the country," Anna said. "Being dispatched to find him was how we first met, if you recall."

"They sent a helicopter and a small army of mercenaries to invite me on board," Harry said. "How could I forget?"

"Ultimately the journalists failed. But they'd done good work before then."

"Which was subsequently taken from them."

Harry met Anna's eyes now, and he knew they both pictured Michael Williams, on his knees and begging for his life before the barrel of Anna's gun. Anna's mouth opened then closed.

"True," she said eventually. "But that doesn't mean it's gone for good."

"Why?"

"Remember the person on the phone... that night? The one from the Company, giving the orders? She's a big fish. Highly-trusted. Rumour was, before being put in charge of such operations, that she'd helped set up the Company's data centre."

"They have a data centre?"

"Obviously I never climbed high enough through the ranks to visit, nor have a clue where it was based. But there's supposedly a facility in which all the Company's most sensitive data is kept."

"They mentioned a data centre in passing," Daniel said. "During one of the meetings in Singapore."

"Any idea where it is?"

"Only that it's in Asia."

"Pretty big place." Harry ran a hand across his freshly-cut hair as he considered. "It's as good a lead as any. Williams and the other one - Jennifer Braithwaite was her name - had been going after the Company for a long time, I believe. Their research could be invaluable. If we gather as much evidence as we can while going after the Three, and put it all together, that should do it. Rupert, have you got any media contacts who could make the actual leak, when the time comes?"

"One, but it's very early days. I'm yet to discern the extent to which I can trust her."

"You've factored the part about us having no idea where the data centre is into your plans?" Anna asked. "Along with the fact that it will be incredibly well-guarded, and extremely difficult to enter, never mind steal from?"

"I have."

"Just checking."

"We'll figure that out later. For now, we have our plan. We take out each of the Three in turn, as quickly as we possibly can before they have time to react. We'll gather evidence, acquire the research collected by Williams and Braithwate too, then release it all together to expose the wider system."

"And be back home for Christmas," Anna said. "It all sounds so straightforward, when you put it like that."

"I'm a straightforward guy."

"Don't I know it."

"Very good, your brother," Noy said to Daniel. "Very, how do you say…" She asked him in Thai.

Daniel considered. "Can-do."

"Very *can-do*!" she repeated, in an exaggerated English accent.

"One last point," Harry said. "I've received a message from an old squadmate, McGinn. He doesn't know all the details yet, but he's willing to help me, whatever I'm doing. We fought together for years, through thick and thin, and I'd trust him with my life. Any objections?" He looked quickly around the room. "Good. Now we just need to decide which of the Three to start with."

"Tinkov," Daniel said. "He's the closest. And we know the most about him."

"Agreed, although I'm assuming he's gone to ground since our little run-in, if he's got any sense at all."

"More than that, old chap," Granville said. "He's left the country entirely. He's fleeing to the safety of Mother Russia's ample bosom."

"Ah."

"And how exactly do you know the movements of Yuri Tinkov?" Anna asked.

"He told me."

"Naturally."

"Tinkov seems to have taken a shine to me, during our meeting in London."

"Of course he did. Who could blame him?"

"We've been in communication ever since. Liaising, you might say." He turned back to Harry. "I believe that he's taking a roundabout route, however, and enjoying a little winter sun before returning east to frigid Moscow."

"Where?"

"Barcelona."

"Ooh," Noy said, turning to Daniel. "I always want to go to Barcelona."

"So we'll get him there," Harry said, voice filled with unaffected confidence. "Everything gets ten times harder if he makes it back to Moscow. How long will he be in Barcelona?"

"Three more days, I believe."

Harry swore under his breath, then quickly apologised to his mother, who rolled her eyes and waved a hand at him. "In that case, it's time to get going," he said. "And once we start moving, we're not stopping until the whole thing is done." He looked around the room, meeting the eyes of each person in turn. Then he nodded. "Let's get to it."

CHAPTER FIVE

Four tickets were booked for the first flight to Barcelona the following morning. The sun hadn't yet risen as Harry, Anna, Daniel, and Noy gathered outside the entrance, each with a backpack containing the few clothes they'd brought to the Chilterns.

"Sorry, popping over to the constituency after this. Needed a few papers and whatnot," Granville blustered as he finally came down the main staircase, carrying a briefcase in one hand and wearing a black coat over his suit. He paused to quickly kiss Sarah's cheek, as she stood with her arms folded and her cardigan wrapped tight around her at the door. "Shall we get a move on, then?"

Harry came forward and hugged his mother, then held her at arm's length. "We'll be fine," he said, in answer to the look in her eyes.

"It's easy to say that. All three of you always said it, before you went off to risk your lives. Everyone's always fine until suddenly they're not."

"We'll give it our best shot?"

"Get on."

Harry saw Daniel standing stock-still as he turned, looming in the predawn darkness. He was watching Harry and not moving. Harry motioned back with his head, almost imperceptibly. Daniel still paused, then finally came forwards. The embrace he gave his mother was very quick.

"Take care," she said simply. Daniel was already turning away, but Harry caught the look on her face and hated it. He could only hope that things might return to normalcy eventually. But that was a concern for the future.

Noy waved a quick farewell, Anna came forward and kissed Sarah on the cheek too, then the four of them were heading to the car.

"This is in a better state than the last time I saw it," Anna said, climbing into the back of the Mercedes.

"Chamberlain still hasn't shut up about that."

"George is *very* fond of this car, as you well know."

"Fond is one word for it." Harry said, getting into the passenger seat beside Granville. "Some would call it obsessed. Almost unsettlingly so."

"All set back there?" Granville glanced over his shoulder and saw Anna on one side, Daniel's bulk on the other, and Noy squeezed between them. "Jolly good. *Vamos, amigos!*"

Sarah waved as they crunched along the gravel near the front door and descended the long driveway. They soon turned onto an A-road and Granville put his foot down, joining the M40 shortly afterwards. The roads were quiet and they made good time heading southeast towards Heathrow.

They reached the airport's vast complex in half an hour. Granville followed the directions on the car's GPS into the car park of a budget hotel on Heathrow's outskirts and parked up. He checked his phone then pointed to a bin on a grassy verge dividing the car park from the road.

"You're joking," Harry said.

"My man thought it the best way. Particularly at such short notice."

Harry leant forward and looked around. "No CCTV on it, I suppose. Although they'll still have the car on film."

"Indeed?" Granville turned to him with a worried expression.

"But the chances of being caught that way are infinitesimal, don't worry. You're far more likely to be betrayed by whoever sorted this for you at the Home Office."

Harry jogged to the bin, reached inside until he felt paper beneath his fingertips, and came back. He emptied the contents of the envelope into his lap, passed Anna one of the passports, and inspected the other himself.

"Harold Mills," he read.

"And Anne Carver. Full marks for creativity, Granville."

"The documents are what matter, not the damned names. A little gratitude wouldn't go amiss."

"We're very grateful... Truly," Harry added, at a look from Granville.

"I should hope so. I only have my contact's word for it that she won't look further into this matter."

They soon reached Terminal 1 and Granville stopped in the drop-off area. "Heard back from Tinkov yet?" Harry asked.

"Afraid not, but I'm sure he's rather busy. Hopefully I'll have something by the time you land." Granville removed a leather driving glove and held out his right hand. "Good luck over there, old chap."

The four of them got through security then, at Anna's suggestion, took an early drink in the departures lounge. Anna asked Noy about her childhood in Burma and she and Harry both laughed at the way she told the story. Daniel smiled often too, even as he remained silent with his eyes cast downwards at her hand in his lap.

Granville's passports saw Anna and Harry through passport control without a hitch, Daniel and Noy using the passports they'd recently acquired from one of his old Organisation contacts. Twenty minutes later they were airborne. Daniel stared out of the window, while Anna read a paper she'd bought. Noy fell asleep, as did Harry before he began to twitch, then talk louder and louder until eventually Anna shook him gently awake and calmed him.

Two hours later they were on the final descent into El Prat, the Mediterranean a calm and beautiful blue beneath them.

To the right of the plane, low-rise Badalona passed by first then Barcelona itself after the Besós river. From above they could see the gridded streets stretching away into the distance until they reached the hills to the northwest. The Sagrada Familia was easily distinguishable and looked like a strange and perfectly-proportioned model from that height and distance.

They moved by mile after mile of beach, culminating in the sail-like W Hotel at the southwestern end after which the sand and the bars on the promenade behind suddenly gave way to the industry of the expansive port area.

The plane touched down a little after midday local time. The four passports were accepted again, and with no baggage to collect they moved immediately outside, the sun and temperature marking a stark contrast to the grey, frigid British winter.

They got stuck into the euros Granville had provided them by taking a costly taxi northeast towards the city proper. They stopped on a street in the Eixample area, not far from Plaça de Catalunya and the upper end of Las Ramblas. The boulevard was broad and lined with tall trees which had shed their leaves. The buildings were all five or six stories tall and had subtle differences in decoration while following the same elegant, modernist style.

Harry had rented an apartment which required neither proof of identity nor a meeting with the owner. He found the right building and pressed a button on the intercom which rang a couple of times before they were buzzed inside.

They went to the third floor and found the fourth apartment. Harry entered a pin code and opened the door into an apartment with tall ceilings and white walls. There was a large dining table, two cream-coloured leather sofas, and two sets of double doors which opened onto Juliet balconies.

They all dropped their bags, and Harry took a laptop from his backpack and connected to the WiFi. He loaded a VPN then logged into the email account he'd recently created and opened the recently-arrived message.

"He answer?" Noy asked, standing in front of Daniel and leaning back against his chest.

"Yes, thank God. Tinkov's still here." Harry's eyes ran over the short paragraph of text, then he grimaced. "He's leaving tomorrow morning. We need to move even quicker than I thought."

"Location?" Daniel asked.

"He's rented a yacht, which Granville assumes he'll be staying on tonight. That's all he said."

"Must be nice," Anna muttered.

"So, we have two objectives. Firstly, find out which yacht he's on, so we've got eyes on him."

"I doubt there's an old school paper trail we can follow," Anna said. "That's not how these super-rich criminals tend to operate. We'll have to do it the old-fashioned way - go down to the port area and poke around. Short of Granville simply asking, which may look a little suspicious, I don't see any other option at such short notice."

"Me neither. The second objective, naturally, is deciding how to take him out."

There was silence in the room but for the low hum of traffic on the street several floors below. Daniel had been staring at the ground as he thought, but now raised his head.

"We use Granville again."

"He'll be thrilled to hear that. How?"

"Get him to send Tinkov a message. Something urgent has come up. Something that could change everything. It's too sensitive to talk about over the phone. He needs to meet in person, and he's flying to Barcelona immediately. It has to be tonight, before Tinkov leaves for Moscow."

"We're gambling that Tinkov thinks Rupert is important enough to be worth spoiling his last day in the sun."

"To an extent. Granville needs to word the message in a way that leaves Tinkov no choice."

"Do we want him on the yacht or off it?"

"Off," Anna said. "Getting him out in the open expands our options enormously. We got to him that way once before. Presumably he'll be a little more careful this time, but we also have twice the manpower."

Harry's phone buzzed in his pocket. He took it out and read the message. "Make that two and a half times the manpower. McGinn's downstairs."

"You're sure this is wise?" Daniel asked.

"I told you I'd trust him with my life. I have done, many times before, and he never let me down."

"He's a mercenary now."

"Some things go deeper than money. Don't they?" The brothers looked at each other for a moment, then Daniel's eyes dropped. "I've thought about this a lot," Harry said, as the intercom sounded. "He increases our chances enormously. If it is a risk, which I don't believe, then it's one worth taking."

Harry looked at each of the other three in turn. Meeting no further objection, he crossed to the intercom and buzzed the main entrance open.

Harry went out to wait for the lift and suddenly felt butterflies in his stomach. Three years had passed since he'd seen his squadmate; his friend. He had just about managed to dismiss the preposterous sensation when there was a ringing sound and the doors to the lift opened.

"Captain."

James McGinn was a little over six foot and had kept himself in excellent shape. His fair hair was cropped at the back and sides, as it had been in the army, but he had grown it out on top.

The Scot's face had immediately broken into a broad grin upon seeing Harry. He came straight out from the lift, dumped his large duffel bag on the ground, and pulled Harry into a tight hug. Harry hugged him back and they stayed that way for several seconds before McGinn stood back and began lifting his arm in an apologetic salute.

"Stop that," Harry said immediately. "Don't be ridiculous."

"Old habits die hard, Cap. I've been thinking the whole way here about the past. Everything we went through out there. The good times. The even better ones. I know I'm one of the bad guys now, one of the greedy bastards, and you'll hate me for that, but I never stopped thinking about our squad, you know, and I'll tell you true that I've still never had a leader like you, Cap, not even-"

"McGinn," Harry said, smiling. "We're in a hurry. There'll be time for all this later."

"Aye, sorry, Cap. It's just so good to see you again, you know."

"Come in."

The others were waiting in a loose semi-circle. McGinn went to each in turn, shaking their hand warmly and repeating each name he was told. His smile had always been infectious and was reflected now in the faces of both Noy and Anna, although Daniel's expression was as impassive as ever.

"McGinn was in my old SAS squad," Harry explained, as McGinn put his bag in a corner. "He was an excellent signaller, and the best marksman I've ever seen."

"Meaning?" Noy asked, looking mystified.

"He was in charge of in-field communications, and liaising between our squad and HQ. And he shot people from a very long way away."

"A… how do you say?" Noy said, holding an imaginary rifle and peering down its scope. "Sniper, no? Ah, so this will be very easy. He shoot this Tinkov from a mile away and we go back to England." She turned to Daniel. "Very smart, your brother, I told you."

"Would that I could be so useful, Noy," McGinn said, grinning at her while she frowned at his broad Glaswegian accent. "Couldn't bring my rifle with me, unfortunately. That kind of thing doesn't go down well at airport security." He turned to Harry. "And I'm guessing we don't have the contacts here to get our hands on one?"

"Not at such short notice. You brought the other stuff with you, though?"

"Best binoculars money can buy, Cap, plus the comms gear you wanted."

"Fantastic," Harry said, clapping him across the back. "Everyone else, take a few minutes. I'll fill McGinn in on the situation." Harry felt Daniel staring at him as Noy and Anna went to one of the Juliet balconies. He resisted the urge to meet his gaze, however, instead leading McGinn to one of the sofas where he began to tell him everything and finding quickly that it felt like old times all over again.

CHAPTER SIX

It was early afternoon when the five of them left the building. All except Noy checked up and down the street by habit as they stepped outside.

It was a mild day and the wintry sun, already on its descent, shone down the southwestern streets at each octagonal intersection. They headed southeast through the Eixample then entered the narrow alleyways of El Born. Local restaurants and cafes on small plazas gave way to touristic shops and more expensive bars the further downhill they went.

Harry walked in front with McGinn beside him. His old squadmate rushed to tell Harry everything that had happened to him since Harry left the army. They had only seen each other once since then, at the funeral for the man who now walked behind them.

After half an hour they passed the soaring gothic facade of Santa Maria del Mar before crossing the broad Passeig de Colom and entering the port area of Barceloneta. They paused there among the crowds, which were thick even midweek in December.

"Any idea where we're actually looking, Cap?"

"Seems like that area's only for sailing boats," Harry said, motioning to the dozens of thin white masts to his right. He looked to his left. "That's where we want to focus."

Half a mile southeast, in the port of Barceloneta proper, they could make out the long, elegant side of a luxury yacht.

They passed a large refurbished warehouse which had been converted into upmarket restaurants and the Museu d'Història de Catalunya before turning right onto Passeig Joan de Borbó. The road was four lanes wide. To their left apartment buildings faced out over the port. To the right was a broad path lined with palm trees and filled with beachgoers and runners, and to the right of that a dozen or more yachts were moored.

"I'll go out on a limb and guess this is the place," Anna said.

"McGinn, can you get a vantage point?"

McGinn looked around, his eyes lingering on the upper stories of the apartment buildings across the road. "No problem, Cap." He snapped off a quick salute before Harry could stop him, winked, then headed in that direction.

"We'll split into pairs. Noy and Daniel, you take the far end of the row. We'll keep an eye out down here."

Daniel nodded, his eyes and some of the worst scarring hidden behind large, black sunglasses. Noy took his hand as they went away along the wide path, Daniel looking twice the size of her at least when the two were seen from a distance.

Harry pressed a finger against the small plastic component dangling just below his earpiece. "Testing." He saw Daniel raise his own hand as he replied. A moment later McGinn checked in too, and Harry heard the noise of a front door to one of the apartment blocks opening. "Everyone stay alert," Harry said. "Whichever Tinkov's yacht is, assume it's being watched extremely closely, even if it doesn't look that way."

He turned to Anna, offering his hand. "Shall we?"

"Why, Mr Miller, you're *far* too forward to be a true gentleman."

Anna put her hand demurely in his and they began walking slowly along the path. Harry saw Anna was frowning.

"What is it?"

"Your brother worries me." Her eyes were fixed on Daniel in the middle-distance, where he towered over the clusters of tourists he and Noy passed.

"He's always been the strong, silent type."

"It's not only that, although I'll freely admit he's a little… disquieting to be around. It's that he's only here because of her. If she becomes disillusioned and leaves, for any reason, he'll go too. And then, dear Captain, we're really up the creek without a paddle."

They walked in silence, although Harry continued scanning from side to side even as he turned over her words. "I'm not sure she's the only reason."

"He adores her. It was obvious at the compound, if you were paying attention, and it's plain for any fool to see now."

"I know that, but I think there's more. He'd never say it - we've barely spoken a word to each other - but I wonder if he wants to make amends."

Anna snorted. "He seemed pretty at peace with it all back in Thailand. And it's not like he's lived a monastic life of penitence and pacifism since all that went tits-up."

"That was before he and Noy were together. Really together, I mean."

"Captain Miller," Anna intoned, turning to him. "I always took you for a realist, not a romantic."

"Can't I be both? You say he adored Noy for years, and now he's with her. That seems like a pretty big catalyst for change to me."

Anna considered. "What you say makes some sense."

"Is that your way of admitting I might be right?"

"It's the closest I'll come."

Harry felt a sudden churning in his stomach, and a lump in his throat. But however absurdly difficult it felt, he forced himself to say the words anyway.

"Perhaps… I wouldn't have believed that myself," he said. "I wouldn't have believed it could be so simple, even a short time ago. But it happened in my own life, and that's what makes it easy to see in someone else's, I suppose. I remember what it was all like before you, and I know how I feel with you now, and it's really a different world. It can change everything."

Harry face's burned. Then he felt his hand being squeezed and turned to Anna. She stopped, looking at him, and he stopped in front of her. "That's a very nice thing to hear," she said, and kissed him.

They walked onwards hand in hand, looking back and forth between the luxurious yachts and the palm trees and the blue sky above as any other couple might who were in love.

The four of them walked in slow patrols along the dock for almost an hour. It was late afternoon and the sky was already darkening across the sea to the east when Harry heard McGinn's voice in his ear.

"We might have something."

Harry and Anna were on a bench roughly halfway along the path. "What is it?"

"Speedboat, coming in fast from the northwest. Looks expensive, not that I'm an expert."

"Keep tracking it."

McGinn spoke again a minute later. "Four occupants. One man at the wheel, three women behind him. The man's short. A bit tubby. They're about half a mile out now. Stand by." Harry felt his heart rate picking up and hope flaring. The seconds seemed to drag by. "It's him."

"You're sure?"

"Positive. I've got all the photos you gave me right here. That's your man."

"Copy. Follow him in."

"Slowing down now. He's approaching your end of the harbour, Cap." There was another short pause. "Right, they're pulling alongside the second yacht in to the right. The Odessa."

"Stand by for confirmation."

Harry and Anna headed back along the row. They reached the penultimate yacht and saw the speedboat tied to its port side just as the last of the slim blonde women was being helped onto the deck of the yacht. A short, fat man was still in the speedboat, a hand fortuitously placed on the young woman's backside to help her up.

The setting could hardly have been more different than that in which he'd last seen Yuri Tinkov, seated on the upper level of a church with the light of a hundred candles flickering across the Russian's round, impassive face. But there was no doubting it was him.

"We have confirmation," Harry said, as Tinkov was helped onto the deck by two burly bodyguards. "Good work, McGinn. Now we just need to figure out how we're going to kill this bastard."

CHAPTER SEVEN

Night had fallen over Barcelona.

Harry stood at one of the Juliet balconies, not noticing the street below nor hearing the rumbling buses and whining scooters upon it. He only saw everything that could possibly go wrong, all the worst-case scenarios playing over and over again in his mind.

The sounds of heavy footsteps approaching broke the spell. But he didn't turn when he heard them, nor when he felt the hand on his shoulder.

"You've changed, Cap."

"Not for the better. Not when it comes to nights like these."

"It's only natural to be nervous, with your loved ones involved."

"It's not as if I didn't care before. When it was you, Cooper, and Davies. We were like brothers."

"We were, but time changes every man. You hadn't lost anybody back then. We all felt invincible. Now you know what loss is, and that makes you fear it."

"You've changed too, McGinn."

"Aye, and not for the better either. Now I'm a fountain of sentimental bollocks, given half a chance."

Harry turned and smiled at his friend, putting a hand on his shoulder. "It's good to have you here. Makes it all feel almost like old times. It's a strange thing to feel nostalgia for a life of killing and violence, but there it is."

"We're strange folk, Cap. All of us who live this life."

The smile was still lingering on Harry's lips, but it faded when he met McGinn's eye and saw melancholy there. His old squadmate was staring downwards. Harry opened his mouth to speak, then - finding nothing to say, and hating himself for it - closed his mouth again and only squeezed McGinn's shoulder.

"We're in position."

All of Harry's apprehension came rushing back at once at the sound of his brother's voice in his ear. He followed McGinn to the large dining table in the living room which had been transformed into their de facto operations centre.

McGinn had packed an impressive amount of hardware into his duffel bag. Black wires snaked across much of the surface and the sockets of two extension leads were filled with plugs trailing off to various screens, chargers, and communications devices.

Harry felt a burst of frustration as he surveyed it all. This wasn't his place. But under pressure from both Anna and McGinn, he had conceded that his gunshot wounds still limited him, that Anna, Daniel and Noy could handle everything at ground-level, and that he would be more valuable directing what might prove a complicated operation from afar.

McGinn seated himself in the middle of the table, where he had a portable monitor beside a laptop. The monitor displayed a map of Barcelona, upon which three blue dots flashed at regular intervals to confirm their locations were being transmitted live.

McGinn took out his smaller earpiece and put on a headset. "Confirm, Alpha," he said, zooming in on the map.

"Alpha in position at Plaça Santa Maria. Southeast of the

entrance to the Basilica. Bravo is northwest of the entrance. Over."

Harry saw that the blue dots were accurate. Both were stationary, roughly twenty metres apart in the small plaza in front of the towering gothic facade of Santa Maria del Mar which they had passed earlier.

"Copy, Alpha," McGinn said. "Charlie?"

"Unlike 'Alpha' I'm not a languages savant, and don't know how to bloody well pronounce it. But I'm lingering in the alleyway next to the Basilica, as instructed by our glorious leader."

McGinn zoomed in again. Anna's dot was slowly moving up and down the narrow Carrer dels Abaixadors which led southwest away from the church.

"Copy, Charlie. Two minutes until target arrives."

McGinn raised his microphone. "We're good to go, Cap," he said over his shoulder.

Harry frowned. "Drop me in again." McGinn clicked, and a ground level view of the plaza appeared on the screen. "Does it feel right to you, Tinkov picking this place?"

McGinn turned the viewpoint through three hundred and sixty degrees. "No," he said. "The plaza's small. Only a couple of wee restaurants and bars. Nowhere near enough people to create a crowd. Plenty of narrow alleyways leading onto it - perfect for mounting an ambush."

"Exactly."

"You think it's all a bluff? Or a trap?"

"Not necessarily. I think Tinkov trusts Granville enough to make the whole setup of an urgent meeting plausible." He straightened up. "But I'd be shocked if he didn't change the location at the last moment. Patch Granville through."

McGinn turned back to his laptop. The ringing sound lasted barely a second before the call was answered.

"Good evening?"

"Rupert. I'm here with-"

"Harry? Listen, old chap, I'm afraid I'm losing my mind back here. I'm still not sure how I got wrapped up in all this, nor that it was a wise idea to begin with, but I must say that I never-"

"We haven't got time for this," Harry said. "You told Tinkov not to mention you by name to anyone else?"

"Well, yes, I-"

"And we'll recover his phone tonight, when the job's done. You'll be fine."

"I fail to see how you can be so sure. This man is-"

"Shut up and listen." Silence followed immediately. Harry could almost feel Granville's indignation. "You've got your phone?"

"I do," Granville said, curtly.

"You're about to get a message from Tinkov."

"I'm not seeing any-" Granville began. "Ah."

"You have it?"

"Oh no. Oh, you won't like this. He's changed the location of our meeting. This is a disaster. He knows we're onto him. We have to-"

"*Granville*," Harry barked. McGinn glanced over his shoulder, grinning. "For the love of God, just tell me what the message says. What's the new location?"

"A place called..." Granville cleared his throat, and affected an accent. "Plaça de Sant Just."

McGinn ran an immediate search on his map then turned to

Harry and shook his head. "Five minutes west of the Basilica. It's too small to be the final meeting point."

"We're keeping you on the line, Rupert. Reply to Tinkov's last message, tell him that's fine, then let us know when he changes the location again."

"I'm not cut out for this, Harry."

"You don't say."

Harry nodded to McGinn again, who lowered the microphone on his headset and relayed the new location. "Be advised, this will not be the final meeting point," he said. "The way they're sending you, you'll have a wide road to cross first then narrow alleyways leading onto the plaza. They almost certainly want to check for tails. Alpha and Bravo, you go together in front. Charlie, you trail by at least twenty metres. Over."

The dots representing Daniel and Noy grew closer then headed straight past Anna as they went southwest along Carrer dels Abaixadors. Anna's dot blinked in place for twenty seconds or so before following.

McGinn glanced back at Harry, smiling. "And so the dance begins."

CHAPTER EIGHT

Anna stepped neatly around a pool of what looked and smelled like fresh urine, then returned to the right-hand side of the alleyway as a couple came in the other direction. The alleyway itself was narrow and devoid of shops or bars, but it linked the Basilica with the large, busy road McGinn had mentioned, and there was a steady sprinkling of people walking along it.

Anna walked slowly with her hands in the pockets of her leather jacket, fingering the blade of the knife which she had strapped underneath. She wore a black baseball cap, and glancing up from under its brim could see Daniel and Noy approaching a quiet road in front.

Momentarily she seemed to be alone in the alleyway, the only noises those of the main road's traffic ahead and her boots on the stone surface. Then she heard somebody approaching from behind.

They were the footsteps of a large man wearing heavy boots and they were drawing closer. Anna kept her head down and continued at the same pace. Casually she reached up as if to scratch the side of her face, and removed the earpiece.

A few moments later the man drew level with her. He was almost as tall as Daniel, although not as broad, and had close-cropped hair. For a second they walked alongside each other. Anna kept looking down, her hunched shoulders covering half of the side of her face, the hat low, and her hands back in her pockets. She sensed the man glancing at her. Then he was past and drawing further away.

Anna relaxed her shoulders, unclenched her fists, and smiled to herself. It was good to be back out in the field. With her senses heightened and playing a game of cat-and-mouse with lethal consequences for the loser, it felt just like old times.

She could hate the Company for its theft of every penny she'd been paid. There was no love lost over the attempted kidnap of her daughter and grandmother either. But there was no sense in tainting all the memories from all those years. They were years in which she'd made good friends and fallen in love; years which had given her Tasha, and in turn a purpose at last.

She had enjoyed the work, too. There was no sense in denying it. The means had been violent. But thanks to the agreed-upon clause with the Company, stating she would only harm those whom she judged to deserve it, she had helped in her own small way to make the world a better place.

She wouldn't say any of that to Harry. She couldn't, after everything the Company had done, culminating in his father's murder, but there was no sense in denying it to herself.

Anna emerged from the end of the alleyway and looked around. She saw Daniel and Noy had turned right here, and were taking the next left. She followed and found herself emerging onto busy Via Laietana.

The road was four lanes wide and heavy with traffic. It ran downhill to her left all the way to the port area. She wondered briefly if Tinkov would be coming from that direction, but they were in the heart of the touristic area now and there were far too many people around to spot him.

She had unwittingly joined a couple of dozen people all waiting at a set of traffic lights. To her right she saw Daniel towering above the crowd, amongst which Noy was barely visible. Daniel's gaze was fixed straight ahead while Noy looked constantly around. Daniel had briefly tried to argue against her coming along, but she had immediately overruled him.

Anna looked to her left. Her stomach dropped as she found her eyes meeting those of the large man from the alleyway.

She thought he had been scanning the crowd, rather than staring directly at her, but it was impossible to be sure. It took all of Anna's experience to keep her face completely expressionless and allow her eyes, after lingering a moment as anyone's would, to drift back across the road.

The light changed. The crowd began to move forward and merge with that coming in the other direction. She stayed at its rear maintaining her prior leisurely pace, and followed Daniel as he turned right upon reaching the far pavement. Her left hand remained in her pocket. With her right she reached up to replace the earpiece.

"Are you there?"

"Here," McGinn replied.

"I've got at least one goon heading for the meeting point."

"Did he see you?" The concern in Harry's voice was touching. There was no sense in denying it.

"Yes."

"Did he recognise you? Tinkov will have shown photos of both of us to his guards, after London."

Anna paused. "I can't be sure." She heard Harry swearing away from the microphone. "We have to go ahead anyway. Who knows when we'll get another shot at him."

This time it was Harry who took a moment. "Copy. Continue as planned, but be careful."

"Great advice," Anna muttered. "All those years of special forces experience really paid off."

"Copy," Harry said; only to annoy her, Anna was sure. She rolled her eyes as she lowered her hand and put it back in her jacket pocket.

The man was behind her again. She was sure of it as she continued up Via Laietana, without needing to turn and despite all the other people around.

They were heading into the lower part of the old town now, and the crowds grew as they drew closer to Las Ramblas. Still Anna kept Daniel and Noy in her sights and maintained the twenty pace distance.

Anna heard McGinn's voice in her earpiece, giving directions. Daniel and Noy turned left off the main road and Anna followed them along a smaller street. Up ahead she saw them entering a small plaza which she assumed was the new meeting point.

"Two men in the plaza," Daniel said. "No sign of Tinkov."

There was a short delay before McGinn answered. Anna heard the calmness in his voice slipping for the first time. "We have a new location. Do not stop walking, or they'll know you're involved. Repeat, do *not* stop walking."

Anna looked ahead with interest from under the rim of her cap. Noy's arm was through Daniel's. With admirable cool Daniel steered her gently to their left without breaking stride. He even pointed at something to his left as they went, which upon emerging into the plaza just as they left it Anna saw was a surprisingly large gothic church tucked away in the small square.

"Alpha and Bravo, one man on your tail now," Anna said, very quietly. "He doesn't look too excited. Probably been told to follow you a little way, then come back."

"Copy."

"Alpha and Bravo, take the next right," McGinn said. "You're close to the cathedral. We're guessing the square in front will be the final meeting point, so stay sharp."

"Sorry to be a spoilsport," Anna said. "But what's the plan when we actually get there?"

"I'm working on that," Harry said. His voice exuded confidence despite the situation, and Anna couldn't help but smile. He would think of a plan, and it would be something simple and effective and it would work. After seeing him in several such situations already she was as sure of this as anything.

They continued onwards in a strange line: Daniel and Noy in front, a disinterested tail behind, then Anna and her own tail bringing up the rear. They all walked, spaced evenly apart, along another alleyway busy with tourists, passed beneath an intricately-carved archway linking the buildings on either side, then abruptly reached the cathedral.

The plaza in which the cathedral was situated, Pla de la Seu, was long and shallow. Cafes and restaurants, each with a dozen or more tables in front, lined the side across from them. The cathedral towered on the near side, two smaller spires flanking a thick central one above a wide, squat facade and the sharply curving main entrance brightly lit.

The cathedral was closed now and the plaza was quiet. Only a few passing tourists lingered to take photos, and the restaurants on the far side looked half-filled.

The lack of people made it easy to see Tinkov's arrival.

He entered the plaza on the far side with two men, both as large as the one tailing Anna. Daniel and Noy had slowed a short distance into the plaza and now stood looking up at the cathedral. Their would-be tail gave them a final disinterested glance then went towards Tinkov and his men. Anna was at least a hundred metres from Tinkov, but kept her head down anyway to hide her face beneath the baseball cap.

"He's here."

McGinn answered immediately. "You're sure?"

"It's a short fat man, wearing an expensive coat, flanked by two gorillas, arriving at the right time and place. I can get closer, but I'm pretty confident."

Hands still in her pockets, Anna continued along the near, shorter end of the rectangular plaza. Tinkov and his men were angling diagonally across the space, from the far corner towards the cathedral. She was more or less level with them, albeit still a hundred metres away, when they came to a halt.

"They've stopped right in the middle. Open ground all around them. Four men with him and a fifth ready to join, if he'd ever leave me alone. Good luck figuring this one out, Captain Miller."

CHAPTER NINE

Daniel stood with Noy, her arm through his. The two of them still faced the cathedral, but he thought only of the group in the centre of the square behind.

"Alpha."

"Here," Daniel said.

"I only see two options. We can wait for them to give up and head back, but they'll be more suspicious than ever when Granville doesn't show. Taking them by surprise in the alleyways after would be almost impossible. And, unlike you, we can assume they're armed"

"Agreed. We need to be direct."

"You have to be sure it's a sensible risk, and one that you're willing to take." There was a pause, then Daniel heard Harry's voice change. "What I mean is that it's dangerous, Da-... Alpha."

Daniel felt a lump in his throat, and swallowed. He reset his face and looked down at Noy. She was looking up at him, and nodded. "Copy," he said. "Charlie?"

"Fine by me," Anna said. "Nice and quick, no messing around. Go hard or go home, as the youth like to say. We could do with a distraction to help us out, though."

Noy had been listening, and looked back up at Daniel. "I can distract."

"I'd prefer if you didn't-"

"Tssk." Noy cut Daniel off with a look of impatience. "I'm here to help, Farang, not just to look pretty. I go over like some of the girls I know in Chiang Rai when they see rich farangs."

"They're getting restless," Anna said. "Time to make our minds up."

Noy looked away from Daniel. "Ready," she said.

"Copy," said Harry, and he could be heard consulting quietly with McGinn for a few brief moments. "Charlie, keep circling the perimeter of the square. Bravo, you move on my first 'Go'. Alpha and Charlie, you close on my second. All clear?"

They all confirmed, Daniel's eyes still fixed on Noy. "Please be careful," he said.

"I'll come back, Farang, don't worry. Not finished with you yet - you still have a lot of apologising to do. I want a lot of nice trips and fancy hotels when we finish all this."

Daniel couldn't quite force a smile, but nodded.

"Ready, Bravo?"

Noy's face resumed its normal frown. "Yes."

"Go."

Noy slipped her arm out of Daniel's, removed her earpiece, turned, and began to walk away. Out of the corner of his eye Daniel saw her placing one hand on her hip and swinging the other back and forth as she headed towards the men. He forced himself to keep looking forwards as her footsteps grew more distant across the quiet square.

"I wish I could film this," Anna said. "It's one hell of a distraction, I'll say that. The men are facing each other in a circle, but one's already looking over."

Daniel half-listened for a response which Noy couldn't give. He waited for what must have been a few seconds, but seemed an eternity, before he heard Harry's voice in his ear.

"Alpha, Charlie."

"Ready," they replied, almost in unison.

"Go."

Daniel felt a sense of release as he turned and began walking across the square.

When Harry had first joined the special forces, Daniel had wanted nothing more than to follow in his brother's footsteps, though he would never have admitted it. Time and disappointment had shown he wasn't cut out for it. He didn't enjoy careful and meticulous planning. He didn't enjoy the buildup to an operation; didn't savour the anticipation. He wasn't made for ambushes or creeping around in the dark. He was made for decisive and violent action. With this now in prospect he felt all the apprehension melting away and in its place a calm certainty.

Noy was twenty metres from the group of four men. A fifth, the man who must have been tailing Anna, had left her now and was coming to join the circle. Unbeknownst to the man, Anna was now following him, just far enough back that he couldn't hear. Daniel saw that Harry's timing had been perfect, with Anna almost exactly the same distance from the circle as he was.

Noy's exaggerated gait seemed so absurd that Daniel was sure the men would be suspicious, or only laugh and assume she was drunk. But the two men facing her were watching with obvious interest as she drew close.

Tinkov, standing in the middle of the circle, glanced over as one of the men called something to her. Noy said something back. Daniel couldn't hear what, but one of the men facing her laughed and even Tinkov smiled.

The circle opened to encompass Noy. All the men were looking at her. Her voice was different to that which Daniel knew as she made a joke at one man's expense that the others all laughed at. Anna's tail was just reaching the circle but the others paid him no attention.

Anna and Daniel were only a few metres away now. As if sensing their proximity Noy was raising her voice to make another joke, as she also reached back to release her long hair from its usual ponytail and tossed it across her shoulders.

Daniel looked across the circle to Anna. Unwittingly he met her tail's eyes first, which immediately narrowed. Daniel's eyes found Anna's, and he nodded. The tail saw the gesture.

The man was just opening his mouth to shout ahead to the circle when Anna grabbed his chin with her left hand and wrenched upwards while there was a flash of metal in her right hand as she slashed across his throat. She had lifted her left hand to cover his mouth as quickly as she could, but the briefest noise of intermingled pain and surprise still escaped.

The group of men all froze then looked towards the sound. Daniel lashed out and punched the nearest man in the back of the skull. He dropped, but the trio of other guards were already reacting with impressive quickness to Anna's attack, drawing their weapons and closing around Tinkov.

Daniel saw Anna stab straight out at the nearest man to her, stopping him from drawing his pistol and cutting him down his lower arm as he parried her attack. The other two had seen Daniel and already had their guns half-drawn.

Instinctively, Daniel charged straight at the nearer one.

He took the man by surprise and managed to grab him around the waist before he could move away then drive him backwards towards his colleague. The man smashed the butt of his pistol down on Daniel's back and shoulders and neck but with the adrenaline now coursing through him Daniel barely registered the blows, nor did the gunshot fired by the other guard, which he felt as a sudden, short streak of fire across his lower leg, have any effect. Daniel only drove onwards, the first man stumbling and faltering several steps then colliding with his colleague, whose second shot was sent off upwards towards the cathedral.

Daniel grunted as he shoved with all his might right before the moment of impact, which sent the first man flying back into the second so that they both fell downwards with Daniel's momentum carrying him down too and onto both of them. Daniel raised his arms to protect his head as the first man scratched and clawed and punched at him, then struggled up a little onto the man so that he straddled his chest with all of his great weight preventing him from moving or turning.

Daniel lowered his arms to reach for the man and immediately took a blow straight to the side of his head.

He didn't feel pain, though that would surely come later. For now his vision only dimmed momentarily and his sense of balance faltered. Blindly he reached out again, and the man shouted as Daniel found his ears and grabbed and felt the crunching of small bones and the loosening of torn skin as he pulled upwards then wrenched downwards again as hard as he could.

He felt the impact and heard the pair of pained shouts even as his vision only began to clear. Both men desperately twisted and fought to get out from under Daniel's bulk and he felt himself beginning to lose his balance and fall to one side then the other.

He grunted as he brought the first man's head up by the ears again and thrust it down with more force, then smashed down again and again and again. He felt the crunching in both skulls, heard the shouts briefly grow more panicked and pained before becoming only moans. When those faded too he finally released his grip and let the lifeless head fall onto the one beneath.

With bloodied hands Daniel pushed himself up and off the first man's chest. His head spun again as he did so and he stumbled sideways, just managing to recover his balance before falling then waiting for his vision to finally clear.

He couldn't see far, couldn't see the details of the restaurants on the other side of the plaza from which the shouts and screams from the tourists had come when the violence began. Now there was silence there, although dimly he still saw the shapes of voyeuristic onlookers.

Daniel's vision cleared enough to see the outcome of the fight. Anna lay beside the body of the man she had attacked. She was motionless, her eyes closed and face bloodied. Her knife lay where it had fallen, near to the deep wound in the man's neck from which blood still streamed.

Daniel's clouded gaze moved up and across until it found Tinkov. He stood with Noy in front of him. One hand was around her neck. In the other he held a pistol pressed to Noy's temple.

Daniel straightened, anger and fear focusing him. Tinkov watched, his face impassive.

"Who are you?"

When Daniel didn't reply, Tinkov pressed the barrel more forcefully against Noy's head. "What is your name? It is a simple question. I don't think you are as stupid as you look."

"Daniel."

"Daniel what?"

"Miller."

Tinkov stared at him for a moment. "Then it was your brother I met. We had an… interesting conversation. He said he was going to take 'the whole damn thing down', if I remember correctly. He had also decided not to kill me."

"Change of plans."

"So I see. Though I must admit, I do not see why." Tinkov stuck his bottom lip out as he thought for a moment. Then his eyes widened momentarily. "Ah. You want to kill us all. All three." A hint of a smile crossed his face. "This is impossible, you know? Kill me and my colleagues will become... how do you say? Paranoid. You won't even get close to them."

Daniel had noticed Anna stirring on the ground. Fortunately she had done so very slightly and without making a noise. She reached for her head and blinked as she looked around. She saw Tinkov, then met Daniel's eyes. He took care not to return his own gaze to the Russian too abruptly.

"We'll see."

Tinkov shook his head. "This is a waste of your time. Trust me, I know these people. I tell you what, Daniel Miller - we make a deal instead. I leave here, with this young lady, and neither of us die." Noy winced and swore at Tinkov in Burmese as the man pressed the gun against her once more.

Daniel's face remained as impassive as Tinkov's, eyes boring into the Russian's even as he saw Anna carefully and silently pushing herself up. "I can't let you leave."

Both of them seemed to hear the first sounds of the sirens at once. A part of Daniel was surprised it had taken them so long to come close enough, but his sense of time had been completely warped by the speed of the combat. Seconds or minutes could have passed since he first approached the group of men.

The sirens came from the city centre to the northwest. If Tinkov had looked all the way around he would have seen Anna crouched behind him and ready with her knife in her hand. But he only half-glanced over his shoulder before turning back to Daniel.

"Looks like you don't have a choice, Mr Miller. You are out of time. Either you let us leave, or we all go to prison."

Tinkov was right. There was no choice. Daniel hated the decision he had to make but saw no other option. "Get him," he said, looking straight at Anna, and Tinkov made the natural but fatal mistake of turning.

Over the prior few days Daniel had only seen Anna lounging on sofas, talking and laughing with Noy and his mother, making fun of Harry. It had formed a false image of her in his mind; had made him forget her past, of which Harry had briefly informed him.

Now she moved with as much quickness and coordination and decisiveness as he had ever seen.

She raised from the ground already reaching for Tinkov's hand which held the gun and, without pausing for a moment, pulled it straight upwards to point into the night sky.

The pistol went off harmlessly even as her other hand was coming around and into the side of Tinkov's head with a brutal ferocity which drove the point of the knife straight through the man's ear and deep into his skull.

Anna twisted the blade. Then she wrenched it free, stepping back to avoid the blood as she let the Russian fall to the ground.

In all his time with the army and working privately, it was as brutal a killing as Daniel had seen.

Daniel came forwards for Noy, who had staggered clear of Tinkov and was now wincing and holding a hand to the ear next to which the shot had been fired.

"Are you okay?" Daniel asked, then again into her other ear.

"Oh yes, perfect, Farang. Never been better."

"We should make ourselves scarce," Anna said, a lightness in her voice which didn't sound forced. She had crouched down to wipe her knife on Tinkov's designer coat, and now waved the clean blade vaguely around the circle of dead bodies. "I've never had a run-in with the Catalan police before, but I doubt they take too kindly to this sort of thing."

"Can you move?"

"Faster than you, Farang," Noy said, still wincing as she clicked her fingers next to her ear.

"Let's go."

Daniel began to jog back the way they'd come with Noy following behind, and reached for his earpiece. "Alpha here."

"Copy, Alpha," McGinn replied. "Status?"

"Target is down."

"Copy. We have a connection to the local police radio. My Catalan isn't great, but it sounds like they're excited about something."

Daniel glanced back as they reached the wide alleyway which ran along the northern side of the cathedral. The sirens had grown much louder and blue lights were flashing off one of the buildings at the far end of the square.

"They're close."

"Not to worry. I'll get you home in no time at all."

Daniel glanced back at Anna as they ran. Her face reflected his own feelings at McGinn's apparent optimism. Past her, he saw the first police car entering the plaza.

CHAPTER TEN

Noy was already panting heavily.

She had been cold every single second she had been outdoors, in both Britain and Barcelona, but now she felt sticky sweat building beneath her clothes. She had always hated exercise and avoided it at all costs. For the first time this decision had come back to bite her.

"Are you okay?" Daniel asked, slowing for her.

"Fine... Farang," she snapped between short breaths. "You just... worry about... yourself. Ten times... weight... of me."

Noy had never been anywhere like Barcelona, and since they arrived had lost all sense of direction. All she knew now was that they were heading uphill, which made it all even worse. All the narrow streets with all their little bars and shops selling silly souvenirs appeared the same to her. Every few moments the farang with the strange accent would say 'right' or 'left' in her ear, then they would turn down another identical street.

There were plenty of tourists around and they all turned to look at the strange trio running by. To Noy it felt as if they were all looking at her in particular, red faced and sweating with her cheeks puffed out.

Her legs were heavy and she felt a burning in her chest and throat. She couldn't take it any more, and it was this as much as anything that drove her mind to make the breakthrough.

"Wait," she shouted, loudly enough that Anna and the Farang stopped and turned to look at her. "Can't..."

Anna stared at her. There wasn't a bead of sweat on her face and she didn't seem out of breath in the slightest. "You know I love you, Noy, and I'd rather you didn't die of a heart attack. But we really can't afford to linger."

"It's stupid," Noy panted.

"What is?"

"The plan… Everyone looking at us right now… Nobody in the world look as suspicious as us… Can't run from police like this anyway… They just… send more people…"

Daniel looked to Anna. "She's right."

"And what, pray tell, do you suggest as an alternative?"

"Split up again. You go one way, we go another. We walk, just like everybody else. We try to…" Noy cursed as she sought the weird English term. "Blend in."

"I'm covered in blood, unless you hadn't noticed," Anna hissed, leaning in so only they could hear.

"Wearing black… can't tell…" Noy said, hands on her hips. "Just look like…"

"Looks like what? I wet myself quite spectacularly? I gave myself a fully-clothed shower of red wine?"

They all looked up as they heard another pair of sirens approaching from a main road nearby. They hadn't seen the officers pursuing them on foot yet, but they couldn't be far behind.

"We don't have a choice," Daniel said. "She's right. We won't out-run them. And we're picking up too many witnesses."

Anna shook her head, then gave Noy and Daniel both a look. "If we end up in that apartment tonight, and not in prison, it'll be a bloody miracle."

She turned ninety degrees and started to walk quickly away

from them, pulling her cap low over her face with one hand as she put the other towards her ear to tell Harry the change of plans.

"Thanks."

"I don't want to see you have a heart attack either."

"Shut up." She held out her clammy hand, and Daniel took it. "Now we walk, like normal people. Think you can try to look normal, Farang?"

"I'll do my best."

They moved off again, at a regular pace this time. Nobody appeared to be watching them now. All the western tourists were too busy buying their stupid souvenirs or drinking like fish at the outdoor bars, even bundled-up in their coats and scarfs and hats. The sweat on Noy's skin was already growing cold and made her clothes cling to her.

McGinn instructed them to continue straight. They had made it less than fifty metres when they heard the first shouts behind. A man and woman were calling to each other. By the speed at which their voices grew louder it seemed they were running.

"Kiss me."

"What?"

"Kiss me, you dumb Farang."

Noy stepped to the side, grabbing Daniel's collar and pulling him down and towards her. He leant forwards and put his arms around her, and they kissed just as the woman reached them.

Noy's eyes were closed but she could hear by the sound of the woman's voice as she shouted that she was looking straight at them. Her breath caught for a moment as the footsteps seemed to pause, then she felt a rush of relief as they carried onwards followed by the man's.

Noy pulled away briefly, gave Daniel a peck on the cheek, then moved away fully. "Could just stay here?" she said. "Stay, have a drink, kiss a little. No more running. What you say?"

"They'll be starting a full sweep soon. I doubt the kissing strategy will work when they have search profiles."

"Shame," Noy muttered, as Daniel took her hand and began leading her again along the street. He checked in with McGinn, who instructed them to turn left in the direction Anna had gone then follow a parallel street to hers. If everything went to plan both streets would lead back up to the Eixample area.

"You know what I love about my village?" Noy said, as Daniel strode up the quiet street and she half-jogged to keep up. "Chiang Rai, Bangkok too?"

"They're all flat."

"Exactly, Farang. You really get to know me at last."

They followed McGinn's directions and found themselves on a busy street running parallel to Las Ramblas, heading up towards Plaça de Catalunya. Large, brightly-lit shops lined both sides and a small crowd had formed around a young busker with a guitar.

As usual, Noy seemed the shortest person around. Through gaps in the towering westerners, however, she could see the end of the street up ahead. There was a large, curved department store to the right and hundreds of colourful Christmas lights decorating the square itself.

"Pretty," she said.

"Apart from the police cars."

Noy lowered her gaze and used one of the English swear words she'd picked up from Anna. Two cars were parked fifty metres in front with their lights off. Four officers were spread in a line looking carefully at every person who passed.

"We need a different route," Daniel said into his earpiece. "Quickly."

"Turn right. Now."

Noy led Daniel by the arm down yet another alleyway. It was taller and wider than those in the older part of the city and had nicer-looking shops, although all of them were closed now.

"Follow that for a hundred metres, then turn left."

"Copy." To the unaccustomed ear Daniel's voice would have sounded as flat and emotionless as ever. Noy had learnt to detect its subtle variations, however, and immediately turned to look at him.

"Farang?"

"We're being followed. Don't look."

"By who?"

"Police, hopefully."

"Why 'hopefully'?"

"They'll just try to arrest us. Anyone from the Company would kill us. We're not dead yet, so it's probably the police."

"What do we do?"

Daniel looked down at her. Then, instead of speeding up or preparing to run, he slowed their pace.

They hadn't gone far before Noy heard two people calling in what she assumed was Spanish. The voices were surprisingly close and getting closer. They switched to English when she and Daniel still didn't stop.

"You! Wait!"

Daniel kept walking as if he hadn't heard. The voices spoke

to each other and she heard the footsteps approaching. They were very close now. She felt Daniel tensing. Her arm had been through his but now she slowly pulled it away.

"Hey!" someone shouted right behind them. In the corner of her eye Noy saw the uniformed arm of a police officer reaching out for Daniel's shoulder.

Daniel spun the moment the man's hand landed. There was no subtlety or intricacy to his attack. He simply turned more quickly than the man could possibly have anticipated, his right hand already in a fist and swinging around towards the man's stomach.

The man let out an exhalation of air and began to double over but Daniel had already moved to the other officer who was drawing her pistol. He kicked out at her hand with perfect accuracy, the gun clattering to the ground while he was moving quickly behind her, wrapping one great forearm around her neck and squeezing while with the other he held her arms tight. Her struggles had just ceased by the time the man was struggling back to his feet, one hand still clutching his stomach. His resistance was ineffectual as Daniel choked him out too, leaving both officers motionless on the ground.

Noy experienced the same confusing mixture of feelings she always did when the extent of Daniel's talent for violence was laid bare to her. Invariably she would hurriedly put any analysis of the feelings to one side, and on this occasion that was particularly easy to do.

"Maybe now we hurry up a bit," she said, looking between the officers and the busy shopping street from which they'd come.

"Agreed."

They stepped up their pace as McGinn guided them into the Eixample area. Ten minutes after the fight in the alleyway, Noy recognised the street on which they were staying.

A figure was lingering near their doorway. Daniel slowed automatically as he saw it, but the next moment Harry stepped out from the shadows. His look of relief quickly gave way to a smile.

"You did it," he said, first holding his hand out to Daniel then shaking Noy's hand warmly.

Anna was waiting for them in the living room with a glass of red wine in her hand, recapping everything from a ground level perspective for McGinn. She smiled as she saw Noy and passed her another glass which she'd already poured. "That's the first of many tonight, trust me. We've earned it. How did you enjoy your first experience of field work?"

"What field?" Daniel was standing over her shoulder and gave her the Thai translation. "Very strange language, English," Noy said. "But yes, very exciting, this field work. I should have been a soldier like you guys."

"You're a natural," Anna said, holding up her glass for Noy to clink. "Cheers."

Daniel hesitated behind Noy. Then he walked over to Anna and offered his hand. "That... What you did. It was spectacular."

She looked up at him, also hesitated, then shook his hand. "Precious few people in the world would describe it like that. But thanks, all the same. Tinkov deserved nothing less."

Everybody looked over at the laptop as a polished voice emanated from it. "I'm not normally one to break up a soirée," the disembodied Granville said. "But I'm having to assume everybody returned in one piece, since nobody has troubled to tell me."

McGinn crossed to the table. "Aye, we're all here."

"Wonderful. And you've recovered the phone, as agreed?" Harry and McGinn looked at each other, and there was a moment of total silence. "The one he was using, which could implicate me in everything which took place?"

"Oh, that phone," Noy said, and produced it from her pocket. "Room of crazy, dangerous spy people, and I'm only one who remember the most important part." She shook her head and made a tutting sound. "Lose Granville, whole operation is over. You guys need to be more careful in the future, okay?"

"When on earth did you get that?" Anna asked.

"When you and the Farang were rolling on the floor and stabbing people. Somebody had to... How do you say?" She looked at Daniel briefly, then clicked her fingers. "Keep their head cool."

Anna held up her glass again. "You really are a bloody natural," she said, and even Daniel - in a rare outpouring of public affection - put a hand on her shoulder and squeezed lightly.

"Thank God," Granville said. "Thank you Noy, more importantly. That's it then, Harry, I presume?"

"Not to be a party pooper, but there's one last thing," McGinn said. "CCTV. I presumed you already had a plan for it before I arrived."

Harry and Daniel looked at each other. Then Harry looked away and shook his head. "We didn't need one."

"The footage will never make it into police hands," Daniel said. "Or, if it does, it won't last long. They'll take it."

"The Company?"

Daniel nodded, eyes resting on the ground. "It's their MO. If incriminating CCTV gets disseminated publicly, it sparks an international manhunt. We're caught, eventually, and we end up in the hands of law enforcement. If that happens, we get offered deals."

"And tell them everything we know about the Company.

Which then gets leaked and made public. It's their worst case scenario."

"Well, that's a relief," Anna said. "In that case, all we have to worry about is the criminal gang with unlimited resources hunting us down and murdering us on the spot."

Nobody looked at each other, and there was silence in the room. Noy broke it. "This is a problem for the future," she said, shrugging. "For now, we do what we wanted. Kill a very bad man. Make the world a better place. Complete our first objective. Only two to go, and the computer stuff, and we're done. Anna is right - tonight, we deserve to drink."

"It took me forty years, but I finally found my soulmate," Anna said, lifting her glass to Noy once more. "I bloody well am right, and so is she."

"Hear, hear," Granville said, voice clearly echoing into a glass of some description. Anna and Noy poured wine for everybody, even Daniel accepting a small one, and they all held up their glasses. "I'm sure there's plenty to worry about just over the hill," Anna said. "But, for now, we celebrate while we still can. Cheers, everyone."

CHAPTER ELEVEN

Rupert brought the car to an abrupt stop outside the house, jogged up the steps, fumbled for his keys, and was already kicking off his shoes as the door slammed closed behind him.

He went upstairs to his and George's bedroom, stripped, went into the ensuite for a thirty second rinse and gave his teeth a thirty second brush. He put the same suit back on in the bedroom with fresh underwear and a clean shirt then went back down the stairs.

His feet had just hit the floor of the hallway when he heard George calling from the kitchen. "I *do* still exist, you know."

Rupert sighed and dropped the shoes he'd picked up back to the ground. George was sitting at the island in the kitchen, long legs easily reaching the ground from the high stool. He lowered his head to peer at Rupert over his glasses.

"Ah, hello, Rupert Granville MP," he intoned. "I'm George Chamberlain, your partner of some decades now. I hoped you might remember me, but-"

"I'm in rather a hurry."

"With matters legal or illegal, dare I ask?"

"I'm needed at Number 10 imminently."

George considered Rupert's evasive answer, then nodded. "I made you breakfast."

"I'm sorry, George. I really don't have the time." Rupert headed back towards the doorway. He stopped there, stood still a moment, then walked slowly over to the island. "That was very kind of you."

"Join me. Even if it's only for a minute."

Rupert did so, forcing down the panicked feeling which had been lodged in his chest ever since Harry and the others set off. He'd hoped the operation's successful conclusion would have settled this anxiety. All that had followed was a sleepless night running through the many potential consequences of their actions.

"You look like death itself," George said, as he fetched a plate of toast, eggs, and bacon and placed it in front of him.

Rupert felt a rush of nausea as he looked at the food, but put a small forkfull in his mouth regardless. "You're not looking your best either, dear."

"I'm worried sick about you."

"I refuse to argue about this again. It never leads anywhere."

"If you had any sense, it would lead to you giving the whole thing up."

"I'm doing a good thing here, George. I truly believe that."

"It's impossible for me to disagree, when I know none of the specifics."

"That's your own choice."

"Indeed, but I can infer quite enough to know that - at the very least - you're certainly risking your entire career over this. A career which, on its current trajectory, is heading to the highest level."

"And how do you think that's happening? Not through talent alone, I assure you."

"Regardless, if my worst suspicions are justified, that's only the tip of the iceberg. We can leave my own career aside, which will almost certainly be ruined by proxy, despite my deliberate ignorance, if whatever you're involved in goes wrong. But tell me honestly, Rupert. Are you putting your life in danger over this?"

Rupert deliberately cut off another piece of the toast, put egg and bacon on it, and lifted it to his mouth. He chewed slowly and swallowed before finally meeting George's eye. "Yes," he said. "It's a cause worth dying for, I'm afraid, George. A cause worth killing for, even."

"Sounds like something Miller would say," George muttered. "Our lives were progressing quite smoothly until he came crashing in here."

"I crashed into his life before that," Rupert said. "He had no say in the matter, but we are where we are now, and if you asked him I'm positive he wouldn't change the past."

"And you?"

"The same, George. I believe utterly in what I'm doing, and I'm determined to see it through."

"Then you're a fool. And you're leading us both to ruin, notwithstanding whatever other damage you might do."

Rupert forced a final forkful into his mouth, then placed the cutlery carefully back down on the plate. He stood, began to walk away, paused again in the doorway, and only half-turned back this time. "I'll need the car tonight, George, if you don't mind. And I'll be staying in the Chilterns. Everything is simpler there."

Rupert didn't look back as he left the kitchen. He took his coat from where he'd thrown it over the staircase bannister, opened the front door, and pulled it firmly closed behind him.

Rupert hurried down the front steps and into the Rolls Royce, which was idling outside. "Wherever did you appear from, Charlie?"

"I was waiting at the end of the road, sir," Charlie said, studiously checking his mirrors before pulling away. "I was expecting you five minutes ago."

"Exceptional circumstances, I'm afraid. Thank you for your punctuality regardless. You're the finest driver a fellow could wish for."

Rupert took his iPad from his briefcase and began scrolling through a draft proposal which had been sent over. It was all extremely important - not just for the Department for Digital, Culture, Media & Sport, but for his own credentials as a 'rising star' in politics - yet he found himself utterly unable to concentrate. He re-read the first paragraph several times without absorbing a word, sighed, and tossed the tablet onto the leather seat beside him.

"Everything all right, sir?"

"Not really, Charlie. I'm afraid I may have bitten off rather more than I can chew. My life appears to have become dramatically different within a very short space of time."

Charlie seemed to sense that no response was required. He gave only a short, neutral nod, eyes still fixed forward, and Rupert returned to his ruminations.

They pulled up near Number 10 fifteen minutes later. "I'll need you to hang around, Charlie," Rupert said as he gathered his things. "We'll be going straight back to the house afterwards."

"Sir?" Rupert had been halfway out of the car. He met Charlie's eyes in the rearview mirror. "There's something I ought to tell you."

"Oh?"

"I hope I'm not stepping out of line… But I feel as if my loyalty should be to you, above all."

"What is it, Charlie?"

"Mr Chamberlain, sir. He's been… asking questions."

"What sorts of questions?"

"Where you've been, and for how long. Who you've met. That sort of thing. I hardly had answers to anything he wanted to know. Those I did have, I kept to myself. I don't want to be a grass, you understand, sir, but I thought you should know."

"Indeed." Rupert stared blankly through the windscreen for a moment. "I shouldn't be too long," he said, then gave a quick nod and left the car.

The novelty of visiting Number 10 had disappeared without a trace. Already Rupert barely noticed his surroundings as he was guided deeper into the building from the main entrance. He did focus again, however, when he saw a woman awaiting him outside the door to which he was being led.

The recently-appointed banking representative smiled artificially at the secretary who'd accompanied Rupert. The smile dropped the moment the secretary's back was turned. The representative waited until the woman was out of earshot before leaning forward.

"What happened last night is an *utter* disaster."

Rupert stared at her dully for a long moment before realisation dawned. "Ah, regarding Tin-"

"Obviously, you buffoon," she said, cutting him off before he could finish the name and looking around.

"Certainly it's regrettable, but-"

"Regrettable? *Regrettable?*" she hissed. "You've clearly failed quite spectacularly to grasp the seriousness of the situation." Rupert simply waited for her to continue this time. "The higher-ups are spooked, Granville. They need reassurance, desperately, and it's your job to provide it."

Rupert's mind was sharp again now. He saw that the role he needed to play, for this woman specifically, was clear. He opened and closed his mouth a couple of times, gormlessly, and his eyes flickered from side to side in apparent uncertainty. "Indeed?"

"Yes! That's your job, isn't it? To 'liaise' between the bank and the Company?"

"Ah, well… yes, of course. I'll see what I can do." The woman's glare showed Rupert what she thought of that answer. Before she could retort he looked pointedly at his watch. "I think, you know, that we should…" He reached hurriedly for the door handle and the woman had no time to reply before he pressed down.

Ruth Audmore, the Prime Minister's Chief of Staff, was waiting behind her large desk. She stood as they entered and directed a tired smile towards each of them. Lord Frost was sitting in one of the three chairs in front of the desk. He nodded at them but declined to stand.

"Please," Audmore said, motioning to the two empty chairs. "You'll note that we have one fewer seat than at our last meeting here. Naturally, that's why I've called you in at such short notice." She sat again with a sigh and ran a hand across her face as Rupert and the woman settled. "You've all got your contacts. You'll all have heard the news. Does anyone have any details, yet?"

Nobody spoke for several moments. Rupert looked at the other two, then cleared his throat. "All I know is that he died, I'm afraid. Getting any further information has been significantly more difficult since the war out east began. The Company's been running a tight ship, and controlling what gets out very closely."

"Are we assuming it was deliberate? An assassination?"

"I haven't heard so," Rupert ventured, after looking at the other two again. "But that seems the most plausible explanation."

"Did you know he was in Barcelona, Granville?"

It was Frost who asked the question. Rupert turned to him, affecting surprise. "Me? Of course not. I had no idea. I hadn't spoken to him before we met here, and I haven't since." Frost's grey eyes pierced his. "I'm flattered you think he'd take any interest in me at all, Lord Frost. But I wasn't privy to Yuri Tinkov's private travel plans, no."

Rupert's voice had lacked the usual deferential respect, and he wondered momentarily if he'd pushed too far. He'd taken a calculated gamble at the cocktail party he and Frost had attended; its paying-off might have led him into a false sense of security. He was more surprised than anybody, he was sure, when Frost simply nodded and looked back to Audmore.

"Needless to say, this is an absolute disaster for us all," Audmore continued. "Tinkov wasn't merely one of the three most important figures in the whole Company. He was the closest to this government, by far. I don't mind sharing, in fact, that I'm utterly clueless as to who the surviving members of the so-called Three even are."

"Come, come," the woman said. "*Disaster* is too strong a word, Ms Audmore. At the bank, we believe it to be merely a setback." Rupert couldn't help but look around. But the representative didn't meet his eye, and her artificial smile was shining at full wattage.

"Indeed? Well, I'm reassured to hear that."

"Losing Tinkov is certainly a blow, but we'd expect a replacement to be installed quickly enough?" The intonation of the statement rose into that of a question, and the woman looked at Rupert, still smiling.

"I, ah- Well... Yes," Rupert stammered. "As I say, I haven't had much contact from the Company yet. But I'm positive that a replacement will be found, and business will continue as usual in the meantime. And, if this was indeed deliberate, whoever was foolish enough to execute it will surely be rooted out. My own suspicion, if I may, is that this was a retort from the Operation, in response to the Company's attack on their Manila headquarters. We believed them decapitated, but perhaps there was a last and violent remnant of life left after all."

Frost murmured his agreement. The banking representative nodded slowly. "That sounds plausible," she said. "And, if that is indeed what it was, the threat should be removed soon enough when the last vestiges of the Operation are mopped up. In the meantime, we'd trust the Company to keep this under wraps. Tinkov's death must be announced today, of course, for its impact on his various businesses. But the messaging must be exquisite. The death must seem accidental, natural, to avoid all speculation and any spooking of our investors."

"Quite so," Frost said. "I'll reach out to a contact of my own at the Company. There's a PR firm I've used several times to handle the fallout in such cases. They'll ensure this is handled in the optimal-"

He broke off mid-sentence. Audmore's phone had buzzed several times in front of her already throughout the conversation. On each occasion she had simply glanced at it then back up again. This time her eyes were fixed on the screen and her face had fallen. She looked up at Frost, as if to apologise, then reached instead for a TV control that lay upon her desk.

Rupert heard a television, fixed to the far wall from Audmore's desk, come to life. He and the other two turned in their seats. The TV was already tuned to BBC News. Rupert swore emphatically when he saw the headline in large letters at the bottom of the screen - 'RUSSIAN BILLIONAIRE OLIGARCH ASSASSINATED'.

"How on Earth did they..." Rupert began. "Who told..."

"So much for our exquisite messaging," Frost said. Rupert glanced at him, and saw his normally steadfast face was grim. "This is now a question of damage control. I'll place some calls immediately."

Rupert turned to see the banking representative's reaction. She was staring straight at him. Her eyes were burning. He gave a weak shrug, as if to ask what *he* could possibly have done, then looked back to the screen.

A quarter of an hour later Rupert was back in the Rolls Royce and returning to Bloomsbury. He placed a call and waited for several rings until it was answered.

"Minister? I'm honoured."

"I'm sure. I saw your handiwork on the news."

"And?"

"It was perfect. Couldn't have done it better myself."

"Obviously. What happens now?"

"You sit back, and enjoy whatever clandestine journalistic clout you've amassed from all this."

"Have I passed your little test, then? Will I be trusted with the next juicy scoop you happen to come across? The events of which had no direct involvement with you, of course."

"Oh, believe me, Ms Archer - they'll get far juicier than this."

"Colour me intrigued."

"One last thing. Lord Frost may be in touch soon."

"And, if he asks, you'll want me to deny having any contact whatsoever with you, and any knowledge at all of what happened to Tinkov."

"Naturally."

"Frost has been a big help to me, you know."

"His intentions won't have been purely charitable, I assure you."

"That's for sure. Fine, consider my lips sealed."

"Wonderful work so far, Ms Archer. I'll be in touch."

Rupert ended the call, sat back, closed his eyes, and let out a long sigh. It felt as if his heart had been hammering in his chest for two days straight. He took several more deep breaths and felt it beginning to settle. Then he remembered the inevitable clash that would be awaiting him at the house and his chest tightened again.

He needn't have worried. George had left the car. The keys were on the island in the kitchen, from which he'd cleared the plate with Rupert's breakfast. The house itself was deserted.

CHAPTER TWELVE

Granville was waiting for them outside the airport, more or less in the same place he'd dropped them off.

"Congratulations, old chap," Granville said, shaking Harry's hand. "Hard to believe it's only been a day since last we met."

"I know what you mean. Meet McGinn, our newest addition."

"Your reputation precedes you, sir." Granville offered his hand again and smiled up at the Scot. "A pleasure." Granville welcomed each of the others then turned back to Harry. "It's going to be a bit of a squeeze."

"Don't worry about me, pal," McGinn said, winking. "I'll make my own way there."

Harry felt Daniel looking at him. He avoided meeting his eyes. "You're sure?"

"I've got a stop to make in London, then I'll head up. Won't be more than an hour or two behind you, Cap, don't worry."

Anna was watching him now too. Harry ignored her and his brother as he said goodbye to McGinn and got into the passenger seat. Noy fell asleep almost immediately as they set off back for the Chilterns, and Anna wasn't far behind. Harry glanced at Granville.

"What is it?" Harry asked.

"Could you be a little more specific?"

"Something's wrong. I can tell."

"Oh, no. Nothing really. Naturally I'm carrying rather a lot of stress, between our little clandestine operation, my political positions, liaising between the bank and the Company, and so on."

"It's not just that."

Granville kept his eyes fixed pointedly forwards. They drove in silence for a full minute before he swallowed, opened his mouth wordlessly, then tried again. "All of this is taking rather a toll on my personal life."

"Chamberlain's kicking up a fuss?"

"He has every right to, Harry. He didn't exactly sign up for this sort of thing. A little politicking here and there, certainly, but nothing like this. I'm afraid…" He broke off, and swallowed again. "I'm not sure what I'd do without him. Or if any of this would be worth it, if he wasn't there once it was all done. I know that's an awful thing to say. We're working for a higher cause, after all. But… there it is."

There followed another minute of silence. "You'll fix it," Harry said eventually. "We'll get through this quickly. And once we have, you'll figure it out. You two are… well-suited."

Granville's hands tightened on the steering wheel. He let out a long sigh, then nodded. "Thank you, Harry."

It was a little after midday when they arrived back at the country house. The front door opened as they were crunching up the large driveway and Sarah Miller greeted them all in turn. Harry caught the slight hesitation before she went to hug Daniel and wished he hadn't seen it.

Noy lifted her nose and sniffed as they reached the entrance hall. "I never know food in England could smell so good."

"Don't get too excited, dear. I had nothing better to do this morning."

"Oh, Sarah," Anna said, putting a hand on her shoulder as she moved into the dining room alongside her. "You are a naughty girl."

"It's nothing, really."

Harry shook his head as he saw the large dining table. His mother seemed to have made every single dish in her arsenal and thrown them all together into what, for him, was a feast of childhood memories. There were the spaghetti meatballs she'd cooked after he and Daniel returned from rugby training on Wednesdays; the curry that had been his father's favourite; the lasagna she'd always made on Harry's birthdays.

"You shouldn't have," Harry said, standing beside his mother by the door as the others started plating up.

"I really did have the time."

Something in her voice made him look at her. "Are you okay?"

"Of course I am, dear. Go and get your food. I'll bet you didn't have breakfast."

"Mum."

"It was fine, really. Initially, at least, when Rupert was here."

"And when he wasn't?"

She folded her arms and shook her head with a smile that gradually slipped away. Suddenly the corner of her eye began to water and she reached up hurriedly to wipe it clear.

"I miss him, Harry. It hasn't been long at all since he… since… It's easy to forget, with everything that's been going on, but it hasn't been long. I feel like I haven't had time… Oh, it sounds so foolish, so old-fashioned. But I haven't had time to… grieve."

Harry nodded, staring down at the floor. A familiar scene flashed across his mind; one which he had replayed countless times over the previous three years. He was sitting beside his mother in a long, black car which trailed a hearse supposedly containing his brother's coffin. They hadn't talked before, they weren't talking then, and they wouldn't talk afterwards for years. He had been no good to anybody, not even his own mother, and every time he remembered that morning he felt a stronger wave of self-hatred.

Harry turned quickly, put his arms around his mother, and squeezed her tight. She stood still for a moment, perhaps in surprise, then hugged him back. "I miss him too, Mum," Harry said in her ear. "I know it's not the same. I know I abandoned him - him and you both. But I miss him too. We'll say a proper goodbye when all this is over."

He felt his mother's cheek wet against his. She nodded, squeezed him tight, then patted him hard several times on the back and wiped her eyes as she pulled away.

"I won't quite say that you're a *good* son, Harry. I'm sorry," she said, the hint of a smile on her face. "But you're on the right track. Now go and get some food. You look thin."

Sarah had guessed rightly that none of them had eaten breakfast, and despite its volume the lunch was devoured with relish. Sarah had seen the news of course, but was given a fuller account of what happened in Barcelona. Noy led the retelling, albeit while skipping over the more violent details, particularly involving Daniel. She also failed to mention her recovery of Tinkov's phone, although this was quickly corrected by both Anna and Granville.

McGinn arrived as they were clearing the plates away. He had seen Sarah at Daniel's supposed funeral, but she didn't recognise him and Harry was more than happy introducing him as if for the first time.

Granville led McGinn up to one of the several guest bedrooms, and Anna stopped Harry in the entrance hall. "You're not going to ask him where he was?"

"He's a grown man, who can come and go as he pleases. Besides, he's here of his own volition. I'm not his superior now, even if he still seems to think that."

"You have to admit that it looks a little odd."

"No, I don't." Harry realised that he'd spoken too sharply, and composed himself. "See it from my perspective," he said. "I've vouched for McGinn personally. I've told everyone how much I trust him. I can't then turn around and ask him what he's been up to, where he's gone, who he's seen, every time he's out of my sight for more than an hour."

Anna met his eyes steadily. Then her face broke into a smile, and she patted him on the side of his arm. "It's not easy, being the de facto leader. I'm happy to say I've never had to experience it myself, and hopefully never will. Taking potshots from the sidelines is far more straightforward."

"And you do it so very well."

"Years of practice." She kissed him on the cheek, and carried on to the kitchen.

Granville returned to London after the feast had been cleared away, but everybody else gathered in the expansive living room. It was a dull, oppressive afternoon outside the many windows. Sarah dozed on one sofa while Noy and Daniel sat on another talking quietly.

Harry and Anna sat either side of McGinn at the dining table. "No guarantees this'll work, Cap," he said, as he plugged Tinkov's phone into his laptop. "I'm not much of a hacker by any stretch."

"Unfortunately for you, I haven't got time to find one. Not one I'd trust, anyway." Harry put a hand on the Scot's shoulder and squeezed. "Just see what you can find."

The phone lit up then loaded onto the lock screen. McGinn opened a program on his laptop. "Pal of mine gave me this, when I thought an old girlfriend was cheating on me." He clicked a couple of times. "Probably shouldn't have told you that."

"And?"

"Turns out she wasn't," McGinn murmured, eyes scouring the screen. "Unfortunately she caught me while I was still going through her messages, and that was the end of that."

"Yes, we women-folk tend not to like that kind of thing," Anna said. "Though I can't imagine why."

"Aye, found that out the hard way," McGinn grinned as he clicked several more times. "We're in."

CHAPTER THIRTEEN

Harry and Anna both leaned closer over McGinn's shoulders.

The contents of the phone were displayed as a long list of folders. One was called 'CONTACTS', another 'MESSAGES'. McGinn opened each in turn and found them both to be full. He leant away from the laptop and drummed his hand on the desk. "We've hit the motherlode here, Cap," he said.

Harry smiled, and squeezed McGinn's shoulder again in excitement. He found Daniel looming by his side and watching too. "This is a bloody treasure trove," Harry said to him. "I'm sure this wasn't the only phone he used, but still. We've got names, numbers, messages…"

As McGinn was scrolling through the folders, the phone suddenly buzzed on the table. A notification appeared on the screen, in front of all the other windows. It was a message which seemed to have only just arrived, from a number which wasn't saved on the phone.

McGinn shrugged, and ran a quick search. "Burmese number."

Daniel immediately turned to look at Noy, and Harry wasn't far behind. She had been frowning as she flicked through a newspaper, but sensed their stares and looked up. "What you want?"

"Nothing," Daniel said, and turned back to McGinn. "Open it."

The message was only two words long: 'DANIEL MILLER'.

"What the hell is this?" Anna muttered.

"Any idea who it could be?" Harry asked, but Daniel only shook his head.

Another notification appeared as they watched the screen. McGinn glanced at Daniel this time before opening it. 'YOU CAN'T HIDE.'

The message was followed by a photo, which McGinn opened immediately. It showed a small, one storey, semi-detached house. A metal shutter was pulled down over the front room and out front there was no road or other paving, only light brown dirt.

"That's... my house."

Harry and Daniel looked down to find Noy standing between them. Her eyes were fixed on the screen. Another photo arrived. The shutter had been pulled up now, and a local man stood outside the house with a boy in his early teens beside him. Whoever took the photo had gone closer, and the man was shouting something at him.

"My father," Noy whispered. "My brother."

McGinn looked to Noy this time when the next photo arrived. She gulped and nodded. When he opened it Anna swore, and Noy's eyes widened.

The photo had been taken inside. The shutter seemed to have been closed again, but a light overhead starkly illuminated the room. The man and teenage boy were both tied to dining chairs. Thick rope had been wrapped several times around their bodies and pairs of socks had been stuffed into their mouths. Their faces were bloody and the teenage boy seemed to have been beaten unconscious.

Harry couldn't help but glance at Noy, and immediately wished he hadn't. Her brow, normally furrowed in a near-perpetual frown, had lifted in confusion and shock. Tears fell silently down her cheeks. Anna had already moved to put an arm around her shoulder but Noy seemed not to have noticed.

Daniel's scarred face, normally inscrutable, had formed into an expression of cold fury.

"Hostages," Harry said. "But who took them? The Company couldn't have reacted this quickly after Tinkov. They couldn't possibly know it was us yet."

"It doesn't matter," Daniel said, his voice quiet. "We'll go there and get them. Noy knows exactly where they are."

"They'll have been moved. We'll see what the demands are and work from there."

"We're not negotiating."

"You think I want to? We'll see what they are, and then-"

Harry broke off as another notification appeared on the screen. He'd expected it to be text, beginning to list demands, but saw it was another photo. McGinn let out a long breath, then opened it.

Noy let out a scream then buried her face in her hands before Anna turned her away from the screen and pulled her into a tight hug. Sarah had come over too and was already wrapping her arms around both of them. Harry ran a hand through his hair, feeling his skin go cold but unable to take his eyes from the screen, even as Daniel turned from the screen with a shout of rage, picked up the nearest chair, and brought it smashing down against the floor.

Both the man and the teenage boy were slumped in their chairs, their throats cut and their shirts soaked with blood.

Harry and McGinn were the only ones still watching the screen when the final notification appeared.

'THERE WILL BE NO ESCAPE'.

Anna and Sarah had taken Noy away but her sorrow lingered in the room. Daniel prowled back and forth along the same five metre stretch near the table, his boots crunching over the splintered remains of the chair. It was as agitated as Harry had seen him in two decades.

"Ready, Cap?" McGinn asked. Harry nodded, and McGinn brought the final photo up again. He and Harry looked at each other, expressions equally grim.

"We have to."

"Aye, I know."

"Zoom in on them," Harry made himself say, and McGinn did so. "Clean, fast cuts. Identical too."

"Definitely the work of a pro."

"The boy took a beating, but minimal bruising on the man. The killer kept his cool."

"Kid must have fought back more than he was expecting."

"Show me the bindings."

McGinn moved down towards the pair's midsections. "Textbook. Couldn't have moved an inch."

Daniel had come over. He held one of the chair legs in his right hand like a club. "There was a mirror."

"Where?"

"Top-right."

McGinn zoomed all the way back out and Harry saw that Daniel had been right. When the photo had first appeared his eyes had gone straight to the bodies before the final message appeared soon after. Now he saw that a cracked mirror hung on the wall at around head-height. The photo had been taken at an angle, and the mirror itself was more or less in line with the person who'd taken it.

"Zoom in."

The killer had made no effort to hide his face. He hadn't been looking at the bodies as he had taken the photo. He had been looking in the mirror, straight back at the camera, so that his eyes seemed to meet Harry's.

The lack of an expression on his face felt like an act of defiance in itself. There was no arrogance there, nor anger, nor confidence. There was only the cold clarity, the simple certainty, that had also filled his messages.

"You've got facial recognition? Access to a database?"

"There's someone I can ask. It won't take long."

Harry nodded. "I'm sure nothing will come up, but we can try anyway." He saw Daniel studying the man's face closely, his face tight with hatred. "You recognise him?"

Daniel paused before answering. "No," he said eventually. "But I can guess. I heard rumours, when I worked with the Company. Rumours about a man, codename Vocitus. Nobody I knew had ever met him. He always worked alone. He answered directly to the Three." He met Harry's eyes. "He's supposed to be the best there is. A ghost. A genius. They say he's invincible."

"You think it's him?"

"Few people at the Company knew anything about me. I was sure they knew nothing at all about Noy. I don't know anyone else who could have put it together so quickly. Nor anyone who would have... done it like this."

"What do you mean?"

"You were right before. Anybody else would have kept them as hostages. Used them to draw you out."

"Me?"

"You're the one they want. They're getting to you through me," Daniel said. "But he didn't use them. He just killed them. It's a statement, that he doesn't need to negotiate. Doesn't need to bargain. That he'll find and kill us all. All of us and all of our families too."

Harry didn't show how much Daniel's words chilled him. He nodded slowly, and when he spoke his face and voice remained steady. "We'll just have to kill him first, then."

"How?"

"If he's such a genius, he'll work out what we're trying to do before anyone else. He'll be there waiting for us when we move on the next target. So we engage him, and we kill him."

Daniel's hand tightened automatically on the chair leg. "Agreed."

"We never expected this to be easy," Harry said. "And now we've got three objectives. Take out the rest of the Three. Expose the Company's actions for the whole world to see." He turned to look back at the amplified face on the screen. "And make this bastard pay."

End of Part One

PART TWO

CHAPTER FOURTEEN

It was a frosty night in New York City.

The doorman stood outside the West Village apartment block wearing a long grey coat and with his gloved hands held behind him. He reached for the door and tipped his cap as a man in a tuxedo and a woman in a long, white dress and a fake fur coat passed and got into a waiting car.

The Assassin watched him. He waited for the car to depart, and the doorman to resume his post, before approaching.

The doorman didn't see him coming. But he was professional enough not to jump when, having looked one way up the street, he turned back to find the Assassin in front of him.

"Good evening, sir."

"I'm going inside."

The doorman's frown was so fleeting as to be almost imperceptible. "Do you have friends living here, sir? Or… family?"

"Who pays you to guard this building?"

"I'm only here to open and close the door, sir."

"You know everybody who lives here. You report anybody you don't know as soon as they go in."

The doorman forced his good-natured, welcoming smile onto his face as an elderly woman approached with her small dog. The Assassin turned the other way as she went inside.

"If there's anything I can actually help you with, sir, I'd be-"

"I'm going to see Mr Bohm."

"Sorry, sir, I don't know any Mr Bohm."

"He owns the building. It's his security that you report to."

"I can't just let you-"

"Your name is Martin Harper. Your wife is Sandra Harper. She's alone at your apartment on West 160th Street. If you don't let me inside then I'll place a call and Sandra will die."

"You cold-hearted bastard."

"Move."

The doorman glared, fists clenched at his sides now. Then he stepped aside.

"I'll know if you call the police or tell Bohm's security I'm coming, and Sandra will die. If you call the police after and tell them what's happened tonight, you'll both be killed."

The Assassin's voice was as cold as the night air. He met the doorman's eyes as he walked past him and entered the building.

The lobby was broad and opulent, with white walls, bronze-coloured fittings, and a large chandelier shining over the central atrium. There was a wide mirror directly opposite the door, with pairs of elevators to the left and right.

The Assassin went straight towards the furthest elevator on the right. Unlike the others it had a small black reader rather than a button. He took a white card from his pocket and pressed it against the reader. A green light flashed and the doors opened.

The Assassin kept his face lowered as he entered the lift and turned so that his back was to the small CCTV camera in one of the corners. He pressed the top metallic button and waited as the lift rose to the penthouse.

The lift opened into a small, caged area. The Assassin touched the keypad by the door in the metal frame to activate it, entered a 10-digit code, and heard a lock snapping open.

A guard was just hurrying over as the Assassin opened the door. He had been monitoring the lift's CCTV. Even if he hadn't seen the occupant's face, he knew the man wasn't expected. The fact, however, that the intruder had not only entered the building without any report from the doorman, but entered the lift too, had made the guard confused and suspicious rather than outright aggressive.

"Who the hell are you?" he asked, holding a tablet in one hand on which nine separate CCTV feeds were displayed.

"I'm here to kill your boss."

The man didn't even have time to move before the Assassin punched him straight in the windpipe. He let out a strangled gurgle and sank to his knees, hands clasping at his throat. The Assassin took the tablet from where it had fallen and glanced at it as he continued past the guard.

The bottom half of the long hallway's walls were made of richly-coloured wood. Abstract paintings hung before the dark green wallpaper along the top half, between the closed doors on either side. There were several sculpted busts on tall black stands too, all of which were surely originals.

The Assassin reached the end of the hall and went through the open doorway to his left. The room he entered could have been lifted directly from a finance magazine, or the advert for some aspirational brand.

Wooden walls ran along two sides of the penthouse. The other two sides, to the Assassin's left and directly in front, were all floor-to-ceiling windows. This building was taller than those it faced, and the Manhattan skyline glittered beyond the roofs around it.

The living room itself was enormous, with two separate seating areas in the centre - each with several sofas arranged in squares - and a long dining table with a dozen chairs towards the far-right corner. Classical music played from speakers covertly spaced around the room, although there appeared to be nobody listening to it.

The Assassin crossed the room and slid open a discreet door in one of the tall windows. A man stood on the balcony which ran all the way around the apartment's exterior, impossible to see from inside thanks to the reflections of the lights on the glass. He held a tumbler of whiskey in one hand and his phone in the other.

"We ready to go?" the man asked, thumb racing across the screen. He looked up. "Ah, Vocitus," he said. He finished writing the email, sent it, then put his phone away and looked again. "You're lucky you caught me. I'm meeting a few clients at ten." The Assassin met his eyes. "Not lucky?"

"No."

"And you got in here... how?" Bohm swirled the whiskey in his glass and took a slow sip. He wore a new suit and his hair was slicked back. He was in his early fifties, short, and had a chiselled face which looked skeletal whenever he smiled. "This explains my guy Brown's recent disappearance. You got everything you needed from him, I guess. Is he still alive?"

"For what it's worth. Your security must be improved."

"Fortunately for me, there's nobody else like you out there. And you're already on the payroll."

"Still."

"Still what? Nobody'd be crazy enough to come after one of us three, right?" He took another sip. "That's a joke. Tinkov got sloppy I guess, but sure, we can tighten things up. You'll fix it for me?"

The Assassin inclined his head an inch.

"Spectacular. Hang on a second." Bohm took his phone from his pocket, smiled at whatever he saw, and dashed off a quick response. He looked back up at the Assassin, still grinning. "Know why I'm the best at what I do? Instincts. That's it. Nothing more complicated than that. There are plenty of hot shots with hedge funds out there. My portfolio's the biggest and best because I *know* I'm right, and I trust myself completely." He nodded towards the door. "Come on in, I'm freezing my balls off out here."

The Assassin followed Bohm inside. The expensively-besuited American shook himself, put his glass on the dining table, and blew into his hands. If the Assassin had felt the cold in any way, he didn't show it.

"I'm glad you're here," Bohm said. "It's been over twenty four hours since Tinkov went down, and nobody's told me anything I can sink my teeth into. I've heard it was one guy acting alone. I've heard it was a whole crew. I've heard it was personal. I've heard it was business. What have you got for me?"

"Daniel Miller."

"I know that name. He was out in Singapore. He was there when they got attacked. Fought well, according to that psycho Jansen. I thought he was on our side?"

"He attacked his team in Bangkok, then disappeared."

"Went crawling back to the Operation? Or was he working for them all along?"

"He did it for a girl."

"You're kidding me."

"I interviewed Jansen. Then hacked Miller's laptop in Singapore."

"He didn't wipe it?"

"Not well enough. I got hold of the Operation's records seized during a raid involving Jansen and Miller in southern Thailand. One girl who came into his compound and never left. I found and killed her family. Let Miller know."

Bohm stared at the Assassin for several moments. "Why'd you let him know?"

"To provoke emotion. Emotion clouds everything."

"And you knew he was involved in the hit on Tinkov? How?"

The Assassin paused. "Instincts."

Bohm laughed, took his whiskey glass up once more, and drained the rest of his drink. "Cute," he said. "What's the motive?"

"Unclear. But I spoke to Tinkov shortly before he was killed. He mentioned meeting with another Miller. Harry. Daniel's brother."

"A family affair? That's juicy." Bohm pulled back the sleeve of his tailored jacket and glanced at his Rolex. "Time to motor. Walk with me."

They crossed the lounge, heading back towards the corridor. "So this *Harry* Miller had a problem with our Russian friend, like a hell of a lot of other people," Bohm said. "He brings his brother in, they take Tinkov out together, and that's that. Sounds like you've just gotta find these brothers and put a couple of bullets in their brains."

Bohm stopped in the hallway next to his guard, who lay on the ground. "Was this necessary?"

"It was a test."

"I expect you to handle the logistics, if he's dead." The two men continued along the hallway, entered the lift, and Bohm pressed the bottom button. "So what do you make of these

Millers?"

"Not much. The older one had a good career in the army, but it didn't last. The younger one had a mediocre military career, then looked after a compound in the middle of nowhere for a few years."

"I'm not exactly quaking in my boots. You know the other reason I'm the best?"

The Assassin didn't respond.

"I'm not scared of anything. Nothing and nobody. I've beaten everyone I've come up against. Overcome every challenge. *Confidence.* Sheer confidence can take you a hell of a long way, my murderous friend. Got anything else for me?"

"No."

"Swell," Bohm said, as the lift reached the ground floor. "So, sort out my security, and take out these Miller clowns. Now that I say it out loud, that sounds a bit too easy, especially considering your paycheque. Remind me to think of a harder job next time, will you? Some kind of a real challenge." He led the way across the lobby and nodded as the main door was opened for them. "Martin."

"Mr Bohm," the doorman said, nodding while his eyes remained fixed on the Assassin.

A sleek black car was idling outside. The driver got out the moment Bohm set foot on the pavement and hurried to open the door for him. "What the hell did you do to Martin?" Bohm asked.

"Another test."

"Well try not to incapacitate him too, would you? He's a real gentleman. In fact, maybe just call ahead next time, okay?"

Bohm held out a hand, nodded to the Assassin, and got into the car. The door was slammed closed behind him and the driver pulled away.

The Assassin looked back over his shoulder. The doorman was watching him. The Assassin stared at him until he looked away, then turned and walked off into the night.

CHAPTER FIFTEEN

The world was filled with chaos and violence. Desert winds whipped sand in all directions and through the gritty haze Harry saw the flashes of explosions and gunfire, vehicles going up in fireballs, men fighting and dying.

Harry was unarmed and wandering lost through the midst of it all. He knew nobody, the figures only outlines in the storm, and was unable to focus on the faces even though there were dozens, hundreds of people twisting, shouting, grappling, running, dying.

He found that he had begun to run, although his feet didn't strike the ground. He was heading somewhere specific, knowing what he would find, desperately not wanting to, yet still being inexorably drawn onwards through the maelstrom.

The silhouette of an enormous, wrecked vehicle became clearer in the dust, then he saw the bodies scattered around it as he drew closer still and all of them were dead because of him. The next moment he had stopped, suddenly, in front of one body in particular which was torn and unmoving. He was unable or unwilling to focus on the face but he knew, even as he knew at the same time that it was impossible, that it was the body of his brother.

He felt somebody grabbing at his shoulders, pulling at him, trying to pull him away. He shouted as he fought them off. He was screaming now but the sound seemed distant, unreal. Someone was calling his name, but he tried to cling on to the world and his brother's body even as it all faded around him.

The new world seemed just as unreal as that which he had

departed. It was dimly-lit and, although there had been no true sound in his dream, still seemed shockingly silent. He found himself sitting up and breathing very quickly and his naked body covered in sweat. A hand was on his shoulder, cold against his wet skin.

"Harry."

Still panting, he turned. Relief and shame coursed through him as he found Anna's face inches from his own. His throat was dry, and he swallowed with difficulty before trying to talk. "I'm sorry."

"I wish you'd stop saying that," she said softly. "Come here."

Anna turned him by the shoulders and made him lay down on the damp, dishevelled towel covering his half of the bed. He turned towards her to hug her as a child might. She put one arm around him and ran the other hand across his hair.

"What happened?" she asked quietly.

"The usual. Was I loud?"

"It doesn't matter."

"I don't understand. I don't know why…"

"The human mind is a great and complex mystery, Captain Miller, and I doubt you'll be the one to solve it. But still, it wouldn't hurt to talk, even to a psychoanalytical know-nothing like myself."

"It was the same as always. The ambush. Dead soldiers. Daniel at the end." Harry shook his head. "I thought it would all stop after I found out he was alive. But I'm literally sharing the same house as him, and it's still…" Anna didn't reply, and Harry raised his eyes to look up at her. "Tell me. I won't throw a hissy fit."

"Well, if you insist," she said, and gave him a brief smile. "He's still alive, in a literal sense, but you've said yourself that he's a completely different person. The brother you knew *did* die in that ambush. Your subconscious might be struggling to catch up with that, even if you're trying to navigate it all as best you can in your conscious state."

Harry stared at the wall as he turned over her words. Then he nodded, his head still pressed to her breast. "You're right."

"Always."

"Perhaps that goes away in time. I hope so. But the others... the other men who died that day." Harry trailed off, closed his eyes, and let out a deep breath. Carefully he broke free, then straightened up and sat on the edge of the bed. He looked back at her. "There's no psychoanalysis needed. They died because of me. I'll never get over that."

Anna met his gaze, then something in her face softened. She sat up too and came to drape her arms around his neck.

"No. You won't," she said, trailing her fingers along a scar on his torso. "And there's nothing I can do to change that. But I'll be there waiting for you in the mornings, when the nightmares are over. And I'll be there in the nights, once you're done playing the big, fearless leader for the day, if you ever do want to talk about it. That's all I can offer."

Harry nodded, smiled, and ran a hand across her cheek.

Harry and Anna descended the staircase together. As they reached the entrance hall they heard arguing in the living room. The voices raised in pitch and intensity, each cutting the other off before one seemed to make a final declaration.

They couldn't help but look in that direction, and each met the eyes of George Chamberlain as he stormed out of the room as quickly as his long legs would carry him. He paused when he saw them, his face pink and mouth tight.

"Good day to you both," he said, clearly trying to master the emotion in his voice. His eyes lingered on Harry, who couldn't help but feel as if Chamberlain blamed him for something; for everything, perhaps. After that long moment, however, Chamberlain only gave a terse nod before sweeping across the entrance hall and slamming the front door behind him. With the Mercedes still left for Granville, despite it all, Harry heard Chamberlain's footsteps crunching away along the drive towards where a driver was presumably waiting.

Harry looked towards the living room. Anna shook her head and led him instead towards the kitchen, where they found Sarah was preparing a large breakfast. She smiled at them as they entered and came over to help. Harry kissed her on the cheek, then began cracking eggs into a large bowl.

"I presume that was George slamming that door?"

"How long was he here?"

"All of five minutes. I fear for them, you know. Trying times like these can push even the most loving couples to the brink."

"Have you seen Noy?"

"They haven't come down yet." Sarah's hand hovered over the onions she'd been chopping, then she lay down the knife. There was a tremble in her voice when she spoke again. "What a horrible, horrible thing. I can't imagine… Not like that."

"We'll find the man who did it. We'll make him pay."

"Yes. That's how it works in the world you all inhabit, isn't it? A never ending cycle of violence, one bad turn deserving another."

"What do you want us to do?" Harry said sharply. "Let him get away with it?"

Sarah paused. "No," she said. "I suppose I wouldn't, just as I don't want the people responsible for your father's death to 'get away with it'."

"That's good old fashioned human nature for you," Anna said, putting several pieces of bread into a large toaster. "You're a woman of logic and reason, Sarah, and I respect you for it, but the desire for revenge is inherent to us all. Someone pushes you, you push them back. It's instinctive - we're born with it. Did I ever tell you that I killed my own father, for what he did to my mother?"

Sarah's eyes widened. "I think I'd have remembered."

Anna shrugged. "Never regretted it. Not for one solitary second. The person largely responsible for the death of Tasha's father is still out there too, still working for the Company. Forced me into cold-blooded murder, when I was out in Bangkok with this one." She slapped a hand on Harry's shoulder. "You can be certain that killing her is still on the old To Do list, and you can be damn well positive that I won't regret it afterwards."

Anna pushed the toaster's plunger down with a flourish, turned to fill the kettle, put it on, then winked at Sarah and left the kitchen. Sarah stared after her for several long moments, then turned back to find Harry watching her from the corner of his eye.

"Yes?"

"Nothing."

"I know what you think, and you're wrong." Sarah said. "I like her."

"Really?"

"Very much. And I wouldn't just say that. She's... not like the girls who used to come for dinner, when you were younger."

"Not exactly."

"But you inhabit a very different world now. A world I largely hate, and a world she's very much a part of, but she's... real. Genuine. Very, very strong. It must be so difficult, to be forced apart from her daughter and grandmother in circumstances like these, but she never complains. She's more sympathetic than she lets on too, beneath the tough exterior. She understands people. She understood enough to give us a rare moment alone, without making a song and dance about it or even bothering with an excuse. That's her to a tee, I suppose, from what little I've gathered."

Harry felt a boyish grin spreading across his face and fought to suppress it. Many years had passed, but he well remembered his mother's lukewarm responses to each girlfriend he had brought home. He went back to beating the eggs and heard his mother chopping the onions again.

"I'm... struggling with your brother, Harry."

Harry kept his head down and his voice level. "I noticed."

"Has he?"

"No idea. He's a little hard to read. Even more so than before."

"I feel like the worst mother in the world. I just... It hurts to look at him. I don't just mean the scars. He's a different person. He was always quieter than you, more withdrawn, but there was a sweetness there too, a sensitivity, a vulnerability deep down if you knew where to look. Now... I just don't see it. I don't want to tell you this, to put it all on you, really, but I... I have nobody else to tell any more."

"I understand."

"Lord knows you've changed too, and getting used to that after you finally deigned to grace your father and I with your presence again was a struggle. Don't think I'm letting you off the hook."

"I didn't, but thank you for the confirmation."

"This feels different, though. There was still enough of you left to get a handle on. Enough to anchor all of the changes. I can't find that with him. He feels..." Sarah dropped the knife, and rested both hands on the worktop. Harry swallowed, lay the whisk against the side of the bowl, and moved to put an arm around her.

"Like a stranger," Harry said. "I know. I feel the same way, but he's not. It'll never be as it was, for any of us." He managed to keep his voice level as he said it, and hoped his mother had no idea how much it had cost him to do so. "It can't be," he continued. "With Dad gone and everything else that's happened. But it can be better than this. We have to finish what we've started. It's more important than any of this, and any of us. But once it's done, we can focus on… us. I haven't got a bloody clue what it'll look like, but we'll find out together."

They both heard the heavy footsteps descending the stairs. Harry let his mother go. She looked at him, nodded, and wiped her eyes on the sleeve of her cardigan. "Thank you, dear. Now stick some oil in that frying pan, get the tea and coffee ready, and lay the table."

Harry drew himself up and gave her a sharp salute, then smiled as she rolled her eyes at him.

It was a beautifully sunny winter's morning, but the light which poured through the windows was powerless to lift the atmosphere at breakfast. Instead it seemed only to throw the drawn, tired faces of the room's occupants into sharper contrast.

Granville had been sat in an armchair when they entered, facing out towards the grounds with his chin resting in his hand. He bid them all good morning, but had not joined them.

Noy sat in the middle of the table, back straight and chin high but not touching the food in front of her. Sarah kept glancing at her, trying to be covert but not succeeding. Daniel only occasionally cut small squares of omelette and ate them quickly, as if caught in a silent struggle between gratitude for his mother's cooking and solidarity with Noy. Only Harry, Anna, and Sarah ate properly, though their fledgling attempts at conversation quickly died away.

"Where's McGinn?" Anna asked, after the latest silence had stretched for more than a minute.

"Already gone when I got up," Granville said from his armchair, without turning. "Must've been off very early indeed."

Anna looked at Harry. He put down his knife and fork, and looked back at her pointedly. "I'm not doing this again."

"I don't want to 'do' anything, but you have to admit-"

"No, I don't. I've told you all that I'd trust the man with my life. That should be enough."

"But it's not just *your* life you're entrusting him with, is it?"

Harry's eyes dropped. He shook his head, momentarily at a loss for words.

"We'd all love to come and go when we pleased. You think I wouldn't like to pop and see Tasha every day? Maria's worried sick about her, about me too. The rest of us are all-in here, Harry, so if McGinn's going to-"

"All right."

Harry's voice cut through the room like a cracked whip. He felt everyone looking at him, closed his eyes, and let out a deep breath.

"All right," he said. "I'll talk to him."

The breakfast continued in silence for another minute, until Sarah lay down her cutlery, told Harry to tidy the table, and put them all out of their misery.

By the time Harry returned to the dining room he found Noy and Daniel already leaving to walk hand in hand across the lawn. Anna and his mother had their heads together and made no effort to hide the fact that they were talking about him. Granville hadn't moved a muscle.

"Give it a rest, would you?" Harry said to Anna and Sarah, who were still watching him as they muttered to each other. "I swear to God it was a hundred times easier managing idiotic, testosterone-charged, adrenaline-fueled men in their teens and twenties than my own bloody friends and family."

"They probably couldn't call you a moody, aggressive, brooding bastard whenever they felt like it," Anna suggested. "Just a guess."

Harry looked to his mother, but she only shrugged and nodded.

CHAPTER SIXTEEN

Harry stood outside the front entrance to the manor house, hands clasped behind his back and looking out along the driveway. There was no sign of McGinn. Harry took his prepaid phone out once more to check for messages, and resisted the urge to call McGinn. Again, he forced himself to retain the old trust.

"You're not making this any easier on me, you bastard," Harry muttered to himself. He took a last look towards the hedge which screened the property from the road, then turned and went around the side of the house to look for Daniel and Noy.

They were just returning across the lawn, her arm through his and gazing into the middle distance with that same unfocused stare. Daniel caught Harry's eye and nodded to him.

They all convened in the living room a couple of minutes later, but for McGinn. It had only been a couple of days since Harry and the others had hatched their plan. The atmosphere had been charged then with excitement and anticipation, despite the gravity of the situation. Now a dark cloud lingered over the room. There was no chatting from the sofas where the others were sat as Harry paced back and forth once more, brow furrowed while he sought the right words with which to begin.

They all looked up as the front door bell rang. Harry found McGinn standing there. He held a small travel bag in one hand, was rubbing the back of his head with the other, and had a sheepish grin on his face.

"Morning, Cap."

"Just about."

"Aye, sorry about that. Things... overran a little, down in London."

Harry wanted to smile at McGinn's childish look of guilt, but Anna's words ran through his head and made him pause. The conflicting emotions only made him more annoyed, at himself and her, and then he realised that an angry expression had crossed his face and that McGinn was looking at him with confusion.

"What's going on down there?"

"Ah, you know. A young lady. I've known her a while now, on and off. She's really lovely, Cap. Great patter, too. You'd like her."

Harry met McGinn's eyes. There was a moment in which he weighed up the man's words, even as his face remained neutral. "Good for you. But knock it on the head for now, would you? I want to keep the circle as tight as possible until all this is over with."

"Aye, of course, Cap," McGinn said straight away. "That's it now, until we're done."

They went straight to the living room, and Harry saw Anna's face tightening when she saw them. He gave her an almost imperceptible shake of the head, and she rolled her eyes and looked away. He looked around as McGinn dropped his bag near the door then went to sit on one of the sofas, and saw Daniel staring at him too. His meaning was clear, and it was very similar indeed to Anna's.

"Right," Harry said loudly, looking deliberately away from his brother.

Granville and Noy had been staring listlessly in different directions. At the sudden, sharp sound of his voice each looked at Harry vaguely.

"There's a lot going on, for all of us," he said. "Some of us have already lost important people in our lives. Others are separated from their loved ones, and rightfully despise it. Still more have put their entire livelihoods on the line, for a fight that wasn't directly theirs. But I'm going to ask you the impossible. I'm going to ask you to put all that aside and try to forget about it entirely. Not forever. There will be a time for us all to grieve, to try and regain what we've lost, or to start over again. But, just for now, we need to forget all of that. For a little while at least. It's a horrible thing to ask, but I have to. Can you do that?"

Harry's gaze moved between each of them in turn. One by one, with varying degrees of swiftness, they nodded; all except for Anna, who rolled her eyes before reluctantly shrugging her assent.

"Thank you," Harry said. "So, let's crack on. We're off to a very good start, with Tinkov already out of the way. That leaves us with the two remaining members of the Trio, plus the data centre."

"We do the American target next," Daniel said, answering Harry's question before he could ask it.

"Why?"

"The woman running Asia is the most important." Daniel said, looking towards the ground. "She'll have the toughest security. I'd rather take out the easier target first. What are your plans for the data centre?"

"I didn't have any. Not yet."

"We should do them together."

"Do what? How?"

"He's right," McGinn said, nodding. "If we go for the data centre first, the Company will work out our whole plan and mobilise to stop it. So we need to save that for last. Security for the third target will be ramped up across the board after we take out the second, whoever it is, so we'll need to move incredibly quickly to give ourselves the best chance. I'm with your brother - we try to hit the data centre and the third target concurrently, or as close as we can, to stop them catching their breath in-between."

"The data centre's in Asia too," Anna said. "Or that's our best guess, at least. It makes things the slightest bit easier, logistically speaking, if we try to implement that ridiculous plan and assassinate this extremely powerful and dangerous lady together. While we're discussing pipedreams, that is."

"True," Harry said. "And thank you for your enthusiasm."

"Any time, Captain."

"So, we go for the head of the operation in the Americas first, assuming there are no objections." Harry met each pair of eyes once more, and hid a smile when his mother shook her head. "Wonderful. Now, we have to figure out who the hell the target actually is."

"I've heard it's a man," McGinn volunteered. "And the rumour is that he's based in New York."

"You've got nothing else?"

"Sorry, Cap."

Harry nodded. "In that case, our first order of business is to find someone who can tell us." Silence descended upon the room. "Don't all rush to bombard me with ideas at once," he said.

"Can't you just find him online?" Sarah said. "You can find out anything nowadays with a computer."

McGinn grimaced. "I did have a wee look into all this already, but the Company's got things locked down tight. There's no mention whatsoever of them above-board. Even the less... legal parts of the internet haven't got a detail worth mentioning."

"The direct route, then," Harry said. "Who can we get in touch with, that might realistically know?" The room went quiet again. "Anything at all?" he asked, not bothering to hide the frustration in his voice.

"Jansen," Daniel said, quietly.

"Who?"

"My CO. From my time at the Company. Hated me, and the feeling was mutual. But he's high up now. He'd have a better idea than us."

"Where is he?"

"Singapore, the last I knew."

"I'm guessing he wouldn't happily pick up your phone call?"

"Only to say that he was going to kill me."

"Heading to Asia and hunting him down would take time. Any alternatives?"

The silence began to stretch once more. Then Harry saw Granville slowly straightening up, rubbing his eyes as if waking from a deep and troubled sleep. "It seems the burden will fall on me."

Granville's voice was so uncharacteristically heavy that, for a moment, Harry wished he could protest; could leave the man to all the other burdens he was already dealing with, not least of which was the apparent disintegration of his personal life. "How?" was all he said.

"I'm acquainted with two people who might know this crook's identity. I'm far from sure, in either case, but unfortunately it seems we have no other options." Granville adjusted his sleeve, cleared his throat, and finally looked back at Harry. "The first is Lord Frost - one of the nation's most powerful men, even if nobody knows it, and certainly one of its best-connected. The second is the recently appointed representative from the bank which launders the Company's money. Another rather important figure. Moving against either would be risky, to say the least, but I suppose we're far beyond worrying about that."

"That's for bloody sure," said Anna.

"Good, Rupert. Very good. Could you convince either of them to tell us willingly?"

"As opposed to what, my dear chap?"

"The faster approach," Daniel said.

"Ah, I see," Granville said, listlessly. "I'm quite sure Lord Frost would tell anybody anything, so long as the deal was balanced heavily enough in his favour. Dealing in information is more or less his 'MO', as you military types say, so far as I can make out. As to the deal he might actually seek…" He grimaced. "Lord only knows. And to even ask would truly put myself in his hands."

"And this lady from the bank?" Sarah asked. "Didn't you fall out with her already, at Number 10?"

"She certainly delivered something of a wrist-slapping," Granville said. "Frankly, I fail to see how I would strike any deal at all with her - for this sort of information, anyway. He could be the boss of her bank, or at least a major part of it, for all we know. And the only interaction I've had privately with her was hardly chummy, as Sarah says."

"So we'd have to beat it out of her," Anna said. Granville turned to look at her, and she winked back at him. "You don't want to say it, but that's what you're dancing around."

"The cordial approach would seem riskier, if easier on our collective conscience."

Harry frowned, his arms folded and brow furrowed. "Well," he said. "Unless anybody's been struck by a sudden brainwave, they're our two options. The cordial approach with Frost, or the faster approach with the banking representative."

"You know where I stand," Daniel said.

Harry looked to Anna. "Snatching the poor posh lady is the speedier option," she said, shrugging. "And it's not like we're trying so very hard to stay on the right side of the law here."

Harry checked on Noy, but her eyes were glazed and still staring into a dark, unseen distance. Finally, he came back to Granville.

"There's no benefit to striking an alliance with Frost?" Harry asked. "It could be helpful later on."

For a moment, he thought a look passed over Granville's face which he hadn't seen in some time. It was one of calculation, akin to that which he had often fleetingly worn when first negotiating with Harry. But then, if it ever had been there this time, it was swiftly gone again.

"Harry, old boy," Granville said heavily, and let out a long sigh. "I've already been forced far closer to the man than I'd like. Much of it on your urging, I should add. He might be old, but have no doubt - he's very intelligent, extremely powerful, and highly dangerous." With that he sank back into the seat of the sofa, his arms folded but his eyes still on Harry.

"I believe that qualifies as a 'no'," Anna said. "Looks like we're snatching the rich bitch. Could you at least find out where she is, Granville, if we ask very nicely?"

"I'll set up a meeting," Granville said. "I'm sure I can lure her in with the right words, despite our highly uncomfortable prior encounters. As I already did with Yuri Tinkov, I might add."

"We all remember," Anna nodded. "And we're all *extremely* grateful."

Granville sniffed, and turned his head pointedly away. Harry clapped his hands together and forced a smile to his face. "Wonderful. Looks like a quick stop in London, then we're onwards to New York. Let's get ready, boys and girls."

Anna gave him her customary mock salute, and she and the others stood to leave. Granville went towards the doors facing out onto the grounds, phone already in his hand. Harry moved to stand behind him.

"You think I ask too much," he said quietly.

Granvilled paused, thumb hovering over the screen. "Nothing that you wouldn't be prepared to do yourself. And you'd do plenty more besides." He sighed. "It's simply a difficult time, old chap. But that's true for us all."

Harry placed a hand on his shoulder and squeezed. "You're doing something good here, Rupert. We're doing something worthwhile. Perhaps for the first time in either of our lives."

Granville stared out of the window, then patted Harry's hand. Harry nodded, and went to the door.

He stopped there, and studied Granville as he tapped away on his phone. He stood that way for several long moments, watching the man. Then he silently left the room.

CHAPTER SEVENTEEN

Rupert Granville paced slowly back and forth along Riverside Walk. Lights shimmered in the black Thames towards the far side. Battersea Power Station towered behind him, its chimneys monumental in the darkness.

The weather was frigid, but Rupert didn't appear to notice the latest gust of biting wind. He only walked to-and-fro along the same twenty metre stretch, the path almost deserted in the late night.

His hands were in his pockets. His eyes moved back and forth without appearing to take anything in. His lips moved, forming words without emitting sound. Even his own name didn't register the first time he heard it.

"Rupert?" Harry asked, over the earpiece.

Rupert blinked, and came to an abrupt halt. "Yes. Sorry. I'm here."

"I don't see any sign of her. You?"

"She'll come, old chap. I'm sure of it."

"She's late."

"Were she meeting the Prime Minister, or one of the Trio, she'd be on time. When lowly Rupert Granville's your date, I'm afraid punctuality won't be a pri-"

"Captain." McGinn's voice cut across Rupert's. He frowned with annoyance at the interruption but paused anyway to listen. He had no idea whatsoever where Harry's Scottish chum was perched, but it would be somewhere with a vastly superior view to his own.

"What is it?"

"We've got something. A boat."

"It's the *Thames*, Mr McGinn," Rupert said. "There are plenty of boats."

"I know that, smart arse, but not at this hour. And not heading straight for the jetty a stone's throw from where you're standing."

Rupert turned and suddenly realised that he could indeed hear an engine growing louder. A quick scan of the inky Thames was all it took to see the outline of a small boat approaching, the round, red light at its bow bumping gently over the blackness.

"What have you got, McGinn?" Harry asked. Rupert wasn't sure of Miller's location either, having only been reassured that he was 'close', which was a little vague for his liking.

"Stand by." There was a pause as the noise of the engine grew. "Looks like… four figures, plus the driver."

Rupert's eyes widened. "Four?"

"She was always going to bring security, however politely you asked her to come alone," Harry said.

"It might have been nice for you to share that tidbit with me. Are you sure you're prepared for this?"

The pause this time stretched the slightest bit longer than Rupert wanted. "We'll deal with it."

Rupert pursed his lips, walked closer to the river, and peered out at the approaching vehicle. The driver turned just before reaching the jetty, which was lit by only a single light at the far end, and somebody fastened the boat to it using a rope.

A couple of men disembarked first, though by their outlines

they looked more like great apes. They were followed by a much slimmer man, then a woman.

Rupert saw each of their faces as they moved past the small light. He didn't recognise either of the first two men. The woman was the banking representative, and she was looking straight at him. Rupert swore when he saw the man following her, hands behind his back and eyes seemingly cast carelessly downwards.

"What is it?" Harry asked.

"Lord Frost appears to have tagged along." *The old bastard*, Rupert mouthed to himself afterwards.

"Meaning?"

"How the bloody hell should I know? Nothing good, I imagine." Rupert felt his pulse quicken as the party reached the shore, some twenty metres away, and he saw Lord Frost's eyes fixed now on his. "He knows," Rupert said, covering his mouth with one of his gloved hands. "God help me, he knows. He's come to get me."

"Calm down, Rupert. He-"

"They'll take me away. Come on, Harry. Now." Rupert just managed to remove his earpiece and stow it away, as covertly as he could, before the woman addressed him.

"Mr Granville."

Rupert affixed a nervous smile to his face, and nodded to both her and Lord Frost. "Good evening, Ms... Ah. Never caught your name, actually. Nor that of your predecessor, may she rest in peace."

The woman's lips tightened, almost imperceptibly. "Smith."

"Smith," Rupert repeated, and smiled again. "Of course." He turned to face the slim older man, who wore a typically expensive-looking overcoat. "Lord Frost. I wasn't expecting the pleasure of your company tonight."

"I'm sure." Frost said, as Rupert stepped forward and held out his hand, which he limply shook. He offered no further explanation.

"Shall we take a short stroll?" Granville said. "It's such a lovely evening for it. Perhaps we could leave the muscle here?"

"They're accompanying me wherever I go," the woman who called herself Smith coolly replied. "But they can remain out of earshot, if you're planning to say something valuable enough to merit it."

Smith nodded to the two men, who remained stationary for several seconds as she, Rupert, and Frost began to move slowly away. They walked in a horizontal line, with Rupert in the middle, towards the hulking power station whose thick, white chimneys - made almost ghostly by the pale lighting upon them - loomed up and into the night sky.

"Weren't talking to yourself as we approached, were you, Granville?" Frost asked, looking straight ahead.

Rupert coughed into his glove. "A nervous habit, I'm afraid, Lord Frost. And one which makes me look quite the fool, I'm positive." Frost's lip seemed to curl slightly, but he said nothing. "If I might, Lord Frost-"

"Why am I here? Because I was asked."

"I was under the impression that-"

"Then your impression was mistaken," Smith said. "Assumptions are dangerous at this level, Granville. I thought you'd know that by now."

They were approaching the near side of the power station. There was a shadowy patch of ground to their right, near to the path. Rupert thought he saw one of the shadows there moving, but looked hurriedly away. He glanced at Lord Frost on his left, who - inevitably - was watching him now, although his face remained inscrutable.

"Not that I'd ever begrudge your company for a moment, Lord Frost," Rupert said, before turning to Smith. "But my 'impression' was based on the fact that I specifically requested you to come alone. Perhaps I wasn't clear enough."

"You're behaving very differently to how you do at Number 10," the woman said, fixing him with a stare. "Your way of talking. Even your tone of voice. Who are you *really*, Rupert Granville?"

"I'm quite sure I don't know what you're talking about." Even as another blast of icy wind passed over them, Rupert realised he was sweating beneath his coat. He also became increasingly aware of the footsteps following them. "What I *am* sure about, however, is that you're deflecting my question. A tactic that won't work 'at this level', I'm afraid."

"I invited Lord Frost because I don't know you, and I don't trust you. Is that straightforward enough? I wanted another pair of ears to witness whatever you came out with. Not to mention another opinion on the specifics, which must be highly important to merit such a clandestine meeting."

Rupert saw the shadow moving again, off to his right. He was sure that the men behind would have noticed it too, but didn't hear them react. He could feel Frost's eyes upon him, even as he kept his head turned towards Smith.

"Lord Frost already knows everything that I do, and vastly more besides."

The woman forced out a scoffing laugh. "I can guarantee he doesn't believe that, any more than I do. Now, whatever you have to say, spit it out. You're cutting into what little sleep I do tend to manage."

They were drawing level with the nearest corner of the

colossal structure now. It was the point at which Rupert had been told to act.

Suddenly he felt very alone. He wished he'd been given a more inconspicuous earpiece, which he might have left in. He had no way of knowing now whether he had been abandoned. He realised too that, if he had been, all the others would disappear without a trace, even taking Sarah with them. Above all, he was struck with the realisation that he had entrusted a large part of his livelihood, and perhaps his very life, to almost complete strangers.

"Something caught your attention, Granville?"

Rupert looked around, feeling that his face was pale and filled with guilt. "Lord Frost?"

"You keep looking into those shadows. Wouldn't be some wild animal over there, would there? Something *dangerous*?"

Rupert looked away from him. He swallowed, then began to talk in a clear voice. "Arms and the man I sing, who, forced by fate and haughty Juno's unrelenting hate-"

"What on earth are you babbling about?" Smith asked sharply. "Have you lost your marbles, Granville?"

"Expelled and exiled, left the Trojan shore," Granville said, a note of panic entering his voice as nothing seemed to happen; nothing except at least two pairs of eyes, one on either side, now fixing upon him, and the footsteps behind speeding up as the guards saw the rapidly increasing confusion and discomfort of their charge.

"You'll be sorry about this, you blathering fool," Smith said, stopping in her tracks and talking over Granville even as he carried on. "Clearly you think it's highly amusing to waste my time, but I assure you it's simply sad, not to mention incredibly ill-advised."

"Long labours, both by sea and land, he bore," Granville

continued. He saw a person clad all in black emerging from the mass of shadow to his right, but the eyes of Smith and her two men were still fixed on him. "And in the doubtful war, before he won the Latin realm…"

Frost was clearly looking ahead now too. "What in the name of-" Rupert heard him saying, before the old man gave a muffled grunt and fell heavily to the earth.

Everything began to happen too quickly for Rupert to follow.

Two more figures joined the first who had attacked. He had no idea where they came from, but they were also dressed entirely in black and caught Smith and her men in a triangle.

The woman herself reached for something in her handbag, but was immediately knocked down by the slimmest figure of the three. She screamed as she fell, and Rupert heard shouting from at least two directions. It came from strangers he hadn't previously seen, and rather than looking he turned instinctively away and kept his face turned downwards to avoid being recognised.

The slimmer figure, who he guessed to be Anna, was straddling Smith's chest now, her knees on the woman's upper arms and one hand clamped over her mouth while she struggled to take a gag from some hidden pocket.

Rupert's eyes flitted up from there and from side to side, trying to follow the two separate struggles which had formed between the guards and their assailants, the larger of which caught the fist of one of the guards as he went to punch him and began to squeeze. The guard's eyes widened in alarm, and he began to shout as the larger man continued to apply more and more pressure.

Rupert winced as he heard the cracking sound starting. The guard lashed desperately out, but the larger man had obviously anticipated the flailing attempt. He used his left arm to bat away the blow with apparent ease, then released his grip with the right which promptly shot straight out and squarely into the guard's nose. Rupert looked away instinctively but couldn't avoid hearing the second crunching sound which was noticeably louder than the first, and which, ominously, was not followed by any shout of pain from the guard.

He didn't particularly want to watch the other fight either, but felt himself morbidly drawn to it. The black-clad assailant was slightly shorter and less broad than the guard he faced. Unfortunately for the latter, he fought with a speed and ferocity which Rupert had never imagined possible.

This was nothing like the carefully choreographed fights of the Hollywood movies which he'd occasionally enjoyed in his youth, before George drummed the habit out of him. It was two men of violence fighting with every tool at their disposal, every ounce of strength and energy they possessed, as if their very survival truly did depend on it.

Rupert winced again as the guard jabbed out and connected with the side of his opponent's head, but it appeared only to be a glancing blow which the other man immediately shook off before coming straight forward again with his fists held high, not pausing for a moment as he feinted to his left while cocking his right fist, hidden, and bringing it sweeping around and into the side of the guard's torso.

The sound wasn't as monstrous as those from the first fight, but the impact seemed to make the guard simply crumple. The other man still didn't stop, hitting the guard in the left side as he went to cover his right. The guard let out a soft gasp and stumbled backwards, but still the first man didn't stop. He closed the distance again, grabbed the guard by his ears, wrenched his head down and brought his knee up and into the centre of his face.

Again, it was the sound which Rupert could not escape even as he looked away. He let out a whimper as he began to retreat from the scene, not caring where he was going, a hand against his stomach as he felt a sudden wave of nausea sweep through him.

Somebody else's hand landed on his shoulder and arrested his stumbling flight. "Where do you think you're off to?"

Rupert recognised Anna's voice and her eyes through the gap in her black balaclava as he turned. "I was simply, ah…"

"If you're going to vomit, please turn the other way."

"Indeed. No, it's only that… I'm not really cut out for this sort of thing. Violence never particularly agreed with me."

"I'm shocked," Anna said, looking him up and down obviously. "You had no trouble being a part of it from afar, back when you were a true stooge for the Company. Now stop whining and give me a hand."

Whatever Anna had done to Smith, she was now lying still on the ground. Frost lay nearby, also motionless. The two other black-clad figures were already carrying one of the guards between them back into the shadows. Anna crossed to the other guard, stooped, put her hands under his armpits, and looked up at Rupert.

"Surely you can't be serious."

"Give the whole delicate flower act a rest. Let's get on with it."

Rupert wrinkled his nose in disgust and avoided looking at the guard's bloodied face as he bent to pick up his legs. With a grunt he helped lift the man, and stumbled along after Anna onto the grassy verge beside the path. When they returned the larger man already had Smith thrown over his shoulder, and the other had his hand towards his ear.

"Ready for extraction." Rupert recognised Harry's muffled voice through the balaclava, and fumbled to put his own earpiece back in. There was a note of pain in the voice, and Harry's spare hand was pressed to the wounds he'd suffered only a short distance away and a short time before.

"Copy, Cap. Already on my way."

"Come on." Harry motioned, and he and Daniel led Rupert and Anna up the broad path towards the road. Rupert chanced to look around as they went. Whoever had shouted before seemed to have fled, but the next moment he made out the whine of sirens quickly approaching.

"Oh, Lord in heaven," he moaned. "This is it. The end of everything."

The other three ignored him, and he panted to keep up as they broke into a jog. The sirens were quickly growing louder now, and Rupert, for the first time in many years, felt blood and adrenaline pumping through him in a heady cocktail of fear, physical exertion, and - perhaps - excitement.

A white van suddenly turned a corner to Rupert's right, driving very quickly before drawing to an abrupt stop on the road in front. Harry ran up to wrench the side door open, and Daniel dumped Smith unceremoniously inside before getting into the back himself with Anna following close behind. Harry had been facing towards the sirens, but now he turned and looked quickly around before his eyes settled on Rupert.

"Stop dawdling and get in the bloody van!" he shouted, and got in the passenger side. Rupert caught a glimpse of McGinn in the driver's seat as he did so, who grinned and gave him a thumbs-up before the door was slammed closed.

Rupert muttered to himself as he clambered clumsily into the van's interior. Somebody slid the door closed behind him, throwing the space into darkness, and he immediately took an undignified tumble as McGinn accelerated away.

CHAPTER EIGHTEEN

McGinn had spent a large portion of the afternoon planning an escape route which would largely avoid London's overwhelming CCTV coverage. All Harry could do was trust him.

Ten minutes later McGinn stopped beneath an underpass covered in graffiti. They left the stolen van there, carried the unconscious Smith down two litter-strewn alleyways which were thankfully deserted, and got into a people carrier McGinn had rented under a fake name. From there it was another twenty minutes north, up across Waterloo Bridge and into Bloomsbury.

Harry caught sight of Granville's face as they ascended the steps to his townhouse. His skin was pale and his expression that of a condemned man. Harry moved behind him as he reached the door and put a hand on his shoulder.

"If there's anywhere else we could have gone-"

"Then I'd have been grateful. As it is, I understand. Time is of the essence, and you wanted somewhere both known and secure. I do understand, old chap, but the ramifications for this, against yours truly, will be..." He trailed off, forced a smile, and turned the key in the lock.

Despite the late hour the lights were on downstairs. Harry followed Granville along the corridor and into the kitchen. Chamberlain sat on one of the chairs near the far windows, one long leg crossed over the other. There was an empty tumbler on the small table beside him, and he appeared to have been staring into space. He showed no sign of surprise at their arrival, only raising his head as they entered then looking slowly between them.

"Good evening, George," Granville said. The formality with which he spoke grew more excruciating when Chamberlain merely nodded back. "I'm going to ask something of you, and I don't wish for you to argue."

"Don't you, indeed?"

"I want you to come upstairs with me, right now, and not ask any questions."

"How very romantic. And what will be going on down here, pray tell, once I'm out of the way?"

"Better you don't know."

"There are so many things going on which I'm better off not knowing. I feel as if I don't even know *you* any more, Rupert. Am I better off for that?"

"We're in rather a hurry," Granville said. "We can discuss this upstairs. Please."

Chamberlain gave Harry a long, piercing look over the top of his glasses. Then he slowly stood and went towards the hallway with Granville and Harry following.

The doors to both the house and the people carrier beyond were still open. Chamberlain looked out as he reached the staircase, and Harry was sure he saw everything. He paused with his foot on the first step, and turned to give Granville a withering look.

"You've let them push you entirely too far, Rupert," he said. "You've lost all track of who you are and where your limits lie."

"Please, George," Granville said, his voice almost pathetically quiet.

Chamberlain looked once more at Harry with a cold hatred he no longer disguised, then proceeded up the stairs. Granville followed, shoulders slumped and not looking back. Harry watched them go for a moment, closed his eyes and let out a deep breath, then turned to face outside again.

Rupert closed the door to the master bedroom with a soft click. He took a moment on the landing, then went downstairs.

"That was quick," Harry said, as Rupert came to stand beside he and Anna in front of the open doorway down to the wine cellar.

Rupert didn't reply for several long moments. He cleared his throat, but when he spoke his voice still emerged as a croak. "George is 'done talking', as they say nowadays."

"Meaning?"

"Merely that my life is crumbling. Not that it'll matter, because I'm going to be arrested and imprisoned anyway."

"There's a chance you won't be."

"Very reassuring, thank you. Unfortunately, even if your Scottish chum did make his calculations correctly, Lord Frost's sudden appearance means my goose is well and truly cooked."

"Play it off as a kidnapping," Anna said. "You're a capable actor, based on your behaviour when we first met on Company business, compared to what I've seen since."

"Not with him," Rupert said. "I've no idea how much he truly knows, but it's clearly more than I gave him credit for. The very fact that he tagged along with Smith shows that." There was a definite tremble in Rupert's voice now and his eyes were shimmering again. "I can't do this, Harry. It's all become too much. Look at this. Look at what it's come to. The love of my life scorned. One of the most powerful men in politics, attacked by my accomplices. A high-ranking employee of one of the world's biggest banks, tied up in my basement. I- I can't-"

"We're ready down here, Cap," called McGinn.

"Come on," Harry said. "Let's get this over with."

Rupert turned his wide eyes upon him. "I'm not going down there."

"Yes, you are," Anna said.

"But I- I can't- I want no part of-"

"You're going, Granville, because there's no telling what you'll do if we leave you up here alone."

Rupert looked at Harry with indignation. But Harry could only shrug and turn away.

The three of them descended the staircase. The wine cellar was square with stone walls five metres long on each side. The wall by which the stairs emerged was bare, while the other three were lined with wooden racks housing a collection amassed over many years.

A dining chair had been placed in the centre of the space, to which Smith had been tied with her arms behind her back. McGinn had wrapped the jumper he had been wearing tight around Smith's head, and a scarf had been tied around her mouth.

"Lord above," Rupert said, stopping dead on the stairs. "This is barbaric. I won't allow it. I can't-"

"Stop waffling," Anna said, pushing him down the last couple of steps. "This is just how it's done. You can bet your fanciest bottle of red that she's been involved in plenty of little interviews like this, though indirectly of course."

"Ready, Cap?" McGinn asked. Harry nodded as he came to a stop a couple of feet in front of the chair, his arms folded. The Scot took a large bucket of water from the floor, hoisted it up, and emptied it over Smith.

The woman crashed immediately back to consciousness, straining at her bonds and letting out muffled shrieks of shock. The soaked jumper clung to her face, and Rupert felt a wave of nausea and panic sweep over him as he involuntarily imagined the feeling of suffocation.

McGinn was watching Harry. He nodded, and the wet jumper was removed and dropped to the ground. The woman's eyes were wide and bloodshot, her hair wild, her skin wet with water and sweat. Her eyes darted around the room, still breathing heavily and grunting against the scarf. Rupert looked away when her eyes met his.

Again, McGinn looked to Harry. Again, he nodded. Rupert guessed this wasn't the first time they'd been in such a situation. McGinn untied the scarf, and Smith took a number of deep breaths but said nothing.

"Do you know who I am?" Harry asked, using a tone of voice which Rupert hadn't heard before.

The woman tried to speak, but could only cough. "I can guess," she managed the second time.

"Then you know what I'm capable of."

"Laying waste to a sizable chunk of London? Murdering at will in the process?"

"I've done this before," Harry said, his voice cold and sharp. "Everybody talks eventually. I'd advise you to do so quickly, to save us time and yourself pain."

"Very admirable. Unfortunately, I don't know-"

Harry gave another nod, this time to Daniel who stood to Smith's left. He slapped her hard across the face. Rupert turned away, wincing at the impact and Smith's shriek of pain, and found Anna standing to his side with her arms folded as she watched the scene dispassionately. Not for the first time that evening, Rupert wondered who in the world he'd gotten involved with.

"Don't lie," Harry said. "We don't have the time. We'll still get our answers. We'll simply need to inflict the pain more quickly. Do you understand?"

Rupert turned back to see a line of blood dribbling from the woman's mouth and a pink mark across her face. But where he expected a look of burning hatred in her eyes, he found only fear.

"Good. Tell us about the two remaining members of the Trio. Who's running the Company now?"

"I don't kn-" the woman began, and flinched as she saw Daniel lifting his hand again. "Wait!" she shouted, and began to talk very quickly. "I don't know anything, really, about one of them. They say she created the whole thing in Asia, only brought the others on board when she wanted to go global, but I've never heard a name, never heard anything else about her. That's the truth."

Harry's eyes bored into hers. "The other one?"

"What do you want with him?"

Smith cried out louder this time as Daniel slapped her again. "We ask the questions, you answer them," Harry said, over her ensuing moans. "Tell us what you know."

"I... I...," Smith said, tears falling from her eyes and mixing with the mucus and saliva around her mouth. Rupert swallowed. It was hard to believe this was the same woman who'd lambasted him at Number 10 such a short time ago. "He's a man, obviously... Based in New York..."

"We know this already," Harry said, and Daniel raised his hand.

"Wait!" Smith cried again. "He works in finance. Hedge fund manager. Incredibly rich."

"We need a name."

"A name? His name..." Her desperate eyes flitted from side to side. Daniel took a step closer to her. "I can't... I'm not trying to..." Her eyes widened still further, and she almost shouted. "Bohm!"

"Richard Bohm?" Rupert asked automatically.

"Yes!"

Harry turned. "You know him?"

"Not personally, but he's spectacularly successful." Rupert shrugged. "He'd certainly fit the bill."

"There, you see!" Smith almost shouted. "I gave you what you wanted. Now for the love of God, you brutes, let me-"

The woman let out another shriek and struggled uselessly against her bindings as McGinn moved towards her, at another signal from Harry, and tied the scarf back around her mouth. Harry didn't look at her again, instead walking straight back to the stairs and out from the cellar.

Rupert was the last to leave. He stood alone for a moment with the woman, twisting his hands in front of him like a boy as her frightened eyes met his. Then with a wave of shame he turned away, Smith's muffled, pleading shouts following him up the stairs.

Harry waited for Granville at the top of the stairs then closed the door behind him. He tried to catch his eye but Granville stared straight at the ground. He appeared to be heading towards the kitchen door when Daniel spoke.

"Where shall we do it?"

Granville stopped and turned. "Do what?"

"Just go, Rupert," Harry said.

"Do *what* exactly?"

"She can't live," Daniel said. Not with condescension, nor any hint of argument; only as if stating a fact.

"You're not serious." Granville looked to Daniel first, then McGinn, then Anna, all of whom looked straight back at him. Finally he turned to Harry. "This would truly be murder, Harry. Cold and indisputable."

"Oh, save your whining and your judgement," Anna said. "Your little labels too. I'll remind you, firstly, that it's not exactly Mother Theresa down there we're about to knock off. Secondly, what did you think was going to happen, once we'd finished our little chat?"

"I... Well, I hadn't thought about it. I assumed you would have a plan, for... afterwards."

"Welcome to the plan. What would you like us to do? Let her skip out of here humming a pretty tune? She wouldn't go to the police, as you well know. She'd go straight to her Company goons, we'd likely be dead this time tomorrow, all your precious houses would be smouldering ruins, your partner would certainly be murdered, and your career-"

"I get the picture, thank you kindly."

"I don't love it either, Rupert," Harry said. His voice was uncharacteristically soft, and unrecognisable from that which he had used downstairs. "But we don't have a choice. Surely you can see that. And Anna's right - this woman's hardly a saint."

"She's only part of the bank. Not the Company, directly."

"She launders their money. She's complicit in an untold amount of misery. I'm not saying..." Harry frowned, and looked away. "You have no idea how I've struggled with this sort of thing," he resumed, more quietly still. "But it has to be done. After that, it's up to you how you justify it - if you even feel that you need to. For better or worse, all four of us have done this sort of thing plenty of times. I'm sure all four of us deal with it very differently."

"I don't want to 'deal with it' at all," Granville said. The tone of his voice made Harry's stomach twist.

"One bitch's life to help prevent the suffering of countless others," Anna said, matter-of-factly. "What you're suffering is the classic meat-eater's dilemma. You're perfectly willing to enjoy the burger, but you'll weep to see the cow slaughtered. It's something that all politicians - those that didn't serve, at least - have in common."

"It's for a good cause, Rupert," Harry said, his voice still soft. "You can't deny that. We had to take her, for everything else to succeed. If and when it does, it will have been worth it. The ends will more than justify the means."

Granville stood with his arms hanging loosely at his sides, looking older than Harry had ever seen him before. He could only guess what was going on behind the tired eyes, though, for once, he was sure no calculations were taking place.

"Don't do it here," Granville said at last. "Not in the house that George and I share. Give me that at least, won't you?"

Daniel opened his mouth, clearly about to make the logistical case for doing just that, but Harry raised a hand. "Of course," he said. Granville nodded, and slowly left the room.

Harry looked to Daniel, and saw nothing. McGinn gave him a consolatory look. Anna shrugged. Harry sighed, suddenly feeling the weight on his shoulders to be almost unbearably heavy.

"I'll do it," he said. Then he turned, opened the door, and began the descent back down to the cellar.

CHAPTER NINETEEN

The wipers of the cramped Mercedes were operating at full tilt. Still the rain beat down in a torrent that almost completely obscured the motorway in front.

Rupert hadn't said a word since they set off. He felt Harry looking at him several times but didn't react, only driving onwards through the downpour in steady silence. There were large bags under his eyes, but that was true for all of them.

It took them almost twice as long to reach Heathrow this time. Anna, Daniel, and Noy got out and jogged for cover.

"I'm just having to assume you haven't forgotten about me." McGinn's muffled voice could just about be heard from the boot, where he had cheerfully volunteered to pass the journey.

"One second," Harry called, and turned to Rupert. "I won't ask if everything's all right. But is there anything you need to tell me? Anything you need to talk about?"

Rupert stared out through the streams of water running down the windscreen. "Lord Frost got in touch."

"Not exactly a surprise."

"Indeed. I'm off to meet him now."

"How's he going to play it?"

"Judging by the fact that he's chosen to call me, rather than have me arrested or slain where I stand, I assume he wants to cut some sort of deal. That or learn what he can from me, before having me knocked off."

"I could've come with you."

"We're both to come alone. He was most insistent on that point."

"You think he will?"

"I do, actually."

They heard McGinn again. "This isn't the easiest place in the world to, y'know… breathe."

"Coming," Harry said. He sighed, and put a hand on Rupert's shoulder. "Stay safe. I'll be in touch." He opened the door, the sound of the storm becoming suddenly clear and real. "And Rupert," he said. "I'm sorry, for last night. Not that it had to happen, but for the way it did."

Rupert kept staring forwards. Then finally he turned, met Harry's eyes, and gave a slight shake of his head. "Don't be," he said.

There had been no discussion on where they would meet. Frost had told Rupert the location, then hung up. Rupert followed the car's GPS away from Heathrow and north to the Colne Valley belt of greenery west of Uxbridge.

The postcode he'd been given took him down a B-road, then a narrow country lane. He saw a lay-by as the satnav told him he'd reached his destination. A silver Range Rover with tinted rear windows was parked there. With some difficulty, Rupert edged the Mercedes up onto the dirt on the far side of the lane.

Rupert turned off the engine, and the sound of the rain hammering on the roof swelled. He stepped out, buttoning the coat he'd already been wearing in the car, then circled around to the boot and took out the large, black golf umbrella George kept there.

He crossed the lane. The Range Rover was empty but he could feel the lingering heat from the engine. There was a metal gate on the far side of the car. Looking beyond it, Rupert saw a tall, slim figure wearing a long coat. The man stood still under his own umbrella, a hundred paces or so into the field. Rupert opened the gate and began to cross the long, wet grass.

Frost stood completely still as Rupert approached, grey eyes following him. Rupert stopped a few metres away.

"We couldn't have met at a club?" Rupert asked. "You must be welcome at every one in London. My feet are soaked."

"I've learned, Granville, that I can't be too careful around you."

"That's quite the overstatement, but flattering nonetheless. This way, I suppose we're at equal risk of meeting our fate. At the hands of pneumonia, I mean, rather than thugs clad in black. Speaking of which, how's the head, Lord Frost?"

"It's been better. How's our acquaintance from the bank?"

"She's been better." Rupert shrugged. "Or so I assume, at least. Naturally I had nothing to do with that awful kidnapping last night. I was just as shocked as you were."

One side of Frost's mouth twitched. It was impossible to tell whether it was a smile or a grimace. "I'm sure."

"Might I ask what you hoped to gain from this meeting, Lord Frost? I'd prefer to cut to the chase before we both freeze to death."

The two men stood looking at each other, the rain pattering down on their umbrellas. Frost's eyes bored into Rupert's. Rupert met his gaze steadily.

"Quite the transformation," Frost said. "Remarkable, really. Your tone of voice. Even the way you carry yourself."

"I'm sure I don't know what you're talking about."

"It's not a criticism. I underestimated you, Granville, and that doesn't happen very often."

Rupert paused, considering. "When did you begin to suspect?"

"Oh, I certainly never took you at face value. I observed the subtle differences in your behaviour around others, when you were unaware I was watching. It was only the business with Tinkov, however - with whom I believe you had a closer relationship than you let on - that pushed me into full-blown suspicion."

"Of?"

"I remain unsure. Something sizable, clearly, involving the Company and the bank. I contacted our mutual friend from the latter, and persuaded her to alert me if and when she received your request to rendezvous."

"Did you share your suspicions with her?"

Frost's mouth twitched again. "Don't be foolish. You know me better than that, Granville."

Rupert nodded. "Well, lessons learned for the future, I suppose," he said brusquely. "You're yet to tell me what you sought from this particular 'rendezvous'."

"I'd have thought that was obvious. I want to know what you're up to."

"And why would I trust you? No offence, Lord Frost, but you're hardly known for dealing with people face to face."

"If your plan is worthwhile, then I'll provide assistance. And few people provide more effective assistance than I. Your next question, I suppose, is what counts as being 'worthwhile'. I would assume you're moving against the Company. On the surface, that would seem as idiotic a thing as a person might do. But ambition should never be dismissed out of hand, and - what's more - you've proved yourself surprisingly capable. In short, you've made yourself worthy of not only my attention, but my involvement."

Rupert switched his umbrella to his left hand, and put his right hand inside his coat pocket. He looked off over Frost's shoulder into the hazy middle distance. "That's very flattering."

"Sarcasm is the lowest form of wit, Granville."

"So I've heard, but that wasn't it. Truly, I'm flattered. I've admired you, from afar, for a long time now. I've learned a lot from you. Perhaps more than you'd wish. I'll carry those lessons forward with me."

"I have plenty more to teach."

"No, Lord Frost. I don't think you do."

Frost cocked his head to one side, picking up on the change in Rupert's voice. His eyes narrowed at the different look on Rupert's face.

"I won't be taking any more of your lessons, I'm afraid. I've received quite another sort of education recently, from very different sources. It's been... difficult for me to learn, but I'm glad for it all the same."

Frost's gaze lowered. "What's that in your coat pocket, Granville?"

"Oh, there were a couple of them lying around the house this morning. Quite disconcerting, when you're not used to that sort of thing, but... The others, my accomplices, couldn't take them along to New York, you see."

"New York? So..." Frost paused. "That's it. You're planning to kill them all."

"And a little more besides." Rupert shrugged. "Which would have sunk you anyway, when it all came out. So it's for the best."

Rupert let the umbrella fall to the wet ground, then drew the gun from the inner pocket into which it had been awkwardly stuffed. Calmly, he raised the weapon in both hands, one supporting the other.

"You've lost your mind," Frost said, his eyes - for once - slightly widened.

"Quite the opposite," Rupert said. "I see everything more clearly than ever. If you have an objective - something that you *truly* want - you do *everything* within your power to achieve it. The morality we're taught is a lie, and one ignored by so many. It's merely an obstacle to overcome. And learning to do so is... liberating. At last, it allows one to truly trust one's own judgement."

"And what *judgement* has led you to threatening me in this preposterous manner?"

"It's a terrible cliché, but I'm afraid you know too much. Your offer of assistance was generous, but I simply can't trust you. Nothing in your lengthy track record would lead me to do so. I'm therefore left with no other option."

Rupert flicked the safety off the gun with his thumb. Frost attempted to sneer. "You don't know how to use the blasted thing."

"Unfortunately you're quite mistaken. Harry Miller taught me one evening, when he was cleaning this gun specifically, I believe. Oh yes, I forgot to mention - he's been staying at my house for some time now. That's one thing you didn't know, isn't it?" Rupert looked down at the barrel. "I was horrified the first time I held one. But it's only a tool, after all."

Fear filled Frost's grey eyes for the first time. "Now look here, Granville-"

"I'm sorry, Lord Frost," Rupert said. There was a tremble in his voice, and his hands shook briefly before he took a deep breath and steadied them. "I wouldn't have thought this possible myself, only a short time ago. But the ends will justify the means. It really is that simple. I've come too far to let you jeopardise everything I've worked for now."

"I won't tell a soul, Rupert," Frost said, beginning to take small steps backward. "I'll disappear, if that's what's required. Truly. Send Miller or whoever else you please after me if I-"

"I'm truly sorry," Rupert said again. "Truly."

Then he fired the gun.

It felt as if he only tapped the trigger, ever so lightly, but the thing jumped ferociously in his hands and suddenly his ears were ringing and both of his arms and shoulders hurt and his hands were numb.

And when he blinked, although he was still deafened and disorientated, he saw Frost lying there in the long, wet grass. His feet carried him forward automatically, stopped, continued.

Frost's face turned slowly towards him. He looked very old, and the expression on his face was terrible.

The bullet had only hit him in the shoulder. Rupert let out a choking sound when he saw. Then he swallowed, raised the gun, and fired again.

Rupert had headed for the nearby river after collecting himself, correctly judging the weather would ensure that the area was deserted.

With a grunt he pushed the body towards the water by the shoulders. It stayed stuck in the muddy bank. Rupert cursed, looked around, and came back with a large stick. "Lord above, how has it come to this?" he whispered, even as he prodded the body through the sludge and out into the water. With a final push he sent it out into the shallows, where it soon began to float downstream. He threw the stick out afterwards, then the gun.

Rupert made his way back up the grassy verge, through the trees, and to the road. He saw no cars in either direction, and hadn't heard any passing either. Not that he had noticed anyway. But perhaps, when he was still standing there on the bank with the body before him...

He caught sight of his face in the rearview mirror as he got back into the car. It was as pale as he'd ever seen. He looked away again, took out his phone, and called the Prime Minister's Chief of Staff.

"Ruth? It's me." Rupert took several loud, short breaths. "I'm worried, Ruth. Have you heard from either of them? I've tried calling. I've sent messages, but... I'm really worried. After everything with Tinkov, and all the business with Miller before that-"

He waited for her to cut him off before he could mention any other highly sensitive names over the phone. "Meet? Yes, I think we should. At Number 10, or...? No, yes, that's for the best. Okay, Ruth, see you there."

Rupert waited for her to hang up, then placed his phone on the passenger seat. He leant back against the headrest with his eyes closed. He took in a deep breath, and let out a long, ragged sigh.

Then he turned the engine on, swung the car around, and accelerated away, his eyes flickering upwards as he saw the headlights of another car half a mile or so in the distance.

He swallowed, shook his head, and pressed on for London.

CHAPTER TWENTY

The five of them didn't so much as look at each other as they went through security at Heathrow. They stayed far apart in the departures lounge too, in three separate groups: Harry with Anna, Daniel with Noy, and McGinn on his own.

"This all feels a little silly, doesn't it?" Anna said, as she watched Noy walking past en route to her seat further down the plane, followed by Daniel who filled the aisle. "Are you sure it's necessary, Captain Cautious?"

"Probably not. But I'd prefer not to take any chances." Harry briefly exchanged a look with McGinn as he saw the Scot stowing his bag near the front door of the plane. McGinn gave him the smallest of nods before sitting down. "It's not like we're missing out on a ton of conversation, anyway."

Anna looked at him with an arched eyebrow. "Catty. What's that supposed to mean?"

"I've been part of teams with better chemistry," Harry muttered.

"I doubt they've been in stranger circumstances."

"Perhaps. But bigger challenges tend to bring groups closer together. In my experience, at least. We barely even communicate now."

Anna put a hand on his arm. "A lot's going on, if you hadn't noticed, and it's not just run of the mill war stuff. Every one of us has either lost someone or been separated from them. Except for your pal McGinn, that is, and he's hardly helped matters with his toing-and-froing."

"Don't start with-"

"I'm not, my delicate flower. I'm simply highlighting the issues you're dealing with here. None of it's your fault, as far as I can see... Well, perhaps I wouldn't say that, but..."

"Thanks."

"The point, Captain, is that it's no reflection on your leadership, per se. Being a part of your team isn't always a barrel of laughs, I'll freely admit-"

"Thanks again."

"But everyone's still on board, and determined to see the job through. We're all still following you, and that's what you want, isn't it?"

"You make me sound like an egomaniac."

"I knew it the first time I saw you."

Harry smiled, and looked at her. She laughed and squeezed his arm. "It's a silly thing to fret about, Harry. You've got far bigger problems to focus on."

"You really are a fount of motivation today."

"I try my best."

With the five hour time difference it was only a little after midday when they landed at JFK. They took separate taxis and checked in separately to the same hotel.

Fifteen minutes later, McGinn knocked on the door to the room Harry and Anna shared. He set up his laptop at the small desk pressed against one of the walls and they chatted for another minute until Daniel and Noy arrived.

"Right," Harry said. "McGinn, have you contacted your man?"

"Yes indeed," McGinn said cheerily. "I'm meeting him within the hour. He couldn't get everything I'd have liked, not at such short notice, but we'll have a decent amount of kit."

"Want any of us to go with you?" Anna asked innocently. "Just in case?"

"Nah, I'll be fine. We go way back."

Harry gave Anna a look. She'd been about to reply, but closed her mouth abruptly and nodded to him. "Excellent," he said, trying to inject his own voice with some of McGinn's enthusiasm. "The rest of us will try to stake this Richard Bohm out. Any idea where in the world we should go?"

"Didn't find a reliable home address, Cap, as you'd expect. But I've got the place he's supposed to work out of."

"Show me."

Harry and Daniel both went to look over McGinn's shoulder. He dropped a pin on a map of central Manhattan. "Right in the thick of it," he said. "Technically he works out of a big bank's office."

"The same bank the Company uses?"

"I couldn't believe it either. As for whether he actually works for them, or it's just to give him some layer of credibility, your guess is as good as mine."

"How's his reputation?"

"Fan-bloody-tastic, on the surface. His daddy gave young Richard a private education, then sent him off to Harvard. Landed straight in a big bank. Turned out to be a financial whizz. Built up his portfolio, one thing led to another, and now he's a billionaire. Property investments all over town. Dishes out charitable endowments so he looks like a good guy, makes political donations so he has his say at the big table. All the usual rich guy stuff."

"Anything at all connecting him with the Company?"

"Not that I could dig up. Pretty clear he's not a straight shooter

- he's been accused of insider trading multiple times, even if he's never been done for it. But nothing on that kind of level. Not that I could find with a few hours and a ban on reaching out to any of my other pals, anyway."

"Is that a note of dissension I detect, McGinn?"

"You know me better than that, Cap."

"We're putting a lot of trust in the word of that utterly conniving and criminal lady from the bank," Anna said. "Perhaps this Bohm was some old enemy of hers, and she sensed a chance to set some incredibly eager and violent dogs on him."

"This is what I would do."

Harry couldn't help but turn with surprise at the sound of Noy's voice. She was sat on the edge of their bed. Her eyes were unfocused and staring as usual, but she shrugged. "I'm not this kind of person. But if I was…" She drew a finger across her throat. "Get one enemy to kill another. You don't have to… how do you say?" She frowned. "Lift a finger. Smart."

"It's entirely possible," Harry said. "But we're here now, and we're pressing on with the assumption this Bohm is one of the bastards in charge of the whole thing. We'll stake him out, learn what we can, and hope to get more confirmation as we go."

"A lot of 'hope' in this plan," Noy muttered.

"That's what we're operating on." Harry looked at the map again. "The building's right in the middle of the block. We'll head over to the office in two teams and set up fifty metres or so from the door on either side. Between us, we should see him if and when he goes in or out."

He paused, briefly. "Anna, you're with Noy this time," he said, keeping his voice as casual as possible. "I'm with Daniel. You go first and we'll follow five minutes later. McGinn, can you see your contact now?"

"Near enough."

"We're all set then."

They sat in the back of a taxi through Midtown Manhattan. Harry had no particular liking for New York, but after a long time away it was hard not to crane his neck upwards like a fool.

"Remember the first time we came here?" Harry asked, not turning around. "With Mum and Dad?"

"2001. A month before the towers were hit."

"Different world, then. In a lot of ways. You didn't come back since, did you?"

"No." There stretched several long moments of silence. "You?"

"A couple of times."

"Working?"

Harry turned, caught his eye, and smiled.

"You're not a part of it any more."

"That's true enough. Old habits die hard, I suppose." Harry shrugged. "I did some training near here. Came for a few nights out in the city with the-" He cut off, and glanced forward at the driver who didn't seem to care less what they were saying. "With my colleagues," he finished. "Do you like it here?"

"No."

Harry let the silence pass more easily this time. He was learning anew how a conversation with Daniel - especially with this new Daniel - worked.

"I don't like cities any more," Daniel resumed. "If I ever did. Too many people."

"And that's a problem?"

"It is now."

Harry looked over at the slightest change of tone in his brother's voice. Daniel paused, then waved a hand slowly, vaguely, over his scarred face.

"Everybody looks at me. Everybody. At the..." Daniel's eyes flickered towards the front this time, before returning to his lap. "At the 'place' in Thailand, the men were used to it. To an extent. I could forget about it. That's more difficult when there are dozens of strangers all looking at once." He drummed a large hand up and down on his knee unconsciously. "Probably an exaggeration. But that's how it feels. Between the size and the scars, I draw a lot of attention. Everywhere I go."

Harry felt a strange swelling of emotion in his stomach. "I hadn't thought about that," he said. "Do you think you'll stop noticing? Or just stop caring?"

As usual, Daniel paused before answering. "Both, perhaps," he said. "But I'd prefer not to deal with it at all."

"So it's a life in the country for you, when all of this is done?" Harry smiled, despite himself. "It's a little hard to imagine you tucked away in some quaint cottage, baking bread in the morning, gardening all day... an afternoon break for tea and crumpets."

There was the faintest flicker of movement in one corner of Daniel's mouth. "Hard for me, too."

"Then what?"

"Whatever she wants," Daniel said, responding more quickly this time. "I owe Noy more than you can imagine."

Harry looked at him. But nothing more was forthcoming, and he decided not to press the issue. "How is she?"

Daniel's hand began drumming on his knee again. He looked at it absently, then turned to face the window. "Putting a brave face on it, now," he said. "But it destroyed her. Utterly. To see it happen that way…" The hand formed into a fist, squeezed so tight that the skin went bright white.

"We'll find him," Harry said, not leaving a gap this time which Daniel might fill, unthinkingly, with something the driver shouldn't hear. "Soon enough. Or he'll find us, and the result will be the same."

Daniel remained as he was, staring out of the window, his face tight. Then he gave a single nod, and the thick fist gradually relaxed.

They passed the rest of the journey in silence, albeit one which, for Harry at least, felt more natural than before.

CHAPTER TWENTY ONE

Harry and Daniel stood outside a pharmacy where Lexington Avenue met East 53rd Street. It was almost five o'clock and the streets were busy with working men and women bundled up in long coats and scarves. The sun had long since disappeared through the gaps in the skyscrapers to the west, and from where they stood they could see hundreds of windows lit up in the buildings towering around them.

They were diagonally across the street from the building McGinn had identified, which was enormous, grey, and glassy like all those which surrounded it. A mile or so down Lexington Avenue, the upper third of the Chrysler Building could just be seen. Much closer at hand were Noy and Anna. They stood a hundred metres further along the street, and appeared to have been talking since they arrived.

Four lanes of seemingly never ending traffic stopped and started in front of Harry. A gust of wind blew down the avenue and he zipped the jacket he'd brought with him right up to the top, hands thrust deep into the pockets.

"The quicker we can get out to Asia, the better," he said. "How's Hong Kong this time of year?"

"Dry season, but not the hottest. Mid-to-high teens."

"Well I'd bloody well take that right now."

"Look."

Harry had been facing up the broad street. He turned now and looked across the intersection. A sleek, black car had pulled up in a narrow parking lane on the far side of the road, parallel to the two storey atrium which formed the building's main entrance.

"So? We've seen tons of cars stop. Every big shot in that building has a driver, I'm sure."

"Not just the car. The entrance."

At least ten metres of concrete separated the street from the revolving doors leading into the building. It had been less than a minute since Harry had looked over, and the space had been empty but for workers leaving. Now a man stood there, easily distinguished next to the entrance behind the individuals, pairs, and small groups departing the office building.

He wore an overcoat, a zip-up sweater, jeans and leather shoes, all of which were black. His hands rested near his hips and his feet were spaced shoulder-width apart. His hair was short, his face angular and clean-shaven. He looked to be around six feet tall and lean beneath the winter clothing. He was slowly turning his head from left to right and seemed to be absorbing every detail.

"Look away. Quickly," Harry said. He turned, but Daniel stayed facing the same way. "Now," he hissed. Finally, Daniel turned to face the pharmacy.

They stayed that way for a good thirty seconds until Harry chanced to look back. The man still stood there but he was looking back towards the entrance now.

A shorter man, expensively-dressed and with an even mixture of grey and black in his hair, was striding across the space between the building and the street. Harry recognised Richard Bohm immediately from their online searches. Another man, a foot taller and twice as broad, followed him across the concrete and into the waiting car.

The car remained in place, the emanations from its exhaust clear in the cold air. The first man still stood there, appearing to watch the pedestrians on the nearer pavement closely. Then, unhurriedly and with his hands still near his hips, he crossed the space and also entered the car, which pulled away a moment later and joined the northbound traffic.

Harry took his phone from his pocket and opened a note. He recited the car's licence plate, as he remembered it. Daniel nodded, and he saved it.

Then he brought up the photo they both wanted to see. It was a screenshot from the video they had been sent. An expressionless face stared back at them through a cracked mirror, Noy's murdered father and brother out of shot in the cropped image.

"It was him."

Daniel took the phone from Harry, and stared at it. He nodded again. "Good," he said.

Harry looked ahead for Noy and Anna. Anna was watching him, seemingly for confirmation. Harry couldn't see Noy's expression but Anna had an arm around her shoulder. Harry nodded, and Anna immediately raised her free arm to hail a taxi.

An hour or so later there was a knock at the door to the room. Harry broke off from talking to McGinn, and opened the door to find Anna standing there with Noy. She paused to kiss him briefly on the cheek as she entered. Noy went to Daniel, who had been looking out of the window in silence. She took his arm in both of her hands and leant her head against it.

"How did it go?" Harry asked.

"Swimmingly," Anna said, unwrapping her scarf and unbuttoning her coat then throwing both on the bed. "We tailed them all the way, and I didn't use the phrase 'follow that car' once."

"Congratulations. What happened?"

"The driver left, but three of them went in. The ape, the rich bastard we're here for, and the other, more murderous bastard who's about to receive a very severe comeuppance for his crimes. You're sure it was him too, I take it?"

"Yes," Daniel answered, before Harry could.

"Good."

"Anything else?" Harry asked.

"Nothing worth noting. Seemed like a swanky enough place from the outside, but we didn't want to push our luck."

"Address?"

Anna told him, and McGinn met Harry's eye. "Same place the car's registered," he said.

"Right. We've got our man, and we've got his house."

"Wonderful. Now all we need to do is figure out how to kill him, plus the scum who seem to have latched on. Fortunately," Anna said, with a sweet smile. "That all falls under your jurisdiction, Captain, although I'm sure your other ex-military pals will help out. In the meantime, Noy and I are off for a drink."

Everybody, including Daniel, looked to Noy. She shrugged. "I like this way of working," she said. "Much easier than in Thailand. Make sure I'm the one who kills that man in your plan," she said to Daniel, patting his arm before following Anna out of the room.

Harry, Daniel, and McGinn all watched the door closing shut, then the other two looked at Harry. He shrugged and crossed back towards the desk.

"Can you find the schematics for that building, McGinn?"

"Already on it, Cap."

In the corner of his eye Harry saw Daniel coming to stand over McGinn's other shoulder, as he had before. For the first time in a long time, he found that he was genuinely glad not simply for his brother to be alive, but to have him there - as the person he now was - beside him.

"These are for the right building," McGinn murmured. "But we obviously don't know-"

"The penthouse," Harry said. "I'm sure of it."

"Good call." McGinn clicked a couple more times, brought up a full-screen floor plan, and let out a low whistle. "I'm no architect, only a wee lowly soldier, but that looks like a bloody nice flat if you ask me."

"Agreed." Harry's eyes moved over the sharp lines of the black-and-white plan. "Only one way in."

"Looks like a private lift."

"Balcony around the outside, though."

"Mmm," McGinn murmured. He brought up a ground-level image of the property and hovered the cursor over the buildings to either side. "Both lower, though…"

"Fire escape?"

"Internal, and it'll be alarmed. Twice over, I'd guess."

"Is there a building against it to the rear? Same height?"

McGinn found a ground-level view of the parallel street. "Looks the same, aye. You're liking the balcony approach, eh, Cap?"

"If we're taking him at the apartment, that's the easiest way in." Harry frowned. "Could be cameras on the roof, though." He pointed at the line separating the living room from the balcony, which was a lighter shade than the other dividers on the plan. "And I'm guessing these are all windows. If anybody happened to look out…"

"We've nae idea how the door's secured, either. If he popped outside, of course…"

"Then we'd be in business. I could come down from the roof, assuming we did something about the cameras, but…"

"Aye. It's not ideal."

"This would all be a hell of a lot easier with a great, big sniper rifle."

McGinn grinned. "Tricky things to get your hands on at short notice."

"True. Anyway, good stuff," Harry said, squeezing McGinn's shoulder. He caught the look on the man's face as he did so. "What is it?"

"Ah, nothing, Cap. Just a wee flash of deja vu. Setting the circumstances aside, it's nice to be doing this again, isn't it? Just like old times." He shrugged, and glanced apologetically between Daniel and Harry. "Obviously things didn't end very nicely, but still… We had some good times together out there. We did good work."

"We did," Harry said. "And I'd be lying if I said I hadn't missed it, every now and then. Not the killing itself. But the times like these, with you and the others. I've missed those times."

"We're all still alive, you know, Cap. Alive, and fit, and we're still young… ish." Harry suppressed a smile as he recognised the old pattern of faster words and a sudden increase in hand gestures. "Have you thought, I mean… When all this is done, have you thought about the future? Because I was thinking, you know, that you, me, Cooper, Davies, we could get together and start-"

"McGinn," Harry said, softly. "There'll be time for all this later."

McGinn stopped in mid-flow, his mouth hanging open for a moment before forming into a familiar grin. "Aye, sorry Cap."

"We will talk about it later. I promise. For now," Harry turned to Daniel, who had remained silent and motionless throughout. "Thoughts?"

Daniel kept looking at the screen, then his eyes fell downward. "This isn't my area," he said. "Planning. Operations."

"Nonsense. Tell us what you think."

His brother shrugged his thick shoulders. "We take him in the open. It worked with Tinkov. It seems more straightforward than getting inside."

"That's for sure," McGinn said.

"This is assuming he leaves the building again tonight," Harry said. "And if he does, where do we hit him? If that bastard who killed Noy's family is anything like as dangerous as you say, he'll be on the lookout non-stop. And you can bet *they'll* have guns with them."

"Sorry again, Cap," McGinn said, head hanging.

"That wasn't a dig. My point is that we can take knives, but we'll get gunned down before we're anywhere near being able to use them.

"So we follow," Daniel said. "Just like in Barcelona. Wait for a better opportunity."

Harry walked slowly to the window and stopped there, arms folded and looking down to the internal courtyard of the hotel. "I don't love it," Harry said. "But I suppose we don't-"

He took his phone from his pocket. "Granville," he said, took the call, and was unable to even finish his greeting before being cut off. He listened. "You're sure about this?" he said, then winced and held the phone a little further from his ear. "Jesus Christ, Rupert. All right, I had to check. Get to bed, would you?

Sounds like you need a bloody good rest."

Harry stared at the phone for a moment, bemused, then looked back to Daniel and McGinn. "There's something wrong with him."

"Aye, Cap. He's aristocracy. All that lot are-"

"Not that," Harry said. "He was... different this morning. Anyway, he had some information, even if he refused to say where he'd got it. The Company are locking down, starting at midnight. All the top execs are being made to stay home, and with more security than they'd probably like."

"Including our man."

"Almost certainly."

"Strange," Daniel said.

"What is?"

"It can't be because of Tinkov. They wouldn't have taken so long."

"Smith's disappearance must have spooked them."

The frown remained on Daniel's face. "Perhaps."

"You think something else happened?" Harry asked, but Daniel only shrugged. "Regardless, if we were in any doubt that we had to strike tonight, this seals it."

"Aye," McGinn said. "But it also gives us a bit of a guarantee."

"How?"

"I did some research into our man while the four of you were out. He's a textbook playboy. Loves getting out on the town. Always in the gossip mags and popping up on social media, being spotted in the swankiest New York venues."

It took a moment for Harry to grasp McGinn's meaning. When he did, he smiled. "Perfect."

"What?" Daniel asked.

"A lockdown like this, for someone like Bohm... He might as well be stuck in prison, as far as he's concerned."

"Right," McGinn said, grinning. "If he's about to be housebound indefinitely, however big and fancy his flat might be, he's definitely having one, last, big night out. Giving us the chance to make sure it really *is* his last night out."

CHAPTER TWENTY TWO

"This takes me back," McGinn said.

Harry's hands were buried in his jacket pockets. "Our old stakeouts were usually in hot countries."

They stood on the far side of the street from the building to which Anna and Noy had followed Bohm. It was a mid-sized apartment block, its red-brick exterior hinting at a historicity which - even through the lower windows which offered glimpses into modern, minimalist apartments - Harry could see the residents hadn't stuck to.

A doorman stood outside the entrance wearing a long, thick coat which Harry eyed with envy. Every so often he would step gracefully forward to open the door for a resident coming or going, offering a smile and a tip of his cap before resuming his post.

"Must be even worse for you," Harry muttered, half-turning towards Daniel while keeping his eyes on the doorway. "Three years in Thailand. You lose all your immunity to this kind of weather."

Standing between them, Daniel left his usual pause. "I suppose I'm made of stronger stuff than you."

Harry glanced instinctively at his brother, wondering if it had been a deliberate stab at humour. Daniel's face was as expressionless as ever, but McGinn chuckled.

"He's got a point, Cap. Look at you, shivering there. You're not as tough as you used to be, that's for bloody sure."

"Cold is cold, you dunce. It's got nothing to do with your toughness."

"We're not shivering."

Harry turned back to the entrance and put a hand towards his earpiece. "Delta, Echo. Everything all right?"

"No," Anna replied. "We were kidnapped by a band of scoundrels while you weren't looking. Come and rescue us, Sir Miller."

Harry looked twenty metres or so to the right of the entrance. It was incredibly unlikely Bohm would emerge alone, but he had stationed Anna within striking distance just in case. Noy stood beside her, and was smiling for the first time Harry could remember.

"A simple 'yes' would suffice."

"*Yes*, Captain. We're completely fine, as you can clearly see. Are you really that bored?"

Harry lowered his hand and put it back in his pocket. "Tough night."

"That's the life of a leader, Cap," McGinn said. "You're always a target."

"It's supposed to be behind your back." He cut McGinn off before he could reply. "Yes, I'm sure that happens too, thank you. And I'm equally sure who leads the charge."

His eyes returned briefly to Anna, expecting her to be muttering something about him to Noy. Instead he saw her looking towards the doorway and her hand already towards her ear.

"It's him."

Harry followed her eyes. The man was still dressed completely in black. Again he stood outside the entrance, head turning slowly from one side to the other.

"Everybody move," Harry said. He, McGinn, and Daniel turned immediately and began to walk slowly away without looking back. Looking to his left, Harry saw Anna and Noy doing the same.

He left it ten seconds before glancing back. The man was standing opposite the doorman, hands crossed in front of him and facing the entrance. He nodded, and Bohm emerged followed by two large men. The same car as before drove past Harry and came to a halt just as Bohm and his bodyguards reached the kerb, the black-clad man following several paces behind.

"Taxi coming," Anna said.

"Take it. We'll get the next one. Let us know where he stops if we lose sight of you." Harry saw Anna and Noy getting into the taxi, which pulled away a few moments after Bohm's car.

Since arriving in New York, Harry felt as if he'd seen taxis everywhere he looked. Now, naturally, there were none to be found. He felt the frustration building as he waited, neck craned back down the one-way street.

"They'll get there before us anyway now, Cap," McGinn said. "We'll get the address then."

Harry nodded, though his fists were clenched with frustration. He began to walk, the others following and all of them looking around. Another minute passed and the feeling of impotence grew.

Finally, he heard Anna's voice in his ear. "We're here."

"Where?"

"A club, not too far away. We just hit a patch of bad traffic."

"Address?"

"No idea. Hang on, I'll ask." The earpiece went suddenly silent, before she came back on and told him. "Bit of a queue. Want us to wait for you or get stuck in?"

"Go inside and try to get eyes on them. We'll meet you there. Don't forget to dump your knives."

"Sound advice. Right you are, Captain."

A vacant cab finally stopped half a minute later. Harry gave the driver the address. The man turned when he heard it. "For real?" he asked, incredulously.

"Just get on with it."

The driver looked pointedly at the plain, warm clothes they wore. He made a clicking sound with his tongue, shrugged, and turned back. "You got it, man. If you're paying me, I'm taking you."

They got stuck in the same traffic as Anna and Noy, crawling along beside other cabs wedged between large, shining SUVs and sleek saloon cars. The man turned off the main road, then again, then once more.

"This'd be the place, then," McGinn said.

The entrance to the club was inconspicuous enough. There was no sign over the two sets of large doors with tinted glass, each of which had a pair of bouncers outside. The one on the left, clearly a VIP entrance, had no queue at all. The line for the right-hand entrance went halfway along the block. Harry studied it as they drove by and saw Anna and Noy almost two-thirds of the way back.

They were deposited at the end of the queue, the taxi driver giving them a parting *'Good luck'* as the door closed. "Give me your knives," Harry said quietly. He put them under his coat, walked to the next corner, and dumped them as innocuously as he could in a rubbish bin.

Several more people had already joined the queue when he returned to Daniel and McGinn. "Aye, this takes me back too," McGinn said. "Bit further back than before, I'll admit. Many's the time I froze my balls off on the streets of Glasgow, waiting in line for a club I had no hope of getting into."

"I've got cash," Harry said.

"Have you now? Some of the posh boy's spending money?"

Harry gave a half-nod and craned his neck around the people in front. "Can you see them?" he asked Daniel, but his brother only shook his head.

They edged forward. At least ten minutes passed before Harry heard Anna's voice again in his ear.

"We're in," she said, the music already audible in the background. "We'll just knock back a couple of vodka cokes, have a quick boogie, then get right back on task."

"Very funny."

"I assume they're tucked-away in some sort of rich guy's booth, with enough champers, coke, and prostitutes to last most men a lifetime. But I'll let you know when that's confirmed."

After another ten minutes, Harry, McGinn, and Daniel were next in line. As this fact struck him, Harry turned to McGinn. "You do the talking," he said, pulling a fistful of cash from his pocket. "Here."

"Why do I have to do it? You're the leader."

"You're likeable."

"These aren't even dollars, Cap. They're pounds."

"I used the rest of the dollars I had in the taxi. They won't care."

"Next," a deep voice called.

The money still in his hand, McGinn's hands still very much in his pockets, Harry came forward with the other two following.

The bouncer was as tall and broad as Daniel, and had a similarly dispassionate expression. He looked the three of them over briefly, and shook his head. "Naw," he said.

Harry forced a smile to his face and opened his mouth, but was immediately cut off by the other bouncer. "Where you think this is? You can't come in *here* looking like *that*." His eyes moved past Harry. "Next."

"I've got, ah..." Harry said, and nodded down to the cash he still held near his waist.

The first man's eyes flickered down, then back up. "We can't do that no more," he said. "They got cameras watching us now. What you got there anyway, euros? Get the hell out of here, man."

"Now *this* really takes me back," McGinn said, as they went back past the onlookers who'd observed and heard the whole exchange.

CHAPTER TWENTY THREE

"What? Hang- Just hang on."

Anna motioned for Noy to follow and made her way through the crowd surrounding the bar and back into the corridor. "Right, go on." Her lips curled into a smile. "You're joking. No, we'll be completely and utterly fine. I just hope the same can be said for your poor ego. I'll keep you updated while we're doing all the actual work."

"They not coming?"

"They were turned away at the door. Their clothing wasn't up to scratch."

Noy looked between herself and Anna. Both were dressed casually, and for warmth. "We don't look... how do you say? Million dollars."

"Noy, my friend," Anna said, putting an arm around her as they slowly headed back towards the main room. "Sexism is very much alive and well in this world, and at least ninety percent of the time it's a frustrating, upsetting, terrible, thing."

"But women always get into nightclub. This in the ten percent, right?"

"Precisely. In this case, it simply means we'll have to take care of business ourselves. The objective remains the same - keep searching until we find the bastard we're looking for."

"The two of them."

They pushed through the thick double doors, the music ramping immediately back to its full intensity, and went to stand by the corner of the bar. The entire central room of the club was one dark, cavernous circle, with a larger ground floor and stairs up to a mezzanine overlooking it. Bars lined most of the circular wall, broken up only by other sets of double doors leading to different corridors along which were smaller rooms.

The bar by which Anna and Noy stood ran for twenty metres or so and was raised a little so that it afforded a view of the entire space. But between the dimness of the lighting and there being at least two hundred people on the dancefloor, it was impossible to make anybody out.

Noy turned to Anna and shouted something. "What?" Anna yelled back over the pumping music.

"I never see anything like this," Noy shouted into her ear. "Only on TV."

"We can have those drinks and a dance after all, if you like. I haven't been to a club in years."

"But you use to? When you were crazy girl?"

"Sure, when I was young and in London. When I worked for the Company too, sometimes. If we had downtime, on an assignment, a group of us would go out, let our hair down," Anna shouted. "The first time I talked to Andrew, that was in a club, actually. Now I think about it, the last time I visited one, that was also with him. Before he went and knocked me up, of course."

"Who's Andrew?"

The reminiscence had been more for herself than Noy. It took Anna a moment to realise what she'd said. "Tasha's father," she shouted. "He worked for the Company too. We'd been on assignment before. But the first time we really interacted was in a club."

Noy studied her with a raised eyebrow before leaning back towards her ear. "Interacted?"

"Come now, Noy. We're grown women. We've both interacted with a man or two in our time." Anna felt the memory of that evening, from so many years ago, come rushing back to her all at once. She felt a sudden pressure on her eyes and a twisting in her stomach. She turned away for a moment, then smiled at Noy. "Anyway, enough chatting. If we're not going to party, we should probably crack on with the task at hand."

With their backs propped against the bar they scanned the pulsating mass. The actual faces were almost impossible to discern but for the momentary flashes of white strobe lighting.

"Very hard to say," Noy shouted. "But... I don't think they're here."

"It's unlikely they would be anyway, but I wanted to check."

"Why unlikely?"

"Between Bohm's status, probable arrogance, and limitless fun-times fund, he's unlikely to be moshing with the commoners. Chances are, my friend, that he and his gorillas are up there."

Noy followed Anna's finger towards the mezzanine. "*Oh,*" she said, as her eyes passed along the metal balcony which ran around the upper level and was lined with men and women all expensively dressed and groomed. "You can go up there," she said, pointing towards some stairs towards the far wall. These did indeed curve upwards, but were manned by the largest bouncer they'd seen yet. "We look pretty and they let us in, like outside?"

"I don't think that'll cut it this time, unfortunately. My educated guess is that you'd need to be invited up, to enter that way. The rich folk would have to judge for themselves, whether you were pretty enough, then offer you the opportunity to be seduced by them."

Noy wrinkled her nose. "Any other option?"

"There are two. We could find another route. I doubt the likes of Bohm are having to mix with the peasants at any point, on their way upstairs. There'll be some kind of back passage, for the customers who actually matter."

"Or?"

"We just go up this staircase anyway."

"Second way sound quicker. Easier too. Just need to make a little distraction, no?"

"You're quite right, Noy, that does sound easy. All you need to do now is figure out the distraction."

"Me?"

"It's your idea."

"You can… how did you say? Seduce him."

"I'd really rather not, if there's any other option, as much to avoid the embarrassment of failure as anything. Which seems likely, given I seem to be at least a decade older than any other woman in this club."

"Fine." Noy frowned. "Okay, let's go."

"You've got a plan?"

"No. But I don't want to wait any more. We think of something on the way."

Noy turned and began to walk off, either not hearing Anna's protestations or deliberately ignoring them. Though shorter than almost everyone she passed, Noy navigated the crowds around the bar area with ease, while behind her Anna alternately pushed past, paused for, asked permission from, or swore at everyone who barred her way.

There was an empty arc in front of the bouncer guarding the stairway, as if an invisible barrier of wealth or status were in place. Anna watched as Noy walked straight up to the bouncer without pausing.

The enormous man had to bend almost double to hear as she spoke to him. He looked at her incredulously the first time. She beckoned him down again and said something more. To Anna's surprise, Noy pointed at her directly. The bouncer asked Noy a question, and there seemed to be an expression of sympathy on his face. He looked around the room as he considered, stared hard at Noy, and glanced at Anna. Then he spoke a few more words and stood aside. Noy turned to beckon an incredulous Anna closer, and they passed the bouncer and began climbing the stairs together.

"What on Earth did you promise him?" Anna asked, leaning towards Noy but not looking back. "Or don't I want to know?"

Noy wrinkled her nose. "I promise nothing," she said, her offence plain.

"So?"

Holding the handrail of the curving staircase with one hand, she waved the other dismissively. "I tell him my boyfriend up here with another girl, and I want to catch him. You helping me."

"That worked?"

"He say he understand. His last boyfriend cheat on him too. Just tell me not to beat him up or do anything too crazy in the club."

Anna looked at her, her incredulity momentarily doubled. Then she stuck out her bottom lip, shrugged, and followed Noy up the steps.

The mezzanine ran in a full circle above the ground floor. There were no bars, staff coming instead to each area to take orders. Most of those areas consisted of small, round tables with a few chairs. Others had larger tables with three sofas around them.

Noy paused as they reached the top and looked at Anna. "Don't understand," she shouted.

"What's that, dear?"

"This the same club, right? Music same, room same. Why people pay more money to be here?" She looked around, frowning. "Less people. Less fun. No… atmosphere. Way worse here, no?"

"You're completely right, and I have absolutely no idea. We have an expression in England, 'more money than sense'."

Noy nodded. "I like this expression."

Anna looked around. The whole floor was almost filled. The men were in their thirties or forties and many wore suits, albeit with the tie removed and top button undone. Most of the women were much younger, and wore little.

"There."

Anna followed Noy's gaze straight across the mezzanine and saw Richard Bohm. He was dressed in a slim-fit suit with the top few buttons of his white shirt undone. He sat on the outward-facing sofa, languidly reclined with his elbows on the low backrest and one leg crossed over the other.

A couple of younger men, identically dressed, sat on the sofa to Bohm's left. They leant forward and hung on his every word. Bohm himself faced the other way, towards a pair of long-legged girls who must have been in their early twenties at most, both of whom seemed to laugh every time he finished a sentence. There were several bottles of champagne on the rectangular table between the sofas, in front of which two of Bohm's men stood with their arms crossed in front of them.

"Miller?" Anna said, pressing her earpiece close. "Harry? Can you hear me? Yes, we're in a club, of course it's bloody loud. Listen, we've got eyes on Bohm."

"But I don't see…" Noy said. Anna looked at her again. Noy was still scanning the faces of the hundred or so people across the mezzanine.

"He's got two of his big boys with him," Anna shouted, not entirely sure what Harry could and couldn't hear. "No sign of the psychopath, though."

"He's here."

The change in Noy's voice made Anna turn to her immediately. Her friend was looking a little to the right this time. A pair of the double doors had just opened and the Assassin was passing through them, his walk unhurried. He stopped next to one of the bodyguards, who leant down to hear what he said.

"Miller?" Anna said. "The psychopath's here too. He must've been doing a sweep of the floor. We're going to get somewhere a little less exposed, and- Oh Jesus."

Her mouth hung open, and it took her a moment to reply to Harry's hurried questions. "It's Noy," she said. "She's going straight for them."

CHAPTER TWENTY FOUR

Anna's eyes had been fixed on the black-clad figure. Noy was already ten paces away. She wasn't walking particularly quickly, moving instead in a steady, determined manner.

Anna went to catch up with her, resisting the urge to run and thus draw attention to herself. Immediately she almost crashed into two girls dancing next to their table. She swore at them instinctively, and they swore straight back at her as she carried on, uncaring.

Noy was halfway around the mezzanine when Anna drew level. Still trying to act casually, she took Noy's left wrist - on the far side from the Assassin and the others - and tugged.

"What the hell are you doing?" she shouted.

Noy was making no attempt at subtlety. Her eyes were fixed directly on the group. Rather than anger or excitement, Anna saw a cold certainty within them. She said something in Burmese, her mind elsewhere, then translated. "Revenge."

"How, Noy? We have no weapons, no backup. What on Earth's the plan here?"

"No plan. Sure they have weapons we can use."

Noy went to move away, but Anna pulled her back again. "You've lost your bloody mind," she hissed, straight in Noy's ear. "They'll kill us."

Noy shrugged. "As long as I kill him first." She went to carry on, looked down at her wrist, then back up at Anna. "Let go."

"I can't, Noy. This is utter madness. It's-"

"Nobody hold me back now. Not any more. Let me go."

Anna let out a moan of exasperation. Then she released her grip, and Noy immediately turned and started forward. "Miller," Anna said. "There's about to be trouble. Whatever half-plan you did have just went straight out of the window."

She began to walk forward, finger pressing her earpiece as far in as it would go. "I can't hear you. Hopefully you can hear me. This is utter madness. God knows something must have changed in me. I should want to live, at all costs, for Tasha. But I can't let her go alone. I've gone soft, and I'm sure it's all your fault somehow."

Noy was three quarters of the way around the circle. Anna, close behind, spoke even faster now. "There's a very good chance I'm about to die. Please look after Tasha if I do. And know..." She swallowed. "That I love you. I didn't tell you before, but I really do."

Anna lowered her hand, and took a deep breath.

The nearest bodyguard had seen Noy. Other people nearby had been walking past or dancing in front of Bohm's area. Something in Noy's walk or her face, however, made the man take notice. He began turning towards her, and unclasped the hands which had been held in front of him. As he did, the flash of a strobe light illuminated a pistol on his hip.

"Jesus," Anna muttered. "This whole stupid operation was your idea, Miller, and now I'm the one about to get a bullet through the bloody head." She broke off and quickened her pace as Noy drew level with the bodyguard.

Noy kept walking by in front of the man, for a step or two. Then she turned to her left and started to go past him.

The bodyguard automatically went to block her, holding out an arm, and Noy suddenly pushed him. She was half the man's size, but he was caught completely off-guard and stumbled back a couple of paces, then his heel struck the bottom of the nearest sofa awkwardly and he fell backwards onto it.

The entire scene froze in front of Anna, only for a moment.

The pounding music seemed to disappear, the constant movement of the club to cease. The whole building faded away so that there was only that small, square space. Even the Assassin and the other bodyguard were momentarily stilled. The eyes of everyone in the immediate area fixed onto the slight figure who remained just in front of the table, standing over the sprawling bodyguard.

It was Noy herself who broke the spell.

With the same clarity and determination she stepped forward, grabbed an empty champagne bottle by its neck, and went straight at the Assassin who stood motionless to the right of the table. Within a couple more paces she had reached him and was swinging for his head.

The expression on the Assassin's face didn't change. With calm eyes and a smoothness which made his movements look deceptively slow he merely leant backwards and let the bottle pass by.

Noy went to swing again, but Anna didn't see the result. The second bodyguard was frozen in place as he watched the bizarre scene unfold, but the first was pushing himself up off the sofa with his eyes set on Noy. Anna snapped out of her own absorption with Noy's assault, turned to her left, reached the bodyguard within a couple of strides, and slapped him hard across the face with the back of her hand.

The bodyguard's head turned with the force of the blow and he fell backwards again, a hand rising instinctively to his cheek. Anna quickly knelt on the armrest before he could recover and punched him straight in the groin. He let out a long, pained breath and doubled over, hands reaching downwards and leaving the pistol unprotected. Anna grabbed the weapon, already raising it and flicking off the safety as she turned.

The Assassin had one hand around Noy's neck and pressed the broken top of the champagne bottle against her throat. The rest of the bottle lay smashed on the table in front of him. He watched Anna, his face still expressionless as if nothing at all had, would, or could surprise him.

The second bodyguard was reaching for his own weapon. Anna aimed at him, and shook her head. The man smirked and began to lift the gun from its holster anyway. Anna lowered her aim and shot him in his thigh.

The gunshot was distinctive and clear even over the din of the music, and the screams started immediately. Anna ignored them, turning the gun back towards the Assassin. His eyes were still fixed on hers and the jagged glass still pressed to Noy's throat. Anna swung left, so that the gun pointed straight at Bohm's head.

"Let her go," she shouted, the gun held steady while her eyes turned towards the Assassin. For the first time his own eyes left hers, and flickered to his right. "He's your charge, isn't he? You kill her, I'll kill him, and I don't think your bosses would be too happy with that. Your *boss*, I should say, since you'll be down to one after that."

The Assassin's eyes flickered back and forth once more. Then, without appearing to move a muscle to prepare himself, he shoved Noy hard in the back.

Noy stumbled forwards towards Anna, who took one hand from the gun and grabbed her to stop her falling. By the time she looked up again the Assassin was already heading for the nearest door and pushing Bohm in front of him. In doing so he had joined a stream of other people who Anna hadn't even noticed fleeing after the gunshot had sounded, many of them looking back at her in terror, the shouts and screams that filled the air audible even over the music which played on.

"Kill him!" Noy yelled, head turned towards the door now too.

"I haven't got a bloody shot, you maniac!"

"So we follow him!"

"*That* we can do."

Anna realised she had forgotten completely about the first bodyguard whom she'd initially incapacitated. She looked around now and saw him running away with the two girls Bohm had been entertaining, the younger besuited men following close behind.

When she turned back towards the table, Noy had disappeared. Anna looked forward again just in time to see her entering the press of people passing through the door. "Jesus Christ," she muttered, hid the pistol under her jacket, and ran after her.

The people nearest Anna as she entered the corridor had been watching her and went quicker to get away. As Anna descended a broad staircase though, and joined the main crush of people on the ground floor pushing to escape, she became anonymous. She also immediately lost sight of not only Bohm and the Assassin, but Noy too.

Anna swore, and raised her free hand towards her earpiece.

CHAPTER TWENTY FIVE

"Look sharp," Harry said, lowering his own hand. "They're coming out."

"Them and everybody else," McGinn said.

He, Harry, and Daniel all watched the steady stream of well-dressed men and women hurrying from the two sets of double doors at the front of the club. At least a couple of hundred had already made it out, and stood - like the three of them - on the far side of the road facing the building.

The music inside had just been turned off and the air was filled instead with the sound of hushed, fearful conversation and approaching sirens. Several police cars had already arrived, their lights flashing across the anxious crowds. The officers had parked across the road in both directions to block off the traffic and were now marshalling the escaping clubgoers across the street.

"There," Daniel said, and nodded towards the VIP entrance on the left. Bohm, his shirt untucked and hair dishevelled, was pushing through the crowd. He turned to his right and moved a few steps clear of the mass, saw the police cars blocking the road, paused, then took his phone from his pocket.

"Calling his driver," McGinn muttered. "We're going to have a pretty small window here, Cap."

"You follow at a distance, in case they double back. Daniel, you're with me" Harry started moving slowly along the opposite side of the street from Bohm, hidden behind the line of people standing on the pavement and watching the club.

He and Daniel paused when the man in black also stepped clear of the crowd and came to stand directly behind Bohm. A few moments later one of the bodyguards jogged over too, though the other man with whom Bohm had left his apartment was nowhere to be seen.

Bohm finished talking on the phone, exchanged a few words with the Assassin and his bodyguard, and motioned to his right. The three of them moved off along the pavement and passed the first pair of police cars which were now being joined by several more, sirens wailing as they came to a halt and men and women quickly exiting then hurrying towards the building.

Harry began to follow with Daniel on the far side of the road. For now they were blocked off by the police officers and the departing clubgoers who preferred to leave the scene entirely rather than wait to see its outcome.

Harry and the others walked parallel to Bohm and his two men. They were around ten metres past the final police car when Harry heard Anna's voice in his ear. "Miller! Watch her!"

He looked around. Daniel was already running across the road, which was free of traffic having been blocked off further along. Harry looked past him and saw Noy sprinting down the pavement with Anna trailing behind and shouting after her.

Bohm and his men had paused and turned at the shouting. As he began crossing the road after the others, Harry saw the man in black standing completely still and taking a moment to assess the entire scene.

The Assassin half-turned, and said something to Bohm and the other bodyguard. Bohm nodded to the larger man, and they both turned and began to run. The Assassin was left standing on his own in the centre of the wide pavement. He remained motionless, feet shoulder-width apart and hands held loosely by his sides as he watched Noy come closer.

The streetlight caught what seemed to be a shard of glass in Noy's hand as she reached the man and swung for him, screaming. The Assassin merely leant back once more to let the impromptu weapon slice by, then kicked straight out into Noy's stomach. She stumbled backwards clutching her midsection, but the Assassin was already moving past her.

Harry saw Anna had drawn a gun, and - unable to get a clear shot - had been holding it half-raised towards the man as she ran. She tried to bring it up now, but had been only a few paces behind Noy, and had not expected the Assassin to advance so quickly towards her.

The man slapped Anna's right hand forcefully with his left the moment he was within range, knocking the weapon into the empty road and putting her off-balance. Still he didn't pause, bringing his right hand up to punch her across the face and send her spinning in the same direction. The gun clattered to the ground a split-second before Anna did.

Daniel reached the Assassin immediately after, charging straight for him with the intention of tackling him to the ground. The Assassin had barely a second to react after knocking Anna down, but by the moment Daniel reached him had still somehow reset himself with perfect balance and his hands raised.

His timing exquisite once more, he ducked under Daniel's lunging arms, grabbed onto an arm as he turned so that his back faced Daniel just as the larger man made contact, and yanked forward. Daniel's own momentum combined with the pull sent him momentarily onto the man's back. The man pushed upwards with his legs, sending Daniel flying briefly through the air and rotating slowly forwards before landing heavily on the pavement behind.

Harry had paused a few feet from the pavement. His mouth hung open. Three people had been running straight at the Assassin a few moments before. Now all three lay on the ground, and the man himself was back in his deceptively relaxed stance once more.

The Assassin met his eyes, steadily. Then his gaze flickered downwards. Harry followed it and saw the gun of which Anna had been divested lying there on the road. There were around ten feet between them, and the pistol was slightly closer to Harry than to the man in black. They looked back at each other, both completely still. Then the Assassin exploded into action, Harry moving a split-second later.

Harry had gone instinctively for the gun, and was momentarily surprised as he saw the Assassin running in the opposite direction. Harry raised the weapon as the man in black sprinted away, his overcoat kicking up behind him, and aimed for his head.

"Cap!"

The voice broke through Harry's concentration, and he looked around to see McGinn jogging over. "Not to second guess you, Cap, but you've got a half-dozen NYPD cars in one direction and a crowd of civvies in the other."

Harry looked ahead along the road and saw McGinn was right. Another line of curious people had clustered towards the end of the road in front, just before the intersection. He quickly flicked the safety back on and stuffed the gun in the back of his jeans. The Assassin had already reached the onlookers, who hurried to create a gap through which he ran without breaking stride before turning right at the intersection and disappearing around the corner.

Harry glanced back at the pavement. Daniel was on his side and nursing his shoulder where he'd fallen. Anna lay on her back with a hand to her face. Noy had tried to struggle to her feet and was now on one knee, cradling her stomach. It was Noy's eyes on which Harry's lingered. They looked at each other for a moment, then she nodded to him. He nodded back, then half-turned over his shoulder.

"Go," he said to McGinn, and began to run, ramping quickly up to a sprint and hearing his friend's footsteps pounding behind him.

They arrived at the corner around which the Assassin had disappeared at least ten seconds after him. He was already a few dozen metres in front.

"Nippy bastard, isn't he?" McGinn grunted.

They accelerated again after turning the corner. Harry had no idea where they were, but it was a large, busy avenue with a broad pavement from which people scattered in both directions as they saw Harry and McGinn charging towards them, many having only just gotten out of the Assassin's way.

All those people were merely a blurred background to Harry, whose eyes remained steadfastly upon the Assassin as his legs and arms pumped and the adrenaline of the chase raced through him.

He gave a half-grin, half-grimace as he saw the Assassin attempting to cross a road which led onto the avenue in front, and nearly getting run down by a taxi. The driver barely managed to stop in time, the front of the car nudging the Assassin and sending him momentarily stumbling. He recovered his balance, ignoring the furious driver's beeping horn as he ran once more, but even the brief delay allowed Harry and McGinn to close the gap by at least ten metres.

Harry saw the Assassin lifting a hand towards the side of his head as he ran, and guessed he wore an earpiece too. The man glanced left to the far side of the one-way avenue. On the fourth and furthest lane of traffic the same sleek, black car Harry had seen earlier was just pulling to a halt. The man slowed, and looked all the way back to Harry and McGinn. Then he veered left, cutting straight out into the road.

"He's a crazy bastard too!" McGinn shouted, but Harry barely noticed. He barely even glanced over his own shoulder before he also turned sharply left.

McGinn's yelled curse didn't register, nor did the sudden blaring of a horn as the first car which was about to run him over screeched to a halt. Harry turned to look in the direction of the traffic, and barely managed to accelerate clear of a taxi, the driver of which had been unable to see him behind the first car and slammed on his own brakes just in time.

As Harry reached the final lane of traffic the driver of the next car turned his headlights on full beam, blinding Harry and forcing him to raise a protective arm, before accelerating as quickly as he could towards him.

The gap was only around ten metres, which - although it meant the vehicle couldn't pick up much speed - also gave Harry no time to move clear. He could only jump over the large grill at the front of the car to land heavily on the bonnet, before the continued acceleration made him roll up along it and into the windscreen.

The impact was heavy enough to knock the wind out of him, but Harry reached anyway for the pistol which, thankfully, had remained wedged in his jeans. He looked through the windscreen and saw the Assassin in the passenger seat, regarding him with complete neutrality.

Harry didn't recognise the driver, but the man's eyes widened as he saw Harry bringing the gun up and around towards him in one hand. He slammed on the brakes. Harry reached instinctively for something, anything, to hold onto, and - finding nothing - was sent straight back down the bonnet and thudding heavily onto the road. He heard the engine revving again almost immediately, and despite his body's protestations just managed to force himself to his feet and dive clear, rolling awkwardly on the pavement as the car missed him by a foot or less.

The driver didn't pause, reaching top speed quickly and continuing on down the avenue. Harry rolled onto his front with a grunt of effort and pain, watching the car pulling further and further away. The left indicator began to blink. The car was about to disappear from sight.

"On your feet, Cap."

Harry felt McGinn's hand on his shoulder, rolling him over onto his back, then he helped heave Harry to his feet. Dull pain throbbed through Harry's torso where he'd hit the windscreen then the pavement, and the bullet wounds from London burned fiercely, but all of that could wait.

"Come on," he said, grimacing.

"We'll struggle to get a cab driver to take us like this. Your hands are bleeding, Cap. Your clothes are dirty, and-"

Harry pushed McGinn's arm from his shoulder where it had lingered, and looked back along the road. He held his arm up for a taxi, then another, and was ignored both times. The third slowed to a halt and McGinn followed him into the back.

"Next left," Harry said. "Go." He leaned forward to look along the road.

"You see anything?"

Harry shook his head. "But we know where they're heading."

"Back to the flat?"

"Safest place to hole up. I'm sure they've already phoned in for backup," he said, beyond caring what the driver might hear. "We need to take care of business before the reinforcements get there."

Harry gave the driver the address of Bohm's apartment and told him to hurry. He tried to reach Anna, but either his earpiece or hers had been damaged. He sent her a message instead, simply reading 'Where he lives. Now.' Then he put his phone away and leant forward again.

"Hurry, I said."

"We go as fast as we can, sir. I will not get arrested for you."

Harry felt something in him threatening to snap. He reached for the pistol which was wedged uncomfortably beneath his backside.

"Cap," McGinn said, putting his hand on Harry's arm.

Harry met his eyes with a scowl. Then he closed his eyes and let out a deep breath, and forced the sudden anger back down. "This should already be over," he muttered. "There must have been a way, before or after the club. At the very least, we should have got the Assassin. Bohm's a sitting duck without him."

"I don't think this Assassin's that easy to 'get', Cap," McGinn said, quietly. "But we'll do it now. We'll get Bohm, in his fancy flat, even with his freak of a bodyguard. It doesn't matter. We'll get him. We've done this plenty of times before, with plenty of other mad, nasty bastards."

Harry felt the briefest hint of calmness settle over him. He glanced sideways at McGinn, met his eyes again for a moment, and nodded. When he looked forward again he saw they were turning onto the quiet street on which Bohm lived. The black car was parked up opposite his apartment building with its lights off, and as they passed by Harry saw that it was empty.

Harry gave the driver the few dollars he had left, then looked to McGinn once more. They exchanged a nod, opened their doors, stepped out, and began to walk across the street.

CHAPTER TWENTY SIX

"What the hell's going on out there? Where are they?"

The large man shrugged helplessly and waved a hand towards the laptop screen, which was divided into nine squares. One showed the cage outside the apartment's private lift, by which the driver was stationed with a gun. Two of the squares were black. "No idea, boss. They took out the camera over the entrance, and the one in the lobby."

"So that's it? All the money I paid for this place, and for idiots like you, and that's what I get? 'No idea, boss'?"

Bohm took a packet of cigarettes from the inside pocket of his jacket and lit one then drew on it, all in one swift, agitated movement. He took his phone out, checked his messages, and swore under his breath at whatever he saw there.

"They come inside, we'll see them, boss."

Bohm gave a fake laugh. "Briefly, sure, then they knock out your little cameras and go bye-bye again. I thought those things were tiny anyway, 'impossible to spot' one of you goons told me."

"They are. These guys just knew where to look."

"What are you suggesting? They were told?"

"No," the Assassin said, and both of them turned to look at him. "They know because they're professionals. When you know how other professionals operate, tasks like that are child's play."

A brief silence followed, as it tended to whenever the Assassin spoke. The bodyguard looked to Bohm. Bohm, in turn, looked at the Assassin as he blew out another cloud of smoke, before turning back to the bodyguard. "Whatever," he said. "Just watch out for them, you buffoon. Do what the hell I pay you for. Protect me."

"You got it, boss."

The Assassin followed Bohm away from the vast dining table where the bodyguard had his laptop set up, and across the living room. Bohm stopped in front of a standing table crowded with various bottles of expensive spirits. Cigarette wedged between two fingers, he unstoppered a decanter of whiskey, poured himself a glass, saw it off, smacked his lips, then poured another.

"That's better," he said, and turned to the Assassin. "When's that backup getting here?"

"Fifteen minutes. Maybe less."

"Swell. We can hole up here that long. One way in, one way out, right? We keep those wolves away from the door, wait for the big boys to roll in, and we're home dry."

Bohm crossed to the floor-to-ceiling windows separating the living room from the balcony, the Assassin following. He blew a final cloud of smoke onto the glass, then dropped the cigarette onto the laminated floor and ground it out with his polished, black leather shoe.

"I'm guessing this is the work of those Miller brothers you mentioned."

"Yes."

"Seems like they brought a few friends along for the ride."

The Assassin didn't respond.

"Know why I'm the best, Vocitus?"

"You gave two reasons last time."

"Well here's a third for you. I don't underestimate *anybody*." He glanced over his shoulder, as if to gauge the Assassin's reaction. Finding none, he turned back to the windows. "You might think that sounds crazy. I just told you I'm the best, right? Well, it's not crazy, and it's not arrogant, if that's what you're thinking. When I was coming up, I went against everybody I could - institutional traders, private traders, didn't matter - and I came out on top. I ever saw anyone doing better than me, they became a target, and I beat them.

"That's how I got dragged into this Company business in the first place. Think I wanted to get involved in that kind of crap? People trafficking, money laundering? Hell no." He shrugged. "But she roped me in anyway, that sneaky bitch of a genius out in Hong Kong. Played on my ego, you could say. Told me I could go way past *everybody* on my level. Stop just being rich, and become *wealthy*, you know? Like the old families of this country."

Bohm nodded to himself and drank the rest of his whiskey. "She was right about that, but I wish to God I'd never bothered. I've had enough already. It wasn't worth the ballache, just to add another zero on the end. Then there's that old bastard, my conscience. If there is a hell..." He trailed off, stared into space for several seconds, then looked back up at the Assassin. "Anyway," he said. "Point is, you think maybe you might have underestimated these Millers? This older brother, the ringleader, especially?"

"Clearly."

"Good. Don't let it happen again - I'm not ready to die just yet. I've gotta make my peace first, you know?" He poured himself a third whiskey and swirled it around the ornate tumbler.

"Think that's why they're here? To kill me? Maybe they're trying to kidnap me or something, get some kind of-"

"No," the Assassin said. "They're here to kill you."

Bohm's face fell, only for the briefest of moments before he smiled again and raised his glass. "To honesty," he said, and took a sip. "What makes you say such a scary thing?"

"They want to kill all of you. Tinkov before. Patel after."

Bohm's eyebrows raised over his glass, and he choked on the whiskey he'd been drinking. He coughed into his hand, watering eyes fixed on the Assassin. "That's a hell of a concept," he said. "What are there, like four of them? What makes you so sure?"

"Instincts."

"That's cute. Care to expand?"

"The speed of it. The directness. The risks."

"But... why? Why would they want to kill us? Why would they want to kill me?"

The Assassin met Bohm's gaze. His eyes bored into the billionaire's. The silence dragged. "Is that a serious question?"

"That's cute," Bohm said again. "Who wouldn't want to kill us, right? That's fine, if you look at it all in a certain militant leftie-liberal kinda way. But to take these risks, like you said, to even try this thing, even if there's no way in hell it'll work. Seems to me like it's personal."

"There was the girl's family I killed. To provoke the younger Miller."

"You mentioned that."

"The Millers' father was also killed."

"Oops. Your handiwork too?"

The Assassin shook his head. The ghost of a scowl crossed his face. "That whole episode was foolish. Clumsy."

"This is as close to mad as I've ever seen you."

"Incompetence angers me. Failure, in general."

"What else?" Bohm asked, but the Assassin only looked at him then away again. "I pulled your file, by the way, Vocitus. After your last visit. Realised I knew next to nothing about you. Then I read it, and felt like I knew even less."

"Which file?"

"Your army one first. Boy, that was a joke. Somebody read that, they'd think you were really harmless. What are you down as in that, a janitor?"

"An engineer, I believe."

"I guess they can't just write 'Assassin' in big letters, huh?" Bohm finished his latest whiskey and looked thoughtfully into the empty glass. "So that led me onto the second file - ours. The Company keeps them on everybody we ever come into contact with, and these ones aren't sanitised. They're the real deal. Boy, they've got everything in there. That's why only a handful of people ever get to see them. You on that list, amigo?"

"It's how I got onto Daniel Miller's trail."

"Ever look at your own file?"

"No."

"Talk about a body count. I'm glad you're on our side." Bohm grinned, then went to refill his whiskey again. He poured himself a larger glass this time and held it up to the light. "What I don't get," he said, voice starting to slur as he studied the amber liquid. "Is why. Somebody's daddy beat them when they were young, they end up dishing it out when they're older. I get it. You grow up around violence, it becomes a part of you, then you can't shake it, right? Well that file on you is pretty long, buddy - goes all the way back - and I didn't see anything like that. Any reason at all. So what gives?"

The Assassin's eyes bored into Bohm's again. Unperturbed, Bohm motioned with his glass. His face had grown pink and some of the contents of the glass sloshed over the side. "Well? Why'd you do so much killing? It's a simple question." The silence dragged. "Technically, I'm your superior. I can order you to tell me, if you want things done military style."

The Assassin's eyes were cold now as they remained fixed on Bohm's. Finally, they slid away towards the windows over Bohm's shoulder and towards the downtown skyline. "I hate people."

"You surprise me. You always seemed like such an affable guy. What happened, some good old fashioned childhood trauma? My old pops beat my mom, but I didn't become a mass murderer over it."

"My parents raised me properly. It wasn't their fault."

"So when did it start?"

"It didn't start. It's been that way for as long as I can remember. I used to get angry when I was young. I hurt the other children."

"I was wondering why you had so many schools on your file. Mystery solved."

"It became less frequent as I grew older. I became better at controlling it. Even if I didn't know why I should have to." The Assassin paused. "Then I joined the military. I thought I wouldn't need to control it any more."

"And clearly nobody told you about friendly fire when you did sign up. How many times did you get investigated for assaulting your comrades? Five in the first two years?"

"On the record."

"But rather than kicking your ass out of there, or sending you to jail where you belonged, they turned you into an... 'engineer'?"

"An arrangement which suited both sides. I was allowed to operate alone, and use the talents I'd been blessed with. They gained a valuable asset."

"So everybody's happy. Not the guys they sent you to hunt down, granted. But you got your job satisfaction, at least."

"For a time."

"And yet, here you are, working for us. I remember when she first told me about you, you know. She's never happy, never satisfied, you know that. It's one of the things that makes her so great at what she does. But that was about as thrilled as I'd heard her."

"You know the rest of the story, since then."

"But not what happened in between. Why'd you leave the military? Your choice or theirs?"

"The situation became unworkable."

"You go rogue? Break off that little leash they kept you on?" Bohm waited briefly for an answer as he downed half the whiskey in one gulp. When none was forthcoming he nodded to himself, then frowned. "What does that mean, anyway, that you *hate* people?"

The Assassin kept staring out of the window. Then, slowly, he turned to fix his eyes on Bohm's.

"As it sounds. I can't be around other people for long. When I am, I feel..." The Assassin paused, but his eyes never left Bohm's. "A rage. It builds up inside me. And I need to lash out." His eyes momentarily lifted up and to the side, as if in thought, before settling once more. "It's always been that way. It was natural to me. I used to fight against it, then I saw there was no need. If I have an outlet, that's enough."

"Do you hate me?"

"It's nothing personal."

Bohm laughed. He checked his phone again. Again he frowned at the screen, before looking back up.

"What about... that old bastard I mentioned, conscience? I tell you, I used to sleep like a baby, whatever stress I was under. Ever since I got involved with this Company..." Bohm's eyes fell and suddenly he looked old. "I can't die yet, you know, because eternal damnation's waiting. I know that, as sure as I know my own name. I've got to atone, somehow. I know I do, I just don't know how yet." He looked up at the Assassin again, a sheen to his eyes now. "How do you justify it?"

"I don't need to."

"To yourself, I mean."

"I don't need to. I'm at perfect peace with who I am. Morality doesn't factor in. It doesn't exist. It's an invention to govern behaviour."

"It's all very well to say that, buddy. I took a philosophy class at college. But you just *feel* it, don't you, when you've done wrong. When you've done evil."

"I don't feel anything. That's why I'm the best... at what *I* do."

Bohm forced an uneasy grin. "That's cute," he muttered, and turned to face the skyline himself. The Assassin watched his back and saw him shaking his head to himself, then Bohm called across the room. "Anything to report, hotshot?"

The Assassin had felt the guard's eyes on him too as he'd spoken. The man cleared his throat now before replying. "Nothing. Elevator's still on this floor. Randy's got the door covered."

"All the windows intact? Nobody using one of those laser cutter things, like in the movies?"

"I don't know if they exist, boss."

"I know they don't exist, you idiot." Bohm looked at the Assassin over his shoulder. "Do they?" He emptied the rest of his glass and put it down roughly on the dining table. "Not an ounce of humour between the pair of you. I'm going out for a smoke."

"Your phone," the Assassin said.

Bohm paused. "What about it?"

"You keep checking it."

"So what if I do?" Bohm considered. "It's that wily old British bastard, Frost. He's not responding, and I don't like it. Not so soon after the Ruskie bit the dust. Can I go smoke now, please?"

Bohm slid open one of the doors. The Assassin went to follow him, then paused as he drew level with the table. He looked at the laptop screen. The guard glanced at him uneasily.

"What?"

The Assassin stared at the screen. The slightest crease appeared on his brow. "He knows we're here. He'll know we have reinforcements arriving."

"So? Maybe he gave up. I'm sure he'll be back to try again another time."

"He would never give up. And he knows there won't be another time." The Assassin's frown deepened. Then his eyebrows lifted. "The roof."

"What?"

"Do you have cameras on the roof?"

"Why would we-"

The Assassin had already turned to look out at Bohm. The guard's head snapped around too at his boss's sudden shout, clearly audible through the gap in the door which he'd left partially open.

Bohm's head was raised and he was backing away along the balcony. The next moment a figure dropped down in front of Bohm, who backed away faster before collapsing under the weight of a second shape which also fell from the roof.

CHAPTER TWENTY SEVEN

The guard sprang up from the table with a shout to answer his boss's. His chair had been closer than he'd thought to the glass window behind him. It struck the surface, and when it unexpectedly stopped moving backwards he promptly tripped over the front-right leg and went sprawling to the ground.

The Assassin had begun moving the split-second after the first man fell, and was already halfway out of the door when the guard tripped. He went straight for the second man to have dropped, who was larger than the first and bearded and was trying to straddle Bohm's chest so that he could strangle him while Bohn twisted and clawed at him.

The Assassin reached the second man before the first could intercept him. There was no need for tactics, nor guile, nor anything more measured than a swift blow to the head, which the Assassin delivered squarely to the side of the man's skull. The man grunted and fell to the floor in the opposite direction, legs still awkwardly stuck over Bohm's torso.

As Bohm began scrabbling to break free the Assassin turned to the other man. The right half of his face was illuminated from the light inside. He recognised Harry Miller easily enough.

The Assassin had anticipated a full blown charge, and had turned to meet the tackle from a low position. But Miller had stayed back, and his kick was already coming around towards him. The Assassin tried to turn away but the toe of the boot still caught the lower part of his face and sent pain shooting through him even as he turned his head to soften the impact.

The Assassin staggered back a couple of paces, then straightened and put a hand to his mouth. It came away bloody. He considered it, then looked up.

Harry Miller was helping the other man to his feet, who held a hand to the side of his head. The Assassin recognised him from his research into Miller. John McGinn. Signaller and marksman in the SAS, under Miller's command before going private. A brilliant sniper, but there was nothing in his file about hand to hand prowess. He wouldn't prove a problem.

There was a pause as all four of the men stood still on the narrow balcony. The Assassin was towards one end. Bohm had just regained his feet behind. Miller stood a few metres in front beside his former comrade, who glared back at the Assassin, grimacing.

It was Bohm who broke the silence. He looked back towards the doorway, where the guard was hovering and seemingly awaiting instructions. "You just gonna stand there and watch the show?" Bohm shouted. "Where's your gun?"

"On the table."

"Your walkie-talkie, to get the other idiot from down the hall?"

"That too."

"Jesus Christ!" Bohm screamed. "I'll get them myself. Do your job, moron!"

The man was large enough to fill the doorway, but he was clearly out of his depth and he knew it. He looked back and forth from Bohm's snarling face to the two intruders. Miller and McGinn looked at each other. Without speaking they swapped places, so that McGinn was closer to the doorway and Miller was lined up opposite the Assassin.

"Now!" Bohm yelled at the bodyguard, as he went to run across the middle of the scene towards the living room. Miller reacted with impressive speed, coming forward and simply sticking out a foot to trip Bohm, who swore as he fell straight to the floor, but Miller hadn't paused. He was advancing straight towards the Assassin with fire in his eyes.

Confronted with the ferocity of Miller's expression and the manner of his approach, the Assassin almost stepped backwards. Instead he set his feet shoulder width apart, perfectly balanced and giving no clue as to what he would do next, and waited. In his peripheral vision he saw the bodyguard closing with his target. It looked like McGinn was smiling as he did.

Miller raised his fists as he advanced and began to move with his left foot in front of his right. He was around the same height as the Assassin but broader. He closed within striking distance, and still the Assassin didn't move. He merely met Miller's eyes, and saw in turn that they continued to burn.

Miller's first strike was a conservative jab with his left hand. It was somewhat telegraphed and not particularly fast, and the Assassin dodged it easily. Miller threw a right hand jab which was equally simple to avoid. He continued to inch forward as he feinted several more times and kept the Assassin at the same range as he backed him up along the balcony.

With surprise, the Assassin realised that Bohm had been right. He had underestimated Miller. Not only the extent of his doggedness and determination, which were factors he'd been foolish not to assume from his military record, but his talent for violence too. The Assassin automatically noted a series of factors, from Miller's balance, to his patience, to his calm intelligence, with the latter being the most dangerous of all.

The Assassin knew the plan which Miller had instinctively formulated. Miller would keep him at arm's length, continue to throw punches without pause, and force him along the balcony. Then he would have him against the wall, which even now was only a couple of metres away, and that would be a very difficult position to fight out of.

The Assassin smiled.

It wasn't a deliberate ploy. It happened naturally. But it was enough to make Miller pause in surprise, confusion, or quite possibly disgust.

The Assassin smiled because he felt that he might finally have encountered somebody worth his effort. Not an equal, perhaps, but at the very least a challenge. Somebody who was not incompetent. Someone with whom he shared commonalities. Someone he didn't need to hate.

Still smiling, and feeling a flickering of excitement for the first time he could remember, the Assassin stopped his retreat, raised his own hands, sunk into a crouch, and joined the fight.

Miller didn't slow his advance at the change in stance, wanting to keep pressing his advantage. The Assassin waited for the next jab to come and flicked it aside with his right hand then punched straight out with his left. Miller didn't seem to have anticipated the move, but his instincts were clearly formidable and his reflexes took hold. He moved his head to the side just in time to let the blow pass by and instantly countered with a punch of his own.

The smile stayed on the Assassin's face as the sparring continued. He wasn't throwing everything into the fight, and neither was Miller. Each was sizing up the other. Either would accept a lucky hit, of course, but neither expected it. Instead they probed and feinted, their punches controlled and both of their positions held.

The Assassin realised he was truly enjoying himself. The rest of the world had faded. There was only the dance with Miller. He had forgotten all context and circumstance and was lost in the fight.

The inconvenient truth of the situation and why they were all there to start with came crashing back with a sudden, desperate yell from further along the balcony.

The Assassin took a couple of steps back with his hands held protectively in front of him and chanced to glance past Miller. McGinn had already dealt with the buffoon. He was half a foot shorter and the bodyguard would surely have beaten up any regular thug on the street. A special forces operative with over a decade of life or death combat experience was another matter entirely.

The bodyguard's face was bloodied and filled with panic. The panic was understandable, since he was currently halfway over the edge of the balcony, shrieking with his eyes wide as he took in the sheer drop down to the street. McGinn must have pushed or tripped or swung him in that direction but had now grabbed the back of the man's trousers to stop him falling. The Assassin observed all this within a split second and looked back just in time to block a blow aimed squarely at his head.

Miller, recognising that the voice wasn't McGinn's, had not turned at the shout. Instead he had quickly closed the small gap the Assassin had created and seemed determined not to lose his momentum again. The smile dropped abruptly from the Assassin's face as he inwardly cursed himself for allowing his attention to slip.

Miller let forth a series of punches which were no longer light, testing jabs but heavy blows which forced the Assassin to retreat, their relentlessness giving him no chance to counter attack this time. He backed up, attempting to cover himself as Miller alternated his aim between head and torso, and felt another sensation shoot through him which he hadn't experienced for a very long time. It was the thrill of danger; the threat of defeat. His heel struck the wall at the end of the balcony.

Both of them stopped this time at the sound of another shout.

"Get down!"

The Assassin looked towards the doorway just in time to see Bohm emerging. He held a pistol loosely in front of him, and the driver who had been guarding the lift followed close behind.

But before anybody else could react, before either the Assassin or Miller could drop to the ground, McGinn was upon Bohm.

The first bodyguard had been saved from falling but now lay unconscious on the ground. With Bohm's attention clearly focused on Miller and the Assassin, McGinn had waited then sprung forward as the pair burst out. His timing was immaculate, reaching Bohm the moment he came out onto the balcony to chop down with force on his wrists just as he was raising the pistol. Bohm yelled again, with pain this time, and the gun fell.

The driver, also combat-trained, was less hesitant than the first bodyguard. He quickly recovered from the surprise of the attack and kicked out hard before McGinn could turn to face him. His heavy boot caught McGinn in the side and the Scot folded in that direction with a grunt. Bohm was turning back towards him now too, face pink and swearing to himself as he looked to get in on the action.

The Assassin and Miller looked at each other. Then Miller whipped around, before the Assassin could react, and shot back along the balcony towards his reeling colleague.

McGinn's face was set in a grimace of pain but he had straightened up again impressively quickly. The driver still stood in front of the open doorway, watching McGinn and poised to strike again. The Scot took one look at him, put his head down, and charged. The driver was caught completely off-guard and backed away a couple of steps, putting his hands up protectively.

The bodyguard lashed out at McGinn just before he made contact, but despite its power the punch didn't deter the Scot. McGinn let out a shout as he bowled straight into the bigger man, wrapping him up and driving him back through the doorway into the apartment then down onto the laminated wooden floor.

Bohm picked up the pistol and followed them inside, then stooped down and used the weapon to beat at McGinn's neck, his shoulders, his head, the blows all wild and largely ineffectual but enough to trouble McGinn as he tried concurrently to cover his back and subdue the driver on the ground. Miller arrived a moment later and didn't pause as he reached down and grabbed the collar of Bohm's shirt in both hands then hauled him off to the side, the gun falling and skidding across the floor towards the door to the main corridor.

The Assassin had walked along the balcony and stood now in the doorway. He contemplated the scene, the four men scrabbling and grappling on the floor of the shining, modernist, minimalist living room, and felt the adrenaline and excitement desert him.

The thrill of his fight with Miller disappeared as quickly as it had come. Although the four men before him all fought for their lives, there was no more artistry to it than a schoolyard scrap. He sighed inwardly as he came forward to join the fray, the smile on his face now replaced with an expression bordering on apathy.

The Assassin went for Miller, since he remained more or less atop of the pile. He saw Miller glance sharply to the side just as he was stooping to haul him off. Too late, he realised Miller had been watching the reflection of the scene in the tall windows, and waiting for him. The man's elbow crashed into his face before he could react, and sent him reeling.

The Assassin's vision dimmed as pain flooded through him, and he immediately felt his nose filling with blood. He heard shouting. When his vision cleared he saw Bohm sprawled near the doorway to the balcony, his face also bloodied. Miller was choking out the bodyguard on the ground while McGinn went to retrieve the gun from near the door.

The Assassin didn't pause, nor did the shooting pain stop him as he came forward. He reached for Miller just as he was about to drop the unconscious bodyguard to the floor and took him immediately into a hold of his own. Miller was strong, and a ferocious fighter, as the Assassin had learned to his detriment. But even he was unable to shake free, however hard he fought.

With difficulty, the Assassin wrenched Miller around to face McGinn. The Scot advanced slowly with the gun raised. The Assassin began turning and backing away in a wide circle, using Miller to shield himself.

"Shoot... Bohm... you... idiot," Miller spluttered, struggling against the wrist across his throat.

McGinn seemed to have forgotten his mission entirely. He paused, nodded, and turned the gun towards Bohm who stood bloodied and helpless in the doorway.

"Shoot him, and I'll break Miller's neck," the Assassin said, calmly. "It would be very easy from this position."

"Don't... listen to him... Shoot... Bohm." Miller's face was growing red now and his voice was weak and rasping. "What matters... Why we... came..."

The four of them stood there, frozen. The Assassin, Miller, and Bohm all looked to McGinn. McGinn remained completely still, the gun still half raised towards Bohm but his eyes turned to his friend.

A sudden, metallic crashing sound broke the spell.

It came from the far end of the main hallway but was still clearly audible. McGinn's eyes flickered upwards to meet the Assassin's. The noise came again, louder, and this time was followed by shouts and the sounds of footsteps as the cage in front of the private lift was broken down.

The pause in the living room ended abruptly. McGinn lowered the gun towards the Assassin's feet. It would be an easy way to incapacitate him, and displayed admirably quick thinking on McGinn's part.

The Assassin reacted just as quickly, however, releasing his grip on Miller and shoving him forwards, hard. Miller went stumbling towards McGinn and blocked his friend's shot. Then, seeing that he had no other choice since Miller was his only protection, the Assassin followed after him.

He rammed Miller forwards, straight towards McGinn who had been standing only a couple of metres away. Glancing over Miller's shoulder, the Assassin saw that McGinn had remained cooler than he'd anticipated. Rather than going to catch Miller, or stumbling backwards, he stepped neatly to his left and fired.

The Assassin dodged to his own left just as he saw the trigger being squeezed. He felt an impact to the right side of his skull followed immediately by a streak of pain. He stumbled sideways, in surprise as much as anything, and raised a hand towards his head. It was a pointless gesture, and McGinn could have followed up and killed him there and then.

When the Assassin looked up, however, hand still pressed to his head, he saw McGinn running for the doorway onto the balcony. Bohm had already fled in that direction, and the Assassin's first thought was that the man was a fool.

Then he realised he'd had no other option, since McGinn would have easily had enough time to shoot Bohm if he'd tried to cross the expansive living room. The balcony was Bohm's one hope of buying the few seconds he needed for the reinforcements to arrive, which they were now doing in force.

Still dazed, the Assassin heard the footsteps pounding down the corridor then into the room, but didn't register them. He saw the men and women beginning to charge past in his peripheral vision, but his eyes were still focused forwards.

Through the windows and the reflections of the illuminated room he saw Bohm rounding the balcony at the corner of the building and beginning to run along the far side. He would be trapped at the end, but his saviours would arrive in a few short moments.

Miller and McGinn pursued Bohm, Miller a couple of steps ahead and shouting something which McGinn acknowledged. They turned the corner and McGinn, to the Assassin's surprise, threw the pistol onto the roof before leaping and grabbing onto the lip above. The Assassin saw him beginning to clamber upwards, then looked down and to the right again.

Bohm had reached the wall at the end of the balcony, and was turning to fight. The first reinforcements were already passing through the doorway, semi-automatic rifles raised in front of them.

Miller sprinted straight at Bohm, who took a wild swing at him. Miller finally slowed to duck underneath the blow before grabbing Bohm's head in both of his hands. Then he brought it forcefully around to the side before bringing it swinging back again and smashing into the concrete wall behind.

Bohm instantly sagged, but Miller didn't pause. He wrenched Bohm into the waist-high wall of the balcony itself, and stooped to haul him up and onto it. Bohm seemed only semi-conscious, but still screamed something. Then Miller tipped him over the edge.

The Assassin caught a fleeting glance of mortal terror on

Bohm's face before he disappeared from sight. But Miller was already turning back towards the apartment and looking up to where McGinn, only his arms visible to the Assassin, reached down for him from the roof.

Miller jumped and grabbed onto McGinn's wrists, planting his feet with a thud against the windows then pushing himself up and off them, McGinn pulling him up too... and then suddenly, just like that, he was gone.

The Assassin watched the first of Bohm's operatives rounding the corner, her weapon raised towards the roof, but she didn't fire. There didn't seem to be anything to aim at.

She moved along the walkway to study the red patch on the wall, then peered over the edge of the balcony. Her face, when she turned back to look at the next colleague to arrive, was a picture of shock. A third person arrived and shouted at the other two, pointing towards the roof.

The Assassin watched the scene play out, not caring about the blood dampening his hand, the throbbing along the side of his skull where the bullet had grazed him, the pounding headache from Miller's elbow, nor about the pursuit which would inevitably end in failure.

Failure. The word reverberated in his mind. Fury began to build.

Slowly he crossed to the door then moved along the balcony, ignoring the operatives who grew quiet when they recognised him. He stopped where Bohm had disappeared and looked over the edge for himself. From that height the body was merely a strange, broken thing with a pool of red already formed around it. Several people had gathered nearby. One was on the phone, presumably to the police. Another, also on her phone, was filming everything.

Failure. For the first time.

The Assassin's fists opened and closed reflexively. He felt his lips twitching. The operative nearest him stepped away and turned to his colleagues as the twitching became a snarl which spread across the Assassin's bloody face.

Then he calmed himself. Only fools gave themselves over to emotion. It was a tendency he had preyed on time and again.

He closed his eyes, took a deep breath, shut the whole world out, and began to analyse. He started at the end, at what had happened most recently, and worked backwards, concentrating on each and every detail. He didn't notice the operatives leaving him.

His eyes snapped open when the image came to him of Bohm, looking down at his phone several times for a message which never arrived.

He turned, hoping that the phone had been dropped during the fight, and saw one of the operatives passing it to the other. He fought down the other emotions too, of relief and excitement, as he walked slowly back along the balcony towards the living room.

The phone would tell him everything he needed to know. And he was sure that what he needed to know began with Lord Frost, who had gone silent so very suddenly, and ended - somehow - with Harry Miller.

End of Part Two

PART THREE

CHAPTER TWENTY EIGHT

Rupert Granville twisted the ring on his finger. The skin beneath was depressed, and whiter than that to either side.

"Trouble in paradise?"

The noise of the bar suddenly returned. Not that it was a noisy bar, by any means. The sounds which Rupert had inadvertently tuned out were those of lowered voices, the specifics of the words further obscured by soft lounge music.

"I'd always assumed a correlation between age and personal stability. A nice, straight, forty-five degree arrow. Alas, I've since discovered it's not so straightforward."

"I didn't even know you were married."

"We never went the whole way," Rupert said, and looked up. Ms Archer sat on the stool opposite, one leg crossed over the other and a glass of red beside the open notebook on the high table between them. "Merely a civil partnership, and we sealed that particular deal long ago, when there was no other option."

"Still not ready to take the leap? And at your age, too?"

"I'll attempt not to take offence at that. And no, we never saw the need."

"You kept all of this bloody quiet."

Rupert shrugged as he gave the ring a final twist. "Sorry to disappoint you, but it's nothing calculated. I'm sure the British public couldn't give the slightest damn about my sexuality;

nor the political establishment, in truth, for all their perceived fuddy-duddiness. I only wanted to keep my private life just that - private."

"How very pure of you." Archer raised her glass by its stem and took a slow sip. "Although that desire for privacy clearly doesn't apply to all aspects of your life."

"Whatever do you mean?"

"Oh, please." Archer motioned to the room at large. The lighting was kept low, even over the bar near which they sat. Booths ran along the walls with dim lamps hanging high above. Almost all of the clientele wore formal clothing. "You think I've never been here before?"

"And who'd have brought you?"

"Have I pricked your delicate ego?"

"A politician's ego isn't so easily damaged. The decades of public insults and private humiliations give us a tough hide, whether we like it or not." Rupert lifted his own wine glass, and took a much longer drink than Archer had. "Besides, your coyness is unnecessary. I can guess for myself. Have you seen Lord Frost recently?"

"Depends what you mean by recently."

"Quite," Rupert said. He took a smaller sip, then set his glass down deliberately. "I'll play the first hand, I suppose, rather than drawing this little dance out."

"Care to unmix that metaphor?"

"I'm afraid this is serious, Ms Archer." Rupert lowered his voice, and glanced around. "I've attempted to contact Lord Frost several times in the past day or so. Normally he responds quickly, as you know. Impressively so, for such a busy fellow. And now, suddenly, he's gone silent."

Archer met his gaze, her face unmoving. "Oh?" she said.

Rupert didn't attempt to mask his annoyance. "I'm proposing that we both lay our cards on the table here-"

"Back to the poker analogy, I see."

"Now really, Ms Archer-"

"I'm only teasing. You know, I seem to remember you being a lot more... friendly, the last time we spoke. Has anything happened since then?"

"The pressures of ministerial responsibility."

"I'm sure. If you must know, I haven't been in touch with Lord Frost the past couple of days, no."

"Is that unusual?"

"In the spirit of laying our cards on the table, yes. He checks in more or less every day, to see what's crossed my radar."

"Di-" Rupert very nearly said 'Did', and caught himself just in time. "Do you tell him about me?"

"You've come up. But I'm no lapdog, you know. Not his rent-a-journo. If I believe another party to be offering a better deal, I'm inclined to take it." Archer made another circular motion with her glass. "That's a roundabout way of answering your next question, as to *what* I told him about you."

"How efficient of you."

"Unfortunately, I won't be answering. You think Frost's sudden reticence has something to do with Tinkov?"

Rupert paused, looking down at the table. "Why would you ask me that?"

"The last time we spoke was after Tinkov's demise. When you gave me the scoop on the Barcelona story."

"A report from which your name was conspicuously absent."

"Journalists working against this 'Company' haven't had a good time of it, from what little I've learnt. Regardless, I'm staying patient."

"For?"

"You promised me more. You promised me something that would really blow my socks off."

"And I very much hope you'll receive it sooner rather than later."

"Hope, Minister?"

"For both our sakes. If you don't, it'll be my pretty head on the chopping block, not yours, trust me."

"Well, consider me quivering with anticipation."

Rupert took another drink. He controlled his gaze carefully as he did so, only glancing between the glass, the table, and Archer.

"You're making a run at it, aren't you?"

"I haven't made a 'run' of any type in decades."

"Hilarious." Archer leaned forward on her stool. "Come on, tell me. Minister, MP, 'rising star', and all of it coming so very quickly. You're going for the top job."

"Whatever gives you that idea?"

"Oh, I don't know. Coming out of absolutely nowhere - to the public, I mean - to suddenly be leading a governmental department? Schmoozing your way around every toff-laden society do, masquerading as a charitable fundraiser, in London? The change in the way Frost has spoken about you behind the scenes, in recent weeks. As if you were a true contender."

"Indeed?"

"Thought you might like that. And yes, he truly has been, before you check."

"I commend your efficiency once more. I'm starting to think I needn't be present for this conversation."

"And then," she continued, ignoring him. "To top it all off, yours truly is invited to the best-known bar in town for politicians wanting to supposedly let off steam, but - in truth - arranging between themselves how the country will be run. And not hidden in some booth either, mind you. No, this meeting with a... *relatively* well known journalist, if I might, takes place front and centre, near the bar, at the highest table around."

"Now that you mention it, I suppose we are a little exposed."

"Not that you'd noticed."

Rupert looked up at Archer, his face suddenly serious. "Very well. I'll be straight with you."

"I've heard some version of that before. Around thirty seconds ago, I believe."

"I assure you it's the truth this time. As you've keenly perceived, I am indeed looking to ascend in this little Westminster bubble we call home."

"How far?"

"I'm certainly not going for the 'top job', as you say. And that is indeed the truth. I haven't suddenly sprouted unbridled ambition overnight. That said, I'll admit that I've enjoyed this small taste of... heightened responsibility."

"Oh, *heightened responsibility*. Let me leap for my quill and jot that gem down."

"May I continue?"

"Please. We were finally getting somewhere."

"My time at the Department for Culture, Media and Sport - Digital too, of course - has been most stimulating. Not to mention rewarding, now that I can finally affect some genuine change in our country."

"But you're not satisfied."

"I believe I can go higher. Not through any delusions of grandeur or genius, mind you. Simply because I think I can do the job, and I enjoy it, and I believe I'd thrive at a higher level." The serious expression returned to his face, and he lowered his voice. "But I have *no* intention of challenging for the leadership. Not now, not in the next few years at the very least, and perhaps not ever."

"You're sure?"

"Quite. I like and respect the Prime Minister. In fact, I believe I could *better* aid John were I given a more influential position. He's encountering some turbulence at the moment, and I'd welcome the chance to smooth the ride."

Archer turned her glass by its stem. Her eyes were fixed on his. He met her gaze steadily. "You *sound* convincing, Granville. But politicians usually do."

"It's because I'm telling the truth, Ms Archer. Which politicians usually aren't."

"No arguments here."

"Not to mention, there's the good of the country at stake."

"Oh, come on. What a mistake, to give even the slightest hint I was taking you seriously."

"I'm serious. A weak- I should say, a *troubled* leadership is bad news for the nation. I did get into this business for the right reasons, whatever might have followed. If I can lend a hand during this crisis, and help John to weather the storm, then-"

"Then *all* is forgiven," Archer said. "I'm not the oldest journo working in this little 'bubble', but I'm just as cynical as the rest, I assure you. As soon as somebody starts discussing the greater good-"

"Very well," Rupert said, holding up a hand. "Dismiss any

notion that I might care about my country."

"Gladly."

"But notwithstanding what you think of my motives, I'm determined to make a success of all this. It's no flattery, merely good advice, to suggest you should come along for the ride."

"Which involves?"

"Sticking by me. Keeping me informed. And, when the time comes, putting the good word out there."

"Which will be *your* good word, naturally. No, don't leap to justify yourself. I'm pleased you're finally being direct. Let's try and keep it rolling, shall we? What might be the nature of this 'good word'?"

"The story of a lifetime, my dear."

Archer had been lifting her glass to her mouth. It paused there as she went to scoff, then she frowned at the expression on Rupert's face. "Really?"

"Oh, quite literally. You'll never see a story like this again, I promise you. It'll be the biggest scandal either our banking industry or government has ever seen."

The glass was still hovering. A light shone in Archer's eyes. "Quite the claim. Both institutions have seen a scandal or two, over the years."

"It's not a claim, Ms Archer, it's a promise. This will catapult you to the highest level of your profession, from one day to the next."

"And where might it catapult you?"

"I won't reveal how or why I'm involved in what's going on. That's my only condition. I can only make you another promise - that the story will have no benefit at all to me. In fact, if anyone dug deep enough, they could find my links to some of the... offending parties."

"So why-"

"For the greater good," Rupert said, immediately. "You can scoff at that and call it preposterous until you're blue in the face, but it's the God's-honest truth. What's going on will punish a lot of very bad men and women. It could spare untold misery; save lives for generations to come."

"And here I was, thinking this would be a run of the mill leak."

"There's nothing run of the mill about this, Ms Archer."

"Oh, I believe you. Congratulations for that, if nothing else." Archer finished the last of her wine and set her glass down slowly on the table. "Fine. I'm in."

"Wonderful. I'll have the contract drawn up first thing in the morning." Rupert finished his own wine, and gave a small shrug. "That was a joke."

"I'm hooting on the inside."

"Shall we?"

Archer put the small notebook which had remained untouched into her backpack, and Rupert followed her out. As they passed along parallel to the bar his eyes finally swept across the room. He made eye contact with a number of people who watched the two of them leave, and nodded to a couple of the more important figures.

Archer folded her arms and grimaced as they stepped out into the night. Rupert's driver was already approaching. "May I offer you a way out of this cold, and a ride home concurrently?" Rupert asked, motioning to the sleek, black car. "As established inside, you can rest assured I won't 'try anything'."

"You'd be pepper sprayed in a split second if you did. But no, anyway. I have a date waiting on me." She laughed at the expression which crossed Rupert's face. "A romantic date, not another player in this great, silly game. You politicians really are the most ridiculous people."

"I won't argue with you there." Rupert took a hand from his pocket and held it out. "Very well. If there's nothing else..."

Archer studied his hand for a long moment. Then she shook it, and turned her eyes up towards him. "You look tired, Granville."

"It's nighttime."

"You know what I mean."

"I haven't slept a wink, the past couple of nights." The words were barely out of Rupert's mouth before he regretted them. Inwardly he cursed at his laxity. It was true that he hadn't slept since the incident with Frost, but that was no excuse. "I mean... you know..." he stammered quickly. "The personal issues, you understand."

"Obviously."

"Indeed. I sincerely hope that your private life progresses more smoothly than mine."

"That wouldn't be hard." Archer rolled her eyes at his expression. "What? We can't both make rubbish jokes? Right, you get in your fancy car and toddle off to your mansion. I'll find a cab like a regular pleb."

"I'll be in touch, Ms Archer. Very soon."

"I'm already on tenterhooks."

Rupert checked his phone in the car. He sighed, seeing nothing but the usual barrage of bureaucratic nonsense from his underlings at the ministry, and tossed it onto the seat beside him. "Haven't heard from George, have you, Charlie?" he asked. "He hasn't been putting any more questions to you about my comings and goings? I'm embarrassed to ask, you know, but..."

"Afraid not, sir. Haven't seen him for a few days now."

"No, he took a suitcase and... Well, you know." Rupert ran a hand slowly down his face. "Back to Bloomsbury, if you would."

"Very good, sir."

They pulled away, Rupert's gaze already glazing over as they passed through Westminster. He sighed and closed his eyes. He didn't hope for sleep, which he knew wouldn't come. He was merely unable to bear the sight of the place for a moment longer.

CHAPTER TWENTY NINE

Noy reflected that, for over two decades of her life, she had never really been cold. There had been no winter in Myanmar, nor in Chiang Rai. In the cool seasons there might be a chill in the air at night. Even that hadn't been present in Thailand's south.

True cold had been a recent discovery, made upon her arrival in England. It had been a shock at first, like most things in this strange, neat, quiet, grey country. Since the video - since her past had come rushing back only to crumble instantly before her - she had grown to embrace it. Only the cold made her feel anything.

Noy stood now on the patio outside the living room, hugging one of Granville's cardigans tight around her. Her eyes were closed to the stark, wintry landscape of the Chilterns a name she had given up trying to pronounce. She focused entirely on the feel of the cold against her skin, which was all that could make her feel alive, and tried to think of nothing else at all.

She frowned as she heard the door, and opened her eyes reluctantly to the long sloping lawn and the morning mist over the gentle, green hill beyond. It might have been Anna or Sarah who had come out to check on her, but she knew it wasn't. She knew it was him. They would have said something, for one thing, instead of standing there cluelessly right behind her.

Noy felt the ghost of a smile approaching her face, and reached back. She found his hand and brought it around to rest on her stomach. As he pulled her close, she put her earlier foolish thought aside. It was not only the cold which made her feel. It was the warmth too, which despite the best efforts of the others at the house only truly came from one place. From the most unexpected place imaginable, she reflected, as she leant her head back against his chest.

"What's funny?" he asked in Thai.

"You, Farang."

"I've been called a lot of things. Never that."

"Not in a good way. Not in a deliberate way."

He grunted, then let the silence stretch.

"But I love you anyway."

He grunted again, and she dug into his ribs with her elbow. "Idiot. You're not funny when you're trying."

Her blow hadn't shifted him an inch. His chest was still against her back and now she felt it moving with silent laughter.

"When's Big Boss's next meeting?"

"Don't call him that."

"That's what he is, Farang."

"And who else was going to be?"

"You? You did it for years in Thailand."

"That was very different. And I hated it by the end. Harry isn't like that. He's always been-"

"A natural leader. I know, Farang." There was another pause. "We spend too much time together."

"Why?"

"Because I can even tell the differences in your silences now. This is your annoyed silence."

"I'm not annoyed. It's just a fact. Harry's one way. I'm another."

"Fine. Be like that."

She felt him move fractionally away. "You're angry."

"No," she said, too quickly. "Yes. But I don't know why."

"Don't you?" She shrugged, arms wrapped around herself again. The Farang turned her, his touch heavy but unintentionally so. "Tell me."

She frowned and made a huffing noise. "It's incredibly frustrating, Farang. He was right there. I still don't believe it."

He nodded. He said nothing else, but his eyes were fixed on hers instead of on the ground where they normally fell.

"I know what happens in movies and on TV. You get your revenge, and it solves nothing. It doesn't make you feel better. It doesn't... Ah, how do they say it in films..." She cast around for the words, then pronounced them in an absurd American accent. *"Bring them back."* She hit him gently in the chest. "Don't laugh."

"I'm not." He took her hands in his. "I'm not," he said again. "I understand. Of course I do. We'll get him, and I'll make him suffer. I promise."

Something in her flinched at the tone in his voice; the look in his eye. She looked down at his hands which were now squeezing hers. Her thumbs looked like a child's as she ran them over the burns. The old confusing mixture of feelings churned in her stomach. As always, she pushed them away.

Squeezing his hands back, she looked almost vertically up at him to meet his eyes, saw the emotion in them which she would never fully hear, and nodded.

They both looked around at the sound of a pointed cough. The Farang had left the living room door ajar and now Anna's head was poking through it.

"Disgusting way to carry on," she said. "Anyway, Big Boss is about to start his latest presentation."

"See?" Noy said to the Farang, switching to English. "Not only me who call him that."

"I did get it from you, though."

Noy held a finger to her lips and shook her head at Anna, who shrugged and opened the door wide for them.

Noy followed her inside, the heat of the living room sweeping over her. She had grown to see some benefits to the cold, but the warmth was still where she belonged, and she gladly shook off the oversized cardigan and rubbed her cheeks as they crossed towards the seating area.

Sarah was already on one of the sofas, knitting. Noy sat beside her and Sarah caught her looking at the small, half-formed jumper in her hands. "You don't need to say it, Noy. It's not my best work, I'll freely admit."

"No..." Noy said. "It's not bad."

"I only hope Natasha thinks so, assuming I ever get to meet her."

"Oh, she won't appreciate it," Anna said, sitting down on Sarah's other side. "Lord knows she doesn't appreciate all the work I've put in for her."

"Well I'm taking the wildest of guesses, my dear, that you haven't specified what that's entailed."

"Oh, to her I'm a travelling businesswoman. There's no doubt in my mind she'd think I was a thousand times cooler if she knew the truth. Alas, it might have some slight effect on her morality, and at a formative age too."

The Farang sat on another sofa, taking up nearly two places at once. His hands were clasped in front of him and he stared mostly at the ground, glancing up occasionally towards Harry who stood near the doorway with Granville. Two large blotches of deep purple were visible on Harry's face, even from where Noy sat, as were the red marks on his knuckles.

Even easier to see were the bags under Granville's eyes. Harry was attempting to talk to him, but Granville seemed uncharacteristically quiet.

Noy hadn't noticed the change in the man's behaviour until their return from New York. Her head had cleared somewhat since then, even if the numbness she had felt after the video had only been replaced with frustration. She'd asked Anna, who told her that Granville and the tall farang with the funny accent and the long name were having a 'domestic'. Noy had nodded, not caring enough to ask what that meant.

"Look at him," Anna muttered. "Checking the door, like a little boy waiting for his daddy to come home."

"Hmm?"

"My beloved. You hadn't noticed that a certain Scot had gone missing again?" Anna raised her voice. "I thought you were going to address this issue directly, Captain."

Harry glanced back, his annoyance plain. "He asked permission, not that he needed to," he called back. "I thought, since he just put his life on the line for all this, that I'd agree to 'let' him pop to London."

"And it doesn't trouble you, that this romantic rendezvous seems more important to him than our mission?"

"It's not some fling," Harry said, his voice growing louder still. "They're engaged, it turns out."

Anna waved her hand dismissively. "The liaison couldn't have waited regardless?"

"I didn't ask. It doesn't *have* to wait."

"Well *we're* all bloody well waiting. I thought speed was of the essence here?"

Harry opened his mouth to retort, then stopped when Granville put a hand on his arm. He stopped, and nodded. "Fine," he said. "You're right."

"Anna always right. Could save yourself a lot of time if you learn that."

"Thank you, Noy," Anna said, nodding sagely to her.

"Leave him be, the poor boy," Sarah said, her needles clicking again.

Harry let out a long sigh and suppressed either a grin or grimace. "Thank you, Mother," he said, and turned back to Anna. "You do happen to be right, on this occasion. I'll fill McGinn in when he gets here."

Anna gave him a mock salute and sat up deliberately straight on the sofa, her expression deadly serious. Harry rolled his eyes, then looked around the room and clapped his hands together.

"Well," Harry said, his voice louder and seemingly filled with an enthusiasm which, to Noy at least, seemed painfully forced. "Firstly, I want to say how pleased I am. With *all* of you… Except you, Mum."

"I'd assumed I wasn't included."

"Obviously it wasn't easy out there, but everybody played their part, and we got the job done. I-"

He stopped as Noy snorted.

"Yes?"

Noy glared back at him, a frown on her face. "Tell me what 'job' got done, Big Boss."

"Bohm, splattered on the New York sidewalk. That's two thirds of the Trio down. Half of all our objectives completed. I'd call that a good job."

"And what about *my* objectives?"

"We all-"

"Yes, yes, we all agreed. All want these three dead," Noy said, waving a dismissive hand then folding her arms again.

"Well... we did. These people have caused incredible amounts of suffering."

"You don't need to... How do you say?" She turned to Daniel and asked him in Thai.

"Lecture."

"Don't need to lecture me, Big Boss," she said. "Who is the only person here to be part of all this 'suffering'? Me. Years I lost, because of them." In the corner of her eye Noy noticed Daniel shifting, but ignored him.

"This has gotten off to a good start," Harry muttered towards the ground, then looked back up at her. There was a forced formality to his voice when he spoke. "You're not the only one to have suffered at their hands, Noy. They took Anna's family, and stole a *lot* of money from her. They kidnapped me too. They killed our father, in case you'd forgotten."

"And you get your revenge!" Noy shouted, sitting forward now. "You go crazy. Go all around London. Kill every one of these people you can find."

"I... I..." Harry stammered. He glanced quickly at his mother. Noy noticed that Sarah had grown very pale all of a sudden, but it didn't register with her.

"Don't argue. Anna told me. You get the person who kill your father. Straight away, right? Then you carry on killing, killing, killing."

"It was... I was trying to take down the whole London operation."

Noy snorted again. "Okay. Well, I want to take down whole Company, just like you. Difference is, you get your revenge. I want mine, but this doesn't matter to you."

"Don't be bloody ridiculous. We're a team. Of course it does."

Harry's voice was raised now too, but Noy spoke louder still. "We're a team, but some people's 'objectives' more important than others, right? You were in the room with him, no? You and the Scottish guy. What, you didn't have one more second to kill him too?"

"He wasn't the bloody priority!"

"He has *my* pri-"

"That's enough."

Anna's hand had been on Noy's arm for several seconds, but this hadn't registered either. It was Granville of all people, in the end, who cut through the shouting. Noy's mouth snapped closed at the tone in Granville's voice.

"It's perfectly understandable that emotions are running a little high," Granville said, hands in his pockets but exuding command as he looked between Harry and Noy. "Needless to say, however, this sort of bickering gets us nowhere. We *are* all on the same team. We *are* all pushing towards the same goals. The foul beast who injured you *will* get his comeuppance, Noy - each of us can assure you of that. In the meantime, we must maintain our composure and our unity. This group has already shown the extent to which it can thrive. Before us lay the two most difficult tasks of all, and exacting your vengeance against this Assassin, Noy, will hardly be straightforward. We must master our emotions for now, all of us, and address them as and when the time is right." He looked between the two of them once more. "Are we in agreement?"

"I'm not the one who started it."

"Oh, that's *very* mature of you, Harry."

"Okay. Yes, fine" Harry said, with a shrug. "Fine by me."

"Et tu, Noy?"

Noy hadn't known this posh, rich farang for long. But the change in him within that short span was remarkable. When they'd first met, in London, he had been affable, subservient, stammering. None of those descriptions could apply now, and Noy wondered if she could really be the only one to have noted the change.

"Fine," she said at last.

"Wonderful. Now, Harry. Why don't you get us back on track?"

Harry briefly glanced over at Noy. She stuck her tongue out at him, and he smiled despite himself before nodding and taking a deep breath.

"*Apart* from killing the Assassin, we have two main objectives remaining. Achieving both should cripple the Company irrevocably. Firstly, there's the final remaining member of the Trio. Did you get hold of any more information, Rupert?"

Granville had sat down on an armchair beside Noy's sofa. He shook his head, and Harry grimaced and nodded. "Hopefully, McGinn can dig up more nuggets on Tinkov's phone. For now, all we know is that she's based in Hong Kong…" Harry said. "Probably," he added.

"Well, I'm certainly reassured," Anna said. "What other information could we really need?"

"Our second objective is to hit the data centre, gather what we can there, and use that for our leak to the press."

"Which I'm pleased to say has been prepared," Granville said.

"Excellent. Unfortunately - and no sarcasm is necessary here - we're not exactly blessed with details on the data centre's location either."

"That's a polite way to put it."

"What did I just say about sarcasm?"

Anna made a zipping motion across her lips and threw the key over her shoulder.

"It may have been prudent, after all, to let the woman live," Granville murmured. "Smith, I mean, from the bank."

Noy felt Sarah stirring on the next seat. "Her too?" she whispered, in a tone that made Noy's stomach twist. Noy looked back to Harry, and saw him scratching the back of his neck.

"Well," he said, quietly. "About that."

"You *must* be joking," Anna said. "You didn't do it, did you?"

"I couldn't, Anna. Rupert was right. It would have been murder, plain and simple. Smith isn't a combatant. She wasn't even collateral damage, caught in some crossfire. It would have been an execution."

"And you couldn't possibly have told us this at the time? Since we're supposed to be… ah, how did you phrase it a mere two minutes ago? Oh yes, a 'team'."

"I should have."

"Too bloody right! Why didn't you?"

Harry looked down at his hands, which were now clasped in front of him. "You'll roll your eyes and call me an embarrassing idiot-"

"That doesn't sound like me."

"But a lot of leadership is about perception," he said, shrugging. "You need to project a certain image, regardless of whether it's how you really act in private or feel beneath the surface. You all had to know - I thought, at least - that I'd do whatever it took. That I felt no sympathy at all, for any of these people."

Silence greeted his words. Noy looked around the room and saw a different expression on every face. Of all of them, it was Granville's which caught her attention.

"I... I really wish you'd let us know at the time, old chap," he said softly, his face even paler than usual. "After what you said, I thought... Well... Too late now." He stood, put his hands behind his back, and walked slowly to the doors facing out onto the grounds.

"It was a mistake not to tell you, and I apologise for that," Harry said. "Berate and insult me as much as you like, when we've got time. For now, the fact is that she's still alive."

"And in which tower, pray tell, might this fairest and most innocent of maidens, apparently so deserving of your mercy, be stowed?" Anna asked.

"She's still in London." Noy wasn't the only one to turn with surprise when she heard Daniel's voice. "McGinn is guarding her. That's why he keeps leaving and coming back."

Anna turned back to Harry, eyebrow raised. Harry held up his hands preemptively. "I know I should've mentioned this too, but obviously-"

"How many secrets you have, Big Boss?" Noy asked.

"That's the last one." His eyes flickered up and to the side. "The last one that's relevant to the mission. For the record, McGinn does have a fiancée in London. He's just been... checking in on Smith too, whenever he was in town." He looked back to Anna. "Okay?"

"*Wonderful*," she said.

"Leaving aside how we actually got here," Harry said. "Smith is alive. And, hopefully, she might be able to dredge up some more details from her memory, if we ask her very… nicely. If not, maybe she can point us in the right direction, at least. Either way, we-"

"Harry."

Noy's stomach dropped horribly at the tone in Granville's voice. She and everybody else immediately turned towards him.

He was taking short steps back from the glassy doors leading out onto the patio and the long lawn beyond. His mouth hung open and he was looking back and forth between the grounds and Harry.

Noy raised herself to a kneeling position on the sofa so that she could see. Anna swore next to her as she looked out too, and she heard Sarah whisper, *"Oh my goodness."*

Three figures clad completely in black were advancing up the lawn towards the house in a line, automatic rifles raised in front of them.

CHAPTER THIRTY

"*Down!*" Harry bellowed as the first shots tore through the glass and into the living room. Noy was momentarily paralysed before Anna roughly pulled both her and Sarah off the sofa and flat onto the ground.

Noy found herself automatically looking back towards Harry. He was crouched behind the sofa furthest from the doors and glaring out. His head whipped around as they all heard a crashing sound coming from the direction of the front door too, and he swore.

"Right," he called, his voice commanding even as bullets smashed through the glass and struck the far wall of the living room. "We've got at most thirty seconds until we're in trouble. Daniel, you take the front door. Anna and I will deal with these three."

"How?!" Granville shouted, flat on his stomach in front of the sofa nearest the doors and eyes wide with fear.

"As best we can. Noy." Harry's eyes were unnaturally calm as he looked at her now. "There's a gun in my bedside table upstairs. Can you get it?"

Noy felt a new wave of fear wash over her, but nodded quickly.

"Rupert, Mum, stay low. Everybody ready?" He looked back out. The approaching trio had already covered at least a third of the lawn. "Now!"

Noy fought down the instinct for self preservation which screamed at her to remain in cover, pushed herself up, and ran for the doorway. She heard a pair of bullets whizzing past before striking the far wall and Daniel's heavy footsteps behind her, and passed Harry who was already moving forward around the far edge of the sofa with Anna crawling behind him towards the doors.

The front door rocked again as Noy ran into the entrance hall with Daniel a few steps back. Through a small window to the side of the door she saw one man lifting back a heavy ram while a woman next to him saw Noy and started raising her rifle.

Noy didn't stop, racing straight up and turning left and left again on the staircase then sprinting along the hallway for the bedroom at the end. She slammed the door into the wall as she burst inside and went to the small table on the side of the bed which had been made with military precision. She opened the drawer there, heard a metallic scraping, and pulled out the pistol. It was the first time she'd ever held a gun. She was struck briefly by its weight, and felt a thrill shoot through her.

Noy left the room, went back along the hallway, and was just starting to descend the final few stairs when the front door burst open in a shower of splinters.

Daniel had been waiting just behind it. He immediately grabbed the frame of the ruined door and slammed it back again straight into the woman who had been trying to enter. She had been looking through the gap with her rifle raised, and Daniel caught her heavily in the shoulder and sent her crashing against the doorframe. The man behind her pushed the door back again and barged his way inside, but Daniel grabbed the barrel of his rifle and yanked him stumbling straight forward then elbowed him square in the face.

Daniel glanced around and saw Noy standing there, transfixed by the violence. "Go!" he shouted, and Noy forced herself to move onwards and back into the living room.

Her breath caught in her throat as a bullet thudded straight into the doorframe as she entered, a matter of inches behind her head. She threw herself onto the floor and started crawling behind the nearest sofa.

Peering up over the headrest she saw the three black-clad operatives mere metres from the smashed glass of the doors now. Granville and Sarah were hiding wide-eyed behind the sofa on which Noy, Sarah, and Anna had been sitting only a minute before.

Harry and Anna were crouched low and waiting either side of the large doors, just out of sight of the approaching trio. Harry caught Noy's eye as she looked at him, and raised his eyebrows questioningly. She nodded, and he made a throwing motion. She hesitated, and he insistently mouthed '*Now!*'.

Noy glanced once more towards the three figures, then cocked her arm back and threw the pistol. The gun spun end over end as it arced across the room, landed a metre or so in front of Harry, and bounced a couple of inches closer. Harry waited. One of the operatives raised his boot and brought it stamping down on the nearest door, and the moment he heard the noise Harry dove for the gun.

Everything after that happened at a level of speed and violence that Noy had rarely seen, and of which she and surely any normal human would have been utterly incapable.

Even to her uninformed eye the operatives were clearly highly trained and well-coordinated. They entered in formation, the man who'd kicked down the door placed in the middle with his gun already raised and pointing forwards and the other two facing in opposing directions.

Understandably, the operative on Harry's side had not been expecting him to dive to the ground right at her feet. Harry landed, grabbed the pistol, flicked off the safety as he raised it, and just managed to fire before she could get a shot off. The sharp register of the gun in the confined space was louder than Noy had expected. She saw a momentary and almost imperceptible spray of red above the woman's head, then, just like that, she dropped limply to the ground.

Sarah must have been watching too, because she let out a strangled involuntary scream. The man who'd entered on the other side of the operatives' formation was grappling with Anna, but the one who'd kicked down the door instinctively turned towards the noise and let off a shot.

Noy whipped her head around just in time to see Sarah falling backwards. Her mouth hung open and she felt as if she should scream. Before she could, a bestial yell which made her hair stand on end ripped through the room. Noy knew logically it must have come from Harry, even before she turned back to look, and even if it sounded completely unlike him. But it was unlike any noise she'd heard.

Noy looked back. The four figures there stood frozen in time. Anna had her hands around the throat of the man she fought with while his hands were locked around her wrists. The operative who'd fired the shot remained where she was as, like the other two, she looked around at Harry.

Slowly, Harry turned his head away from his mother and towards the woman. The expression on his face made her take an involuntary step backwards, the rifle she still held momentarily forgotten.

The woman recovered herself and attempted to raise the rifle, the movement sparking Anna's fight back into life too as the man began grappling with her once more. But Noy's eyes were still on Harry. He simply knocked the barrel of the rifle to one side, but did it so forcefully that the gun fell from the woman's hands. She reacted with admirable quickness, attempting to punch Harry as she backed away, but he batted away her blows as easily as he had done the gun.

Noy looked to the other side as she heard Anna's shouted curse.

The man had broken her hold and caught her across the face in the process. He swung again at her but this time she ducked under the punch, her bloodied nose streaming. As she did, Noy saw Anna's hand shooting out and reaching for something.

The man had a knife in a sheath tied around his waist. Anna grabbed the handle, slid it free, and stabbed the man in the side, straight into the gap between the front and rear of the bulletproof vest he wore. He grunted and reached out. Before he could get her into a hold she withdrew the knife and stabbed him again. Then again. Noy was vaguely aware that her mouth was hanging open, but she was unable to close it. The ferocity with which Anna's arm jerked back and forward, back and forward, and the look of grim determination on her face as she did so made her realise suddenly that she knew nothing at all about this person; this woman she thought she had befriended.

Noy looked away as the man clutched desperately, pathetically, at Anna's shoulders even as he sank downwards and saw that Harry had the other operative flat on her back. He had a knee on her chest and both hands around her throat. The muscles in his forearms strained, the veins bulging, even as his face seemed strangely devoid of emotion but for the eyes.

"No!"

Noy looked around in surprise, along with everybody else in the room. Sarah had gotten herself into a sitting position, apparently with Granville's help. He had also taken a thin throw from the sofa nearest them, torn a strip free, and tied it around her throat. Sarah held a hand to the darkest patch.

"No, Harry." Sarah's voice was weak, her face pale. "I'm not… Don't. Not for me… Please."

Noy felt Daniel's presence behind her, then a moment later he was passing by. He limped slightly as he did so. His fists were bloodied and his shirt torn at the collar.

He came to a stop beside Sarah and Granville, towering over them. His face seemed as impassive as ever as he looked down at his mother and she looked back at him. The fear on her face was unmistakable.

Something changed in Daniel's face. He looked up and to the operative. Noy had only seen that expression once before, when he and his Thai lieutenant Decha were at the height of their mutual hatred.

Harry's hands were still loosely around the woman's throat but the fire in his eyes was gone. He watched Daniel approach, looked between his brother and mother, then pushed himself up and off the operative. The woman raised herself onto one elbow, coughing and rubbing at her reddened throat. Her eyes raised as Daniel came to a stop in front of her.

"Get up," he said.

"Daniel-" Sarah said, then she began to cough and splutter and her subsequent attempts to talk proved fruitless.

"Get up."

The operative looked around the room, making eye contact with every person in turn as if in silent appeal. Noy met the woman's panicked gaze steadily, and found that she felt nothing. It had been her choice to come to the house.

Finally, the woman stood, swaying a little. Daniel stood completely still, watching her. Then he went behind her, the woman visibly shaking as he did so. Sarah let out a weak noise of desperate protest, but nobody else said a word as Daniel reached up, grabbed the woman's head in both hands, and twisted.

He did it so quickly that Noy barely had time to close her eyes. But there was nothing she could do to block out the sound, which was followed by the noise of the body falling, then silence.

CHAPTER THIRTY ONE

The body bumped off the edge of the patio then moved more smoothly across the damp grass. His hands under the armpits, Daniel pulled the dead man backwards easily down the gentle slope.

He reached the bottom then grunted as he lifted the last body up and onto the pile, then straightened up and looked around. There wasn't another house that he could see, and the road was a fair distance away and also out of sight. Certainly nobody would see the pyre, and he was confident they wouldn't smell it either.

Daniel gave the pile a final glance and walked back up the lawn. Harry and Anna's raised voices carried easily through the ruined doors.

It was a bright morning, and it took Daniel's eyes a moment to adjust to the dim living room. Anna sat on the nearest sofa. Harry knelt before her as he dabbed a cut on her face.

"What dirt could this McGinn clown possibly have on you, that you still *refuse* to accuse him?" Anna said. "Where does it end? Does he need to walk in here and shoot you himself before you'll stop believing him? What would your parting words be? 'I *still* trust him with my life!'"

"He doesn't have it in him," Harry said, shaking his head. "I promise you. He couldn't do that to me. Not after everything."

"*Or*," Anna said. "You're so blinded by loyalty that you refuse to see what's right in front of you. But that couldn't possibly be right, could it? Because you've got this *special* bond of trust which non-military folk, us poor silly civvies, couldn't *possibly* understand."

Harry put a large dollop of alcohol on a piece of cotton wool, and Anna winced as he pushed it none too gently against the cut. "And what is really going on? Enlighten me, please."

"He's moved on!" Anna said. "He's been out of the army for years, working and living with these contractor types. His priorities have shifted, his loyalties too. He's being paid - a life-changing sum, in fairness, I'm sure - to infiltrate us poor mugs, report back, and drop us right in it."

"And why now? Why wait this long to hit us, after we've already killed two of the three people running the whole show?"

"How should I know? Maybe they thought we must have been part of a wider operation. Working with *his* old pals, perhaps" she said, waving a bandaged hand towards Daniel. "When they finally realised it was only us idiots, and they couldn't use us to get to anyone truly important, they decided to put us out of our misery before we could cause any more mischief."

Harry opened his mouth to argue, then stopped. He took a plaster, removed the white plastic, and placed it carefully on Anna's forehead.

In the presumably brief moment of silence, Daniel finally chanced a look over to his mother. She was on the furthest sofa, Noy perched on the middle cushion beside her and holding her hand. Her head was turned in his direction, and he found to his surprise that she was looking right at him.

Daniel tried to meet her gaze, but his eyes flickered off to the side. A moment later he found that she was still watching, but she didn't seem particularly aware that he was looking back. She seemed instead to be studying him as if he were something

- not even a person, perhaps, but an animal, even an object - with which she simply couldn't come to terms. Daniel forced himself to look away, his fists clenching momentarily at his sides and a lump in his throat.

"What do you think?" Harry asked, in a calmer tone of voice.

It took a moment for Daniel to realise he was the one being questioned. He cleared his throat. "Anna's right."

"No. I'm afraid she's not."

Granville stood in the doorway holding his phone. He looked like a man whose world had just collapsed around him.

"I just spoke to dear Charlie, my driver. I've had him…" Granville paused, then shrugged. "Well, what of it now? I've had him following George for the past day or so, since he was last in the Bloomsbury house. It's not that I didn't trust my partner, nor suspected him of some affair. More that I didn't have the faintest idea what he was up to. If anything, I was…" He laughed, without humour. "I was worried about him."

He took a few small steps into the room, and put a hand out to steady himself on the sofa occupied by Noy and Sarah. "The fact is that George returned to the house today. Almost exactly as we were being attacked here, it seems. Nor was he alone in his visit. Charlie took photos as best he could, suspecting George to be accompanied by his lawyer. Alas, I almost wish he had been."

Granville tapped the screen, then passed the phone to Noy. Her face fell, and she swore in Thai. "It's him."

Daniel came automatically forward and took the phone from her. There could be no mistaking the face with which they had all grown so familiar. The photo showed George Chamberlain ascending the steps of the Bloomsbury townhouse. He was followed a few steps behind by the Assassin, a bandage wrapped around his head from McGinn's gunshot wound but dressed completely in black as usual, and with a hand already on his weapon as he prepared to enter.

Daniel barely noticed Granville slumping to the ground with his back against the sofa, his mind running instead not only with questions, but also with the possibilities of vengeance.

Noy had taken one look at Daniel after Granville stopped talking, seen that their thoughts were clearly in unison, and walked over to him. Harry went to Granville, who had sunk into his usual armchair with his head in his hands, and put a hand on his shoulder.

"Maria and Tasha are both fine, thank God. No signs of trouble, but I've told them to get to a hotel anyway," Anna said, as she returned to the room with her phone in her hand. "So, please explain to me, fearless leader, how this is possible. We just got back from New York ourselves."

Harry nodded absently. "He's brilliant," he murmured, then glanced over at Noy. "Brilliant at what he does, I mean... Exceptional." He shook his head, then frowned. "Bohm's phone would have been the first thing he checked. He found a connection there, somehow." His eyes roamed upwards, and across the ceiling, before settling again on Anna. "Frost. It must have been."

"Unless your favourite posh boy here has secretly been in cahoots with Bohm all along, of course."

"You don't trust anybody, do you?"

"Only you, Captain Miller." She waved a hand. "I'm joking. Or I think I am, at least. Fine, so he finds some message from Frost on Bohm's phone. And that, somehow, led him to... well, to our posh boy."

"Why me?" Granville asked. He raised his head quickly, and there was a note in his voice that Daniel hadn't heard before.

"Why not any of us, or all?"

"They hit *your* houses simultaneously. The Assassin went to your London home, presuming that's where we'd be, and likely had another team coming around the back which your driver didn't see. He sent his B-team out here, as the nearest alternative. That team will now be completely out of contact, of course, which means that-"

"He'll come here," Noy said, standing up sharply. "Now."

"Listen to me, Noy," Harry said, holding up a hand. "I'm not doing this to spite you, I'm just telling you. There's no chance we can be here when they arrive. We have to leave. Immediately."

Noy's expression darkened very quickly indeed. Daniel put a hand on her shoulder before she could raise her voice. "He's right."

"You serious, Farang? I thought you wanted-"

"I do. But it's one thing surprising a handful of secondary operatives. It's another to fight against this man and his top team. Especially when they're prepared for us."

Harry nodded. Then he looked over to the sofa on which Sarah lay. She was still pale, but conscious. "I'm fine, dear," she said, voice barely more than a whisper.

"You're not bloody fine," he said. "But we'll have to move you anyway, as carefully as we can. We have no choice."

Noy snorted, and sank back onto the sofa with her arms folded. "Always have a choice," she muttered.

"A realistic choice," Harry retorted, his rising frustration clear.

"And to where, exactly, are we beating our tactical retreat?" Anna said.

"We... do have a safehouse."

"And thus another secret is revealed, by this unrelenting man of mystery!"

"In my defence, it's technically part of the same secret. Smith is being held there. McGinn found it for us."

"And who was kind enough to provide it for him?"

"Don't start this again. I'm telling you that I trust him, and we're not exactly flush with options."

Anna opened her mouth to argue, then shrugged. "Fine," she said. "We can have that little chat we wanted, with our fair lady Smith, while we're there."

"That's the spirit. Now let's get a bloody move on. Grab what you need, then we're gone. Anna, can you help with my mother, pretty please? Daniel, take care of those bodies in the garden before we go."

Daniel nodded as the rest of the room stirred into activity. Noy's face was thunderous as she stood and looked at him.

"We'll get him," Daniel said, taking Noy's hand and giving it a gentle squeeze. Then he let her go, took the matches Granville had found for him, and went back outside and down the slope towards the pile of bodies.

CHAPTER THIRTY TWO

The Assassin had known what to expect when they arrived. But that didn't prevent the rage building inside him, which was expressed merely as a slight tightening of his jaw and a light tapping of his finger on the armrest between himself and the driver as the SUV crunched up the driveway.

They had lost communication with the other team almost immediately. As the Assassin and his team drove closer they found the front door smashed in and a small cloud of smoke coming from behind the property.

The Assassin stepped out onto the gravel, the second car coming to a halt behind them. He glanced at the shattered wood of the front door then looked again towards the smoke. He motioned to it and the operatives from the second car jogged off that way, their weapons raised out of caution rather than expectation.

The driver had come to stand a couple of feet behind the Assassin and to his left. It was as close as any of the operatives ever got to him.

"Bring him here," the Assassin said, without turning. The woman left, then the Assassin heard two pairs of footsteps returning. "Well?"

"I- I-," George Chamberlain stammered. The Assassin's jaw tightened again. Even the way the man pronounced that single letter infuriated him. "Come now. I said they would be here.

Here or in Bloomsbury. And, you know, technically they-"

"Where are they now?"

"I haven't the faintest-"

The Assassin motioned again with his hand. He heard an impact, then Chamberlain letting out a wheeze which quickly turned into a moan of pain.

"Try harder."

"How..." Chamberlain coughed, and drew in a couple of deep breaths. "How could I possibly know? I've told you, we have a couple of other small properties too, which you're more than welcome to-"

"No. They know you've betrayed them. Miller knows we'll send teams there."

"*Betrayed* is an awfully unfair word to use, old chap. It's not like you gave me a great deal of-"

The Assassin motioned again and heard Chamberlain falling to the ground as he walked away, unable to stand the man's company for another instant.

The Assassin's lips pursed slightly as he went around to the back of the house. His fists clenched and unclenched. His eyes moved over the ruined doors to the living room, then descended to the bottom of the slope where a pile of bodies was burning. The incompetence of those men and women made him angrier than anything else. He felt the old hatred building inside of him, to dangerous levels.

The team from the second car were standing by the bodies and looking to him for instruction. They saw the expression on his face and, in unison, hurried back up the slope without looking at him again.

The Assassin stood near the smouldering pile as he waited for them to leave. Then he walked closer still. He paused beside the closest body, lifted his boot up, and brought it stamping down on the blackened remains of the dead man's head, over and over and over again, his face set in a grimace of rage but the only noise the crunching of the bone and the squelching of the matter being ground into the earth.

Once the head was ruined and in pieces the Assassin stopped and paused to consider it. Then he let out a deep breath and stepped backwards and away from the pile. He began to walk slowly back towards the house. He didn't check if anybody had been watching, not caring. It had been foolish to accept an assignment which saw him working with others, regardless of the level of payment or challenge. The mistake would not be repeated.

He took his phone from his pocket, scrolled through the list of nameless numbers, and dialled one.

"Who the hell is this?"

"Vocitus."

The Assassin waited a moment for the word to reach Hong Kong. He heard Luuk Jansen swearing to himself under his breath. "Great," Jansen said. "I was just thinking how long it'd been since you chewed me out. You know, I'm not some grunt that the Company just-"

The Assassin hung up the phone, and resisted the urge to throw it down and start stamping once more. He dialled the same number.

"I'm guessing it's you again."

"Give me a report. Nothing else."

He heard Jansen muttering to himself in Dutch, then clearing his throat. "Fine, you moody bastard. It'll be a nice, short one anyway. We're all still here in Hong Kong."

"It would be easier if she left."

"What am I, stupid? I've told her that. I'm bloody sure *you've* told her that. But she's not moving for anybody. Says she's got too much business to attend to here. And that if we can't protect her in our own headquarters, in our own city, where the hell can we protect her? I'm - how do you say - paraphrasing, a little bit, but that's the general message."

The Assassin knew there was some logic to the plan. He searched for any preventative measures with which he hadn't yet tasked Jansen, and found none. "Very well," he said. "Expect contact within the next two days."

"You lost them again?"

The Assassin left several seconds of silence.

"Hello?"

"They'll be heading for Hong Kong. I don't believe they know the location yet. Based on recent events, I assume Miller will find it."

"You and him are the only people I know who could."

The Assassin said nothing once more.

"What now?" Jansen asked. "You can't possibly have started crying again, after that. It was a compliment, you sad-"

"Something isn't right," the Assassin said, talking over the rest of Jansen's insult.

"Yeah, you don't say. We're losing men and women left and right. Two of our three bosses are dead. The whole Company's panicking because a few losers caught us off guard."

"Not only that. We don't have the whole picture. There's something more." Jansen waited this time as the Assassin paused. "Clearly they're seeking to kill the Trio. But Miller's no fool. Neither are the others, whatever you might think. They know that won't be the end of it, even if they kill all three. They know the Company could recover. There's too much money at stake."

"So... what is it? What's the plan?"

The Assassin stared into space for several long moments, then shook his head. "Stay alert. Constantly. I'll give you this number. Phone me immediately if anything happens. I'll remain here another day. If I don't find them, I'll come to Hong Kong."

The Assassin hung up without waiting for a response. He took a cursory look at the ruined doors as he stepped into the living room, where the bulk of the fighting had clearly taken place. He noted a patch of blood near a sofa further from the doors. Someone had been hit.

A couple of the operatives were standing guard near the main staircase in the entrance hall. The Assassin heard footsteps upstairs and furniture being smashed. "You're all incompetent," he said to the man and woman. "Gather everyone, and get out. Stay out until I'm ready."

He returned to the living room and crouched beside the dried blood, contemplating it until he heard the last pair of footsteps moving outside. Then he straightened up and began his search of the house. Miller and the others might be gone, but they had left too quickly to be thorough. A clue would certainly have been left behind, and the Assassin felt all his rage and frustration dispersing as he climbed the stairs to find it.

He found it on his first sweep. The closet in the master bedroom was filled with coats of differing lengths and varying shades of neutral colours. One was halfway off its hangar. The Assassin took it, carefully, and laid it on the bed.

He looked it up and down slowly. The coat was a very dark brown, bordering on black. He saw nothing at first. Then he noticed the slight discolouration on one of the sleeves, and again in a matching location on the other sleeve. He ran his thumbs lightly across both of the small, near-circular patches, and felt the unmistakable texture of dried blood.

CHAPTER THIRTY THREE

Rupert watched dully out of the window as they drove down yet another long street of uniform terraced housing.

"London supposed to be fancy, no?" Noy said. She was squeezed into the middle seat between Anna and Rupert, with Daniel squashed against Rupert's other side. The windows were lowered a couple of inches but it was still suffocating in the back. "That's what everyone always say. Bangkok nicer than this. Even Yangon nicer."

"There are more picturesque areas of our capital," Rupert murmured.

"Like Bluesberry."

"Bloomsbury, my dear. We're not so very far north of there, you know. This is Tottenham."

"I guess rich guys like you never come up here, even if it's close."

"I never had cause to."

"In your whole life?"

"I'm afraid not."

They went by another short row of boarded-up shops, followed by a house with its front windows smashed.

"This, Noy, is precisely the sort of area to which well-intentioned political folk like Lord Granville refer, when they rave about improving the lot of the common people every five years or so," Anna said, waving her hand vaguely towards the small, near-identical houses. "They might even deign to come and visit, knock on some doors, just long enough to take a few selfies before they flee south once more. Then, the instant the election is done with, all memory of the place seems to magically disappear from their minds, the poor souls."

"I had no notion that you were so politically inclined, Ms Cavill."

"You can slap whatever label you like on it, *Mr Granville*. I only say what I see. And what I see right now is somebody seemingly desperate to aid the plight of the suffering masses on the far side of the world. So very desperate that he's willing to risk it all. And yet, not quite so desperate, it appears, to do the same for the people suffering on his own doorstep."

"Now look here, Ms Cavill. I will not-"

"Rupert. You'll wake her." Harry spoke without turning from the driver's seat. His mother was across from him, seemingly asleep and her skin still pale. Harry held her hand on the rest between them as he steered with the other.

Rupert realised he'd raised his voice inappropriately loud for the confines of the car, but still bristled. "As soon as this business is concluded - with my own involvement apparently meriting no recognition from you, Ms Cavill - I fully intend to throw my energies into domestic politics. You can rest assured of that, *not* that I particularly wish to justify myself to you in any way, shape, or indeed form."

"Oh?" Anna asked. "And you're going to right all the country's wrongs from the Department of Culture, Media and Sport, are you?"

"You forgot 'Digital'. As everyone always seems to," Rupert muttered. "I have no pretensions of grandeur in my current position, I promise you. But soon…" Rupert caught himself, and trailed off.

"We're here," Harry said, before Anna could press Rupert. "Thank God."

They stopped outside a house at the end of a terrace. At first glance it looked the same as all the others along the street, albeit with black curtains across all four of the front-facing windows, none of which left a millimetre of space through which someone on the outside could peer in.

Looking again, Rupert also noticed a small camera on the right hand corner of the house, pointing back towards the door on the left. The camera appeared old and rusted and had nothing so obvious as a blinking red light on top. If he was passing along the street, he would simply assume it had been installed by a particularly wary resident some time ago, and had since fallen into disrepair.

"Wait here," Harry said, and got out. He passed through a creaking gate that was even more rusted than the camera, crossed the path in three strides, and pressed a buzzer beside the front door. He glanced at the camera then turned to look up and down the street with his hands in the pockets of his jacket.

Rupert saw the door opening an inch and Harry turning and talking through the gap. He came back to open the passenger side door. "Let's go," he said to them, then woke his mother with a gentle rubbing of her upper arm and led her carefully from the car.

McGinn was standing in the hallway, and offered his hand and a melancholy smile as Rupert entered. "Nice to see you again, old bean. Cap told me what happened. Sorry about the houses." He paused. "And the husband."

"We weren't married. Aren't, I should say."

"Ah, well that's not so bad then." McGinn winked at him, then, seeing the expression on Rupert's face, coughed into his hand. "Aye, too soon for jokes. Far too soon."

McGinn greeted the others in turn, receiving withdrawn responses from both Daniel and Anna despite his recent validation of Harry's trust in him. Harry himself brought up the rear, his mother leaning heavily on him.

"There's at least a bed here, isn't there?"

"Aye, Cap, we've got a couple of wee bedrooms. Just this way."

As Harry, McGinn, and Sarah went slowly up the narrow staircase near the door, Rupert wandered along the hallway after the others. He stopped with them in the small kitchen.

"What's with the expression?" Anna asked.

"It's not what I was expecting from a 'safehouse', I suppose."

"And what were you expecting? High tech gear strewn everywhere? Big computer screens with feeds of every CCTV camera in the area? Assault rifles and grenade launchers lining the walls?"

"Something along those lines."

"It's a normal house, but safe. Mostly because very few people know about it. That's it."

Rupert tried not to wrinkle his nose as he looked around the dingy room. All of the curtains were drawn across the kitchen windows too, which presumably faced onto whatever 'garden' the house possessed. Looking through an open doorway, Rupert saw a small, square, sparse living room.

He was already reflecting that he would really rather spend as little time in this place as possible, when he heard Harry and McGinn's footsteps on the stairs.

"Of course I'm bloody worried."

"I didn't mean it like that, Cap. Only that we *could* take her, but you know as well as I do it'll raise a whole lot of questions. She'll get by, I'm telling you."

"How is she?" Daniel asked, as they entered the kitchen.

"It could've been a lot worse," Harry said. "The bullet passed straight through. The blood made it look more dramatic than it was. No arteries hit. McGinn's right, she should be fine without going to hospital, as long as we keep a close eye on her."

"I've got a pal who could come and take a look," Anna said. "She's done work for the Company before, but I trust her."

"I'd rather not, unless she deteriorates. The Company could be, and probably are monitoring any known associates."

"Discretion is the better part of valour, I suppose."

"The motto I've lived my life by."

"Very funny. Shall we get down to business, then, with our recently resurrected friend from the bank? No offence, McGinn, but this isn't the most homely place in which to pass the time."

McGinn took them back along the corridor. It was barely wide enough to walk in single file, and Daniel's shoulders brushed the wall on one side and the staircase on the other. There was another door to the left of the entrance. Rupert hadn't noticed it before, nor had he seen the large padlock securing it.

McGinn took a key from his pocket and inserted it, knocked a couple of times, paused, then opened the door.

Like the rest of the downstairs, the room into which Rupert and the others entered was cramped and devoid of natural light. Inside there was only a single bed against the wall nearest the door and an armchair in the far corner.

The woman who called herself Smith sat in the chair with a book in her hands. She was noticeably paler than before, and wore an oversized t-shirt and sweatpants. Both had presumably been sourced by McGinn, and made Smith look a younger, vastly less threatening person than that which had harangued him in the corridors of Number 10 such a short time ago.

Smith watched as they entered. Daniel came in last. Smith stood automatically when she saw him and moved behind the chair.

"Relax," Harry said, his voice calm. "Nobody's going to hurt you."

"Oh yes, you're all well known for your aversion to violence."

"We need more information. It's incredibly important."

"I told you everything I know."

"I really doubt that's true."

"And if I think extremely hard, yet still prove unable to be of assistance?"

Harry looked back and nodded to McGinn. He came forward with a phone in his hand and showed the screen to Smith. He made sure she got a good look at the first photo before swiping to another, and another. Smith's hand went to her face so that only her widened eyes were visible.

"My friend did some research on you," Harry said, his voice just as calm as before. "For all the enormous benefits that family brings, it leaves you more vulnerable than anything else by far. I should know." He nodded again to McGinn, and Rupert caught a glimpse of the phone's screen as the Scot withdrew. The last image showed a man holding a boy's hand as they walked along the street just a few feet in front of the photographer; presumably McGinn himself. The boy was wearing a school uniform.

"You really are the most abominable, wretched monsters," Smith said, her eyes watery now.

"It's all for a good cause. You'll have to trust me on that."

"Trust somebody who's had me trussed up like this, and threatened the lives of my family? I don't believe I will, thank you."

"I'm sure it's no less than you deserve," Anna said. "Just a wild guess."

"There's a facility," Harry said, his voice steady and his hand held up for peace. "A data centre. We know it exists, and we know the Company keeps records of all its most sensitive data there."

Smith took a split second too long to respond. "Is there? It's news to me, if so."

"Give me the phone," Daniel said to McGinn. "Where do they live?"

"Oh, aren't you a big, brave boy? Threatening the lives of an innocent man and a child." Smith rolled her eyes, and turned back to Harry. "Obviously, I don't know any details. Why would I? I didn't even know it was a data centre."

"But you've heard of a place."

Smith stared at him, and her lower lip trembled slightly. "What's the point of all this? They'll kill me anyway, even if you do let me go, which I doubt. They'll figure out I was missing, it won't take a genius to figure out who took me, and I wouldn't even know how to hide myself, let alone the three of us."

"You won't need to. There won't be any Company left, after this." Smith rolled her eyes again, then wiped them with the tips of her fingers. "You don't believe me?" Harry said. "You'll be free to leave as soon as we have the information, if you want."

"And why wouldn't I want that?"

"This will be the safest place for you. Personally, I'd recommend sticking around a day or two. Bring your husband and son, if you like." Harry shrugged. "If you don't help us, we'll cut you loose right now. And you're right - they *will* find you, and the psychopathic bastard in charge of the search will treat you far, *far* worse than we have. I promise you that."

Smith stood with her arms folded, staring towards the covered window. She gave a small shake of her head, then talked, her voice strangely detached now.

"The building I heard about was in India," she said. "In the north and far away from anything or anywhere else remotely important. Where nobody would think to look. I can't promise it's your data centre, but it's a safe bet."

"Why?"

"She's Indian, the woman you're hunting. I only just remembered, before you jump on me - you think I'd have withheld that before, with my life on the line? They say she grew up dirt poor. Abject poverty. In Delhi, I believe, or thereabouts. I know nothing of the intervening decades between that and her founding of the Company."

"What else?"

"Nothing."

"You said that last time."

"Well, this time I couldn't be more sure. I believe what you said, about the Company's demise being my only route to safety now. Thanks to your kidnapping of me in the first place, I might add. I also believe he'll kill my family if I prove insufficiently useful," she added, nodding at Daniel.

"Who would know more?"

"Lord Frost." Harry glanced back at Rupert. Smith saw him and looked at Rupert too. "What is it?"

Rupert's heartbeat rose rapidly. He cleared his throat to buy a moment of time in which to phrase his response. "I've been unable to reach Lord Frost."

She arched an eyebrow. "That's unusual."

"Highly."

"What's happened to him?"

"I haven't the faintest idea."

There was silence in the room for a long, uncomfortable moment as Rupert's heart hammered.

"Who else?" Harry said, at last.

Smith considered again, looking down at the ground. Then her eyes drifted back upwards to meet Rupert's.

"There are plenty of people who *might* know," she said. "But I'd be sceptical in each case, and trying would risk both your time and secrecy. I can only think of one person who *would* know." A smile which Rupert certainly didn't like the look of spread across her face. Smith addressed Harry, but her eyes were still on him. "And Mr Granville here is the only one with even the slightest chance of speaking to him."

CHAPTER THIRTY FOUR

Rupert was shown inside and almost immediately found Ruth Audmore striding down the hallway towards him. Every other time he'd stepped foot inside the building she'd awaited him in either her office or the Cabinet Room.

"Rupert," she said, a little out of breath as she shook his hand. "You look... relaxed."

Rupert scratched the stubble on his cheek self consciously. He resisted the urge to also adjust the lapel on the ill-fitting coat he had borrowed from McGinn. It was drab and worn, but it was the only black coat available at the safe house, and therefore the only one which could hide the tiny camera affixed to it.

"My apologies, Ruth. I've been a little under the weather."

"You don't have to beat around the bush with me, Rupert. I've barely slept a wink either, with all of this business with John in the papers, Frost's disappearance too, all on top of the usual trials and tribulations of government."

"Well, your lot is ten times worse than mine at the moment, I'm sure," Rupert lied. "Did you manage to squeeze me in?"

"He's in a meeting, but it should finish any moment. Come on." Ruth resumed her prior pace as she went back along the corridor and Rupert hurried to keep up. "I presume you're still unwilling to give me any hint as to what this extremely urgent business might entail?"

"I'd rather wait, if it's all the same to you."

"It seems I don't have a choice." They walked in silence but for Ruth's heels clicking rapidly against the floor. "Sorry, Rupert. I'm wound up a little tight at the moment."

"No apology necessary, I assure you."

They took a couple of turns, passing besuited men and women holding folders, tablets, and laptops, all of whom greeted Ruth and gave Rupert and his outfit a once over. Rupert recognised Ruth's door as they went by. After one final turn beyond it they arrived at another closed door at the end of a short hallway.

Ruth didn't knock, instead coming to a halt to one side of the door. She gave Rupert a short nod and forced a smile, and he came to stand alongside her.

Less than a minute passed before the handle turned and the door opened. "I'll hold you to that, John," a large, red faced man called back into the room with a smile on his face. He shook Ruth's hand on his way past, nodded to Rupert, then was on his way. Ruth stepped politely back and Rupert went inside.

It had only been a short time since Rupert saw the Prime Minister at the most recent cabinet meeting. But the degradation of the man's appearance seemed to have picked up at an even greater pace.

He was in his early fifties but looked ten years older at the very least. His hair was greying at a remarkable rate; a fact which had not escaped the notice of the tabloid newspapers. The bags under his eyes were darker even than Rupert's and the worry lines on his forehead were visible from across the room. The recent weight loss made him look increasingly gaunt.

Despite it all the Prime Minister put on a seemingly genuine smile as he approached. "Rupert," he said, shaking hands warmly. "You're looking... comfortable."

"My apologies," Rupert said again. "I've come over in rather a rush, John. I'm a little flustered, truth be told."

"So I've heard," John said, with a nod towards Ruth who had quietly closed the door behind her. "I'm all for cutting to the chase, Rupert, if it's all the same with you. I'm on an especially tight schedule today."

"Of course," Rupert said. He remained standing, having not been invited to sit, and tried to ensure his lapel was facing directly towards the Prime Minister. "It's about Lord Frost, you see."

"I had a feeling it might be. I hope you've heard more from him than I have."

"I'm afraid not."

The Prime Minister swore under his breath and his expression darkened. "The media are after me like a pack of baying hounds. He chose a hell of a time to take a sabbatical."

"I don't believe this is a voluntary absence, John."

"Meaning?"

"In the spirit of cutting to the chase, you understand… I believe the entire Company is under threat of collapse. And if it does fall, it will take a lot more with it."

"Jesus Christ. Well, that's for bloody sure," John said, beginning to pace back and forth with his hands in his pockets and his eyes cast downwards. "It'll blow a massive hole in the profits of one of our biggest and most important banks, for starters. Could take them out entirely. Not to mention all the off the books payments to investors. Investors who happen to include some of the most influential and powerful men and women in the western world."

"It's a mere trifle in comparison, of course, but… there would also be the potential exposure of any high ranking figures with Company connections. Not only the private parties, but the…

public ones too."

A smile briefly lifted John's tired face. "You're saying it would be the end of me."

"Of all three of us, most likely. We have to imagine whoever's doing all this has a vendetta against the Company, and those perceived to hold influence with it."

"And what *is* 'all this' that they're doing, Rupert? So far you've only told me that the old man has gone AWOL. Worrying, I'll admit, but not a sign of the end times in itself."

"If it were an isolated incident, I'd quite agree with you. Unfortunately, it's very much not."

"You're referring to Tinkov's assassination."

"Followed by Bohm's disappearance."

"Richard Bohm?" John's face clouded instantly. "Did you know about this?" he asked Ruth.

"I didn't want to bother you until the… specifics were clarified."

"The specifics?" Rupert asked, raising his eyebrow at Ruth. "To put it bluntly, he went splat on the sidewalk outside his penthouse, per the information I received." He turned back. "So you can see, John, why I'm tending towards connecting the dots, given the circumstances. That's two members of the Trio meeting a premature demise within a few days of each other. And now we have Frost's disappearance, in the midst of it all."

"Yes, yes," John said, irritation flaring in his voice as he waved his hand. "I quite agree with your premise, Rupert, you needn't worry about that. The question is what *solution* you're proposing. As we've already concluded, the Company's collapse could have disastrous consequences for all of us. Not to mention the impact on the country, of course," he added.

Rupert swallowed and felt his heartbeat, which had hardly

been sedate, ramp up once more. "I'd never normally ask, John," he said. "I know it's a secret. One of the most closely guarded secrets around, as far as I can tell. But…" He paused. "It's the third, and now final, member of the Trio. I need to know who she is."

Automatically, John glanced at Ruth. He looked back to Rupert and frowned. "Why?"

"Because I wish to help her. I've been involved with the Company for some time now, regardless of whether I was technically an active member or not. With Lord Frost's disappearance, I believe myself to be the only person positioned to provide her with the sort of analysis and advice which straddles the line between governmental, financial, and… private interests. I also have the necessary contacts to act as an intermediary as we try to gather information on this threat."

He finished there and prayed the speech had not sounded entirely rehearsed. He certainly hoped it didn't sound like the result of an impromptu committee meeting, composed of people with the exact opposite intentions of those being stated, tasked with thinking up plausible reasons for the Prime Minister to divulge the information they so desperately needed.

John stood with his arms folded, leaning against the edge of his desk and staring at the floor again. "Give us a minute, would you, Ruth?" he said quietly, and only looked up when he heard the door close. "You're right, Rupert. It is a closely guarded secret. If it even came out that I knew, my career would be over like that." He snapped his fingers weakly. "The only reason I'm telling you is that… well, should the Company collapse, and any information about it leak out, her identity will likely be revealed regardless."

"I quite understand, John. I'd never even think to ask, under normal circumstances."

John's eyes rested on Rupert's. They remained that way for at least ten seconds, by which point Rupert was starting to think that John's exhaustion had got the better of him and he'd simply forgotten where he was.

Finally, John cleared his throat. "Anuradha," he said. "Anuradha Patel. She's one of the richest, most brilliant, most ruthless women on the planet, and almost nobody knows she even exists."

John took his phone from his pocket, unlocked it, then shook his head and muttered something. He went behind his desk and opened the top drawer then took out a different phone. "I'll send you her number," he murmured, tapping the screen. "Well, it's the number I've used on the very rare occasions I've needed to contact her. It's the only one I've got, regardless."

Rupert's phone vibrated in his pocket, and he checked the screen. "Thank you, John."

John closed the drawer again and walked slowly back around the desk. He checked his watch as he approached Rupert. "I'm running late, although that's a prime minister's schedule. I've been running late for the best part of two years now."

"My apologies."

"Not necessary. I'm glad you came." John held out his hand and Rupert shook it. "We're due a proper reshuffle in the cabinet, you know, and I'm more than ready to open up a couple of the top jobs. I'm *sure* that Dan and Nicola are two of the people…" He trailed off, and forced a smile which did nothing to brighten his expression.

"Not to mention," he continued. "If Lord Frost has… well, if our worst fears are confirmed, that will leave another position open behind the scenes. The power behind the throne, you know. Keep this ship sailing as it should, Rupert, and you'll prove yourself an excellent candidate for either type of role. Even both, perhaps."

"Most kind, Prime Minister. I'll get the job done, rest assured."

"Good man."

Rupert gave a short bow, his expression grave, then turned on his heel and left the office. He nodded to Ruth on his way out as she passed in the opposite direction.

Rupert waited until he was not only outside Number 10, but back in the safety of his car, before removing the tiny camera and flicking the fiddly on/off switch. Then he let out a long, slow breath and let his forehead sink down onto the steering wheel.

"I really wish you hadn't gone and done that, George," he whispered. "I really wish I didn't have to go through all of this alone."

Rupert gave himself another minute. Then he composed himself, started up the car, and headed for Tottenham.

CHAPTER THIRTY FIVE

Granville cleared his throat. "Naturally, I don't wish to complain," he began.

"Here we go," Anna said.

"But it *is* getting rather stuffy in here. Are you sure you wouldn't prefer to open a window?"

"It's nothing to do with what I'd prefer, pal," McGinn said, his eyes not leaving the screen. "The windows don't open. Security measure. Short of smashing a hole in the wall, we're not getting any more air in here."

"And does it still count as a 'security measure' if we end up suffocating to our collective demise?"

"I'll gladly break this laptop over your noggin, if you'd prefer a quicker death."

Granville glanced up from his own screen at a noise from Anna's direction. "Found that amusing, did you? The image of my violent murder?"

"Everyone's got their own sense of humour, Granville."

Harry popped the final beer open and brought the four bottles to the table. He gave one each to McGinn, Anna, and Noy, and held onto the other himself. Daniel had a glass of water on the worktop beside him. Granville raised his eyebrows.

"You hate beer," Harry said. "And you declared the wine we bought at the shop *ghastly*."

"Well, you know. The man in the desert... When he's dying of thirst... However that old saying goes." Granville rubbed his eyes underneath his glasses. "I'm too tired for metaphors. Just top me up, would you, old chap? I'll swallow the wine and my pride alike."

Harry returned with the wine bottle and placed it heavily in front of Granville. Noy and Anna sat either side of him, with McGinn opposite. There was barely an inch of room on or around the tiny, square dining table. Harry went to stand beside Daniel, where they could both see McGinn's laptop.

Usually carefree, McGinn's face now was an even mixture of concentration and frustration. Harry placed a hand on his shoulder. "You'll find her," he said. "Be patient."

McGinn nodded briefly but didn't turn from the screen. He was logged in to a database filled with records on tens of thousands of people. Harry didn't recognise the software, but knew better than to ask any questions. He only needed the answers, and had long since stopped caring how he got them.

"You're sure the name's right?"

"Lord above," Granville said. "You saw the footage for yourself."

"No known aliases?"

"I didn't think to ask the Prime Minister of the country whether this international super criminal had any aliases. How foolish of me." Granville looked over the top of his own laptop, the screen of which reflected in his glasses. "Sorry, old chap. I'm rather frustrated with all this Photoshop nonsense."

"Not Photoshop," Noy said. "Photoshop for photos. This is a video. And it's not complicated, what you trying to do. You're just bad. Very, very bad."

"Would you like to take over?"

"I don't know how to change videos. I never own a computer in my life. My mobile phone barely have colour screen. But I know what Photoshop is, and I know this is easy."

"Play it," Harry said, and after a momentary glance at his keyboard Granville hit the spacebar. His muffled voice emanated from the tinny speakers for a few moments, there was a brief pause, then the Prime Minister spoke. "Fine. So just go back a few seconds to when you start talking, hit that button to remove the sound, then click the other button to start the sound again when you've shut up. Noy's right, Rupert. It's not rocket science."

"Oh, very original."

"Keep going and you can have it done in half an hour, even at your speed. Then we'll have a nice, shiny piece of evidence ready for the big release."

"You're trying to tell me my floundering Photoshop tomfoolery is an essential part of this mission?"

"Not Photoshop," Noy said quietly.

Harry turned back to McGinn as the man was taking his phone from his pocket. He glanced down at a message he seemed to have received, then he quickly looked back again, eyes widening.

"Hold on just a wee moment," he murmured, and opened the message fully.

"What is it?"

"Could be nothing, Cap. Or it could be everything we need." He lay the phone on the table, brought up a different website on his computer, and entered some login details from the message he'd been sent. After a moment's pause another database filled his screen. To Harry it looked almost identical to the first, but McGinn clenched his fist and turned to Harry with an expression of triumph.

"Pal of mine came through for me," he said. "And no," he added, looking at Anna, whose suspicions he'd clearly picked up on. "I didn't reveal any specifics. Only asked for one time access, as a wee favour."

"And he just… gave it to you?"

"As he bloody well should have. I saved his life last year, down in the DRC. Anyway, he's an American, had some very good contacts indeed, and now…" He trailed off as he began to navigate the database. "Well, if she's not in here somewhere, I'll eat my proverbial hat."

Harry felt a flutter of genuine hope as McGinn began to type. He began with a basic search for women born in India named Anuradha Patel and puffed out his cheeks when the results came up. "That's a hell of a lot more hits than we had before," he said. "Thousands and thousands of them."

"Narrow it by age," Anna said. "She's unlikely to have created an international web of people trafficking and money laundering in her teens."

"Any idea how long the Company has been around?"

"Not a clear one. At least a decade, at an extremely conservative estimate, and she'd surely have been thirty or more when she got the ball rolling."

McGinn entered a few parameters. "That's narrowed our options. Maybe I can sort them by the amount of tax they pay."

"People as rich as her don't pay taxes," Anna said.

"Good point."

"Try limiting it to people born in Delhi," she said. "That's where our illustrious houseguest believes she's from." McGinn did so, and the list became sparse with no promising results. "Surrounding areas?"

McGinn widened the search. Again, there was little to work with.

"Remove the surname," Daniel said. "It might not be hers."

"Now we've got too many again."

"Put an upper limit on the age," Anna said. "Looking after Tasha is about all my grandmother can manage without getting exhausted."

"If I cap it at eighty now…" McGinn said. "That leaves us with a couple of dozen results. It won't take me long to look through those."

Harry watched as McGinn opened each file in turn and scrolled through the personal details within. The database, whichever American agency it belonged to, was a gold mine of information and all for people living on the other side of the world.

"Well," McGinn said, after a couple of minutes. "You never know, I suppose, but none of these seem like the type. These Anuradha Patels all look like they're in or around Delhi, for one thing, not living the high life over in Hong Kong. The ones who are still alive, anyway"

Harry mused, frowning. He thought for a few moments before something clicked. "The ones who are still alive," he murmured.

McGinn's beer bottle was halfway to his mouth. "What's that?"

"How many times, back in the day, were we given targets supposedly dead yet still very much alive?"

McGinn's customary smile finally began to spread across his face. "Too many times, Cap." He shook his head as he began to alter the database's fields. "Should've thought of that myself," he muttered.

He hit the return key with a flourish. No results came up. "Ah.

No dead Anuradhas, who'd have been between forty and eighty now, in the Delhi area."

"Widen the search," Harry said. McGinn put another fifty miles on the radius, then another fifty. There were still no results. "Keep going," Harry said. A trickle of results began to come in. McGinn opened each file but they were all quickly dismissed by both he and Harry.

McGinn kept adding to the distance until two more results popped up. The first had died of an illness when she was still a teenager. McGinn opened the second file and began to quickly scroll through it.

"Stop," Harry said. "Go back up. Look." He pointed at the lines near the top of the page showing the woman's dates of both birth and death. "She died fifteen years ago."

"Would've been... forty one at the time?"

"Criminal record?"

McGinn scrolled down again, more slowly this time. "Money laundering. Tax evasion. She died while she was under investigation."

"Convenient. Education?"

"University of Delhi. Scholarship. Honours degree in economics."

"Place of birth?"

McGinn found the name and copied it over to a map in a different tab. The map zoomed automatically in on a small village some three hundred miles north of the capital, sitting at the edge of the Himalayan foothills.

"It's her, isn't it?" McGinn said.

"Not only is it her," Harry said. "But that's where our data centre will be."

"You reckon?"

"Smith said it was in the far north, away from everything. It'd make sense for Patel to pick a place she knew."

"Smith also said the bitch was from Delhi," Anna pointed out.

"She studied there. Perhaps she told people that's where she was from. Smith said she was supposed to be 'dirt poor', and the remoteness of her home, along with the scholarship, point to that. Maybe she was ashamed of her origins and lied."

Granville and Noy were both watching. "There's an awful lot of supposition and speculation here, old chap," Granville said.

"McGinn and I did this sort of thing for years," Harry said. "Often without the help of an enormous database. You get a sense for patterns. You learn to listen to your instincts. Trust them."

"I don't question your experience, Harry, and I certainly don't doubt your judgement... In cases like these, at least. For this type of operation, however, isn't it best to be sure? After all-"

"I'm sure," Harry said, his voice flat. "This is her."

Granville's mouth opened and closed a couple of times. "Well," he said, and took off his glasses to clean them. "If you're *sure*..."

"The question then becomes," said Anna. "How do we find this woman who's supposed to have been dead for fifteen years?"

Harry and McGinn looked at each other. The Scot shrugged. "Same way we've always found people," he said. "Research."

"I'm thrilled already."

Anna stood from her stool, took a glass of wine to the neighbouring living room where Sarah lay, then joined Noy and Granville, her focus seemingly on chatting to the former rather than helping the latter. From his place beside McGinn Harry barely noticed, and time began to melt away.

He tried to fight against the nostalgia; the sudden rush of memories of all the times he and McGinn had sat together that same way and for a similar purpose. He fought too against the surprising and sudden sense of loss he felt for the other two members of his team, Cooper and Davis. McGinn said both were still alive, but neither felt that way to Harry. He couldn't push it all completely away, but he at least put it to the back of his mind and concentrated instead on the business of hunting.

Daniel loomed behind both Harry and McGinn and added the occasional suggestion. Harry checked the clock once and saw an hour had already disappeared. The other three had finished their video and Noy and Anna had gone to join Sarah in the living room, all without Harry noticing. He only realised Rupert was standing beside Daniel when the former cleared his throat.

"How are we progressing, chaps?"

"Slowly but surely."

"You've found some clues then, I take it?"

"None whatsoever," McGinn said cheerfully. "But half the battle is exhausting all your logical possibilities."

Harry finished another bottle of beer, placed it on the table, and turned it in place thoughtfully. He looked back at Daniel. "Her name," he said.

"What about it?"

"You mentioned before that she may have changed it. We certainly have her birth name. I'd have thought any marriage would be listed on this database, but there's no guarantee."

McGinn nodded and switched to another of the tabs he still had open. He searched for marriages in the area of the village, involving an 'Anuradha' and within a realistic time frame. There was only one result.

"Fantastic," he said with a smile, and opened the record. "Jai," he read. "That's the husband's surname." He ran a quick search. "And the name she was carrying, it turns out, when the investigation began." He shook his head. "Should've checked that sooner. Sorry, Cap."

"Can you find the husband's file?"

McGinn switched back to the other database and entered the name along with a geographical radius centred on the village. "Got him," he said, and frowned. "Says here they got divorced. That wasn't mentioned in her file either."

"When?"

McGinn paused as he worked out the dates. "A few months before the investigation into Anuradha Patel began."

"Another incredible coincidence. What did he do after?"

"Looks like he had a business in Delhi. Exporting computer chips to… Well, you'll never believe where."

"Hong Kong."

"Bingo."

"Have they still got an office there?"

McGinn hammered the keys of his laptop. "Registered address. No guarantee it's her headquarters now."

"It's a start, though."

The Scot continued to scroll through the details of the husband's company. He stopped halfway down and looked at Harry with a smile. "They've still got an active facility in India. Guess where."

Harry leant forward and scanned the name then looked back at McGinn. He nodded and McGinn switched tabs again, returning to the map focused on the remote village in the Himalayan foothills.

Harry felt Rupert's hand on his shoulder, and the man leaned past him to study the screen more closely. Anna and Noy came to the living room doorway too, having clearly overheard them.

Anna met Harry's eyes. "You've got her?"

Harry exchanged another look with the grinning McGinn. "We're well on our way," he said, trying to maintain more composure than his friend. "I think we have the data centre. We don't know where exactly she's based in Hong Kong, but I'd be shocked if McGinn can't find out based on what we've learnt here."

"You and me both, Cap," McGinn said. "When are we leaving?"

"First thing in the morning. No sense in waiting around."

"Too bloody right."

"Apologies if I sound like a stickler for details," Anna said. "But it appears we'll be trying to accomplish multiple objectives at the same time."

"Right," Harry said. "We'll split into two teams."

"I'd guessed that, Captain Obvious. What I'd like to know is their constitution."

Harry pushed his chair from the table and stood up. He folded his arms in front of him and let out a long breath. "I've been thinking about this."

"Glad to hear it."

"Neither is exactly straightforward, but the data centre is the tougher target. There will be more security, since it's an entire facility. The building itself will be larger, and we can't simply kill a single person and be done with it. We have to get in, get what we need, and get away again before any reinforcements arrive. That's not to say it'll be child's play to take out Patel, by any means."

Anna looked around at the others, then back to Harry. She shrugged. "Sounds reasonable enough. And so, the actual teams are?" She saw Harry's face clouding and rolled her eyes. "Just spit it out, glorious leader. We're all adults here and none of us are going to have it easy."

"Fine. You, Daniel, and Noy are going to Hong Kong. You and Daniel have plenty of combat experience. Noy can help in all manner of ways, as she's shown already in recent weeks, and I'm positive the Assassin will be guarding Patel. If she wants a shot at killing him, that'll be her only chance."

"Good idea, Big Boss," Noy said, nodding.

"It's a regular stroke of genius," Anna said. "Except for the fact that leaves only two of you - I'm assuming Lord Granville isn't joining you to lead the charge - for the part which you just now claimed would be more difficult."

"Well observed."

"Not just a pretty face."

"The fact is..." Harry began, then trailed off. He looked to McGinn, and considered for one final, brief time whether he was still in the throes of nostalgia, or reaching for the only realistic chance they had. "Well," he said. "I'm hoping there won't only be two of us, when it comes down to it. I'm *hoping* we'll have four."

McGinn looked questioningly at him for a moment, then a wry half-smile crossed his face. "I don't know if they'll be up for it, Cap," he said. "They've got other commitments now."

"So we'll see how much the past truly counts for," Harry said. "I'm willing to be disappointed. Expecting it, even. But I hope to God I'm proved wrong."

The full smile spread now across McGinn's face. He nodded and stood up, already drawing his phone from his pocket as he went towards the hallway. "I'll see what I can-"

"No," Harry said, and McGinn stopped. "I'll speak to them."

CHAPTER THIRTY SIX

McGinn ran his hand gently through Mae's firm hair, which bristled against his palm. She stirred on his stomach and spoke, her words lazy with sleep.

"Looking for greys?"

"I wouldn't have to look far."

He felt her mouth widening to a smile against his skin. "Cheeky bastard. You'll be in your forties one day, you know."

"We'll see."

She turned at the tone of his voice so that her face was only a foot or so from his. "It's cruel to say things like that, James."

"I don't want to mislead you, lass. You know that."

"And yet there's so much you won't tell me."

"There's a difference between that and lying, isn't there?"

"The kids at school are always saying stuff like that. I didn't lie, miss. I just didn't tell the truth."

"Wise kids."

She sighed, folded her hands on his chest, and rested her chin on them. She continued to study him. "I'm not going to chase you for specifics, any more than I already have. Just tell me if you're planning to come back to London. If you're planning to come back and really marry me. I'm a big girl. I can handle the truth."

"I'm planning on it."

"Your work," she said. "You do bad things, don't you?"

"That depends on your perspective. I don't think I'm a bad person. Honestly, I don't."

"I don't think you are either," she said. "But it's hard to know, given the circumstances."

"Aye. Of course it is." McGinn looked to the ceiling as he began to stroke her hair again. "I'm not doing a bad thing this time," he said. "I'm sure about that. It's a very good thing, in fact. Better than anything I did in the army. Maybe the best thing I've ever done."

"Will you tell me about it after?"

McGinn's eyes crinkled as he smiled. He saw her purse her lips and look off to the side. "What?"

"I want to hate you for all of this. Nobody would put up with it except me. But you're too bloody..."

"Charming? Funny?"

"Oh, God no, it's nothing to do with your awful personality. You're only too bloody handsome. Dull as a doorknob, and boring as drying paint. But beautiful... in a rugged, rural Highlands sort of a way."

"D'you want me to pluck these greys for you before I go, or what?"

She lifted her hand an inch and smacked him softly. "Idiot." His chest bounced up and down with laughter, and she rolled her eyes and settled back onto it. "Life would go on if we didn't marry, you know," she said, her words slowing and becoming softer once more. "But I truly hope we do."

Mae's eyes were closed now, but McGinn studied her face anyway. "Aye, lass. Me too."

Rupert lay with his head in Sarah's lap, propped up a little on a cushion. The walls of the living room were completely bare. The furniture consisted of the sofa on which they dwelt and a single armchair.

"I do hope they come back soon," Sarah said.

"Of course."

"Not because of any matriarchal tenderness, you understand," she said. "It's the thought of spending more than a minute longer than I need to in this deathly dull purgatory which terrifies me."

"My mind was running along a similar track."

"At least you're permitted to leave."

"I'm required to leave, dear. It would likely raise some alarm bells if a government minister suddenly stopped coming to work. On balance, I might prefer to pass the time here with a good book than be exposed to whatever Company ne'er-do-wells still seek me. Not to mention the usual baying hounds endemic to politics, as John calls them."

"Well," Sarah said, and looked around at the plain walls and the covered window. "I think I'd take my chances with the hounds and murderers."

They stayed in silence for a minute or so. Sarah's hand rested on Rupert's forehead. His eyes were closed as he enjoyed the first moment of peace and comfort he could remember.

"I assume you haven't heard from him."

Rupert didn't open his eyes. He only hummed in response.

"Do you think he's okay?"

"I doubt it," Rupert said, trying unsuccessfully to sound carefree.

"He'd have had a jolly good reason."

"There's no reason good enough, Sarah."

"I wouldn't be so sure," she said. "Things were all fine and dandy towards the end, with my husband... before it all went wrong. But we had so many problems over the decades before that. You wouldn't believe how many." Sarah began to run her thumb gently across the lines of Rupert's forehead. "And yet, now that he's gone, I find myself remembering them all. Every single one. I was usually harsh with him, at the time, and certainly I still think his actions were wrong now. But I can see, with this distance, why he might have done them. And I wish..." Sarah's voice trembled, and Rupert raised his own hand to place it over hers, looking at her upside-down. "I wish I'd been a little more understanding at the time. It's so very easy to say that now. Now that it's too late. It's very foolish. But I wish it anyway, because I really did, you know... I really did love him."

Rupert lifted his glasses and squeezed the bridge of his nose. "You're a wise woman, Sarah," he said, once he had control of himself. "I value your judgement tremendously. But I'm afraid I simply can't discuss that any further right now. There's so much... It's all too much for me, you know. Already. If I were to confront that now, fully, as I eventually must, then I don't believe I'd have enough left to do what must be done. Do you understand?"

"Yes. But don't put it off forever, Rupert. That would be a terrible waste."

Rupert stared at the ceiling. When he looked backwards and up again silent tears were running down Sarah's cheeks, half descending into the dressing across the wound in her neck.

"What is it, my dear?"

"Oh, nothing very interesting, nor very original," she said, smiling. "Nothing that any other mother wouldn't feel."

"They're big, strong boys, Sarah. Very big, and very strong, in fact. If anyone can do it..."

"I know. But I'll still be sick with worry, every second they're out there."

"Did you get used to it, when they were in the army? Or-"

"Never," she said. "Between him, then them, I've had decades of this feeling."

Sarah suddenly looked very old. Rupert reached up and ran the back of his hand down her cheek. "I think this will be the end of it," he said. "For both of them."

"It seems to me that it's in their blood, and not from my side. An addiction to this sort of thing. They've both had opportunities to leave it all behind, and neither has taken them."

"But now each of them has a real reason," Rupert said. "Now each of them has a future."

Daniel finished packing the last of the few clothes they would take into a bag. Noy was sitting on the edge of the small bed, which was pushed against one of the walls. There was a bedside table with a lamp turned on behind her, facing towards Daniel and framing her.

The bed creaked several inches downwards as Daniel sat. "What is it?" he asked in Thai.

"Nothing interesting. I only feel a little sad."

"We'll get him. It won't bring them back, but it will make you feel better. People tell you it won't, but I've taken revenge before. Most recently on the man who gave you away, after the fight at the compound. It felt… How do you say?" He asked her in English, then nodded. "Yes, satisfying. Very."

"I know, Farang. I want him dead, and I'll celebrate when it happens, even if it's not very enlightened of me. But it's not that."

"Then what?"

Noy screwed up her nose and shook her head. "It's hard to explain. And it sounds stupid."

"Tell me."

She held her hand over his and traced the outline of his fingers with one of hers. "My brother and father... That's the worst thing that ever happened to me, in my whole life. Easily. But everything aside from that... Everything since..." She made a noise of annoyance, as if frustrated with herself. "That part has felt... nice. Like being part of a team. Part of a family. It's the first time I had that feeling in a very long time. Years and years." She shrugged. "Big Boss is crazy. Anna's crazy in a different way. I still don't trust the Scottish guy. And I would never trust someone as rich as the posh guy. *Rupert,*" she said, in her finest English accent which always made Daniel smile. "But still, when we're all together... It feels nice, no? Don't you feel that way? It's nice not to feel like you're surrounded by people who want to kill you, or do other bad things. It's nice not to feel lonely, isn't it?"

Daniel covered her hand with his. Then he raised her hand to his lips and kissed it gently.

"What this mean?" Noy asked in English. "Some kind of British code?"

Daniel smiled and kissed her hand again. "It's not code."

"Then what? You feel like that or not?"

He looked down and was silent. "I can't," he said. "I do understand. Maybe I want to feel that way too. But I can't let myself."

"Eh?" Noy said. "It's a good feeling, you dumb Farang."

"Perhaps," he said slowly. "But it opens you up. To a pain that will be just as strong as whatever good feelings you get. No. Far stronger."

Noy frowned and seemed about to argue. Then her brow cleared, and she nodded. "Understand," she said. "Not what you suppose to say, but I understand. Maybe I feel the same, that's why I'm confused. So many bad things happen that you just expect more and more."

Daniel nodded, his hand still resting on hers. Noy stared at the ground, then looked at him. "What about me?"

He smiled. "I knew you would ask that."

"What girl wouldn't, Farang? Sound to me like you're not interested in the good feelings in life, in case the bad follow. This include me?"

"It's far too late for that. If anything happened to you, it would kill me."

Noy sighed, and rested her head on his shoulder. "Same," she said. "Maybe we break up now. This is the perfect time. Then, if one of us die in Hong Kong, the other one won't care."

"You're a genius."

"I know. Very difficult to be such a genius in a group of dumb farangs." She sighed again and shook her head. "Very difficult."

Daniel put his arm around her, the scent of her hair filling his nostrils and the feel of her next to him still making his pulse race.

Anna kicked the bedroom door closed behind her, dropped her toothbrush into the small bag on the floor, and stopped to watch Harry with her hands on her hips. He stood with his arms folded and his back to her, staring down at the lamp beside the bed.

"I'm positive you don't stand that way when there's nobody to see you," she said. "You only want me to view you as some brooding malcontent, with the weight of the world on his shoulders."

"You've figured me out at last."

"Sorry to break it to you, Captain, but it wasn't difficult." She walked over and draped her arms around his neck. "Tell me."

"And open myself to mockery?"

"I only mock you because I know you can take it. That, and the fact that you're so incredibly mockable." She leaned forward and kissed him on the cheek. "Go on. I'm not going to beg you."

Harry put his hand on her forearm. "I could never work out if I missed it all or not," he said. "I didn't miss the death. But even the violence, as you've so astutely observed before... I didn't 'miss' it, logically or consciously, but I slipped back into it so quickly that perhaps, on a deeper level..." He shrugged. "It sounds terrible to say."

"It's just your nature, Miller. It's not terrible or otherwise. And regardless, you can't deny that the people you've fought so far, and those you're going to fight now, deserve it. That's supposed to be very terrible to say too, but I couldn't care less."

"I agree," he said. "But in this case, it's not the violence anyway."

"Obviously. It's the responsibility."

"You really do have me figured out."

"I told you it wasn't difficult."

"Whenever I look back, and remember anything at all except for what happened in the end, with Daniel, it's always the good times that come to mind. The times at base, or returning there after a job well done. I've certainly missed that - the camaraderie. But tonight I realised I'd put the other part of the role out of my mind, the other part of leadership."

"Which is?"

He shrugged again and turned towards her with a half-smile on his lips. "The terror," he said. "The crippling fear that you'll lose someone you know well, someone you care about, and it will all have been your fault. You can be as prepared as you like. You can trust your judgement, and you should. But anything can happen, it only takes a moment, and then you've lost that person forever and you'll never, ever forget it."

"This isn't just because of what happened with your father, at Sherston?"

Anna felt him tense. Then he let out a long breath. "No. I always felt this way, even if I blocked out the memories of it until now. But what happened with the convoy, with Daniel... Then with my Dad too..." He shook his head. "I don't know if I can do this. I don't know if I can deal with the risk again. And I'm sure that, if anything did happen, I'd never-"

"Harry," she said gently, and he stopped. "This is all irrelevant."

"Thanks."

"I'm not mocking you, just this once. It really is irrelevant. None of us are following orders. We haven't been coerced into anything. We're all grown men and women, here completely and utterly of our own volition. You're the one making the plans and running the show because you're the best at it. It's as simple as that. I wouldn't blame you if anything went wrong, and neither would the others. If I got hurt then I'd blame myself, for choosing to get involved in the first place. There is no 'responsibility' in that regard. Your only responsibility is to tell us what to do, when, and where, which is the duty we've given you. What happens after that is up to each of us."

They stayed standing there in silence, Anna's arms pulling Harry to her more tightly now. Finally, Harry reached up and gently broke her grip so that he could turn and put his hands on her hips. "Your microphone was working, you know."

"What on earth are you talking about?"

"That night in New York. When you were in the club and Noy was set on taking down all Bohm's bodyguards alone. You weren't sure your mic was working, but I heard what you said."

To her shame Anna looked away, and she felt a heat spreading quickly across her face. "I was quite sure I was about to die at that moment," she said. "It's rude to remind someone of what they've said, at a time like that."

"Well, since we're both about to head into mortal danger," Harry said. "I can tell you that I love you too."

Anna knew her face was turning rapidly red, and looked down and away from him. Harry put a finger under her chin and slowly turned her face back towards his, then kissed her. "I wish we'd met earlier," he said. "Sometimes I think my life has never felt easier, even if the circumstances have never been harder."

Anna smiled. "I know what you mean," she said. "But we have each other now."

CHAPTER THIRTY SEVEN

Harry and McGinn landed at Indira Gandhi International Airport around midday. They bought a sim card using Harry's fake passport then found a man waiting at Arrivals holding a sign bearing the false name they'd given.

The man led them through the crowd of taxi drivers just outside and to a multistory car park. McGinn checked the car quickly while Harry counted a wad of US dollars. He handed them over once McGinn gave the all clear, and both of them shook hands with the man before driving away.

Harry and McGinn had travelled plenty for their work. Both agreed they had never seen roads like Delhi's, and Harry was very glad not to drive the first leg. The concept of lanes was completely ignored. Horns were used instead of indicators when another driver wanted to turn. Cows blocked entire sections of road, eating from heaps of rubbish or ambling along oblivious to the traffic.

They skirted the western side of Delhi's centre, although it still took them over an hour to leave the city. The roads calmed significantly. They soon discovered the air conditioning didn't work, despite the seller's online claims, but it was pleasant for Harry to have the window down and the warm wind blowing against his face as they cruised along the NH-44.

The uniform brown dirtiness of Delhi gradually gave way to greenery as the hours passed and they continued north. The land was flat, and they went through a constant string of towns in which Harry would never set foot and cities of which he had never heard.

They stopped halfway for food, then Harry took over. A couple of hours after passing Chandigarh the ground finally began to climb. The air cooled noticeably, and they moved through green hills and past forests.

They arrived in Dharamshala some ten hours after leaving the airport. It was completely dark and the roads were quiet.

"Well, that was the easy part," McGinn said. "I'm guessing we're not putting up in some nice hotel here? Breakfast buffet in the morning before we pop out to find this data centre?" Harry looked at him. McGinn grimaced. "A night in the car it is. Lovely."

"Which way's the village?"

"East." McGinn adjusted the map on his phone. "Onwards, Cap. I'll tell you when to turn."

"Any reply from them yet?" The matter had dominated Harry's thoughts throughout the journey, and he couldn't help but ask.

"They'll be here, Cap."

Harry nodded, wishing he shared his friend's confidence. Then he put the car into gear and continued on.

Harry shook McGinn's shoulder. Bleary eyed, the Scot squinted at him then out of the window. He winced as he sat up.

"I was dreaming of a nice comfy bed," he said. "A proper king sized one, with those pillows that you just sink into, you know?"

"No you weren't."

"Well I'm dreaming of it now."

They left the car and breathed in the cool air. They had found a side road late at night and driven off the track and into the forest. Getting the car out again would be its own struggle, but that was a distant concern.

They took their backpacks from the back seats then left the car behind. McGinn opened the map on his phone and took them up through the trees to the top of the steep hill.

"Well, there's the village." McGinn raised his eyes higher, then higher still, and whistled. "Jesus Christ," he said. "That's a sight for these weary, sleep deprived eyes."

Harry lifted his gaze too, and struggled at first to process what he saw. The village itself, in which Anuradha Patel had been born, was tiny. There must have been fifty single-storey buildings clustered together in a central grouping, then another fifty or so scattered around the low hills which ran around three sides. The fourth side, directly across from Harry and McGinn, was open to the Himalayan foothills.

The land appeared to simply drop away beyond the village. The mountains beyond the drop towered up some three and a half thousand feet. Harry found the sheer scale of them difficult to comprehend. His eyes raised to a regular level, where mountains should end, then kept going. The lower halves were spotted with green blotches of grass and miniscule trees, which gave way to grey stone higher up then, at the very peak, black stone starkly contrasted with white snow and the blue, early morning sky finally visible above.

Harry heard scuffling sounds and his head whipped around. "Down," he hissed, and the two of them dropped flat onto the ground.

Harry waited a full minute as the noises slowly passed by then crawled forward to look over the lip of the hill. Two boys were walking away, one hitting the long grass on the near side of the path with a stick. Anna would have mocked him when she saw the boys, Harry knew, but McGinn said nothing.

He remembered, as Harry did, that the people like those they hunted would pay absolutely anybody to serve as lookouts, and he watched the boys carefully until they were halfway down the hill and heading back towards the village.

McGinn used his map to guide them in a wide, counter clockwise circle around and above the village. They stayed off the path near to the cover of the trees, but saw nobody else save for the small shapes of distant villagers walking slowly or sitting together below.

After reaching the eastern side of the village, so that the colossal mountains were to their left, McGinn took them back into the forest. They went directly east and the ground began to descend. After another fifteen minutes Harry saw the trees thinning in front.

"That'll near enough do it, Cap," McGinn said, checking his phone. "Patel's so-called factory is just past the forest."

They walked to the edge of the tree line and looked out.

They had reached the bottom of the hill now, and in front was a plateau of dirt with patches of rough grass that extended for a mile or so. The drop-off, which they had seen past the village, was close on their left hand side with the Himalayas towering beyond. A narrow, well maintained road emerged through a gap in some smaller hills to their right. It hugged the tree line initially, before curving away more or less where they stood, to head in the direction they now faced.

Half a mile in front was a tall chain link fence. It ran from the edge of the cliff on their left, for half a mile to their right, before turning at a right angle to stretch away from them. The road led to a guardhouse and a gate in the middle of the fence.

Harry and McGinn had already taken their binoculars from their backpacks. McGinn laughed to himself as Harry looked to the guardhouse.

"For factory guards, these lads have got some decent kit."

There were two men stationed by the small building beside the gate in the fence, one leaning against the wall and smoking a cigarette and the other strolling back and forth in front of him. Both were equipped with modified AK-47s and bulletproof jackets.

"Definitely former military," McGinn said. "Everything about them screams it."

"Ex-special forces," Harry said. "And they took their guns with them when they left."

"Aye. There's another, look. Two o'clock."

"This is a good spot. We'll settle in here, see what's what, then circle round to get a closer look at the building itself." Harry lowered the binoculars and looked at the small hills to their right. A ridge ran parallel to the right side of the fence. "There," Harry said. "It won't offer much cover, but we'll get a bloody good view of the place."

"Right you are." Both Harry and McGinn settled down a few feet inside the tree line so that they were hidden in the darkness but with their view unobscured.

"Not to be a Debbie Downer, Cap," McGinn said, binoculars raised once more. "But you're sure this is the place? I was picturing something a little... well, bigger."

Harry gazed beyond the guardhouse and the fence to the building a quarter mile beyond. The structure around which the large square of fencing was built looked almost exceptionally nondescript. It was made of unpainted concrete blocks, stood two stories tall, and was at most a couple of hundred metres long. Windows were spaced evenly along both floors, but none were open, nor was there a light or any other sign of life visible.

"I know what you mean," Harry said, still scanning the

structure. He paused at the roof. "Four satellite dishes," he murmured. "Seems a little excessive, for such a small building. No telephone poles."

"No electric wires either. I guess they must be…"

"Underground," Harry finished for him, nodding. "This building is a shell. A diversion. The real action's going on beneath the surface."

"But that bloody offence to architecture is the only way to get down there. The only way we'll find today, at least."

"Agreed."

There was a soft vibrating sound and McGinn took his phone from his pocket. He frowned as he looked at the screen, then showed Harry a series of letters and numbers which appeared entirely random. To the casual observer it would look like simple spam, or a message which had been inadvertently scrambled.

"I was never any good at this mad code, Cap."

Harry shook his head, having spent many an hour trying to drill it into his friend's memory, but couldn't help the smile spreading across his face regardless.

"They just touched down," he said. "And they have a contact in Delhi who sounds a damn sight better than ours was."

"Theirs will get them a car with air conditioning?"

"That and a whole lot more, if we're lucky."

Harry and McGinn spent the next six hours in the same spot. Doing so came harder to Harry than it used to, but gradually his training and practice came back to him and his discipline returned along with them. As a marksman, such stillness had been McGinn's bread and butter for many years, and Harry barely heard him move a muscle.

Each kept their eyes trained on the building and its surroundings, only occasionally raising their binoculars when there was movement. People and occasional vehicles came and went as together they built a picture of the building's security: the numbers, equipment, and patterns of the guards; the surveillance that they saw, and that which was undoubtedly there even if it wasn't visible.

The light began to dim as the sun dropped beneath the forested hill behind them. The mountain to their left became painted in soft orange.

When the light was mostly gone Harry and McGinn finally stood and headed towards the hills on their right. They dashed across the road when they were confident nobody was looking then moved along the far side of the nearest hill where they would be blocked from view. They continued until they believed themselves roughly level with the building then climbed to the top of the ridge, dropped, and crawled to the edge.

They found themselves just behind the building and saw another guard stationed on that side. He sat on a chair tilted back against the wall, smoking a cigarette as he looked out at the other, equally empty stretch of fenced-off area. Both men scanned the guard, then the building itself.

"Well," McGinn said. "Turns out that wee door at the front is the only way in or out of the place. He looked across at Harry, and grinned. "Sounds like a nice little challenge, eh?"

Harry had to force his own smile. He had hoped that being out in the field would settle him. Instead he felt nothing but nerves, at a pitch which he couldn't remember from his army days.

While a part of his mind still analysed and processed and planned automatically, another, larger part thought only of what could go wrong: that they had the wrong place; that the others would never come, or, when they did, that they would betray he and McGinn. He feared ultimately that they would fail, and if they did then Daniel and Noy, Anna and Granville, and his own mother would fall with them.

"You all right, Cap?"

Harry didn't look at his friend. He only gave a short nod then settled in to observe that side of the building. McGinn looked at him a moment longer, then did the same.

When dusk fell they returned to the trees. They waited another hour before McGinn's phone buzzed again. "I *think* this means they're here."

Harry looked at the code and felt another wave of apprehension. "Send our coordinates."

Ten minutes passed. Then they heard the sounds of heavy footsteps approaching behind, and turned. From the moonlight coming through the thick branches above they saw the shapes of two men jogging down the slope. Harry and McGinn moved away from the tree line and towards them, Harry's heart beating quickly.

"Jesus Christ," McGinn said, as the pair drew close. "They could hear you two coming back in Delhi."

"You try stealthing your way through a bloody forest carrying all this lot in the dark," Cooper said, and dumped the enormous duffel bag he'd been carrying to the ground.

"Stealth's my middle name, lad. Or have you forgotten?"

"Anyone can be 'stealthy' when all they do is lie there half a mile away and look through a little scope." Cooper turned, and Harry found himself being analysed. He couldn't help but do the same, his eyes running over the faces that had once been so familiar. His old demolitions expert, Cooper, and his medic Davies looked back.

"You haven't changed a bit," Harry said to Cooper, holding out his hand.

"That's just the bad light, Cap," McGinn said. "He's half grey when you see him properly."

"Half grey's better than being completely ugly."

Harry turned to Davies and held out his hand again. Davies was the youngest of them and had always been the shyest. He looked down at the hand, paused momentarily, and went to shake it.

Harry shook his head. "What am I doing?" he asked. "We were at war together. Come here." He stepped forward and wrapped his arms around Davies. The younger man squeezed back and Harry felt him laughing.

"I missed you, Captain," Davies said as they pulled apart.

"We all did," Cooper said.

"Aww, look at him," McGinn said. "The big, bad demolitions expert, on the verge of tears because he didn't get a hug."

"The verge of tears? I'm about to start bawling my bloody eyes out. I'll alert every guard in a three mile radius if I don't get some love."

"I missed you all too," Harry said, stepping back from hugging Cooper. "More than you know. More than I realised myself."

"What've you been up to then, Cap?"

"Jesus Christ, come on," McGinn said. "We've got a job to do here. You can play chat show host after."

"Easy for you to say. You've been hanging out with him for days."

"And I knew better than to blunder on in with daft questions like 'what've you been up to in the past three years?'"

"It's fine," Harry said, smiling and squeezing McGinn's

shoulder. "The short answer is 'not enough' for almost exactly three years, then a hell of a lot since. We should have the full debrief afterwards, though. McGinn's right."

"Might be the first time anyone's said those two words."

"We only wanted you for the gear," McGinn said. "You and your crap patter can piss off again now while the grown ups do the work."

"Speaking of which," Harry said, squatting down to the bags and the others copying him. "Did you get everything?"

"Get everything? We brought enough presents to cover all your Christmases and birthdays for the last three years, Cap. And we're going to have a proper party to celebrate too."

"Or die trying," Davies added.

"Do you have to lower the mood? I swear, doctors are more obsessed with death than soldiers."

"Not a doctor, just a medic," Davies said. "For the five thousandth time."

"How much did you tell them?" McGinn asked.

"Just enough. The location, the objective, and that I needed them."

"Don't forget the million pound bonuses. In cash."

"Haven't we made enough in recent years, you greedy bastard?" McGinn said.

"Just a little joke, don't get your wee kilt in a twist."

"Oh, that's *very* funny. Can I strangle him now, Cap, and save those lads down there the trouble?"

CHAPTER THIRTY EIGHT

They opened the bags and the four of them geared up. It was nothing they hadn't worn or carried before and they prepared without issue in the dark.

The others were silent as Harry laid out the plan. Then, after testing their comms, he sent McGinn circling around towards the ridge overlooking the building while he and the others returned to the edge of the tree line.

Harry looked up as they went a metre or so into the open. Clouds were just starting to creep across the sky, some already outlined in silver. Soon they should obscure the moon completely and allow Harry, Cooper, and Davies to advance under the cover of darkness.

Harry raised the powerful monocular scope Cooper and Davies had brought and saw the scene slightly distorted and painted in pale green. He adjusted the lens and brought the two lookouts currently manning the guardhouse into focus. They didn't appear to have night vision equipment with them. But from within the guardhouse they had brought out and set up a tall light which powerfully illuminated the area around them.

Focusing on the light with the scope burned Harry's eye, and he looked past it quickly and to the building itself. Another guard was stationed there near to a bare bulb over the door.

Harry had just passed the scope to Davies when they heard McGinn's voice over their earpieces. "In position, Cap."

"Copy. Any other guards?"

"Negative. Only the three out front."

"Perfect."

As he checked on the clouds and saw to his satisfaction that they were already half-covering the moon, Harry realised that all of his apprehension had dissipated without him noticing. In its place there was the old, near forgotten but now familiar cocktail of excitement and fear, the trust in the team he led and the pleasure in their company, and the anticipation of violence.

"We go when the moon's covered," Harry said. "Wait on my order."

"Copy."

Harry checked the magazine on his rifle then loosened and re-tightened the silencer. He heard Davies doing the same while Cooper, having just checked his larger rifle, took his turn with the scope.

"Child's play," Cooper said quietly. "You've lost your ambition, Captain. You could've done this on your own with your eyes closed a few years ago."

"This part, yes. I'm guessing the actual challenge will come once we're inside."

"I hope so."

Harry realised that he did too. Since leaving the army he had tormented himself endlessly with questioning and analysing his past actions and the violence he'd committed. Led in large part by Anna, he had begun to look at it all differently since the kidnapping in Slovenia. Now, with the prospect of combat mere moments away, he found he couldn't wait to get started.

He looked up once more, impatiently. "All set," he said. "We're moving out in three, two, one-"

"Hold it, Cap."

Harry had just started to raise himself from his crouching position and it was all he could do to stifle a groan. Cooper, who had already jogged a few paces, made no such effort. "What is it?" Harry asked.

"Vehicle coming in along the road. Sorry to burst your bubble, but I thought you'd want to know."

Harry and the others went completely still, and listened. The unmistakable noise of a large engine became quickly clearer.

"Can you see it?"

"Not quite. One second." McGinn swore under his breath. "Back of the truck's covered, but it could well be personnel in there. Truck's old Indian army issue. Might've brought in backup. You don't think…"

"Could be that things have gone badly in Hong Kong, yes. Or we've just gotten extremely unlucky."

"Or that psychopath genius figured out the plan."

Harry saw the lights of the vehicle hitting the nearest part of the gap in the hills to their right, then the truck itself came into view. The three of them back in the trees now, the truck rumbled past along the road before stopping at the guardhouse up ahead. Cooper passed Harry the scope automatically, and he watched as one of the guards went to the driver-side door. Harry looked to the open rear of the truck, and swore.

"You were right, McGinn," he said. "I see at least six men in the back. No, eight. Plus the driver."

"One more in the passenger seat. Ten in total. How do you want to play it?"

Harry barely paused. "We take them now."

"Yes," Cooper whispered.

"You sure, Cap?"

"We have to do it at some point. Better here in the open where we can surprise them than at close quarters down below, especially once the alarm's been raised."

"We'll raise the alarm anyway, with this."

"Then we'll have to go even faster."

Harry glanced to his left and right. Cooper nodded at him, grinning. Davies looked down for a moment, then back at him before he nodded too.

"McGinn, keep eyes on them. We're moving up. Go."

Harry pushed himself up and this time broke completely out of cover. He jogged across the flat ground with his rifle held in front of him and heard Cooper and Davies following. The darkness covered their advance completely, but looking up Harry saw the slow clouds already drifting by the moon and a patch of open sky just behind. He estimated they had at most two minutes before the moonlight caught them.

He slowed when they closed to within six hundred metres. Lifting the scope to his eye he saw that the gate had been opened and the last of the new arrivals was jumping down from the truck. The driver had climbed back into the cab, and began to reverse and turn.

"The driver could be going for more men," Harry said quietly. "McGinn, have you got a shot?"

"One sec... Yeah, easy. Poor lad left the window down. Ready when you are."

Harry stopped at around four hundred metres and sank down onto one knee. He would have liked to get closer, but the driver was about to complete his turn and pull away. He would have liked night vision too, but Cooper and Davies had been unable to procure goggles. They would need to rely instead on their targets remaining roughly within the glare of the tall light by the guardhouse.

"I see ten in total near the gate. Confirm?"

"Copy," McGinn said. "Plus that one by the main building, a quarter mile ahead."

"Driver first, then the guard by the building before he figures out he should go inside. Keep an eye on the one at the rear too - he'll come to help out. I'll take the man in the passenger seat and we'll split the others as best we can."

"Sounds like a plan, Cap."

The truck had turned and was starting to head back towards them. They would be caught in its headlights within moments.

"Three. Two. One," Harry said, as he took aim down the scope of his rifle. "Go."

The cracking sound cut through the air and the truck veered sharply to its right and off the road, straight across where Harry was aiming.

Harry had tapped the trigger immediately after hearing McGinn's rifle, his bullets bursting through the windscreen, and he heard the muffled sounds of Cooper and Davies' rifles too. He swore as his scope was suddenly filled by the dark bulk of the truck which rumbled on driverless, and stood up to move to his right, tapping Davies' shoulder and knowing instinctively that he would alert Cooper too to follow in turn. Sure enough he heard Cooper letting off a couple more shots before his footfalls came crunching after those of Harry and Davies.

A moment later there was another crack as McGinn fired upon the guard next to the building. Moving around the side of the truck Harry saw that the seven remaining men were not facing in Harry's direction, although they were not panicking at the sudden attack either. Rather, one man seemed to have taken charge and was shouting orders as he and the others moved quickly towards the building in a line, all with their weapons raised and firing towards the ridge.

McGinn's voice came in over the earpiece, notably louder and less calm than usual. "I'm pinned down here, Cap."

"Copy. Hold on."

Clear of the truck now, Harry went back to one knee, took aim quickly at the rearmost of the retreating men, and tapped the trigger twice. The man fell straight forward, his momentum carrying him into the heels of the next man and sending him stumbling.

The latter called out and he and a couple of the others who had been facing McGinn turned back. One immediately fell dead to Davies' bullet while Cooper sent another spinning. McGinn's rifle rang out again and the man who had been shouting orders collapsed.

The last three men had abandoned all hope of fighting and were now sprinting for the building. Each of them died before they had made it ten metres.

"Push," Harry said, straightening up and sprinting now across the ground. "McGinn," he said, in between breaths. "Keep watching... the road... Assume reinforcements... incoming."

"Will do, Cap. I'll reposition a little further back. Should be able to see any lights coming from a good mile away there. No sign of the lad at the back of the building, by the way."

Harry and the others slowed as they reached the gate. He went into the guardhouse while Cooper and Davies checked the men there were dead. There were live feeds from CCTV cameras facing either way along the road outside. Beside the keyboard and mouse was a red button. A red light flashed beside it.

"Come on," Harry said, and swerved around the bodies as he ran out of the guardhouse and along the road.

They reached the main building ninety seconds or so later, which looked no more impressive up close than it had further away. Hundreds of bugs swarmed around the bare bulb above the door. Harry waved them away uselessly with his rifle and pushed buttons on a nine digit keypad by the door with his free hand, entering a code he and McGinn had seen a guard using earlier. The small LED above the numbers flashed red and Harry swore.

"Looks like we're doing this the old fashioned way."

"I was hoping you'd say that." Cooper came forward, passing his rifle to Harry and swinging his backpack around to withdraw a small package. He placed it over the keypad and fiddled with it then nodded to Harry, took his gun back, and withdrew.

"McGinn," Harry said quietly.

"Here, Cap."

"We'll be going underground, and we'll lose comms. If reinforcements come, do *not* engage. I can't give you orders any more, but I can tell you you'd be throwing your life away if you did. You won't be able to warn us, and you won't be able to take them all yourself."

"That *would* be stupid, even for you," Cooper said.

"Are you listening?"

"I'm listening, Cap. Let's just hope it doesn't come to that, eh?"

Harry looked at the others, who both shrugged at him. He moved to one side of the door, a couple of feet back, with Davies and Cooper on the other side. Harry held up three fingers on his left hand towards Cooper, then two, then one. There was a soft thud and the door opened a few inches.

CHAPTER THIRTY NINE

Harry poked his gun against the metal surface to open the door further, and found himself looking down a long hallway with bare concrete walls.

Corridors led off to either side of the entrance and he swept his aim quickly from left to right, seeing only a few closed doors in each direction. Though he saw nobody along the main hallway either he still took cover at the corner to the right and kept his gun facing forward as he waited for the others to enter.

Davies came first, also looking left before hugging the corner on that side. Cooper went behind Harry and tapped him on the shoulder. Harry started to advance slowly along the hallway with his rifle raised and Davies right behind him. Harry didn't need to look back to know that Cooper would be covering their rear, Davies guiding him with a hand on his shoulder.

The building wasn't particularly deep and the main hallway only ran for around fifty metres. There was an alcove halfway along and as they reached it Harry saw a large lift there.

He had just begun to study the small, black panel beside the steel door when there was a slight scuffing sound up ahead. It was the only warning Harry and the others had before a rifle opened up from the far end of the corridor, the sudden rapid cracking sounds amplified as they echoed off the hard walls.

All three of them had reacted immediately, knowing full well what the first sound had meant, and taken cover before the firing began. The bullets had followed them and now ripped in bursts into the concrete corner of the alcove.

Cooper was the closest to the edge. He stood a foot or less from the turning, ready. Harry knew he was waiting for the gunman's magazine to run out; for that short, deadly opportune moment in which a non-elite operative ran empty without realising he was about to and took a split second too long to get back into cover.

The firing stopped and Cooper moved out of cover. At precisely the same moment there was a ringing sound to Harry's other side and he heard the lift doors beginning to slide open.

Even as he heard Cooper firing Harry turned towards the lift with his rifle raised and immediately began to back away lest he and the others be caught completely exposed by whoever was inside.

"Back!" he shouted, the command directed at Cooper even though he still faced away from him. He knew Cooper would understand, knew he would obey and be moving away too so that they didn't collide even as he continued looking along the hallway towards his target.

The first man tried to exit the lift, already firing. Harry and Davies were in no man's land and it was pure luck that saved them, the man's bullets passing audibly close on Harry's right to strike the wall on the far side of the hallway while he and Davies fired a moment later, the twin bursts catching the man in different parts of his torso. Harry aimed past him at the only other man he could see, who had been about to follow his comrade out but had now made the fatal mistake of pausing, and Harry's shot took him in the forehead.

By their shouts Harry could hear at least two more men inside. The interior of the cargo lift was much wider than its doors and the men had taken cover in the space to the left. The doors themselves began to close, but stopped as they squeezed the first body before opening again automatically.

Harry and Davies managed to get around the corner back into the main hallway before the two other men could emerge. Harry finally took a moment to glance back in the direction of the initial attack which had caught them unawares.

"Did you get him?"

"Did I get him?" Cooper muttered. "I'm almost insulted, Captain."

Harry could hear the two men talking hurriedly inside the lift, although he didn't understand their language. Their meaning became swiftly clear, however, when he heard the subsequent noises.

"They're shifting the body," he said. "Going back down. Grenade, Cooper."

Cooper nodded and came to stand nearest the corner, moving his gun to one side and unclipping a frag grenade from his belt. He pulled the pin, waited two seconds exactly, then moved out and threw it before withdrawing into cover. There was a shout, then a thud, then silence.

Harry swallowed when he saw the interior of the lift, and knew immediately it would be added to the long litany of images that haunted his dreams were he to survive the night.

He made himself look away and to the lift's controls. There were only two buttons, G and -1, and a black panel beside them identical to the one just outside. He removed the glove from his right hand and tried pressing it against the panel. A thin red strip of light appeared around the edges. He bent down to the body which had been blocking the doors, grabbed it by the wrist, and lifted upwards with a grunt. Davies pushed the man's thumb against the panel and this time the light was green. Davies pressed the -1 button, the doors slid shut, and the lift began humming downwards.

All three of them reloaded. "I'm guessing they know we're here now," Cooper said, as he clicked the new magazine into place.

"The chances seem pretty high." Harry looked to Davies. "Everything okay?"

"I haven't seen much combat recently. That's all."

"By choice?"

"Yes."

"I wouldn't have been able to tell."

Davies forced a quick smile. He looked pale. Harry nodded, feeling a short burst of guilt in his stomach. He forced it aside, as he'd long ago learned to do with any and all feelings which might affect his performance, and instead found his focus once more.

The lift slowed. Harry took a position to the right of the doors with Cooper and Davies to the left. The descent came to a smooth halt, they heard the same ringing sound again, and the doors slid slowly open.

They arrived into what seemed like a reception area. The brightly-lit space was square and spacious with smooth stone walls and tall ceilings. A long desk occupied much of the far wall, above and behind which a large sign read 'MUST SUBMIT TO SECURITY SEARCH BEFORE LEAVING PREMISES in English, with the Hindi just below.

The three of them had been primed for contact the moment the doors opened. What they found instead was utter stillness, and silence but for a steady electric hum in the background.

"Careful," Harry muttered, and moved around the edge of the lift and out. The others spread to form a horizontal line, all three of them scanning back and forth as they advanced step by step.

They reached the security desk. It was made of smooth, spotless black acrylic and was empty but for two computers, both of which buzzed gently. Davies slowly made his way around one edge of the desk, took the glove from his right hand, and touched the seat in front of the computer. "Still warm."

Harry nodded and waited for him to return. They stood completely motionless, listening. Wide hallways began on both sides of the desk, each starting in the side walls before abruptly turning ninety degrees to head away from the lift. The turnings made it impossible to see down either.

"Left or right?" Harry whispered.

"Right," Cooper said.

"Left," Davies replied, a split second later.

"Be my guest. We'll meet you further on,"

Harry rolled his eyes and went left, raising his weapon once more and placing his finger delicately on the trigger. His footsteps were precise and silent.

Looking up, he noticed one of the smallest surveillance cameras he'd ever seen, with no telltale light to give it away, affixed in the top corner of the turning there with a perfect view of the desk and the three intruders.

The others followed his eyes, then they stopped too. "Ah," said Cooper.

The next moment they heard the sound of a small, light object bouncing towards them down the hallway. "Back!" Harry shouted, and the three of them scrambled away towards the desk and behind it just as the grenade detonated. It was followed a second later by another explosion, identical but this time unexpected, the second grenade's arrival from the opposite corridor having been masked by the shouting then the boom of the first.

Harry had hidden behind the desk just in time. The sharp bang still made his left ear ring, and he felt the desk shaking with the impact before a shower of debris rained down over them. Harry ignored the ringing and the dust, knowing that now would be the perfect time to strike them and seeing, sure enough, the first man coming around the corner to the right.

Harry had the drop on that man, who required a moment to find and aim at him. Though he held his gun awkwardly crouched behind the desk, he still got two shots off which struck the man in his exposed neck just above his bulletproof vest. The man fell, dropping his gun and hands reaching for his throat, and other hands reached around the corner to drag him back and out of sight. Harry heard both Cooper and Davies firing in the other direction but his eyes stayed fixed on the nearer hallway.

Another man attempted to come around the corner, this one firing wildly in Harry's direction. Harry remained in place and squeezed off several shots which sent the man back behind cover. The man tried again and again Harry sent him back even as his mind raced to find a solution. They were in a terrible position. They could control the ways in for now but would easily be overwhelmed if and when their attackers decided to take the risk of a final, decisive push.

"We have to move," Harry called, without turning. "How many grenades have you got?"

"One smoke, one flash," Cooper replied.

"Give me the smoke." Holding his rifle with one hand, Harry reached behind with the other and felt the cylindrical metallic object pushed into it. He rested it on the floor in front of him and just returned his second hand to his rifle in time to aim and fire and repel another push.

"Ready with the flash?"

"Ready."

Harry put several more shots into the pockmarked concrete of the corner, then quickly put his rifle on the ground, took up the grenade, primed it, and threw it into the hallway. There was a quiet popping sound then a hissing as smoke began to billow out, thick enough that no highly trained soldier, as their attackers seemed to be, would run through it and into gunfire.

"Now," Harry said, still watching the smoke until he heard the pin being pulled behind him and the grenade bouncing into the opposite corridor. Harry was already up with the first sound. He heard shouting in Hindi as he moved past Cooper then Davies, both of whom stood to follow him. The grenade detonated with another thud and bright white flashed against the section of the wall he could see.

The next moment Harry was rounding the corner. There were four men there. Three had run away a short distance and turned, covering their eyes and heads too, when they saw the grenade. The closest to the corner had not reacted in time and was doubled over, rifle held loosely in one hand and the other covering his eyes.

Pity threatened to sway Harry's judgement before clashing with the old teaching that this man would certainly kill him in the same situation. He had no time for moral quandaries, and without breaking stride hit the man in the head with the butt of his rifle, hard enough to knock him unconscious but not so hard, perhaps, as to kill him.

Davies and Cooper were already firing past him, and Harry saw two of the men up ahead falling as they ran. The final man was attempting to reach another hallway which split off to the right of the main one. Harry hit him in the shoulder just as he was turning and the man's momentum sent him spinning into the far wall. He attempted to raise his weapon anyway with a defiant yell, but both the effort and the shout ceased abruptly as Harry put a bullet through his forehead.

Harry glanced down the side corridor down which the fourth man had tried to escape as they passed. He didn't know specifically what he was looking for, but this corridor was short and the doors innocuous. He shook his head and jogged onwards towards a turning to the left up ahead. A quick burst of shots from behind, from the other team no longer delayed by the smoke grenade, made he and the others hurry to avoid being caught out in the open.

As he rounded the next corner Harry very nearly ran straight into a bullet. He had guessed already that this hallway would rejoin the parallel one from which they had been attacked in the reception area. He had not guessed, however, that any of their attackers would have doubled back in an attempt to flank them.

The man who had done so was young and his eyes opened wide as Harry came into view. His weapon was not fully raised, and the second it took to do so gave Harry time to stop his momentum as best he could and drop backwards to the ground.

He heard the bullets whizzing by above his head and attempted to raise his own weapon but the young man was already lowering his aim. Twin bursts from Cooper and Davies took him in the neck and head and sent him down, lifeless, a moment later.

They heard three voices following along the corridor from which they'd just emerged, calling to each other. Another, wider hallway led onwards from where the two side corridors rejoined. Harry motioned to Cooper and Davies to hide along it just out of sight. "Wait until they're all around the corner," he said quietly, reloading his rifle as he talked. "And leave whoever's at the back alive."

They nodded, and Harry went around the corner of the clear side corridor. The voices came closer accompanied by the sound of heavy footsteps. He waited until all three of the men seemed to have arrived, then shouted "Now!" as he leaned out from cover, crouching below where they would expect him to be.

The leading man fell to his bullets while Cooper took the one nearest him. The man at the back attempted to arrest his momentum, as Harry had done a few moments before, and get back around the corner. Harry quickly aimed and shot him in the right leg and the man tripped and fell, shouting.

Cooper was already coming forward, rifle pointed at the man as he tried to roll over and reach for the rifle he'd dropped. "*Leave it!*" he boomed. The man hesitated, then lay on his back and put both hands up.

Davies and Harry advanced. The man's face was contorted with pain and Davies looked to Harry. Harry nodded, and Davies laid down his rifle, removed his backpack and placed it next to the man, then knelt down and removed a bandage.

"How many more?" Harry asked.

The man let forth a tirade of fast, angry Hindi through his clenched teeth as Davies began wrapping the bandage around his lower leg.

"How many?" Harry asked again, interrupting him.

"No more," the man grunted.

Cooper gave Harry a disbelieving look. "Fine," Harry said. "We'll make this very simple. Show us the way through this place, and we won't kill you."

"I'll be killed anyway."

"At least this way you'll have a chance. We'll take you with us, then let you go after."

The man screwed his eyes shut and grunted as Davies tied the bandage tight before straightening up. Davies offered the man his hand. The man looked at him, then took it and struggled to his feet, wincing again as he tried to put weight on the injured leg. Davies took up his rifle in one hand then stooped a little so the man could put an arm around his shoulder.

The man looked around at the lifeless guards. "Why did you come here?" he asked Harry. "Why did you kill all these people?"

"Thousands more lives will be saved. You have no idea how much suffering the woman who runs this place is responsible for."

"You're right. I have no idea. I just get paid to keep this place safe." He said. "Same as all my friends," he added, waving his free hand back towards the bodies. "All you guys are... what? Special forces? Best of the best? You just decide to come here and kill a load of people who never had a chance?"

"We haven't got time for this," Cooper growled.

"I'm sorry about your friends. Really, I am. But we have to move. If you don't want to end up like them, you'll help us."

The man glared at Harry with undisguised hatred. Then, not taking his narrowed eyes off him, he nodded towards the main hallway. "This way."

The hallway ran for another twenty metres before reaching a pair of thick double doors. There was another fingerprint scanner in the wall to the right.

"You got an army waiting for us through there?" Cooper asked, nodding towards the doors.

"I wish. You want me to open it or not?"

The man limped to the scanner and pressed his thumb against it. The light around the edge went green and the doors slid back into the walls. The four of them entered what seemed to be another security checkpoint, although this one also appeared empty.

"We are coming to the main server room."

"*This* is?" asked Cooper.

"No, idiot. Through here."

The man put his thumb to another scanner and the second set of doors slid open. "Bloody hell," Cooper said as they took a few steps inside, and Davies turned to Harry with a quizzical look. Harry could only shrug his shoulders, as he turned his head from side to side.

"It's a bit bigger than I expected," he said.

CHAPTER FORTY

The room went on for at least fifty metres to the left and right and another fifty in front. The entire space was filled with row upon row of computer equipment, most of the black units two metres tall and dotted with green, blinking lights. The ceiling high above the large devices was lined with rows of powerful churning fans.

"What are these? Servers?" Cooper asked.

"Most of them look more like storage devices," Davies said. "But the size of them... The capacity on just one of those... And there must be hundreds of them. Captain," he said, turning to Harry. "What is this place?"

"A data centre," Harry said, frowning. "But there's a *hell* of a lot more data than I was expecting." He turned to the guard. "How can I access it?"

"Plug in a little USB stick. How should I know?"

Harry nodded to Cooper, who dug the butt of his rifle into the man's stomach. "We really don't have time," he said to the grunting man. "I'd prefer not to hurt you. So tell me, *please* - how can I access it?"

"There's a... control room," the guard wheezed. "I will show you, *bhosdike*." He spat on the ground at Harry's feet then straightened with a hand still pressed against his midriff, and with Davies supporting him again he led them to the right.

They cleared the end of that row and turned left, and Harry saw a rectangle of light falling across a gap in the rows of equipment ahead. They turned once more and saw the light came through a window dividing the main space from an office area. There were a dozen desks inside, each with a computer on top.

A woman was watching them. She wore glasses and looked to be in her early thirties. She stood completely still, her face expressionless, but the hand with which she grasped the edge of her desk was white with the strain.

There was another fingerprint scanner to the left of the door. "It won't work," the man said, as he was led over.

"Let's give it a shot anyway." Harry pressed the man's thumb against the scanner, and the light around the outside turned red.

"Breaking news, geniuses," the man said. "I am not the boss of this place. They don't give me access to everywhere."

Harry went back to the window. "Save us some time and open the door," he shouted to the woman. "We're getting in there anyway." Harry was unsure whether she could hear him or not, but either way she remained motionless. "Can you blow it?" he asked Cooper.

"I could give it a shot, but It's made of sterner stuff than the first door. I'm not sure I've got enough gear."

Harry turned back and brought the butt of his rifle smashing against the window. The woman jumped but he didn't even mark the surface. Harry sighed and turned to Davies. "Bring him over."

The man struggled as Davies forced him towards the window then pushed him up against it. Harry lowered his rifle, took his pistol from its holster, showed it to the woman, and flicked off the safety.

"This will be your fault," he shouted to her, and pointed the gun at the guard's head. The woman's eyes were wide and her face was as pale as her hands now. Harry lowered the gun quickly and fired a round into the floor. The sharp crack made the woman jump and the guard began to whimper. Harry raised the gun again and pressed it to the side of the man's head. "Three," he called. "Two. One."

"Wait!"

The woman's muffled voice was just audible through the partition. She stumbled a little as she pushed herself from the desk then walked unsteadily to the other side of the door. There was a moment's pause, then the scanner flashed green and the door clicked.

Cooper entered first, sweeping the room swiftly with his rifle raised before giving the all clear. Harry checked behind them then followed Davies inside with the guard.

"We don't want to kill you-" Harry started, before the woman interrupted him with a panicked, high pitched laugh.

"Oh no! Why would I possibly think that?!"

Harry followed her hand gesture towards the nearest screen, which displayed the building's internal surveillance feeds in a grid. Bodies were visible from almost every camera. The sight of it made Harry's chest momentarily cold. But he collected himself and turned back to the woman with a scowl.

"I'll accept judgement from him," Harry said, nodding towards the man who had lowered himself into a desk chair and was wincing as he ran his hand up and down his lower leg. "There's not a bloody chance I'm taking it from you. He's only guarding the place. Fine - this isn't his fight. But if you're working in *this* room, you know exactly what's going on here."

"I am a computer technician. I monitor the equipment, and-"

"This is a data storage facility. Can we agree on that?"

The woman glowered at him.

"For whom?"

"I just receive my paychecks. Very good ones. I don't-"

"What kind of data is being stored?"

"I don't know. I only monitor the equipm-"

Cooper laughed out loud, and Harry scoffed. "I can answer both questions for you, if you like," he said. "Maybe I'll just be jogging your memory. Your employer is the head of an international criminal organisation which specialises in people trafficking. It makes ungodly amounts of money each year kidnapping and exploiting thousands upon thousands of people. Along with plenty of other stuff, judging by the scale of it, the equipment you're 'monitoring' stores the evidence. And that's what we're here to collect. If you've got an ounce of morality inside you, you'll help us. We can even pretend you really didn't know any of that, if you like, and we'll let you go, along with your wounded friend, when we're done here."

"But they'll-"

"Kill you anyway? There won't be anyone to kill you after this. We're bringing down the whole thing. Take all the blood money they've given you, and go and do what you want with it."

The woman bit the ends of her fingernails as she stared at the ground. She looked up again, her dark eyes meeting Harry's. "What do you want me to do?"

Harry nodded to Davies, who removed his backpack and placed it on the desk neighbouring that at which the wounded man sat. He withdrew an external hard drive and brought it over. The woman looked at it. "We won't get very far with just this. What is it, a couple of terabytes? We have-"

"It's plenty for what we need. Get on with it." The woman went to use the computer showing the security feeds. "Not there. Use the next desk along. Cooper, you keep an eye on the cameras."

Harry went to stand behind the woman. She sat, woke the computer, and entered a lengthy and complex set of login details. She looked from the monitor back to Harry. "Now what?"

"We need proof. As much as we can get our hands on. Just as a reminder, the more proof we find, and the better it is, the higher your chances of survival as well as ours of success. Find what you *think* we might be looking for, and add as much of it as possible."

The woman stared at him for several long moments. "I really didn't know what this place was, when I started," she said. "By the time I found out, it was too late. They had their power over me."

"I know the feeling."

She turned back to the screen. "Very well," she said, and went to work.

The woman brought up the computer's file management program and began diving down through folders and subfolders. All had been given either obscure names or were identified only by letters and numbers, but the woman seemingly knew them by heart along with exactly what each folder contained.

She appeared content to play the game Harry had outlined, presumably seeking out exactly what he'd requested since she didn't request any further direction. She simply shot towards certain folders, scanned their contents, then copied specific files or the folder in its entirety across to the external hard drive.

After a few minutes Harry went to stand beside Cooper and Davies, both of whom were watching the surveillance feeds.

"Anything?" he asked, positioning himself so that he still had a clear view of the woman.

"Not yet. Only a matter of time though, isn't it?"

"Reinforcements will come, but I doubt they had anyone particularly close, and it's a tough area to drive through quickly. We should be gone before they arrive."

"Captain," Davies murmured, leaning closer. "That stuff you said to her…"

"All true. I'll tell you as much or as little as you want to know, but not yet. Let's stay focused for now."

Harry went back to the woman with his rifle held loosely in his hands. She continued clicking and typing, flying between folders and transferring documents by the hundred. Despite knowing it was foolish, since this was the whole reason they had come, Harry felt an illogical frustration building as the minutes passed by. He had not anticipated the tension he would feel between getting as many documents as possible, and not staying so long that they would all be killed.

"How much longer do you need?" he finally asked.

"As long as you like. You already have several thousand documents."

"Show me."

"What would you like to see?"

Harry considered. "Banking transactions. Show me the money being laundered."

The woman swapped to the window showing the data on the hard drive, went down through a couple of folders, and coughed into her hand. "I… believe this may show what you're looking for," she said, clicking once more to bring up a document.

Harry leaned closer. Fifty million pounds had been paid from one private account to another. The former was with a bank based in Hong Kong. The latter was registered in London. "I'm taking a wild guess that this transaction wouldn't have been registered with the financial authorities? That it wasn't declared for tax?"

"That would be my guess. Not that I'd know."

"Are there many like this?"

"Hundreds."

Harry nodded, fighting down a feeling of growing excitement to maintain his focus. "I'm assuming the second account here is under a fake name, or belongs to a middle man at best. Are there any transactions involving… people whose name I might recognise?"

"Oh, not for this much money."

"I'd hope not. Let's try, oh I don't know, the Prime Minister of the United Kingdom, for example."

The woman's hands hovered over the keyboard. She shook her head, as if to herself. Then she ran a quick search and opened a file. Harry saw the name John Haynes near the top of the document. "It's definitely him?"

"In all likelihood," the woman said carefully, and Harry rolled his eyes. "I would guess it's not his main account. But it could be traced to him. Probably."

"Only half a million pounds. The PM needs to negotiate harder for himself."

"There are at least a dozen other documents with transactions to this account."

"It all adds up, I suppose. Who else along these lines has money been sent to?"

The woman opened a series of similar documents. Most of the larger payments originated in Hong Kong. The accounts they went to were spread across the western world, though concentrated in the UK and USA. Lord Frost's name appeared several times, his payments larger than those the Prime Minister had received. There were other names Harry vaguely recognised too, of politicians and business leaders.

"Brilliant," he said eventually, and almost clapped the woman on the shoulder before catching himself. "I need proof of the operational side of things too, though. Of the actual people trafficking. Dan- Someone else mentioned that the bookkeeping at ground level was meticulous for the Organisation. A way for the middle managers and the higher ups to ensure they were all getting their full reward. I'd assume it's the same for the Company. I know somebody else who was kidnapped for trafficking. She said it was standard practice for the traffickers to ensure they knew the names and other details for all their victims. Helped stop them trying to escape, for fear of reprisal against their families."

"I've never heard of this… Organisation. Or this Company."

"Of course not."

"But I think I know what you're looking for."

The woman searched again through the files she'd copied over. She found and opened a specific one. The document ran to some two dozen pages and each was filled with names.

The names were Southeast Asian this time, not western. Below each was an address and date of birth, and in most cases a short list of other people sharing the same surname. At the end of each person's subsection was an emboldened line of text. Some were tagged SALE and had a price in dollars. Others were labelled LABOUR, with an industry - Sex, Factory, Fishing, Hospitality - beside them.

"I take it this is just one minor operation. Out in the Philippines, it looks like?"

"It seems so."

"And this is, what? A year's worth?"

"It appears to be a monthly record."

Harry noticed how quiet the room was. Looking back, he saw Cooper and Davies watching and listening. "You don't need to be involved past today, don't worry," he said. "And as I told our newfound friend, there won't be anybody to come after us, for any of this."

Cooper and Davies looked at each other then back at him. "We're not scared of any reprisals, Captain," Cooper said. "We're wishing you'd brought us on earlier."

Harry smiled and felt a warmth in his stomach. He turned back to the woman. "It's exactly what I was looking for," he said. "There's more of it?"

"Plenty."

"I'll have to take your word for it. The files you've copied over - when they are released, and analysed by others... will it all be enough? Enough to take down the Company, and anyone who's had anything to do with it? Enough to prove the banks knew, and the governments too?"

The woman frowned, and tilted her head from side to side. "Yes..." she said. "But whoever runs this Company won't leave it there. I doubt that she... or he, appears on any of these documents. That would surely be a very important rule. That person would suffer in the short term, if these documents were made public, but would certainly rebuild."

"I'm hoping we won't need to worry about that."

The woman looked at him quizzically, then shrugged. "Very well."

"Captain."

Harry turned quickly at the note in Davies' voice and

found his former medic's eyes fixed on the screen displaying the surveillance feeds. "Reinforcements already?" he asked, coming around the desk.

"For us, apparently," Cooper said.

Davies pointed at a feed in the top right corner which showed a man running as fast as he could while still carrying an especially long rifle. Even from a distance and with the somewhat grainy picture Harry recognised McGinn immediately. The camera, which Harry hadn't noticed during their earlier stakeout, was positioned somewhere near the roof of the building and looked back across the stretch of land between the guardhouse and the data centre. McGinn was halfway across the distance and pushing hard.

"Maybe he got lonely," Cooper said.

"It's possible," Harry said. "It's also possible that he spotted reinforcements inbound, couldn't reach us down here on regular comms, and is now sprinting to save all our lives."

"Either way, we should probably go and say hello."

Davies went to help the wounded guard up, and Harry retrieved the hard drive and put it in his backpack. "Ready?" he asked the woman, who looked up at him hesitantly. "Feel free to take your chances here, if you'd prefer. They'll come eventually, whatever happens next, and you're welcome to try and convince them that-"

"Okay, that's enough, thank you," the woman said, and got abruptly to her feet. "I'm ready."

CHAPTER FORTY ONE

Harry checked the feeds once more and saw that McGinn had almost reached the building, although there was still no sign of anybody else outside. Then he flicked the safety off his rifle and led them back through the enormous, humming server room. The woman opened the pair of security doors and they went in a line down the corridors with Harry in front, Davies with the man and the woman in the middle, and Cooper bringing up the rear.

The woman cried out when she saw all of the bodies. Her cry was loud but unaffected. The vivacity of holes in flesh and blood on the floor was something which the surveillance feeds couldn't capture. Harry didn't turn, not wanting to see the look on her face nor the guard's. Like a coward he avoided looking at the bodies completely as he hurried them all quickly along.

They took the lift back to the ground floor. The heavy doors slid open to the sight of McGinn in cover at the corner in front and to their right, his pistol pointing straight at them and his sniper rifle hanging down in his left hand.

"Nice to see you too," Cooper said.

"Sorry." McGinn came forward, putting the pistol away and raising his rifle again. A harsh lightbulb over the lift made his forehead shine with sweat, and his breathing was heavy. "There are-"

"We guessed," Harry said. "How many?"

"Two trucks. Still at least two miles away when I saw them, and the road up here's a real bastard, but we don't have long."

Harry looked towards the main door without seeing it, his mind grasping instead for a plan that could get them all away to safety.

"Tough terrain for tracking," Cooper mused. "We could give it a go on foot."

"We won't get far with him," Davies said, tilting his head sideways at the man whose weight he bore on his shoulder.

"Please don't worry about me," the man said. "The sooner I get away from you crazy murderers, the better."

"Problem solved," Cooper said.

"Do you have combat training?" Davies asked the woman. "Survival training?"

"What do you think?"

"Just asking," he muttered. "We can't leave her, Captain."

"Well," Cooper said. "Let's not rule anything out."

"Too many of them," Harry said. "They'd surround us eventually. The reinforcements might have better gear than the first lot too. Night vision. Infrared." He stared at the ground. "We have to take the truck," he said. "The first one."

"We shot it up pretty good, Captain."

"The cab, but not the engine. It'll run." He nodded, looking up now. "It's our best shot. Trust me." He met the eyes of Cooper, Davies, and McGinn in turn. After the briefest of pauses, each nodded at him.

Harry led them along the final hallway. McGinn had pushed the door closed, although with the area around its handle destroyed by Cooper's explosives it had already opened again a couple of inches.

All Harry could see through the gap was a pool of bright light from the bulb above the door, then blackness. He set up on the side of the door nearest the gap, the others falling into line behind him except for the guard. The young man had pushed himself off Davies' shoulder and now stood in front of Harry, swaying slightly.

"I'm really free to go?"

"Yes. But I'd advise-"

"You won't shoot me in the back of the head?"

"I promise."

"Like that means anything," the guard murmured, and didn't take his eyes off Harry as he limped to the door, grasped for the edge, and pulled it open.

He had taken one step outside when there was a cracking sound from far away in the night. A brief moment passed before the back of the man's head exploded. He crumpled backwards and downwards, coming to rest in front of the door with his eyes half closed.

Harry swore, and he wasn't the only one. "Just what we bloody need," Cooper hissed. "Where did you say the other exit was?"

"At the back," Harry said. "But we've got no chance in that direction. There's no cover at all, before or after the fence."

"Any… I don't know, secret passages out of here?" Cooper asked the woman.

"Secret passages. Flying carpets. I can provide you with a lot of magical options for escape."

"I preferred you when you were fearing for your life."

Harry looked at McGinn. The Scot was scratching at his beard thoughtfully, and met his gaze. "Can you see the light switches?" he said.

"Here?" Harry looked around. "No. I assume they're controlled from one of these rooms."

"Just shoot the bulbs for me, then."

"You're not thinking about-"

"I'm not thinking about it, Cap, no. I'm going to bloody well do it. Now get the lights." McGinn winked. "Please."

Harry shook his head but took his pistol anyway, leant away from the wall a little, and destroyed the light bulbs outside the main door, inside it, and away down the corridor in turn, the woman jumping with every shot. Clouds had covered the moon outside once more and they were left in complete darkness.

"I'll need one of you to-"

McGinn broke off as there was another cracking sound. It was followed this time by the sound of a bullet striking the ground a few feet beyond the body.

"How rude. As I was saying, I'll need one of you to go out of the back door and around a little way. Just show your face for a moment, then get away again. I hate to ask it from you, but I need to see the flash of his gun. It's the only way-"

"I'll go," Cooper and Davies both said concurrently.

"Count of three?" Cooper said.

"Fine."

There were three rustling sounds.

"What did you go for?"

"Paper."

"Ha!" Cooper said. "Right, I just run out there, show my pretty face, he tries to kill me, and you blow his brains out. Easy."

"Run a quick comms check," McGinn said.

Cooper did so. It didn't work. "Some signaller you are."

"Who brought this crappy equipment along in the first place?"

"If you'd given me more than a day's notice, maybe I could have-"

"Just shut up a second," McGinn said. "We'll do it the old fashioned way. From the moment you go, we'll give it forty five seconds before you leave cover."

"Got it."

There was another distant crack. They all heard the sound of the bullet hitting dead flesh by the door. "Hoping he'll get lucky," McGinn said. "Not a bad idea. At the very least, he keeps us pinned while his mates advance. Ready?"

"Always."

"Three, two, one. Go."

They heard Cooper standing up, placing his hand against the far wall, then guiding himself around the corner and away along the corridor. McGinn moved past Harry so that he was closest to the door.

They heard the sound of the back door being opened, then waited in near silence but for McGinn counting under his breath. Another bullet flew inside and hit the ground further along the corridor.

When twenty seconds had passed, Harry saw the vague outline of McGinn getting down onto his stomach then crawling sideways and into the open doorway.

There was a click as he lowered the stand near the barrel of his rifle, then another as he removed the safety. There were a series of quieter clicks as he adjusted the scope. Harry wouldn't have the faintest clue where to aim. But he guessed McGinn was adjusting it to roughly the range and area in which he instinctively knew the other sniper would be; to where *he* would be, if he was in the other, far superior position.

Harry calculated that thirty or thirty five seconds had passed. There was another cracking sound in the distance. It was followed by the same sound as before, of bullet striking flesh. There was a sharp intake of breath from McGinn. Then his friend let out a long hiss.

"McGinn-"

"Quiet," McGinn said, his teeth gritted.

Several more seconds passed. There was another cracking sound. McGinn began to shout as the second bullet hit him then stifled the sound into a grunt.

"Get back, you idiot! He knows you're there!" Harry shouted. But McGinn remained in place, although Harry could see and hear that he was breathing very quickly now.

Harry had stopped tracking the seconds. He heard the cracking sound again and his breath caught as he became sure that McGinn was dead.

But this time there was no sound of a bullet striking anywhere near them. The sniper had fired at Cooper instead.

He heard McGinn making a quick, slight turn on the ground, then a shorter series of clicks as the scope was adjusted, then the barrel of his rifle flared briefly with fire and the cracking sound was beside Harry this time, much louder and deeper so that he was momentarily deafened, and his ears kept ringing for several long seconds so that when silence descended again it too seemed deafening.

He hardly dared breathe, and remained completely motionless as he waited for the distant, answering shot. But it didn't come. He waited, and waited, and still it didn't come.

"Did you get him?" he whispered.

McGinn was in the same position on the ground, his eye still pressed against the scope.

"McGinn?"

"Shh," was the softly whispered response. "Wait."

They stayed that way for another ten seconds, fifteen, twenty. There were no more shots.

"McGinn?"

There was no response this time.

CHAPTER FORTY TWO

Harry ran as well as he could behind Cooper and Davies. He only had one hand spare to hold a pistol, and had given the woman his rifle to carry. His other arm was wrapped tight around McGinn who was slung over his shoulder.

He had said nothing, and Davies hadn't had time to inspect or help him. They could only run for the truck, get McGinn inside, and take him somewhere, anywhere that could help.

They were a couple of hundred metres from the guardhouse and could see the outline of the truck just beyond when the first pair of burning, bright lights appeared through the gap in the hills ahead, to be joined by another pair a few moments later.

Harry's legs were heavy, his shoulder hurt, his lungs burned, but he forced himself to run faster. His eyes were focused straight ahead on the truck. He knew the approaching lights were getting larger at an alarming rate, but ignored them. There was nothing he could do now, for either himself or McGinn, but run.

They were a hundred metres from the dormant truck now. The approaching vehicles were three hundred metres beyond, the low rumbles of their engines clearly audible. There was a flash from above one of the headlights and the first bullets landed comfortably wide of them. Cooper and Davies both raised their rifles to fire back.

"Don't... bother..." Harry panted. "Just get... to the truck...or we're dead... anyway. You two... push ahead."

They accelerated away with Cooper veering right towards the driver side door and Davies going the other way. The bullets from up ahead were landing much closer now, and it seemed the trucks themselves and all of their occupants would arrive only shortly after Harry and McGinn.

Cooper and Davies were just throwing the two bodies from the cab when Harry reached the truck. He had no time for delicacy, and could only grunt as he hauled McGinn up and into the open rear of the vehicle. He heard the front doors slamming then Cooper trying the engine.

The engine whirred, then died.

The woman threw the rifle inside then clambered up into the back of the truck after Harry, and he saw by the tall light near the guardhouse that her eyes were wide and wild. The roar of the nearest arriving truck was very close now and whoever was in the passenger seat fired again, the bullets striking the metallic side of the cab.

Cooper tried the engine once more. The engine sputtered and died.

"Come on, you old bastard," he said. He tried again. The engine whirred once more, and finally grumbled into life.

Cooper put the truck into gear and put his foot down immediately and Harry and the woman both lost their balance as the truck awkwardly jerked forwards, the woman falling straight backwards and almost out of the back before Harry grabbed her with his left hand and yanked her to momentary safety.

Cooper was pushing the engine for all it was worth, harder surely than it had ever been pushed before. Its low, mechanical protests were very loud directly beneath Harry but he still thought he could hear shouting over them to his left.

A spray of bullets ripped through the canvas on that side of the truck the next moment, and Harry was convinced that he was about to die. He was so certain of it that there was no fear, since there was no point fearing the inevitable, but his instinct for self preservation kicked in anyway and triggered those others honed through all the years of training and experience.

"Down!" he shouted, and pulled the woman to the ground after him as he dove for the floor of the truck. She fell with him as he pulled. By the way she fell he knew she was already dead.

A distant part of him knew that he had also been hit. Multiple times. But it didn't register. The shots had only felt like being hit by a tiny hammer. He only felt the floor of the truck, as he landed heavily upon it, as a larger impact. There was no pain, and no meaning. They had travelled all the way here and fought through and gotten the information they needed, which could have helped so many people, and now they were all dead anyway and that was the end of it.

The bullets moved down the truck as they drove past the first group of reinforcements. Then Cooper jerked the wheel firmly to the left and accelerated still faster as he yelled *"Brace!"*, and a moment later Harry, McGinn and the woman's body were all thrown forward as they forcefully struck the right hand rear corner of the second truck.

Harry realised he had hit his head in the collision on one of the wooden benches to either side. There was still no pain, but his vision came and went. He heard shouting and several screams which must have come from the back of the other vehicle. Their own truck had built up so much momentum that it ploughed onwards, barely slowing, Cooper steering them roughly to the right again to get them back onto the road.

Harry reached around on the ground, found his rifle, lifted it in both hands, and tried to focus. He pushed himself up so that his back was against the partition between the rear and front of the truck and fired back towards the shadows and the noise and the flashes of gunfire. He heard and felt retaliatory impacts all around him.

He felt another bullet hitting him. This one struck him high in his left arm and the rifle fell as his hand opened instinctively. He shouted in frustration, taking his pistol from its holster in his good hand and firing stupidly and almost blindly back towards the dwindling chaos behind.

The chasing gunfire became less accurate, then less frequent too. The truck they had hit didn't, perhaps couldn't, move. The other was turning slowly in a wide circle, the burning headlights coming around to send the first traces of pain through his skull.

Harry closed his eyes, then found that he struggled to open them again. He tried, and tried. But the light was so bright and all of his energy, even that required to simply lift his eyelids, seemed suddenly to have deserted him.

He felt the grip on his right hand loosening too, and the pistol slipping, and he felt that his clothing was damp in several areas across his torso, but there was still no physical pain, only another kind of anguish which threatened to overwhelm him utterly, so that when darkness enveloped him he felt that it was almost welcome.

It was the physical pain which woke Harry. He realised it had been throbbing even in his unconsciousness, and a sudden burst of it finally stirred him from the blessing that had been nothingness. Somebody seemed to be shining a light through his closed eyelids, which made his head feel as if it might split apart.

"Hold still." Harry recognised Davies' muffled voice and felt the pain shooting down the length of his left arm. "There," Davies said, tying the bandage. The light mercifully moved away as Davies took the small torch he'd been holding between his teeth and flicked it off. "I've saved your life, for half an hour at least. You're welcome."

By the bumping and the sound of the engine Harry knew they were still in the truck. Childishly, he didn't want to open his eyes. When he finally did, he saw the open rear of the vehicle and the vague outlines of dark trees slowly passing by. The sky had cleared now, and the gap between the trees above was a silvery black. He was propped up once more against the partition between the rear and cab of the truck.

"What happened?"

"We guessed you were unconscious pretty quickly, so Cooper had to make the call. The truck he didn't smash into like a maniac was gaining on us. Cooper decided to confront them. Said he was the better shot, but really he just has the bigger gun."

"Confront them how?" Harry said, teeth gritted.

"It was quite smart, for him. Clearly he learnt something from watching you all those years. We slowed right down to a crawl, like we had engine trouble. If we'd stopped completely, they'd have known something was up. We swapped places, Cooper jumped out and hid in the trees along the side of the road. He was behind the other truck when it caught up, saw us, slowed down. He had a clear shot at the poor guys in the back. Fish in a barrel, you know. I stopped, jumped out, and got the two in the cab while they were getting down to go after Cooper. That was it."

"Where are we now?"

"Not a bloody clue, Captain. We didn't want to use GPS, just in case. We're going to stay on here and stop at the first proper town we get to."

"Too risky. We need to-"

"There's no debate," Davies said. It might have been the first time he had ever interrupted Harry. "You've been shot at least three times, and they're just the ones I can see. If we don't get you a transfusion soon, you'll die, and if blood loss doesn't get you then the infections from the wounds will. We'll have to find someone we can bribe not to ask questions or turn us in to the police, of course, but let's take it one step at a time."

Harry grimaced as another wave of pain washed over him. It was remarkable how he could be in a state of such constant pain, then suffer more seemingly at random. He didn't argue, and they bumped onwards along the road in silence for another minute.

Since waking Harry had either looked deliberately ahead or remained with his eyes closed, only occasionally glancing up at Davies. When looking forward he had seen in his peripheral vision that the two bodies were still there on the floor, but had avoided looking at them and at one in particular.

Harry felt a lump in his throat. He tried to talk and found he couldn't ask the question. Then he tried again and forced himself.

"McGinn's dead, isn't he?"

There was silence. Then Davies put his hand on Harry's lower leg, and squeezed.

"Bring him over. Please."

Davies paused, clearly not wanting to, then went slowly along the truck anyway. Harry heard him dragging something heavy. When Harry felt the body by his legs he pulled with his uninjured right arm so that the head lay in his lap.

"I want to see," he said. "Just... point your torch at the roof."

A circle of light appeared on the canvas above. Harry looked from it, to Davies' despondent face, to McGinn. It felt unreal, incorrect, for his friend's face to be so still, so devoid of animation and of life. It felt strange to think he would never again see the smile he had seen so many thousands of times before.

The whole right side of McGinn's face was covered in blood, which matted his beard too. His right ear and a large piece of his cheekbone were missing.

"First shot hit the side of his head and went straight through into his lower back," Davies said. "Tough bastard barely moved, did he?"

"No."

"Second bullet entered high up, near his throat, and carried on. No exit wound that I could see, but it must have torn up his internals. Heart, lungs maybe, I don't know. I didn't want to check."

"I don't want to know this," Harry said, his voice cracking.

"Yes, you do, Captain," Davies said. "Because what McGinn did is the most remarkable thing any of us has ever seen on a battlefield. He took the first bullet, and the second, and he stayed. The pain must have been immense. He would have known he was about to die. But he stayed right where he was, with his eye to the scope and his finger on the trigger. And even with all of that, and in the darkness, and with one flash of a rifle to aim at… he still didn't miss."

Harry squeezed his eyes shut and felt the warm tears running down his cheek, his right hand resting in McGinn's hair. He heard Davies searching for something on the ground a little further along the truck, then coming back.

"Open your eyes, Captain."

Harry obeyed the order and blinked several times to clear his vision. Davies was holding the torch in one hand and held the hard drive in the other.

"Is it-"

"It's fine. Completely fine. And if that crazy bastard hadn't done what he did, and that sniper had lived, we wouldn't have made it out of that building in the first place, never mind getting to the truck. If none of that had happened, this hard drive, and the data on it, never would have seen the light of day. And if what you said back at the facility is right, and the data on this disk really can stop all those things you talked about, then McGinn would have voluntarily given his life to get it out of there. He'd have agreed in an instant. No question. Especially..." Davies paused, and seemed to be smiling when he finished. "Especially if you were the one asking. He loved you. And if he had to die, he'd have wanted it to happen with you beside him, and for the best cause imaginable."

Harry knew that everything the man said was right. And perhaps later, if he didn't die and if the others succeeded in Hong Kong against all the odds, and if one day he had time to reflect, Davies' words would bring comfort. He knew, logically, that they were true.

But at that moment they brought no consolation, nor did the survival of the hard drive and the 'success' of their mission.

All Harry felt was emptiness. He had lost a brother, and one he had spent vastly more time with over the past decade than Daniel. Even if he hadn't seen McGinn for almost three years, the simple supposition that he lived - that Harry had not only the memories of him, but the possibility to see him again one day - had remained. Now that knowledge, and the comfort it had always brought, was gone.

The man had been his best friend, and Harry would never have another friend like him. Their shared history was irreplaceable. A sudden hole had opened in his life which, whatever happened next, could never be repaired.

Harry let out a long, ragged sigh as he ran his hand through

McGinn's hair, closed his eyes, and leant his head back against the partition.

CHAPTER FORTY THREE

Anna, Noy, and Daniel landed several hours after Harry and McGinn reached Delhi. The sky was already tinted orange as they descended high above Macao, crossed the enormous river estuary separating it from Hong Kong, then touched down at the latter's airport.

Their reserved seats had been spaced far apart on the flight, and the three of them remained apart as they disembarked and went through passport control then the arrivals area. They queued for the bus separately too, Anna getting on at least a minute before the others.

"Oh, come on," she said, as Daniel walked past her seat towards the middle of the bus without looking over. He stopped, and stared at her. "Sit down, you oaf. On the row in front, if you please. I've had more than enough of being squished alongside you in the back of that stupid Mercedes recently."

Daniel looked around, then back at her. The expression on his scarred face never seemed to change, but Anna got the sense he was unhappy with her.

Anna heard Noy's voice from somewhere behind Daniel. "Sit down, Farang, you're blocking everybody. You're a big guy, if you didn't notice."

Daniel sat on the seat in front and Noy dropped down beside Anna. "Thought flying was supposed to be fun. Most boring thing in the world. And my back hurt." Noy rubbed the offending part of her body and looked between Anna and Daniel. "What you do to him?"

"I blew his cover."

"We weren't supposed to be in contact until it was necessary."

Anna snorted and waved her hand. "Going through immigration and arrivals, that's fine. I get it. But do you really think they put a lookout on every single bus that leaves here?"

"Seem unlikely to me," Noy said.

"Very unlikely. And Noy's been devoid of my sparkling company for over twelve hours, poor thing."

Noy nodded. "This was the only good thing about the flight."

"Charming."

The bus pulled slowly away, and they left the airport complex behind and headed northeast along the coast of Lantau Island. Noy let out a quiet '*oh*' as they crossed the towering Tsing Ma Bridge and Anna smiled at her.

"Impressive, no?"

"Very. This isn't really what I was expecting from Hong Kong."

"What were you expecting?"

"Oh, you know. Skyscrapers, skyscrapers, and more skyscrapers." She looked out of the window at the turquoise blue water far below to either side, and at the forested and low hills of the larger and smaller land masses spaced randomly across the bay. "I'd love to come here with…" She trailed off.

"Tasha?"

"Well, yes. Both of them. Tasha and Harry."

"They still never meet?"

The image of smashed cars and the sounds of Tasha and her grandmother screaming flashed through Anna's mind. "Not properly," she said. "But I think she'd like him. I don't know why. He can be a moody bastard, and he's prone to the odd murderous rampage. But for some reason I think they'll get along." She looked out of the window again, and smiled at the beauty of the view.

They crossed a small island then a much shorter bridge before reaching the mainland. The bus turned south, away from the Chinese border. They saw the first apartment blocks in front, and soon they were in the thick of it.

Before they boarded at Heathrow, when she had been finalising the details of the meeting to which they were now headed, Anna had checked the address she'd been given and had read that Kowloon was one of the most densely populated places on Earth. As they now drove through the district which swallowed up the entire area on the mainland across the bay from Hong Kong Island itself, she could very much believe it.

She had seen plenty of tall buildings in her life, but never so many squeezed together in such a way. There had been skyscrapers in New York of course, only a short time before, but this was different. The buildings were packed so tightly, and the apartments themselves clearly so much smaller and more numerous, that she could almost feel the weight of it all, the sheer mass of humanity, pressing down on her.

The road itself was broad and filled with what was likely a never ending stream of traffic. The streets were crowded with people too, the shops and restaurants and bars they passed seemed endlessly varied, and the whole mad spectacle of it was thrilling and overwhelming in equal parts.

Anna had been so preoccupied with staring out of the window like a gaping idiot that she barely noticed the latest stop being announced. She glanced up at the board towards the front just as the bus was slowing to a halt, recognised the name her contact had given her, swore, and jumped to her feet.

"Off!" she said, pushing Noy out in front of her and whacking Daniel none too gently across one of his oversized shoulders.

They exited the bus just before the driver could close the doors and found themselves suddenly in the midst of the constantly shifting streams of people Anna had been watching from on board, only now there was the heat of the air too and the smell of the fumes and the noise of it all. The streams adjusted their course around them, giving Daniel a particularly wide berth, as Anna consulted the map on her phone.

"This way," she said. "I think."

She led them against the current at first before switching to the correct side of the pavement and finding it slightly easier going, if still extremely slow. They continued along the main road, the sky in the broad gap between the towering buildings gradually growing golden. She took them off down a side street which was closed to traffic but heavy with people, then they turned again onto an alleyway which was deserted but for two children kicking a football between them.

"This is the place," she said, looking up. "Apparently."

"Very nice," Noy said, nodding towards the door, the narrow glass windows of which had been smashed then boarded over. "Hope inside is just as nice."

"You'll never know, my sweet. I've been instructed to go alone."

Noy stuck her bottom lip out as she considered the chipped plaster and filthy facade around the entrance. Then she shrugged. "Well, if you say so. Come on, Farang. I see a bar at the corner. You can buy me a drink while we wait."

"It's that kind of solidarity which makes me positive *our* team will succeed, even if Harry's doesn't," Anna said.

As she'd been instructed, Anna pressed a particular button on the intercom as Noy led Daniel away by the hand. There was a brief crackle of static then the sound of the lock. Anna nodded to the camera at the top of the intercom as she went inside.

The only natural light disappeared as the door closed. The narrow, mouldy hallway was lit only by a single, flickering bulb above. Anna went along it to the small, square central atrium and pressed the button beside the lift. Nothing happened.

"You must be joking," she muttered, and pressed again more insistently as she looked up through the gap in the middle of the staircase. The apartment was on the 18th floor.

Ten minutes later Anna arrived at what she hoped to God was the right doorway. The staircase had no ventilation whatsoever and she was drenched in sweat. She ignored the bell and banged heavily on the door. Locks clicked and chains tinkled before the heavy door opened.

A slim, beautiful woman at least ten years Anna's junior opened the door. "You're the girlfriend, are you?" Anna asked, wiping her hand across her forehead. "Talk about a bloody cliché. Take me to Archangel, would you?"

Anna followed the woman along a corridor, passing several closed doorways. They turned left through the open door at the end and Anna raised her eyebrows. The owner had knocked through into the apartment next door and converted the whole area into one large storage unit. The floor was filled with low stacks of plastic, hard cased boxes of various shapes and sizes, all arranged in neat piles.

Two men were standing near the small window just inside the storage space. Anna addressed the older one. "In the movies, arms dealers live in mansions on private islands, you know. And I'm pretty sure they have lifts that bloody work." Both men stopped talking and looked at her. "I assume you're expecting me," Anna said. "You are Archangel, aren't you? You look the type who'd choose a name that-"

"I believe you are looking for me."

Anna turned and found the younger woman smiling at her.

"My name is Chu. My father started his work under the Archangel alias, and I kept it after he died. Brand continuity can be so important in business, wouldn't you say?"

"I'm... Well..." Anna said, feeling her face reddening all over again as she stared at, by reputation, one of the most dangerous arms dealers in Asia. "I'm not the person to ask," she finished, lamely.

"Take it from me," the woman said. "The lifts have been deactivated for some years, since the attack which claimed my father's life. Gives us more time to prepare, should we see unwanted visitors coming in."

"Smart thinking," Anna said. "Listen, about what I said..." The woman watched her, smiling expectantly. "It's been a long journey. I'm not at my best."

"So I see," the woman said, eyes scanning Anna's sweaty face. "Not to worry. I don't have the thinnest skin in the world, as you might guess. And the man who vouched for you carries a lot of weight in my book. The Company has been one of my best clients for many years now. He, in particular, has been an excellent customer. Have you worked for them long?"

"A few years."

"Yet you're not here on Company business, according to him."

"Not exactly," Anna said. "I've worked alongside your favourite customer for a long time. Saved his life once, out in Rio, and he's owed me a favour ever since. I had rather a pressing need for some hardware, so I claimed that favour in the form of an introduction to you. No questions asked, from him at least."

"Nor shall you have any from me, since he's vouched for you.

Now," Archangel said, and waved one arm gracefully towards the stacks. "What can I do for you?"

Harry had made Anna memorise the equipment she was to ask for. The younger of the two men made short, coded notes on a piece of paper as she relayed the items.

She finished her recitation and the woman looked at her. "Is that everything?"

Anna paused. "Yes."

"Are you sure?"

"No."

"People have usually made up their minds before placing their orders."

"Are you able to drop off the equipment?"

"We insist on it, for larger items. We have an agreement with the police. But even they would need to intervene, should they receive too many reports of people strolling out of here with .50 cals. Just give us an address, anywhere in Hong Kong, and we'll get it there." The woman folded her arms. "I do have other business to attend to."

The plan Harry had concocted was fine. Anna knew that. But an alternative had come to her on the journey which would simplify matters.

Anna nodded absently, focused on the woman, and asked her the question. The woman's eyebrows raised.

"When?"

"Tonight. Along with all the rest of this junk."

The woman turned her head slightly and had a rapid conversation with the older man, presumably in Cantonese. Anna understood not a word. She turned back. "It's possible. Not cheap, but possible."

"Money is no object," Anna said. "Well, that's not strictly true. But the budget will stretch." She had absolutely no idea whether or not this was the case. The balance of Granville's offshore bank account, the existence of which had been reluctantly revealed during their final night of planning in London, had not been shared with her.

"Naturally you're not planning to use it *in* Hong Kong."

"Of course not."

The woman nodded, and gave another short, sharp instruction to the men. One took a laptop, tapped away, then beckoned Anna over. It was all Anna could do to stop her own eyebrows raising when she saw the price at the bottom of her shopping list.

Anna coughed into her hand. She had no deep affinity for Granville, but would still prefer not to be there when he saw the bill. The man switched to a suspiciously barebones banking website, created a new transaction, entered the amount, and looked up at Anna. She took a slip of paper from her jeans on which Granville had written the details, and typed them in.

The screen went white. A spinning circle appeared in the middle and remained there for half a minute, Anna barely breathing. Finally the screen refreshed to display a line of Chinese characters. The man turned to his boss and nodded.

"Give him the address, and your preferred delivery time," the woman said. She offered her hand and smiled sweetly. "You'll forgive me, I'm needed elsewhere. It's been a pleasure."

Anna found Noy and Daniel sitting at one of two dozen plastic tables outside a bar. Noy had just finished one glass of beer and was in the process of ordering another.

"Absolutely not," Anna said as she arrived. "We're on duty."

Noy pulled a face. "Another big boss. Great. Duty didn't start yet. We have hours."

Anna considered. "Damn it, you're right. I really have been spending too much time with the Captain."

"You want or not?" the rotund waitress beside the table asked them loudly.

"Yes indeed. Two, please, and make them big ones."

Anna sat opposite Daniel, saw the look on his face, and stuck out her tongue. He rolled his eyes. "Did you get everything?" he asked.

"Sure, I placed the order. It'll be delivered to the agreed place, at the agreed time."

He stared at her. She found her eyes flickering away momentarily. "Did you follow the list?"

"Jesus Christ. It wasn't exactly the most complicated task of my life, you know." Fortunately, the woman reappeared at that moment. The top part of each beer sloshed onto the table as she placed the glasses heavily down. "Ah, here we go," Anna said, taking hers up and holding it out to Noy. "To holidays with friends."

"Cheers," said Noy, clinking her glass to Anna's. Anna knew Daniel was continuing to stare at her, even as she looked away, but he said nothing more.

CHAPTER FORTY FOUR

After the drinks the three of them walked down to the harbour. The beer had banished the travel fatigue which had been creeping up on Anna, and she found herself suddenly enjoying the madness and energy of the place. She had thought Bangkok possessed plenty of both, but Kowloon was on a different level.

They reached Victoria Harbour. The sun had set out of sight to their right, and in the clear sky above there was a gradual progression of bright blue to soft orange.

Directly south, across the bay, was the skyline of Hong Kong Island. All along the bay the glassy towers of varying shades of silver and grey reached up towards the dimming sky, with Victoria Peak looming over it all. The lights of the skyscrapers were already starting to come on. The water of the bay itself was growing dark with the sky, and was surprisingly quiet but for a mid-sized ferry making the crossing and a solitary junk boat with red sails sailing westwards.

The Kowloon side of the harbour was filled with tourists, but they found a space along the railings. The couple who had been alternating kissing with savouring the view moved a couple of feet further along as Daniel came to stand next to them.

"This," Anna said, sweeping her hand across the harbour. "Is what I had pictured for Hong Kong."

"Don't like big city, normally," Noy said. "But not bad. Even I admit."

Barely thirty seconds had passed before Daniel coughed, obviously. Anna ignored him. "We should go," he said, when that didn't work. "We need to find-"

"I know what we bloody well need to find," Anna said. "Can't a woman have a minute to savour one of the world's great views?"

Daniel stared at her. She tried to look back across the harbour, then gave up. "You've ruined it now. I'd managed, for a moment, to forget the whole place was built on naked capitalism and colonialism, probably by people very similar indeed to the one we're here to hunt down. But fine, come on. Let's clamber into the belly of the beast."

They went west a couple of minutes to the nearest pier and took a ferry across the water. The scene had looked like a picture postcard from Kowloon but now the buildings towered over them as they approached.

They alighted from the ferry near the Convention Centre then headed south away from the water, taking a walkway across an eight-lane road filled with taxis and sleek saloon cars. Soon afterwards they were amongst the skyscrapers. One wrong turn aside, Anna guided them all to the address McGinn had found within ten minutes.

"Hmm," Noy hummed, looking up at the enormous, circular, white building. "A little more information would have been nice."

"You don't say." Anna craned her neck straight upwards and could still barely see the top.

"Address just say this building?"

"We've got '24th Floor' too."

"Useful. What now?"

"We wait," Daniel said. "And hope she comes out."

"*Hope*," Noy repeated. "Always lot of hope in our plans. Maybe she doesn't even come here herself. Maybe she's a real big boss, and doesn't do anything."

"Possible," Daniel said. "But unlikely. Operations this complicated, with this much money on the line. Whoever started them usually likes to stay in charge, for as long as they can."

"But risky, no? If not, we waste the whole night."

"We don't really have a choice," Anna said. "Loathe as I am to agree with your beau. It's a little late in the day to pursue a full investigation."

Noy frowned, but shrugged. "Fine. Thought this would be exciting, but obviously I was wrong."

There was a far more upmarket bar fifty metres along the street than the one at which Noy and Daniel had waited in Kowloon. Only two of the dozen tables at the front were taken, both by small groups of besuited young men.

The three of them sat at the nearest table to the building. Anna and Noy reluctantly ordered non alcoholic drinks, and they settled in to wait.

"At least we're not freezing our arses off here, like in New York," Anna said, early on. That was one of two differences. The other was that, while Bohm had shown up relatively quickly, there was no sign whatsoever of Anuradha Patel.

Hours passed as they kept a constant watch on the tall, glassy entrance. First a stream, then a flood, then a slowing trickle of workers issued from the building. Most walked away, although many were collected by waiting cars.

The sky overhead went from orange, to pink, to a blue-black. They had sat down at around six thirty. It was a little after nine and nobody had left the building for a quarter of an hour or more when Anna sighed and turned to Daniel.

"You're from the family of great military minds. Now what? It seems our genius plan has foundered."

Daniel nodded. "So we need to adapt."

"That's more of a statement than an idea."

He fixed his eyes on her. The scarred side of his face was lit brightly through the window of the bar. "They must have persuaded her to stay home. Understandably. We only have one contact who might know where that is. Or, failing that, who could find out."

It took Anna a moment to twig. "You're not serious. I didn't exactly make the best first impression, truth be told, and Archangel would never take the risk anyway."

"These people will do anything if the price is right."

Anna stared at him. He looked steadily back at her, face typically impassive. She sighed. "If Patel does come out, you follow her then we rendezvous back here in two hours," she said. Then she stood up and went back the way they had come.

Daniel and Noy were still there when she returned an hour later. Yet another round of soft drinks sat untouched in front of them. Noy had folded her arms on the table and fallen asleep. She stirred and looked up, blinking, as Anna came to stand beside her.

"What's wrong?" Noy asked.

Anna shook her head. "I got the address. Let's go."

Daniel watched her as he eased his large frame out of the seat, cracking his neck to relieve some of the discomfort. "What was the price?"

"She didn't want more money. She wanted information."

Daniel stopped. "What kind of information?"

"My information. My name. My address. The names of my family members."

A brief frown crossed his prematurely lined brow. "Not for blackmail."

"Of course not. I haven't *got* anything that she could possibly want. She wanted the information as collateral. She wanted *me*. And the assurance that I would do as she asked, when she chose to do so."

"Did you give it to her?"

"Like I had a bloody choice," Anna snapped, and the occupants of the nearest two tables turned to look at her. "I got the information," she said, her voice lower now but still charged. "That's all that matters, isn't it? Never mind the possibility of my poor family being dragged into danger yet again. We'll just worry about that later, won't we?"

She closed her eyes, let out a long breath, and gave a slow shake of her head. "Let's get this done. Or bloody well die trying. Actually, that sounds like a blessing right about now."

CHAPTER FORTY FIVE

"We not taking a taxi?" Noy asked, with a hint of hope in her voice, as they began to walk.

"No point," Anna said, not turning. "Archangel sent people ahead to move the drop point. We need to arrive after them."

They didn't talk again after that, only walked. They went west for a while, through the financial district and then to the central area.

There they took the series of covered, outdoor escalators upwards which Anna had seen on TV and in movies. Under normal circumstances she would have gotten a kick out of being conveyed upwards past people's apartments and entire, busy streets filled with bars and restaurants. Now all she could think of was how the romanticised, Happy Families future she had briefly allowed herself to envision seemed already to have been snatched from her. In its place was only more blackmail, more danger.

They reached the end of the escalators and continued upwards on foot, making the steep ascent of Victoria Peak alongside tourists with the energy and fitness for the climb or simply lacking the money for a ride up. They paused when they reached a large, paved area. An old fashioned tram unloaded tourists next to a viewpoint, and there were the inevitable souvenir shops, cafes, and restaurants nearby.

Anna checked her map, and moved them on. They continued to climb, upwards and away from the crowds. They soon saw only a few people as they turned onto roads with what were presumably some of the most expensive properties in the city, perhaps the continent, almost all with an unrestricted view across the metropolis.

They were approaching the island's peak, and had seen nobody else for at least a minute, when Anna turned them abruptly left off the street, between some trees and into darkness. They walked across uneven ground alongside large water pipes, the only faint light coming from above. They passed an industrial building, then reached a small plateau.

A man was standing there twenty metres away, his figure framed against the light-polluted sky. He was turned towards them, although they couldn't see his face. They stopped there, and he seemed to watch them for several long moments. Then he turned and walked away down the far side of the hill, disappearing into the blackness.

Anna led them across the grassy ground. As they came closer they saw the man had been standing beside two duffel bags, one much larger than the other. Daniel went to open them, but Anna stopped him.

"Not yet," she said, and he straightened again. "We don't have much further to go."

She took up the larger bag before he could, hauling the strap over her shoulder with a grunt, then took out her phone again and checked the route she had been given. They would take the same path as the man had. It was invisible in the darkness, impossible to find for those who didn't know it existed, but led to the perfect spot.

"I never see something like this," Noy whispered. Anna hadn't looked away from their immediate surroundings since they arrived on the plateau. She looked to her right now and saw the entirety of Hong Kong laid out before them, hundreds upon hundreds of buildings and thousands upon thousands of lights. They were above even the tallest of the skyscrapers and above them was only the sky, with the bottoms of the low clouds lit up by the combined electric force of the city.

Objectively Anna knew it to be the most spectacular sight she had ever seen. But it provoked no feeling in her.

"Come on," she said, and started down the far side of the hill.

They descended for five minutes before a deserted street came into sight, lit by closely spaced streetlights. Across the road were expansive properties with tall walls screening them from the road, and looking out over the city on the far side.

Anna stopped and checked her map. "That's it," she said, nodding down towards the house directly across from where the path emerged.

From their current vantage point, only the bottom of the near side of the house was blocked by the surrounding wall. They could see the rest of the property, which was long and two stories tall. All of the windows were floor to ceiling, and on the far side there was a large terrace jutting out over the hill from the upper story, supported by tall pillars.

Only a couple of the nearer rooms were illuminated, and they saw nobody through the windows. On the terrace, however, a group of figures stood or paced about.

Anna put her bag down and Daniel did the same. She unzipped his, took out a scope, and put it to her eye. "Well," she murmured, twisting the lens. "We came to the right place. I've got at least a dozen thugs here, all armed."

"Is she there?" Daniel asked.

"You'll be shocked to learn I was just checking that."

The quality of the scope was excellent, and despite the figures being a couple of hundred metres away she could see their faces clearly. "Well, they all appear to be men," she said. "And with a similar build to you. Unless our Anuradha had some rather drastic surgery-" Anna paused. "Hold your horses. Someone else just came out." She stopped moving the scope and adjusted the focus again. "Well, would you look at that."

Anna took her phone from her pocket and opened the only photo McGinn had been able to find. Decades had passed since it was taken, but there was no mistaking the strong jawline nor the thick, tumbling hair, though its blackness was artificial now. "Either my eye is deceiving me, or I'm witnessing a miracle. Anuradha Patel has risen from the dead."

Anna passed Daniel the scope and turned towards Noy, placing a hand on her shoulder and squeezing. Noy wasn't looking at her. "Is he there?" she asked.

Daniel didn't speak for several seconds. "Yes."

"Let me see."

Noy took the scope, not bothering for a second to turn it towards the one female figure clearly visible even with the naked eye. Instead she focused the way Daniel had been pointing, towards the far corner of the terrace where a solitary figure stood.

"The Assassin?" Anna asked. "You're sure?"

"Of course I'm sure. I don't stop thinking about his stupid, ugly, evil face since the video."

"Well," Anna said. "This has worked out perfectly."

Daniel looked at her. "It makes killing Patel more difficult."

"Not with my plan. We can simply kill both of these nasty birds with one particularly explosive stone."

"How?"

"I gave up shopping years ago, you know," Anna said, squatting down. "It was simply too dangerous. I'd get into a store and lose my composure completely. Start thinking of all this new stuff I desperately needed, which of course I didn't really." She began to unzip the heavier bag which she had been carrying. "On this occasion, though, I'm quite pleased with my impulse purchase."

Anna finished unzipping the bag, pulled the edges back, and with some effort hauled out its main content. Noy had to step back hurriedly to avoid being struck by the rocket launcher as Anna settled it onto her shoulder.

"Say hello to my new plan," she said.

"Jesus Christ," Anna hissed, half a minute or so later. "Would you stop complaining and get on with it?"

"No," Daniel said.

"Give me one good reason why not."

"Only one?"

"I'm assuming you learnt how to fire one of these back in the good old army days, before your abrupt career change?"

"Yes. Years ago."

"Well, they say that firing a rocket launcher is like riding a bike, don't they."

"You're being ridiculous."

"Maybe, but who cares? Something can be effective, without being all neat and tidy. Tell me a more effective plan to solve all our problems than this."

Daniel made the mistake of meeting Noy's eyes. "You can't possibly-"

"Of course I do!" she said, a little too loudly. "We come here to kill the evil woman and the murderer of my family. This does both."

"If I hit, yes. If I miss-"

"Then they'll make a break for it, guaranteed," Anna said. "That's what you do, when your charge is under threat. You get them away to safety. And while they're attempting to do so in this case, we hit them out in the open."

Daniel shook his head. "This is insanity."

"That doesn't make it wrong. Harry and his army boys will be slinking about in their fancy formations, with their expensive gear and elaborate hand gestures. It all seems a bit unnecessary to me, when we can just blast these bastards to pieces and be done with it."

"And afterwards?"

"We party. What do you mean 'afterwards'?"

"Our escape. The police are unlikely to take kindly to all this. Rocket launchers being fired in their island's richest district."

"God, you fret far too much for a hardened criminal. Auntie Anna's taken care of that too. Don't worry your massive head about it."

"Come on," Noy said, her face set and voice firm. "Let's do it. We're all here, and we're all ready. Now or never."

Daniel looked to the sky, and ran a giant hand across his closely cropped hair. He looked back down at Noy, met her eyes, and shook his head. "Give it to me."

Anna took up the RPG and handed it over. Daniel turned it back and forth in his hands then held it up and looked through the sights. "How much ammo?"

"I purchased three... rockets? Are they rockets?"

"These are very slow to reload. I might have time to fire two before they run."

"Hit with the first and you won't need to worry about it."

"Good advice."

Daniel knelt to take a projectile from the bag, and inserted it. He fiddled with something on the side of the weapon in the darkness then straightened again, lifting the weapon onto his thick shoulder effortlessly and looking through the iron sight on top. "Is she still there?"

Anna raised her scope and scanned the group. "Yes. She's the one talking to the Assassin now, in the corner. The rest are all in a group."

Daniel turned the weapon to the right a little. "Only a couple of metres between them and the guards," he said. "If I aim correctly..."

"Why don't you just worry about the target?"

"Because I'm also worried about our escape. I'd prefer not to be pursued by a full dozen guards."

Anna prepared to argue again, but Daniel spoke before she could. "Ready," he said, then let out a long breath. "Three. Two. One."

She saw him squeeze the trigger.

The back of the RPG flared then the flare grew bright and large and white so that it momentarily seemed as if the weapon itself had exploded. A moment later she saw the briefest burst of smoke from the front and something fly out from it.

She turned her head as quickly as she could to follow the object whose hiss was loud to begin with then faded as the rocket shot away leaving a thin trail of smoke behind. She saw the missile fly across the road, the wall, past the side of the house. Then it hit.

There was no towering fireball, as Anna had subconsciously anticipated. Instead there was the clear and heavy noise of the impact and a great cloud of thick, black smoke was thrown instantly into the air over the terrace.

Daniel was already kneeling to reload. "Well?" he asked.

Anna had the scope to her eye and scanned the scene. The cloud was already thinning and lifting. She saw figures moving and could hear the sounds of men shouting even from there.

"You certainly didn't kill them all."

"Not yet," he said, as he inserted the second rocket into the launcher and straightened. "Can you see the targets?"

"I can't make anyone out individually. All the bloody smoke makes it a little tricky. Wait. There!"

"Where?"

Anna saw one figure carrying another in its arms across the terrace, past the bodies and parts of bodies on the ground. "Middle. Going inside."

"I see them."

Anna heard the whoosh again but kept her eye to the scope. She saw only the figures first, with several more trailing behind as they all stumbled towards the house. Then the rocket passed briefly across her line of sight before another cloud of smoke was thrown up.

"I haven't got a clue, before you ask," she said. "It looked a little behind. More time on the RPG shooting range for you, when you get chance."

"We need to get down there."

"Do we?"

Daniel had dropped the RPG and was already kneeling beside the other bag. He took a pistol and two magazines and pressed both into Noy's hands. "I need you to fire too. No choice. Sorry," he said quietly.

"Fine by me, Farang."

"What's the plan here, out of curiosity?" Anna asked.

"Two on the hill across the road. One on the street near the gate. When it opens and they run for it, we hit them from both directions."

"Now you're getting into the spirit of things."

They all looked around as they heard loud and panicked voices, closer now and on the near side of the house although the wall blocked their sources from sight.

"I'll get onto the street," Anna said. "Try not to shoot me." She left before Daniel could argue and took the narrow path down from the small section of flat ground on which they'd stopped.

There was a large gate in the centre of the wall at the front of the house, which was already sliding open as Anna reached the pavement opposite. She ran across the road diagonally away from the gate, to take a position behind a parked car a few metres from it.

She heard an engine revving as she flicked the safety off her pistol and raised the weapon to take aim just as the noise of the engine became a roar.

A black car shot out through the gap in the gate which was still opening and Anna squeezed the trigger. She fired again and again, adjusting her aim as the car passed by and the driver turned sharply to the left, the tyres screeching and the engine revving again as the car skidded sideways a couple of metres with the rear tyres kicking out before the vehicle straightened.

Anna had caught a glimpse through the front windows and seen the driver, face covered in blood and looking grimly forwards. The Assassin was beside him, and his eyes and Anna's had met for the briefest of moments. His expression had been completely neutral, as if this was all perfectly ordinary. The rear windows at which Anna had instinctively aimed were completely tinted, and her bullets struck them and made cracked, whitened webs in the blackness without penetrating.

Two other pistols fired from higher on the hill, but the noises barely registered with Anna. She focused instead on the newer sounds of higher pitched engines revving and was already moving forward as two motorbikes burst forth through the fully opened gate. She heard the bikes whining then screeching once more as they made the sharp left hand turn but didn't turn to watch them, nor did she stop to wait for Daniel or Noy to finish firing.

The time for discussion and planning, with them or anybody else, was over. In the past she might have waited. Perhaps all the times seeing Harry in action and talking to him had changed her, because now there was no hesitation nor any thought of consequence. There was only the objective and the best way to achieve it, and she followed her instincts unthinkingly.

Anna sprinted straight through the gate, not checking before she entered the square parking area in front of the glassy house, but nobody fired at her or shouted. She saw what she sought immediately, and reached the single remaining motorbike within moments.

The logical part of her brain told her that she hadn't ridden a bike in years, that she had a child and grandmother at home, that she would be outnumbered even if she were able to catch up to the fleeing group without a fatal crash along the way.

She ignored it all, mounted the bike and kicked away the stand, squeezed the brake as she turned the key in the ignition then released it as she turned the handle as gently as she could, the bike still jerking away beneath her and nearly throwing her backwards off it before she forced herself to lean forwards and into the machine's momentum.

Noy and Daniel were in the road as Anna emerged. She put her foot down as she stopped and spoke to them quickly. "There's still a car there. Drive fast and you'll catch up." Then she turned the handle again and was away before they could reply.

CHAPTER FORTY SIX

Anna drove hesitantly at first. Then she pushed all that aside and forced herself to trust in her instincts and judgement and turned the handle further towards her, engaging the clutch with her foot as she went up a gear then did so again and again.

The steep downhill gradient of the road aided her acceleration and the world sped up all around, her long hair kicking up and tossing behind and the houses and parked cars and street lights all becoming meaningless blurs. All that mattered was the road directly in front and its twists and turns into which she leaned instinctively, knowing that a single misjudgement could cost her life yet disregarding the fact completely.

She had been so focused on the road itself that she failed to notice the pair of motorbikes until she had already closed to within fifty metres of them. They were cruising down the mountain behind the car, the whole convoy having slowed to a legal speed once it seemed the imminent danger had passed.

Anna slowed immediately to match their speed. Both riders wore helmets and hadn't heard her yet. They hadn't seen her either but she knew this wouldn't last long. Again she had no time to plan. Again she didn't care.

She accelerated once more as quickly as she dared and pulled out alongside the driver to the right. Holding the accelerator in place as tightly as she could with her right hand, she took her left hand from the handle, leaning a little in that direction to take her within arm's reach of the rider. His eyes caught her in his peripheral vision, and he did a double-take as his brain caught up with what he'd seen.

He took one of his hands away too and reached for the pistol in a holster on his hip, but it was too late. Anna leaned over as far as she dared so that the bikes were mere inches apart then pushed out. Her own bike zig-zagged beneath her and her heart skipped a beat as it seemed she'd taken herself out, but she managed to right it and, within that moment, the man she'd pushed had crossed involuntarily into his companion's path.

He went sideways across the other rider, the bikes colliding and flying away from beneath their riders, and Anna just saw the men and their machines falling to the ground and rolling with muffled shouts and mechanical whines before she was forced to face forwards once more. The bikes had only been going thirty miles an hour and both men would survive the fall, more was the pity, but Daniel and Noy would surely catch them up and overtake them before they could recover.

Even over the noise of the wind Anna heard the thin cracking sound in front. Her eyes hadn't lifted from the road just ahead, but they shot upwards now and she saw the Assassin hanging from the passenger side window in front with a pistol pointed straight at her.

She saw him about to fire again and turned sharply to the right just as the gun fired, almost losing control of the bike once more before desperately managing to right it. The Assassin kept firing and Anna accelerated to get on the right hand side of the car and pressed herself low to block his view.

Light suddenly filled her vision, and she heard a heavy horn honking. She looked ahead just in time to see she was mere moments from striking a truck head on. Fear almost paralysed her, but she overcame it just in time to throw the bike left before the fatal collision, the horn temporarily deafening as the angry driver passed before growing fainter behind, and then there were the pistol shots again, and more traffic on the other side of the road, so that Anna was forced to stick close to the rear right of the car and lean down as low as she could over the handlebars in a desperate effort to hide from the gunfire.

The right hand lane cleared and Anna was able to resume her original position out of sight of the Assassin, buying herself fleeting moments to decide what to do. The momentary peace was broken by the unmistakable sound of a loud whining whose pitch grew and died, grew and died. Sure enough, looking a little further ahead to a curve in the road she saw red and blue lights playing on the buildings there.

Anna dropped back several metres to trail the car, the driver of which also slowed. Three police cars came around the bend, each with its siren on and travelling quickly. Anna faced straight forward and held her breath and prayed they wouldn't see the earlier bullet holes she'd put in the car. She resisted the urge to look at any of the police cars as they came closer, drew alongside, went by. A few seconds passed, and all three sirens seemed still to be receding.

Anna was about to accelerate once more when she realised white lights were flashing from behind. She turned and saw another car, identical to that in front but for the bullet holes, only a few metres away. Daniel was in the driver's seat, Noy beside him and waving. Then she realised Noy was pointing frantically ahead, and as she turned back she saw the driver had accelerated again and was already building up a significant gap. The bike surged forward as she turned the handle and she heard the deeper noise of the car engine behind also revving.

As the car in front grew closer once more Anna realised that the hill was finally levelling out. She raised her view and saw that the relatively peaceful mountain road was coming to an end.

The skyscrapers were suddenly in front of them. On the one hand this meant straighter streets and not having to worry about skidding out every time she turned. On the other hand it meant traffic.

Even as she looked ahead the black car had to brake suddenly as it reached an intersection to avoid smashing into the side of a red, double decker bus before accelerating again to get through the crossing before being rear-ended by a taxi. Anna slowed too and swerved to the right just behind the taxi, then left to get in front of an SUV and onto the next straight stretch of road.

They were quickly into the central district and the dark, glassy buildings towered all around them. The car joined a long, broad carriageway and Anna saw the harbour ahead through a gap in the buildings. Clearly the driver was trying to reach a specific destination. Despite having no idea where that was, Anna felt sure she must stop him doing so.

The carriageway was several lanes wide in each direction. Despite the late hour it was still heavy with cars and vans, taxis and buses, but the car kept finding gaps to shoot through and Anna, only a second or so behind, managed to follow. They passed endless shops, bars and restaurants on their left and tall palm trees growing in the divider separating this road from the other on their right. Grey walkways and blue signs written in Chinese and English whooshed by overhead.

They hit a relatively empty stretch of the broad road and the driver put his foot down. Anna saw that they were less than a mile from the harbour and whatever salvation awaited Patel and her posse there. She could only think of one, foolhardy way to get past the bulletproof glass protecting the car, and this was her last chance to try it.

Anna withdrew the pistol she'd stowed in the back of her jeans with her left hand, keeping the speed and the direction of the bike steady with her right. Then she closed the gap one final time, pushing right up to the car's rear bumper before swinging out to the right.

She managed to keep her course steady as she drew level with the driver side door and reached out with her left hand, holding the gun with difficulty with her thumb and three of her fingers while extending her little finger to wrap around the handle. She prayed to a god she'd never believed in that in all the confusion the driver had not remembered anything so basic as locking the doors, then she pulled.

There was a click, and the door opened an inch. Her finger felt as if it would break or tear off completely as the wind pushed back against the door, but Anna put her strength into her shoulder and wrenched as best as she could, and the momentum of her pull swung the door open so that it nearly knocked her off the bike before she could pull away. She just managed to steer clear of it, and glanced ahead to see that the road was still mercifully clear even as she raised her left arm straight out.

She looked back into the car. The driver was reaching out blindly with his right hand for the door while still facing forward. The Assassin beside him was raising his gun, his expression neutral. Anuradha Patel sat in the rear left hand seat looking straight at Anna with a strange mixture of fear and defiance. Beside her was a large, extremely muscular man with several visible scars, who grinned at her.

Anna fired before the Assassin could get his shot off.

The bullet hit the driver high in his left arm, and he sagged. The car jerked in that direction and the Assassin dropped his pistol as he reached immediately for the wheel. He didn't just straighten it, but jerked it all the way to the right so that the car veered straight for Anna. She swore and automatically dropped her own gun so that she could wrap her left hand around the brake and drop back just in time.

Then the wounded driver's foot seemed to press involuntarily down on the accelerator, and this time the Assassin couldn't turn the wheel back fast enough. The car struck the partition in the middle of the road at a slight angle, the open driver side door hitting first. The door sparked against the concrete then swung closed as the Assassin pulled the wheel back the other way. The accelerator was clearly still pressed down, and the engine whined and the car fish-tailed as the Assassin forced it straight.

Then Anna saw the door on the right side opening again. The car slowed briefly and the next moment she saw the driver struggling and shouting as he was forced from the car. She swerved to avoid striking him as he was pushed out entirely, rolling and tumbling forwards and sideways. The car sped up again and continued in a straight line with the Assassin clearly having taken control.

Anna looked ahead and saw they were at most half a mile from the abrupt ending of the tall buildings and the start of the harbour. Over her shoulder she saw that Daniel was following close behind, and dropped back, Daniel lowering his window as she pulled alongside.

"Gun!" Anna shouted. Daniel's reticence was sometimes frustrating, and frequently unsettling, but in this case welcome. Without pausing or saying a word he held his hand out to Noy who had both pistols in her lap. She passed him one and he held it out to Anna.

"Be ready," she called, and accelerated forward once more.

The Assassin had just passed through the final junction on the main road before the turn onto the road running parallel to the harbour. The traffic light was already yellow when Anna went through, and by the beeping horns that followed a couple of seconds later she guessed it was red by the time Daniel crossed the junction.

Anna closed the distance quickly, the world blurring by again on both sides and her eyes set only on the car which grew closer by the second. The Assassin began to make the long, arcing turn left onto the harbour road, still carrying plenty of speed, just as Anna was forcing the bike into a final burst of acceleration which brought it to the right of the car. She released the accelerator and switched the gun to her right hand, aimed, and squeezed the trigger as many times and as quickly as she could.

The first bullet missed but the second, third, fourth all struck the front right tyre of the car. The vehicle spun abruptly with the other tyres screeching, and for a moment Anna feared that was all that would happen, but then the car's momentum lifted it onto two wheels then the left side kept on lifting before it started to roll, turning over and over again as it flew across the broad road before finally landing onto its back and skidding with a metallic shriek across the tarmac.

Anna had been travelling at speed when she fired and even after releasing the accelerator the bike kept rolling along the road. The upside down car was still skidding in the direction of the water when she heard a horn extremely loud and surprisingly close.

She looked round and saw the white truck heading towards her with its lights flashing and blinding her. The driver was braking but he had seen her too late. She reached for the accelerator automatically while still holding the gun which clunked clumsily against the handle, and by the time she had dropped the weapon it was too late.

The driver tried to turn at the last moment but struck the rear wheel of the bike anyway. Anna was spun violently around with the bike for half a second before she went flying, her body spinning and turning in space and time seeming to slow as the world also turned around her and she waited for the impact.

CHAPTER FORTY SEVEN

Anna landed on her left shoulder, hard. There was no pain to start with. Then it came all at once. She cried out, which she never did. The entire left side of her body felt as if it had been systematically pounded with a hammer then dragged across gravel, the pain burning and throbbing all at once.

Anna shouted again as she was turned over by a strong hand. She realised her eyes were still closed and found herself needing to force them open. Daniel had straightened up and was looking in another direction. Noy was crouched beside her.

"That look painful," Noy said.

Anna raised her head, tried to speak, and only coughed.

"I don't know you can ride bike like that."

"Neither did I."

"You stand up?"

Anna lay her head back on the tarmac, and sighed. "I've met more sympathetic people."

"Now time to fight. Sympathy later."

"I'll hold you to that." She turned her head an inch or two to face Daniel, her body protesting even at that slight movement. "Put all that muscle to good use, would you?"

He barely glanced at her as he squatted down, his eyes still focused further down the road. Then he put one arm under her legs and another beneath her back and lifted her as if she were a child. She moaned like one too when the new and subtly different pain struck her, before he set her down on her feet.

"Where?" was all she could say, grimacing. Daniel nodded in the direction he'd been facing.

Spots danced in Anna's vision. She blinked a couple of times and strained her eyes that way. The car was still there, on its roof. Most of the road's sparse traffic moved slowly around it. A couple of cars had stopped but nobody had gotten out to investigate.

Even as Anna watched, she saw the first figure crawling from one of the smashed windows. Daniel was already striding towards the crash, Noy beside him. "Heaven forbid I have a single moment to rest," she muttered. She sighed, and ignored her body's desperate protestations as she followed as quickly as she could.

Still somewhat dazed, she looked around towards the various beeps that pursued Daniel, the drivers either braking or driving around him and Noy and he paying them no attention at all. Her gaze passed across the ground near her fallen bike and she saw a gun lying there. It took a moment to realise it was hers, and she slowly and carefully stooped to collect it.

Then she heard shots from up ahead. Whoever first emerged from the car had now taken a position behind it. Daniel fired back, his bullets striking the vehicle inches below where the outline was and making the other man duck down. A little to the left Anna saw the larger more muscular man had also emerged from the car and was stooping down behind it. He helped a woman to her feet, and Daniel got two shots off before both retreated behind cover.

"That's all of them, then," Anna said to herself, her voice sounding strangely muted. "And in a wonderfully awful position as well." Remotely, she noticed the reactions of the nearby drivers had differed at the gunshots. Some had sped up to get past. Some had stopped, either frozen in fear or from simple curiosity. One woman had been caught halfway between Daniel and the overturned vehicle, and had abandoned her car and was now fleeing towards the city.

Daniel continued to advance, his gun held high. Noy was still beside him, her pistol raised far less expertly. Anna followed a couple of metres behind. There was no movement at all from behind the car ahead. Then they made their move.

It was the larger man who rose up first, utterly without fear. He squeezed off several shots without pausing to aim, and his misplaced fire gave the three of them the chance they needed to veer sideways and behind the car which the local woman had abandoned.

The shots followed them and thudded into the vehicle's body. Anna popped her head over the car's rear and saw the Assassin ushering Patel towards the harbour. His gun was raised in one hand, his other around the woman's shoulder to push her in front of him. He fired twice at Anna, the shots disturbingly close. She ducked, then moved out from behind the rear of the car and fired back. Daniel was also returning fire, but both of them were forced behind cover once more by the barrage of shots which flew in their direction.

"Wait for them to reload," Daniel said calmly, and Anna did so. There was a pause in the shots, and Daniel said, "Now," then they were up again and around the car.

The Assassin and Patel were already some hundred metres ahead and visible only as dark shapes behind the streetlights now, already halfway up the grassy bank which separated the road from the bay. Patel's other, larger bodyguard was close behind and running quickly after them while fumbling to reload his gun.

He caught them up just as they were cresting the bank, the shots fired by Anna, Daniel and Noy too as they ran all missing their targets. Then they had disappeared and Daniel lowered his gun and ran faster, his long strides covering the distance more quickly than Anna or Noy could manage. In the distance, Anna heard the sounds of sirens approaching.

The three of them left the road and the lights behind and reached the bank's short stretch of darkness. Daniel was in the lead by at least ten metres even with Anna and Noy running as quickly as they could. He reached the top and disappeared briefly from view. Then Anna heard a great roar that certainly did not belong to Daniel.

She crossed the crest and began descending. The harbour was a surprisingly short distance in front of them, and she glimpsed the lights of a few boats on it and of Kowloon's reflected skyline before her eyes switched automatically to the two shapes twisting on the ground.

One was Daniel, and he wrestled with a man clearly shorter than him but at least as thick and broad. Both men grunted as they twisted and punched and kicked and scrambled to get on top of the other. The shorter man caught Daniel with a blow to the nose which sent him reeling, although he didn't shout. Both got to their feet, breathing heavily.

"Well hello there, Scarface!" the shorter man said in a Dutch accent. "Did you miss me?"

Daniel stood and stared for a moment in the darkness. "Jansen," he said.

"The one and only. I'd been hoping to run into you, you ugly bastard. I owe you, for a lot of things."

Daniel only stood there, stock still.

"Still working the strong, silent act, eh? Well, it's time to-"

Anna almost jumped out of her skin at the sound of the gunshot right beside her. With her heart beating wildly she looked around and saw Noy's arms raised, the lights from the harbour glinting a little on the gun.

Noy glanced at her. "What? Aren't we in a hurry?" She grunted as she looked forward again. "Was aiming for his stupid face."

Turning back, Anna saw that Jansen had sunk to his knees with one hand pressed against his throat. Daniel hadn't moved at the sound of the gunshot. Now he came forward and began to circle Jansen. The man tried to swing for him but only fell forward onto the grass with a grunt. Daniel knelt down so that his knees were on the ground either side of the man, and put his hands on both sides of his head.

"I'm going to enjoy this," he said. Then he twisted.

Anna winced at the sound and Noy made a noise and looked away. Daniel let the body drop, and stared at it for a moment. Then he pushed himself up, cast around briefly, picked up his gun from where it had fallen when Jansen tackled him, then came to stand by Noy.

"That was... surprising."

"You can say that again," muttered Anna.

"Don't like him calling you Scarface and ugly," Noy said. "Nobody can bully you except me."

They all looked back in the direction from which they'd come as the sirens halted there. Though blocked by the slope they were still only a short distance from the road, and could distinctly hear the sounds of car doors opening and voices shouting.

"Good to know. Come on." Daniel turned and jogged down the slope, and Anna forced back the pain which had briefly stilled as she followed. They reached the promenade and looked from side to side. There were a couple of dozen people walking along or gazing across the harbour.

Noy pointed. "There."

Anna saw the two figures, more easily visible now in the tall lights which lined the promenade. They were crossing from a jetty onto a small boat.

Daniel began to run, even as the sounds of the boat's engine reached them. "Wait!" Anna called, and he stopped and turned back. "Now's probably the time to tell you I made one more little request, from my new best friend here in Hong Kong."

"Okay."

"Well, nobody else seemed to give any thought to how we'd actually get away, once the job was done," Anna said, as she took her phone from her pocket. She found the correct number and dialled. Her call was answered after the first ring. "We're ready. I'll send you our location," she said, and whoever heard her immediately hung up.

"We taking taxi?" Noy asked.

"A very fast one," Anna said, tapping her phone screen.

"How much of posh guy's money you spend?"

"As much as I could, in the time I was given."

Daniel had turned halfway back to them, but he still looked along the promenade. His face was tight as he watched the boat leave its mooring and move slowly away, heading east. His body seemed to be pulling him that way. "I hope you're sure about this."

"Positive," Anna said, wishing she was. "In theory our ride has been awaiting us along the shore. We'll catch up."

Daniel started to pace up and down as they waited in agonised silence. Thirty seconds passed before they heard two noises growing concurrently closer.

The first was shouting from further up the hill, the voices clearly having just cleared the crest. No knowledge of Cantonese was necessary to know that they belonged to the policemen and women, at least a dozen by the sounds of it, hunting for whoever had caused the chaos back on the road.

The second was an engine, much louder and more powerful than that which had accompanied the departure of Patel and the Assassin. Anna held her illuminated phone screen in the direction of the noise and waved it back and forth as she jogged towards the nearest jetty, every step jarring her injured shoulder.

The boat arced towards them and came to a perfectly judged stop by the platform. The pilot was the only person inside. He didn't turn as they climbed on board. He only looked around when he heard the shouts reaching the promenade. Turning too, Anna saw several powerful torches pointing straight at them. The pilot faced ahead again, pushed the throttle forward, and they were away.

CHAPTER FORTY EIGHT

With difficulty Anna made her way to the front of the boat as it began to cut through the water. "We're not finished yet," she shouted over the wind. The man showed no sign of having heard her. "There's another boat ahead. We need to catch it. I was told you'd take us wherever we needed to go."

The expression on the man's face didn't change. But after a moment he reached down and pressed a button on the console beside the wheel, then flicked through a couple of screens. A detailed, colour coded radar screen appeared, which Anna doubted came as standard issue with the boat. Their vessel was a triangle in the middle of the screen and she saw a dozen or so other, smaller triangles spread across the bay.

"There," she said, and pointed to the only one east of them within a reasonable distance. It seemed to be angling northwards, heading for the eastern part of Kowloon. The man glanced down, adjusted the wheel to the left, and pushed further forward on the throttle.

Anna stumbled and reached for the side as they began to bounce across the water. Pain shot up her left arm as she grabbed a handhold there and she cried out, but the sound was carried immediately away by the wind which was now whooshing by and sending her long hair whipping across her face.

She settled into an uncomfortable and ungraceful half-crouch, still holding onto the side, as they raced across the bay. The close-packed towers of Kowloon rose ahead and to their left with their thousands of lights reflecting in the water.

The triangle they chased across the map appeared to be almost at the far side of the bay, where Anna was sure their prey's salvation waited. Then the pilot tapped a button on the screen to zoom in on the map, and Anna saw the boat was still a short distance from the shore and apparently only a little ahead of them.

Then she saw it. The Assassin had turned off any screens or lights on the boat, so that it was visible only as a dark patch passing across the reflections in the water. The shape grew rapidly larger even as she watched and ten seconds later they were upon it.

The pilot slowed his speed to match that of the boat, following closely behind and to the side just out of its wake. Anna could see the outlines of two figures standing near the prow and facing forward. They didn't seem to have heard or seen the approach.

"Pull alongside when I tell you," Anna said, right into the pilot's ear, and moved carefully back to Daniel and Noy. "Ready?"

"For what?" Noy asked. "We shoot them?"

Anna looked to Daniel. He looked back at her, and gave a shake of his head. She grimaced, and nodded.

"The bastard driving that thing seems almost superhuman. If we shoot and miss, which is more than possible bouncing around like this, then we don't just lose the element of surprise. He'll shoot back, and I doubt he'll miss."

"So we jump," Daniel said

Anna opened her mouth to argue, then met Noy's eyes and saw the younger woman looking up at her with a strange smile. Anna rolled her eyes and shrugged. "Sure," she said. "Why the hell not jump from one moving speedboat onto another? That's the kind of night it's been."

Anna returned to the front of the boat and clapped a hand on the pilot's shoulder. "Now's the time, my good man. Let's see if you can really sail... or drive. Whatever this counts as." For the first time he looked at her, one eyebrow raised. "Just go," she said, slapped him on the back, and went back to Daniel and Noy.

"Ready?" she shouted, as the boat sped up again.

"I'm dreaming of this since he send that video," Noy shouted back.

"This specifically?"

"Maybe no. But result is the only thing that matters."

"That's the spirit."

The boat surged across the water. The shapes of the two figures grew clearer in the lights from Kowloon and still they hadn't heard or seen their pursuers. Within moments they were very close, the pilot expertly narrowing the gap metre by metre, and Anna saw now that the other boat was at least half as large again as theirs.

Daniel steadied himself against the edge of their boat as its nose drew level with the rear of the other. The driver looked back. Daniel waved his arm forward and got ready to jump. The driver accelerated once more and then they were completely level.

The Assassin saw them. Even under the circumstances Anna couldn't help but feel a surge of pleasure at the look on his face as he turned to see their boat pulling alongside and Daniel looming on the gunwale. She had never seen his expression change before. Now his eyes opened and his mouth parted and both grew wider still as Daniel leapt. The Assassin let go of the wheel and turned away instinctively as Daniel's great bulk dropped from the night sky towards him.

Then Daniel hit him and they both went sprawling sideways onto the floor, one of them knocking the steering wheel so that the boat began to turn slowly through the water. The pilot followed it as best he could but the gap was still wider than it had been.

This fact didn't seem to deter Noy in the slightest. She crouched on the edge as Daniel had, and jumped without even looking back at Anna. She landed with surprising smoothness halfway back along the boat with Patel, who remained pressed against the side opposite the brawling men, watching her warily.

Anna went to the edge too. She hesitated there, testing her shoulder as she rocked herself back and forth. Then she saw Patel stooping down and reaching out for a gun, and she rocked herself back one more time and leapt.

CHAPTER FORTY NINE

It was a curious sensation to jump from one moving vehicle to the next, and an endeavour for which Anna was completely unprepared.

She had intended to land a short distance in front of Patel, and either get to the gun first or knock her down before she could reach it. Technically she accomplished the first objective. But she also completely failed to find her balance, and twisted her ankle as she stumbled forward across the tossing deck and collided straight into the older woman.

They went down in a heap, and Anna was just fighting to disentangle herself when the fight between the two men spilled over towards them and an elbow or knee, which or from whom she wasn't sure, struck her in the side of the head. She fell to her left and shouted as her shoulder hit the ground hard.

When the worst of the pain had faded Anna turned onto her back and looked up at the clouded, light polluted, impassive night sky beneath which they passed. For a moment, she considered that it simply wasn't her night.

She heard Noy shouting her name and saw Patel coming towards her. Daniel and the Assassin were going at it hammer and tongs towards the front of the boat, but Anna was more concerned with the black leather boot that had just been planted by her side and the other which was being raised to kick her in the head.

She moved away just in time, grunting as she rolled over her injured shoulder, then pushed herself to her feet with her good right arm. Patel stood before her. She wore a long thin coat over a white buttoned shirt which was tucked into her trousers. Her thick dyed black hair billowed behind her. Her eyes were fixed on Anna's, and in them Anna saw no fear, only arrogance.

"You've gotten far closer than anyone else ever managed," Patel said. She didn't shout but her clipped voice still carried easily over the wind. "But I'm afraid you won't finish the job. I won't allow it."

"I don't plan on giving you a choice."

"There's always a choice. And I don't believe I've ever made the wrong one."

"Well, there's a first time for-" Anna began, before suddenly being hurled sideways.

The fight between the two men had been continuing as a background flurry behind Patel, with Noy lingering nearby with the gun raised and waiting in vain for a shot. One of the men had grabbed hold of the wheel as he was knocked backwards, jerking the boat to the left and straight towards the Kowloon harbour wall and sending Anna and Patel flying.

Anna managed to steady herself with her right hand before she went tumbling over the edge of the boat, while Patel sprawled to the ground. Anna advanced towards her, but stopped short as Patel aimed a sharp kick straight towards her stomach before climbing to her feet with surprising quickness. They looked at each other for a moment, then the hairs on Anna's neck stood up as Patel let out a scream and charged her.

Anna swung for Patel before she made contact. The blow landed, if only on her shoulder, but did nothing to slow the older woman. She knocked straight into Anna, sending her staggering back to almost lose her footing again on the bouncing boat. She'd barely regained her balance when Patel came forward again.

There was no subtlety to the way Patel attacked her. There was no technique, no evidence of any formal training nor even of experience. The older woman only fought, in the most primitive meaning of the word. She used every tool which nature had given her which could inflict pain on another person, and brought them all to bear against Anna. She fought with a mania which her appearance belied. She fought with the unflinching confidence of a woman who had built so much and the desperation of someone now faced with its destruction.

The brutality and ferocity of the attack worked initially. Anna had never been in a fight like it and was forced almost automatically onto the back foot in the face of such aggression.

But as the seconds passed she not only regained her composure but felt a calmness descend upon her. The setting and all of the circumstances fell away. This was still only fighting, and she had done plenty of that in her time.

She stepped backwards quickly with her arms held protectively in front, letting Anuradha come to her again. Then she stopped and lowered her guard. Her eyes wild, Patel charged in as Anna had known she would.

Patel lifted her right hand back ready to scratch Anna's eyes out with her long nails, but she was still too far away. Anna was at least ten inches taller, and was able to lean back on her left foot and kick straight out with her right before Patel reached her. Her boot landed with a satisfying impact right in the woman's stomach. Patel's progress was halted immediately and she fell straight to her knees with her mouth gaping.

Her opponent incapacitated, if only temporarily, Anna glanced ahead to the front of the boat. Immediately she found herself unable to look away from what she saw.

What Daniel and the Assassin were engaged in wasn't merely a fight, as hers had been. It was a battle which both men knew would go to the death. She had never seen anything like it. Had never seen combat with such brutality and power. As far as she knew the two men had never exchanged a single word, and yet they seemed to fight with what could only be hatred; whether for the other person or for something else entirely, something deeper, she couldn't say.

Each man's face was bloody. That was clear even in the inconsistent shifting lights from the skylines in front and behind. Both landed heavy hits to the shoulders, the arms, the ribs of the other, but neither seemed to feel them despite the power in the blows.

The Assassin seemed almost superhuman. He moved faster than anybody Anna had seen except for Harry, but it wasn't only that; it was the decisiveness of his movements, machinelike in their precision but also with a fluidity and flow that made them seem almost choreographed.

Daniel's frame made him seem too large and surely too slow compared to the Assassin's lean build, and yet he was more than holding his own. He protected himself more carefully than the Assassin, the blows striking his thick arms like water crashing against rock. His own punches were heavy and powerful, and despite the Assassin's own obvious strength he was sent backwards with each punch that landed before immediately regaining his ground.

Noy stood halfway between the two of them and Anna. Her gun was raised and pointed at the Assassin, but the speed with which the two of them moved back and forth, grappled then broke apart, made it impossible for her to get a clear shot.

Patel got to her feet, stumbling a couple of steps to the side before coming forward at Anna with another scream. Feeling a flicker of annoyance at the distraction, Anna rocked back and kicked out again.

Patel was ready this time and caught Anna's leg before it made contact. The two women looked at each other for a moment. Then Anna squatted down before jumping up and kicking out with her other foot. She caught Patel squarely in her nose this time and the woman screeched. Anna had a split second to regret her decision before she landed on the deck, hard, and swore loudly at the protests in her left side.

Anna grunted as she pushed herself once more to her feet, and vowed - uselessly or not - that it would be the last time.

She saw their course had taken them closer to Kowloon than she had realised. They were travelling northeast but still heading diagonally towards the shore, and closer all the time to the imposing stone wall of the harbour. She doubted they had more than thirty seconds before the impact.

She looked back to her right just in time to see the Assassin catch Daniel in the chin with an uppercut that sent him reeling backwards. At last, it seemed like a decisive blow.

Noy's shout was audible even over the whipping wind. The crack of a gunshot soon followed, now that she finally had a clear target.

The Assassin didn't pause, nor even flinch. Instead he went straight towards the gun, covering the distance in a couple of long strides. Noy fired again, and missed again, and then the Assassin was on her, grabbing her wrists and wrenching them straight upwards then kneeing Noy hard in the stomach. He wrested the gun away, and Anna was suddenly sure that they would all be killed.

The realisation brought clarity. She would love nothing more than for the Assassin to die, particularly for Noy's sake. But Patel was the priority, and it wasn't even close.

Daniel was stumbling back towards the Assassin with one hand held to his cut and bloody chin. Anna began advancing towards Patel, who still lay on the ground only a metre or so from where Noy was on her knees, wheezing.

The Assassin lashed out with the gun and caught Daniel a glancing blow to the side of the head which sent him falling forwards. He didn't even pause before turning his attention immediately to Anna just as she was within striking distance of Patel, and raising the gun at the same time.

Anna's eyes fixed upon the barrel of the gun. The moment seemed to stretch. Then the Assassin fired.

Anna felt the impact somewhere towards the right side of her stomach. It burned but didn't hurt, per se. And yet she still found herself stopping almost automatically and falling to one knee, reaching out her right hand to steady herself, then falling onto her injured left side. When that didn't hurt either she realised she was in trouble.

Rather than despair, Anna found that a natural defiance kicked in. She could go down, certainly, but not like this.

She began dragging herself forward. It was very difficult to raise either of her arms to pull herself along, even though there was still no pain, but she forced herself. Teeth gritted, she looked up and saw the Assassin watching her. He was the last person still standing on the boat. For the first time, she saw a small, unnatural smile on his face.

The Assassin's chin was high and he looked down upon her. Then he turned away, dismissively, towards where Daniel had fallen.

As she continued her mechanical crawl forwards Anna saw that Daniel had wrapped a thick arm over the side of the boat and was attempting, slowly and with great difficulty, to haul himself upwards. The side of his head was streaming with blood.

The Assassin took a couple of steps forward and raised both arms with the pistol held in front of him once more. The gunshot rang out. Dimly, Anna realised that it had come from the wrong place.

She was only a metre or so from the Assassin, and stopped to look up at him. He was standing completely still. But instead of looking at Daniel his head was now turned downwards. He took his left hand from the gun, pressed it against his chest right over his heart, then lifted it up to stare in disbelief. Anna saw the glint of the rapidly approaching lights of Kowloon against the dark liquid on his fingers.

The Assassin stumbled a little as he turned towards Noy. "You bitch," he said, his voice deep and his enunciation precise. He began to raise the gun again, and then there was a roar and Daniel was upon him, wrapping the Assassin up and the gunshot flying harmlessly off into the sky. Daniel drove them both forwards before the Assassin could react, across the two metres or so which had separated them from the gunwale, then over the edge and disappearing into the water with a heavy splash.

Noy shouted something that Anna didn't understand and ran to the rear of the boat to look back. By the clarity with which she could see Noy, Anna realised they were very close to the lights of the shore now. Looking up, she saw the towers of Kowloon suddenly rising above them and the sea wall only a short distance ahead.

Then she saw Patel rising from where she had been briefly forgotten. The older woman reached towards her boot and Anna saw the flash of a knife.

Anna had reached the front of the boat. She was too far away to stop Patel. Even if she was closer, she felt that she lacked the strength to overpower a child, never mind a crazed, grown woman fighting to save her life and her life's work.

Patel moved down the boat. Noy was still looking back to where Daniel had disappeared. Anna hauled herself up using a ridge which ran above a series of instruments beside the wheel. She looked at the wheel itself, then at the wall which was flying past on their port side, close enough now that she could make out the shadows of the individual stones and hear the engine rebounding against them.

Anna reached for the throttle and pushed it forwards. The boat surged. She straightened. Her hands drifted. It felt as if a weight were pushing down on her chest, but she took as deep a breath as she could.

"*Noy!*"

Noy turned. She looked at Patel first, who was barely a couple of metres in front, then past her to Anna. She saw Anna's left hand resting on the wheel.

"*Jump!*" Anna screamed. She waited a half second for some sign of recognition on Noy's face. It came almost immediately, and she felt a brief surge of gratitude at her friend's quickness.

Then she jerked the wheel downwards with her left hand as hard as she could, sending the boat abruptly towards the harbour wall.

She didn't try to fight the momentum of the turn, stumbling gladly in the opposite direction and tumbling straight over the edge of the boat and into the water, blackness filling her vision and an abrupt but welcome cold sweeping over her as she heard the low sound of a heavy impact nearby.

CHAPTER FIFTY

Anna found that it had taken all of her strength merely to turn the wheel, and that now she was spent. She hoped that the job was done. But if it wasn't, she had nothing left to give. She lacked even the energy to fight for the surface.

Then she felt small hands on the back of her shirt and pulling her above the water. She tried to breathe and instead began coughing uncontrollably. There was a bright, searching light, then an engine coming closer. Strong hands hauled her up and onto a hard surface. There was a larger person there beside her, not moving. Whoever had pulled her onto the rocking boat went back to the edge and turned the light back and forth again.

There were voices. One was Noy's. They spoke English, Anna thought, but the words didn't register.

The light turned. The man operating it called out. There was splashing, going away then coming back. The man bent to pull someone else up and laid the person on Anna's other side. Finally the man helped a small figure onto the boat, and Anna recognised Noy's voice again.

Noy went first to the larger figure. Anna heard her talking softly and with concern. The figure stirred, there was a pause, and then after a bout of coughing she heard Daniel's voice, deep and halting. He sounded confused; finally, Anna thought, they had something in common.

She closed her eyes, and when she opened them again Noy's face was hovering inches above.

"Still alive?"

Anna tried to reply and started coughing again. "I almost… wish I wasn't."

"I can… how do you say? Put you out of misery? Throw you back in water, if you want, like a fish."

"It's a kind offer…" Anna winced as the first wave of pain from her bullet wound swept over her. "Before I accept," she said, teeth gritted. "I'd like… to know that… we achieved… what we set out to."

"Kind of."

Anna blinked as she tried to focus on Noy's face. "Explain."

"On your right."

She frowned, and turned her head in that direction. Anuradha Patel was lying next to her. Her eyes were closed and her clothes torn.

"Dead?"

"No."

"Help me."

Anna began to struggle to her feet. Noy nodded to someone behind her, and she felt the strong hands again under her armpits. She swayed a little as she turned, and saw the boat's pilot already returning to the bow without looking at her. She turned back to Noy.

"He save you," Noy said. "Well, I save you first. But he bring the boat and help."

"My thanks to you. But not to him." Anna looked to where the pilot scanned the water. "He didn't do it out of the goodness of his heart. He did it for his boss. I'm an asset to her now."

Noy hummed, then shrugged. "Anyway, still alive."

"For better or worse. How's our special guest? Conscious?"

"Sometimes. I can try wake her up."

Anna stumbled around to stand beside Patel. Noy considered the woman. Then she squatted down and slapped her face hard.

Patel stirred. From above, Anna could see that she was in very bad shape. At least one leg was pointing the wrong way and the skin across her body was gashed in places and scraped all over. Noy slapped her again and Patel's eyes flickered open.

The eyes were red and the pupils dilated. Patel seemed oblivious as to where she was, or with whom. Then her eyes focused and realisation dawned.

"Congratulations," she murmured.

Anna bit her lips to stop from crying out as the pain swept all over her.

"Thanks," she said. "For what, exactly?"

"Absolutely nothing."

The woman tried to laugh, then spluttered. A line of blood dribbled from her mouth.

"You couldn't find a court in the world… that would convict me. There's not a country… whose leaders I don't… have information on… or could get hold of in no time."

Anna exchanged a glance with Noy. Patel saw them, and frowned.

"I think you might be a little confused, as to what this is," Anna said.

"Very confused," Noy said.

"We're not here to arrest you. Your crimes will be exposed, don't worry. We have plenty of evidence. Everyone will know who you are and what you did. But if you think you'll get a single word in to defend yourself, you're very much mistaken."

A coughing fit seized Patel, and she spat blood down her front. "You wouldn't," she said, looking back up.

"I will."

"It can't..." Patel's eyes flickered back and forth, widening and narrowing at random as she seemed to gain and lose focus. "It can't end like this. After everything." She looked back up at Anna. "You have no idea... what it took. What I had to give. And the scale of it. The scale of what I've accomplished. To build something like this, from the ground up. Something so enormous, and yet with so very few people who knew about it."

Anna shrugged, with her right shoulder at least, her left no longer responding. "Sure," she said. "One day people might look back on what you've done with admiration. The suffering is always forgotten once enough time has passed. Only the... 'accomplishment', as you put it, is remembered." She struggled to keep her own eyes focused as her vision dimmed. The wound had become a dull, distant throb now. She held out a trembling hand towards Noy, and felt the cold weight of a gun being placed onto her palm. It cost her more effort than she showed to bring the weapon around and up.

"Anuradha Patel," she said. "You've exploited a broken, corrupt system, and you'll never be charged for it. Congratulations again. But you've directly caused more suffering, and been responsible for more misery, than perhaps any single person currently on this planet. You should be paraded in front of the world, so that everybody can see your crimes and hate you for them. But you're correct. If we tried to do things *the right way*, you'd only spend or blackmail your way out of it, as the wealthiest criminals do. So we're left with this. Few people indeed would say that you deserve to live, although they wouldn't be willing to pull the trigger themselves. I am willing, and to tell you the truth I couldn't be more delighted to do so. Do you have any final words?"

Patel opened her mouth.

Anna pulled the trigger.

The gunshot drowned out whatever Patel had started to say and sent a shockwave up Anna's feeble frame that made her stumble backwards, where Noy caught her.

"Easy," Noy said softly. "I've got you."

Perhaps they had been there already without Anna noticing. But now she became aware of the sound of sirens, and looking around she saw the flashing blue and red lights approaching across the harbour.

Their pilot didn't put the speedboat into gear to flee, as she expected. He only watched the lights coming closer, then reached for an intercom at the front of the boat, raised it to his lips, and had a short conversation. The lights and the sirens kept coming closer.

Then the sirens stopped and the approach of the lights slowed abruptly. The police boats themselves came to a halt a few hundred metres away, and Anna could almost feel the inhabitants looking at them. Quietly, the boats turned and went away again.

With Noy's help, Anna turned back around. Anuradha Patel lay flat on her back, her open eyes staring up at the night sky, the lights of the city she had made her home reflecting in the pool of blood gathering around her head.

"So," Anna said. "It's done, then."

Then she finally gave in to the blackness which had been encroaching on her vision, and sank downwards into oblivion.

CHAPTER FIFTY ONE

"You're sure?"

"How could I be *sure*?"

"You know what I mean. Don't be irritating."

"All I can relay to you is what I've been told myself."

"That he's good to go?"

"It *seems* that way, but-"

"You can't possibly be sure."

"Now you're getting it."

Sitting in the back of the large car, legs crossed in front of him, Rupert straightened the fold on the trousers of the suit he'd been given. The assistants he'd also been given continued squabbling on the seats to either side.

Rupert glanced up and met Charlie's eyes in the rear view mirror. There had been something odd about the man's expression this morning. He looked almost proud.

"Any sign of this traffic easing up, driver?" called the young man whose suit was too big for him. Charlie raised his hands off the wheel in response, not bothering to turn.

"Looks like it'll clear in a couple of junctions," said the young woman, panning along the map on her phone.

"What if we're late?"

"Then we'll be late."

"You don't think they'd-"

"What, start without him? How would that work, you dunce? It's rather important that he's there, wouldn't you say?"

"Do you want to run through your speech again?"

It took Rupert a moment to realise the young man was talking to him. He looked slowly around, smiled, and shook his head.

"Your answers for the presser?"

"I'll be quite all right."

The assistants went back to arguing. About what, Rupert didn't know or care. He went back to looking out of the rain spattered window as central London dribbled by.

Given the circumstances he should be as nervous or excited as he'd ever been. This was the day of all days, after all. As it was he felt only a strange detachment, as if it were all happening to somebody else.

One part of his brain told him this lack of joy in a supposedly crowning moment of his life was due entirely to the things he'd done to make it happen. The larger, more cowardly part silenced it. Then insisted he'd been brave, not cowardly, and that it was well known that to make it anywhere in politics you needed to get your hands dirty.

"Mr Granville?"

"Call me Rupert, for goodness' sake."

He had only murmured it, but the young man looked as if he had been slapped across the face. It was going to take time, Rupert realised, to adjust to the weight his words now carried.

"Sorry... Rupert," the young man forced out. "Just wanted to say that we're almost there."

Rupert looked back out of the window and realised he had been lost in his thoughts for some time. They were only a couple of streets away.

"Everything ready?" he asked, and the assistants rushed to assure him it was.

He felt the first flicker of nerves as they turned onto Whitehall and he saw the crowds ahead. Some were cheering. Many more were booing. The fight or flight part of his brain kicked in and told him to make a run for it. That this was a step too far, much too far, and it wasn't too late to back out.

The black gates opened and they drove through a gap in the line of police. People were pressed in close to the metal barriers as they left the road, seemingly several lines deep everywhere Rupert looked and every single one of them staring at him. Then they were pulling up, the door to Number 10 on their right and a mass of photographers and journalists to their left.

The car door was opened by an enormous security guard before Rupert could collect himself. "Smile!" one of the assistants called after him, and Rupert forced the specific smile onto his face that he'd been instructed to use by the PR woman they'd given him. Not jubilant, certainly not given the circumstances, but still positive, reassuring, statesmanlike.

He turned to face the press and saw only a solid wall of flashing lights that made him want to wince or close his eyes completely, but he'd been instructed not to, been told that he must stand there and raise one hand in greeting and turn slowly from side to side so that everybody could get a good shot, with the foolish, fake smile plastered to his face the entire time, as if anybody could truly enjoy this.

And all the while everybody seemed to be bellowing the same two words at him - *"Prime Minister!"*

"Thank you," Rupert read from the autocue. He nodded and used the smile again as the scrupulously crafted speech, of which he had written not one word, drew to a close.

Nobody applauded, as he had been warned they wouldn't.

There were only the flashes again and a few journalists hopefully calling "Prime Minister!", although they knew full well he wouldn't respond.

Rupert raised his hand and turned to make the short walk towards the famous black door, concentrating more than he ever had in his life on simply putting one foot in front of the other. The door was opened for him and he proceeded down a long corridor lined with people there to welcome him with a handshake.

He was led to the office in which he'd met John only a short time before. No personal effects remained, but he was given no time to consider this or get accustomed to the place before a series of important people were brought in for him to meet, each of whom seemed to follow the same pattern of first congratulating him, then quickly introducing their own agenda, before declaring they hoped they could 'count on his support'.

Then he was being taken away and thrown into the lion's den of the Number 10 press briefing room. The cameras flashed again as he ascended the podium. The journalists were still taking their seats, most chatting to each other and paying little mind to him.

Rupert's Press Secretary, with whom he had never exchanged a word, entered the room and gave the journalists a quick rundown of the format to which Rupert, suddenly overcome with all the nerves he should have been feeling earlier, paid no attention. Then somebody was talking to him.

Rupert blinked. "I'm sorry. Could you repeat the question?"

There was scattered laughter and a few of the journalists muttered to each other.

A woman's voice came from somewhere in the first few rows. "Are you excited to be standing here today, Prime Minister?" It was a deliberately easy question, as agreed upon between the Press Secretary and the reporter. Rupert's pre-prepared response immediately deserted him.

"Excited?" he repeated, as he cast around for the nonsense they'd programmed into him. The moment dragged on, and he gave up. Instead he cleared his throat, found the woman, and directed his response straight towards her.

"I'd have preferred to stand here under different circumstances, certainly. But I'm excited by the opportunity I've been given to help the country heal, and to lead it forwards into what I'm positive will be a bright future."

"About those circumstances, Prime Minister," said a man, seated further along the same row as the woman and with a far less friendly tone. "You've been a member of the party since you were at university. You've worked directly for the party for well over a decade now, including with senior figures. Most recently you were a cabinet minister, and an MP. Taking all of that into account, are you seriously asking us to believe you had no idea what was going on behind the scenes all this time? There have been rumours online, in fact, that it was *you*, yourself, who first leaked the story to Michelle Archer."

Rupert adopted the serious expression he had practised in the mirror for several minutes that morning, and changed the tone of his voice.

"Those rumours are utter nonsense. And I'm asking you to believe that I didn't know, because it's the truth," he said. "I'm as appalled by the recent revelations as anybody else. We've all read and heard, over the past few days, about how the recent events have eroded the people's trust in their government, and their financial institutions. It's *my* job, now, to help rebuild that trust, in a transparent and democratic manner, and ensure *nothing* like this happens again."

"Prime Minister." Another man's voice came from several rows further back, near the bright lights which were already starting to cause Rupert a headache. "You talk about democracy, but you obviously haven't been elected as the country's leader. You've only been chosen by your own party members."

"Hardly the first time that's happened."

"Granted, but surely you'd agree there are two differentiating factors this time. Firstly, as you say yourself, the country's trust in this government has just been dealt a massive blow. Shouldn't they be allowed to elect a new one, if they see fit?"

"There are no plans to hold a general election at this time. This party's mandate from the people still has three years to run."

"Secondly," the man continued, as if Rupert hadn't spoken. "There are the questions surrounding *you*, Prime Minister. To put it bluntly, a few months ago nobody in the general public had ever heard of you. First you're suddenly a backbench MP, parachuted in to a safe seat at an unexpected by-election. Then you're a minister. Now you've suddenly got the top job. It's fair to say your family has moved in the upper echelons for generations. You yourself have been photographed at charity fundraisers and other highly exclusive events almost constantly in recent weeks. Wouldn't you agree that this 'rising star' narrative smacks of political manipulation and opportunism at best, and behind-closed-doors cronyism at worst? What deals have been struck here, Prime Minister? Aren't you making a personal mockery of our so-called democracy?"

Rupert forced a smile as he gathered himself. "I have full faith in my abilities to do the job. If I didn't, I'd never have stood for the leadership," Rupert said, repeating the phrase that had been drilled into him for just such a question, although, in the test runs, it hadn't been phrased quite so mercilessly. "A long established democratic process has been followed. The party members have had their say. Three years from now-"

"Oh, come on, Prime Minister. *Surely* you must-"

"Next question," interrupted the Press Secretary. There was general muttering around the room before the first woman spoke again.

"Can you tell us any more about the investigations, Prime Minister?"

"The public inquiry is set to begin imminently," Rupert said. "Its head should be announced tomorrow morning, I believe, and the government will be happy to provide any and all assistance we can. As for the police investigation, you'd have to ask Scotland Yard."

"We've all read the stuff in the papers, Prime Minister," said another woman. "We're the ones who wrote it. The public want to hear *your* version of events. From the horse's mouth, you know."

"We're still gathering the full facts, and await the results of the investigations along with everybody else."

"I'm sorry, Prime Minister," the woman continued, cutting off another question. "But the public demands a proper answer. The people have a right to know, don't they?"

"And they will know, when the investigations have concluded and the information made public." There were sighs around the room and more muttering. Rupert discovered that it was harder than it looked to knowingly spout obfuscating nonsense to a room full of people who knew exactly what you were playing at, not to mention millions more watching at home or online.

"That being said," Rupert continued, and ignored the Press Secretary who looked at him sharply. "I would be happy to give you my own summary of the events, although I'm afraid it won't differ much from what you've already read. Or, in your case... *written*, as you noted." Rupert paused for a ripple of laughter, which was not forthcoming.

"Again, as you've likely read, it appears an international operation, colloquially known as the 'Company', has been behind much of the enormously profitable people trafficking business in Asia, albeit with connections to other parts of the world too, for years now." For the first time in the press conference, there was a rush of flashes from the photographers gathered behind the reporters. "This was led by three prominent figures, none of whom can now be found. Unfortunately…" He paused. "Other parties were also - allegedly - involved in this operation. There are charges of money laundering against at least one major financial institution. Further allegations have been made against dozens of individuals around the world, including a number of well known figures in this country. Obviously, the most high profile, in our case, was the former incumbent of this office."

Rupert placed his hands on the lectern, and leaned forward.

"I might have joined the cabinet only recently. But I can certainly say that, if the allegations are proved to be true, I'm *ashamed* that this could have happened. That our leaders in politics, finance, and business could have been involved in such ghastly dealings with such an evil enterprise. I can *fully* understand why these revelations might have eroded the public's trust.

"But I can *assure* you that that sort of thing stops *now*. The government I lead will be one of transparency, honesty, and directness. We won't earn back the people's confidence overnight, but I firmly believe that we will be able to do so in time. Our goals are not political. They are to do the right thing. Abroad, we will do everything we can to help ensure that the horrendous cycle of people trafficking is well and truly broken, and the misery of millions ended. In this country, we will seek to rebuild, and usher in a new era of fair play, compassion, and morality. I will be at the helm of this endeavour, and both the wider government and myself have three years in which to achieve these goals. We will work around the clock to do so. The British public will then judge whether or not we have succeeded. Either way, I hope only to leave this country a better place than I currently find it. Thank you."

CHAPTER FIFTY TWO

Rupert suffered one of the largest adrenaline crashes he could remember after the press briefing, but he was not given a moment to recover.

From there he was whisked to a meeting with his new closest advisors, most of whom he barely knew, to discuss his imminent cabinet reshuffle. Then he met the larger team at Number 10 who would form the engine which handled the logistics and bureaucracy of top level government. Then there were individual interviews with a handful of the nation's most prominent journalists, then more meetings with donors in his office who he knew very well indeed, interspersed with congratulatory platitudes from world leaders over the phone. And so it went until Rupert looked out of the window during his final meeting of the day and saw that night had fallen.

He made his weary way to the residence on the third floor. A mixture of his belongings from the property in the Chilterns which was currently undergoing a dramatic and costly renovation, and the London house had already been unpacked for him. He had barely sunk into an armchair when there was a knock at the door. He groaned, hauled himself up, and went to open it.

"He's here, Prime Minister."

Rupert looked at the armed woman outside his door in momentary confusion. Then he remembered. "Oh, yes, wonderful. Send him straight up and in. You can stay out here," he said. "If you wouldn't mind," he added.

He returned to the living room and looked around, clueless.

His eyes alighted on a decanter and several tumblers and he poured two glasses of whiskey. He took a sip of his and grimaced at the pleasurable burning in his throat, then heard the door opening and closing and the sound of footsteps.

It was only the second time Rupert had seen Harry since he'd left for Delhi. They had met briefly when Harry returned, first to send the banking representative into hiding with a suitably frightening threat, and finally to take Sarah home.

If anything, Harry looked even worse now than he had then. He stood strangely, in clear discomfort from the obvious multitude of injuries all of which he refused to discuss. The bags under his eyes were visible from across the room, and for once neither the hair on his head nor his face had been tended to.

Rupert felt a sudden rush of emotion. He tried to smile, then to talk. "Harry," he said, and his voice trembled. He gave up and weakly beckoned him over.

Harry limped to the desk, one arm kept stiff beside him, and accepted the whiskey with his other hand. Rupert clinked their glasses and Harry put away the first drink in one gulp. He grimaced, without any hint of the pleasure Rupert had felt.

"Rupert," Harry said at last, his voice somehow strained.

"No need to ask how you are, I suppose."

"You can probably guess."

"It killed me, you know… That I couldn't go to the funerals. If there had been any possible way, without…"

"I understand."

"I trust all the military… procedures, and so forth were… to order? That your father and Mr McGinn were given a proper send off, you know, befitting their-"

"Rupert," Harry said again, bringing the decanter over and refilling both glasses. "Why did you ask me here?"

"Well, I… I wanted to see you. I *had* to see you, after everything that happened."

"It's done now. It's all over."

"Come on, old chap. It can't be that way."

"How would you like it to be? You're the bloody Prime Minister, and I'm…" He trailed off.

"Well… there's how I would like it to be, of course, and then there's what's possible. What I would like is for the world to know what you did. How much pain and suffering your personal actions have saved. What you had to go through, to accomplish it all. What you had to give."

"Breaking God knows how many laws in the process. Which brings us to what's possible."

Rupert opened his mouth, and closed it again. "It all seems so unjust, somehow," he said, lamely.

Harry shrugged, then finished his second glass.

"Fortunately I couldn't care less, so you don't need to do either. I wanted to do something, something I thought was very important, and I did it. With plenty of help along the way, of course."

He poured himself a third glass.

"Was I prepared for the price?"

He stared at the drink.

"No," he said. "Would I have done it all again, if I'd known what it would cost?" He paused again. "That, I don't know," he said quietly. "It's stupid to think like that, anyway. Pointless."

"But natural."

Harry shrugged again. The silence began to stretch. Rupert

found it very hard to look at the man before him.

"I saw your speech."

"Oh, goodness."

"It was good." Harry paused, and half smiled. "I hardly recognised you."

"They say the camera adds ten pounds. That's what I've been telling myself, anyway, whenever I've glimpsed a clip."

Harry looked up suddenly and straight into his eyes. "How much of it was planned, Rupert?"

"How much of what, old chap?"

"You don't just chance into being Prime Minister."

"Well, perhaps you do, sometimes. I'm the living proof."

"I don't care either way. I'd just like to know the truth."

"And you have it. Of course I'd always had idle dreams of the top job, like anybody in politics. But come, my friend. I couldn't have planned it this way if I'd tried. In the end I only saw the slightest opportunity and went for it."

"They're saying there was nobody else left. That the evidence happened, directly or indirectly, to incriminate all the cabinet's top brass."

"Nobody else left," Rupert repeated, forcing a chuckle. "I've had more hearty congratulations today."

Harry stared at him. Rupert tried to meet his gaze, then took a sip of his drink and looked away.

"The timing of Frost's disappearance was interesting."

Rupert looked back at him, too quickly. "Was it?"

Harry turned to rest against Rupert's desk, sighing as the clear struggle to keep himself upright was somewhat relieved. Rupert watched him. "Harry..."

"I'm sure you were careful. And I'm sure you had your reasons. I won't be the one to judge you, God knows. In some strange, perverted way it made me think more highly of you. At least you got your hands dirty."

There was a pause.

"So you knew."

"Of course. Your behaviour changed from one day to the next. And you didn't need to be a genius, to piece that together with what happened at Battersea, when Frost was our unexpected guest."

Rupert turned to rest against the desk as well. "I try desperately not to think about it."

"I know the feeling."

Rupert finished his second glass and placed it on the desk between them. Harry refilled it automatically. Rupert's head was starting to feel a little light, and despite the subject matter he was more relaxed than he had been all day.

"There are perks to the office, you know," he murmured. "The night I won the leadership election, you and the rest of our little team came immediately to mind."

"We're all flattered, I'm sure."

"I'm serious, Harry. I already 'put the feelers out', as you might say, with somebody I trust. A plausible story can be concocted for your brother, for example, should he choose to formalise his resurrection. Captured and kept in captivity, returned in a prisoner swap, that sort of thing. If not, an entirely new identity can be created. I'd be greatly indebted to you if you'd ask him, next time you cross paths."

"I'll be sure to bring it up over the dinner table."

"Regarding Noy, I plan to have a lifetime visa granted for her, if she'd like it. She didn't seem overly impressed with old Blighty, particularly regarding our weather, but still. Should make things easier for her and Daniel, you know, whatever their plans." Rupert reached for the glass and took a longer sip than he should have. "As for you-"

"I don't want anything," Harry said, and Rupert looked at him. "I'm not being ungrateful. It's just the truth. All I want is to be left alone, to be done with all of this sort of thing, to finish with this life. And it seems that might never happen."

"Surely the Company is-"

"Not them. Anna got caught up in something out in Hong Kong. Better you don't know."

"I'd say you're probably right."

Harry looked around the room. "Nice digs. And it looks like you've got them all to yourself."

"I presume that was a veiled query after George?"

"Perhaps."

"He's out," Rupert said, and felt a pathetic burst of pride at how level his voice had sounded. "Our relationship was predicated on trust. That trust had survived for many years, but I'm afraid this whole business stressed it to breaking point."

"You're sure about that?"

"Completely. He's moved his things out of the houses. We've said our tearful goodbyes, and now it's full sail ahead. Albeit on a... solo voyage."

Rupert's voice betrayed him before the final sentence. Harry put a hand on his shoulder.

"I think it's the right choice. For whatever that's worth."

"It's worth more than you could possibly know, old chap. I do wish you'd come along for the ride here. I could get you onto the security team in a heartbeat."

Harry did seem to consider. "Who knows, one day," he said. "But not right now."

He squeezed Rupert's shoulder. "I doubt we'll see each other like this for a very long time. But get in touch, if you need to. I mean it. Leadership can be incredibly lonely, even when you're surrounded by people."

Rupert found that his eyes were suddenly watering, and hurriedly turned away. "I wanted to thank you, you know," he said, facing now towards a door in the side of the room he hadn't even noticed before. "Perhaps that's the real reason I asked you here."

"For what? You've had nothing but trouble since I turned up on your doorstep that day."

"And yet I wouldn't have changed a thing. What I want to thank you for, Harry, is giving me the opportunity to make a difference. A true difference. It's something that the political system makes deliberately difficult, you know. Even the smallest change requires endless hours of planning and negotiation and compromise. There's good reason for that, of course, but still. Despite all the hardships, it's been incredibly, enormously rewarding to help genuinely achieve something, in my own small way. To achieve something meaningful. I might have gone my whole life without doing so, if you hadn't turned up on that doorstep."

"Well, we couldn't have done it without you. Not just the financial backing, but your contacts, your accommodation. And your bravery, Rupert. You were braver than I'd have ever thought, the first couple of times I saw you. Although of course that wasn't the real you."

"And which is the real me? Sometimes I lose track myself."

"This one."

"You sound so very sure."

"I've known you long enough. I can see through the acts."

Harry finished his whiskey. There was some colour in his cheeks now and he didn't hold himself so rigidly. "I should go. You can't get drunk your first night on the job."

"I suppose you're right, though I wish you weren't."

They both stood, and Rupert followed Harry in silence along the carpeted corridor and to the door. Harry stopped there, turned, and cleared his throat.

"Well-" was all he managed before Rupert stepped forward and hugged him hard. Harry tried to put one arm around him before grunting with pain and pulling back a little. "Ow," he said. "You know I got shot, don't you? A number of times."

"Sorry, old chap. You did keep all of that to yourself."

"I thought it was obvious."

"This is it, then? For a while, at least."

"Yes."

Rupert wrung his hands in front of him. "You've become a true friend, you know. The… the only one I have."

Harry looked at him, and Rupert was unsure if he'd heard.

"What is it?"

"I was remembering again when we first met, in Canary Wharf. Then again when I came to Bloomsbury, and we truly first met. They both seem so long ago now." Harry shook his head. "It's been a hell of a time."

"And we've achieved so very much."

Harry nodded, his eyes still not focused. Then he looked at Rupert, and smiled.

"What now?"

"Don't take this the wrong way, Rupert. But I'm shocked that I've come to like you."

Harry put his good arm around Rupert, and Rupert hugged him back as softly as he could. They stayed that way for several moments, Rupert with his eyes closed and his chin on Harry's shoulder.

Harry pulled away and opened the door. The security guard turned immediately, saw them both, and stepped aside.

"Goodbye, Rupert," Harry said, and limped away with the guard following a short distance behind.

Rupert leaned against the doorframe and watched him go, and suddenly felt completely and utterly alone.

CHAPTER FIFTY THREE

Great Britain sits separate from Europe, close to the continent but alone in its own dark blue seas.

Seen from space, the main island is a green but bizarrely shaped stretch of land, with smaller islands dotted around it at random and a larger, more aesthetic one off its western flank.

Middle England is comparatively unremarkable, lacking the dramatic coastlines or the beaches, the mountains or lakes which usually distinguish the British landscape. It is a breadth of relatively flat greenery, albeit rich in rolling hills and market towns.

Shropshire sits in the western part of middle England against the invisible border with Wales. It is a quiet county, with no cities and only a couple of larger towns. Lying somewhere in the middle of the county is a mid-sized village, with a church, a high street, and a couple of thousand inhabitants. It is an in-between place, the main road through it used mostly to get from one of the larger towns to the other.

Branching off from that main road and quite close to the church is a smaller street called Manor Close. This road turns a couple of times before ending at the gate to a large field. On the right side of the road, near to the field, is house number twenty.

It was an unusually warm winter's day, and from above several people could be seen in the garden of number twenty. Another was running up the street towards the house, his form unsteady and irregular. He slowed as he approached it, then stopped outside and lingered there with one hand wrapped across his chest. He started jogging again, along the street to the end, then finally returned, went up the drive this time, and opened the door.

Harry paused and listened just inside the hallway. Hearing only the faint voices from the garden, he closed the door as quietly as he could and went to ascend the staircase.

Then he stopped with his foot on the first step, closed his eyes, let out a long breath, and shook his head. He went instead down the hallway, through the kitchen, and out into the garden.

His mother sat at the table with Maria, Tasha's great-grandmother, opposite her. Tasha herself was dribbling a football towards Noy, with Daniel standing in front of a small, red, metal framed goal. Despite not being used in some two decades, the goal had never been thrown away, and someone had retrieved it from the shed at the end of the garden while Harry was out. Tasha went past Noy and hit the ball. The shot dribbled towards the goal. Daniel kicked it easily away, and Noy let forth a torrent of angry Thai.

Harry's mother had been talking to Maria when Harry came outside. The two women were roughly the same age, and both sat under blankets. Sarah looked up now, and smiled. "Good run?" she asked. "It's very pleasant out today, isn't it?"

Harry had been watching Tasha. "What?" he said.

"Your run, dear. I *had* suggested it mightn't be the wisest idea, after being shot multiple times, but you insisted."

"It was fine," he lied.

"Are you joining us?"

He glanced at Tasha again, then at Maria who watched him. "I'll just shower and change," he said, and went inside slowly to show that he wasn't running away.

Harry stayed in the shower at least ten minutes then shaved slowly, having to stop several times. He stared at his ruined torso in the mirror. The wet bandages and the old scars. Then he returned to his old bedroom and put on a pair of jeans, a faded t-shirt, and a hooded sweatshirt, all of which he'd had since at least his early twenties. He went towards his door, stopped, turned back, sat on the edge of the bed, and put his head in his hands.

The door opened and footsteps crossed the floor. He felt her hand on his shoulder.

"You really are pathetic."

"Charming, as ever."

"We barely knew each other. It was only, what, a couple of months."

"You know it's not the length of time. It's what happens during that time. You weren't with Tasha's father that long. Not properly."

"And I never got over it."

"That's reassuring."

"But I did move on. So will you."

"I don't want to."

"Don't be a baby. It's not about what *you* want any more. You've made a commitment, haven't you? Even if you haven't told anybody yet. You want to look after her, and that'll be pretty tricky if you're moping around for weeks or months on end."

"It's impressive that you're still able to bully me, even now."

"Well, that's your choice really, isn't it? And anyway, I always knew that you could take it. You're a big, tough boy."

Harry shook his head in his hands, wiping the tears from side to side across his face. "I don't want that any more. I don't want to be tough. I can't. I've lost too much. I feel… broken. Like one more blow would completely destroy me, if I'm not destroyed already."

"It's not a choice, Captain. You just *are* tough. That's how you've achieved what you have. Leave aside all the military stuff, if you like, but you can't discard what you've done here. There *will* be more blows, you know there will, but you'll get through those too. Not only because you're strong, but because you don't have a choice any more. That's the terrifying and wonderful thing about being responsible for a child. You *have* to be strong, always, for them. Whether you want to be or you don't. Whether you think you can or not."

"Sounds liberating, in a way."

"You know it is. You've had plenty of responsibility in your time. You know how freeing it can be to put the lives of others before your own."

"Exhausting, too."

"You should be used to that by now. And you wouldn't have it any other way, if you're honest with yourself."

"Aren't I being, right now?"

There was silence, but Harry still felt the hand on his shoulder. Truly, he felt it.

"Noy told me what you did," he said. "With the bike. Then on the boat."

"All the result of too much time spent around you. I used to be far more sensible."

"She said you were incredible. Even Daniel said it. They said it was all you. That none of it would have been possible without you."

"People are always so very nice after something like this happens. Not that I'm disputing a word of it." She paused. "I'm sorry, though, to have stuck you with the situation in Hong Kong."

"I wouldn't know what to do with myself, without some criminal forcing me into violence for the lives of my loved ones."

"Really, I'm sorry. Perhaps afterwards-"

Harry smiled. "I'll have a quiet life?"

"Is that what you want?"

He paused. "I don't know. But I'd like there to be less death."

"I'll have a word with the man upstairs. See what he can do for a good looking, conflicted young man whose heart's in the right place after all. I won't mention all the killing, don't worry."

Harry heard the bottom stair creaking and knew immediately by the weight of the tread and the interval between that one and the next that it was his mother.

"Don't leave," he said.

"I won't go far. I'll be lingering to irritate and insult you for as long as you'll allow, Captain."

Harry smiled, and the hand left his shoulder as the knock came at the door. His mother waited a couple of moments for any protests, as she always had, then entered.

Harry still sat with his face in his hands, but heard his mother cross the carpeted floor and felt her sit down on the bed beside him. Gently she pulled his hands away, then she reached up and wiped his eyes with her sleeves.

"Two men were here," she said. "I don't recall their names, but I know they were at your friend McGinn's funeral. I invited them inside to wait, but one of them said *'We'll find him'* in that typically serious, extremely silly army tone. Then the other one gave me a wink, which was a little strange."

"Davies and Cooper respectively," Harry said. "They caught up with me."

"What did they say?" his mother asked. "You can tell me honestly. I'd rather not be left in the dark about these things any more."

"That they would always be there if I needed them."

"And will you?"

"I hope not. But it's good to know, and I believe them. And it's good…" Harry broke off and smiled, not meeting her eyes. "God, I feel… I don't even know…"

"Take a breath. Okay. Now tell me."

"I don't know how you see me any more. One moment I'm giving orders, charging headlong into danger, fighting and shooting and all the rest of it. The next we're sitting on my bed with me in tears. As if twenty years never passed."

His mother put his hands in her lap and ran the palm of one of her hands over the scars there. "Don't overthink it. Just tell me how you feel."

"It's nice to know that I still have friends, I suppose. Wherever they might be in the world, and whether they're prime ministers, mercenaries, or whatever else. I wish that I'd kept in touch with them all. We went through so much together. McGinn…" Harry shook his head. "He was the best friend I ever had. And I just threw away three years of that friendship, as if he and both of us would live forever. And I'll never get that time back."

"I won't tell you you're wrong, Harry, because Lord knows I've felt the same in my life. But all that matters now is that you learn from it, and you carry that forward into all the other relationships you have. Which you will, because you're a smart boy and you've got a good heart. Despite... well, everything."

Harry nodded, then raised his eyes to her face. She looked old, suddenly. He swallowed.

"What about you, Mum?" he said. "I've been so wrapped up in everything that I haven't asked how you are."

"Nobody ever asks how the mother is," she said wistfully, turning her eyes to the heavens before looking back at him with a smile. "I'm not sure, truth be told. Losing your father was such a blow... and yet there was so much going on at the time, and ever since of course, that..." She tapped a finger on his hand. "This sounds so very callous, and you must understand that I miss him dearly. I haven't slept more than an hour or two each night since it happened. I miss him... quite terribly."

Sarah stopped and quelled the tremble in her voice with a deep breath. Then the words began to tumble out in a way Harry had never heard before.

"But it feels as if we missed the window to grieve. And now he's just... gone. The shock of it has worn off, and now there's only that gaping hole. Which will never go away, I'm quite sure... But the time for being the weeping widow has passed. And whenever I do start to trend in that direction, I tell myself... I *know*, I mean, that being the person he was, with all the damned military breeding, if he'd been offered the choice to die as some part of a cause like this, he'd have done it, the fool. And although I'm far from being an expert in these matters, nor do I want to be, it seems to me that what happened that night may have set you on the path which led to everything that happened recently. Which, however I might feel about the details, is quite obviously the single most impactful thing that I or anybody else here has ever been a part of." She looked at him. "Does that make sense?"

Harry placed one of his hands over both of hers, and smiled. "Of course it does. And it's a good way to think, I suppose. I've struggled to do anything but wallow in the misery of it all since it happened."

"But you really can't, Harry. It's really *very* important that you don't," his mother said, her expression changing. "I've been watching the news, almost non-stop. I know you don't want to see it or hear about it, so I've been quite covert about the whole thing. Only watching it downstairs when you've been out on one of your very long walks, or in my room when you're in the house. But the things they've uncovered in that data... The scale of the entire operation those three evil people were running..." She shook her head. "A part of me feels conflicted. The way you went about it flies in the face of everything I thought I believed in, especially when I was young. I feel almost as if I've lived three lives, you know. There was the idealistic, pacifistic girl. When she accidentally fell in love with a soldier, she was thrown into several decades of almost constant struggle and confusion, theoretically clinging to her beliefs but helping to raise a military family regardless."

"And now?"

"And now," she repeated, and shook her head again. "I hated violence when I was young, so very much. I found the thought of killing for any cause abhorrent. Redundant, perhaps, since we should surely have evolved beyond such barbarity by now. But having read all these figures about the number of poor people involved. Having read all the stories that are coming in now, from all the people they've freed from the camps and the ones they've tracked down who had already been sold, and the slaves they were using for themselves. Not to mention the fact that our own bankers, politicians, and God knows who else have been complicit in the whole thing. Benefiting from it." She had been staring at her hands under his, but now met his eyes. "I hope I'm not exaggerating embarrassingly. I don't think I am. But whatever you did to make all of that happen, I'd struggle to think of many more instances of such a small group, helping to improve or outright save the lives of so very many people, with so comparatively little blood spilled. And if this really does mark the beginning of the end for trafficking around the world, at least on this sort of scale... Which they're saying it might, you know, since the data shows precisely how it's done and who's likely to be involved. Then Harry..." She squeezed his hand. "I honestly can't say that I particularly care how you did it. The important thing is that you *did* do it. This incredible, miraculous thing. And I'm so very, very proud of you."

Halfway through her speech Harry had already found himself unable to look at his mother any longer. At her final words he turned away completely so that she wouldn't see his face. Any brittle walls he might have built over the past fortnight now felt as if they could crumble completely.

Then the walls finally did fall, and he put his head in his hands and his shoulders rose and fell as he was racked by silent sobs that felt as if they might never stop. He felt his mother put her arm around him and squeeze but she didn't say anything, didn't try to comfort him or help him to stop, only hugged him and put her head on his shoulder and gave him all the time he needed for the emotion that had built and built to pour out now, through him and out of him until gradually, at last, the sobs slowed of their own accord, then stopped. And then, knowing that he didn't want to feel any more of a child in that moment, she went away and gave him time to compose himself before coming back with a packet of tissues and putting them in his hand, not looking while he cleaned his face. When he was done she put her arm back around his shoulder and waited until he was ready.

"I-" Harry began. He cleared his throat, then tried again. "I know that you're right. I know what we all achieved. I know it objectively. It's just... very hard to feel that way when you were the person, or people, who actually did the thing. Who made the sacrifices. I can read about the hundreds of people being brought to justice. The thousands of people freed. All the others who hopefully won't have to go through all that in the future. But I don't *know* those people. These are amazing, wonderful statistics, but they're only statistics. I *knew* McGinn. I *knew* Dad. I *knew*..."

He put a tissue to his eyes and laughed quietly. "It's so strange... I shouldn't... But then you were honest with me before, I suppose. It's so strange, that she's the one I miss the most. The one I can't stop thinking about. Really, I can't stop replaying all these memories over and over in my head. Even imagining that we're still together now. I knew McGinn for years, well over a decade. Dad was... he was my Dad. I loved him. I only knew her a couple of months..."

"It's because she was the future," his mother said. "Of course she was smart, and charismatic, and beautiful, and strong. But your father and your friend were a part of your past. If you felt the way about her which I believe you did, then you intended her to be a large part of your future."

"All of it," Harry said. "I can't tell you what a difference she made, Mum. You saw how I was after Daniel's funeral, and I didn't change at all for the three years after. Right up until I met her. She pulled me out of it all. She made me..."

"She made you happy again."

Harry nodded, and put his head onto his mother's chest. She ran a hand over his hair.

They stayed that way for some time, neither showing any inclination at all to move. Finally, Harry's mother cleared her throat. "I've seen how you look at Tasha, you know. With fear. Or apprehension, perhaps. As a responsibility, but one you're scared to accept."

"Nothing ever did get past you."

"So you're going to take care of her?"

"If Maria agrees."

"From the hints she's dropped, I don't believe you created the best first impression."

"That's for sure."

"But you were discussed regularly in the Cavill household thereafter. Anna tried very hard to bring Maria round, and was already succeeding before all of this. Now it seems you have quite an admirer, and rightly so."

She put a hand under Harry's chin, and lifted his head to meet his eyes. "But you won't be doing it alone, you know. I want both of them here, in this house. Maria doesn't want to stay in that apartment in London, after everything that's happened, and I've already made enquiries at your old school for Tasha."

"You have been busy."

"Oh, yes. I want Daniel and Noy to come back as often as they can, too. And the same goes for you." His mother stroked his freshly shaved face. "I've had enough of this only being a house, full of memories and nothing else. I want it to be a home again."

"I think it's an excellent idea."

"In that case, you'll need to be a big boy and have a chat with that little girl out in the garden." Harry smiled, nodded, and began to stand up. "And one more thing," his mother said, making him pause. "You'll need to learn to say her name again."

"Tasha?"

"Not that one."

Maria's face had been dark, her eyes staring far into some unseen middle distance. She smiled when Harry's mother put a hand on her shoulder, before resuming her seat and starting a quiet conversation which had Maria laughing within moments. Harry watched his mother with something like a newfound awe, seeing her at last, for the first time, for who she really was. Then he looked around at Tasha's giggling.

Harry had heard Noy crying in the bathroom or Daniel's old bedroom several times over the past fortnight. Now she had been to the shed again and returned with two rusted, cheap badminton rackets and a shuttlecock, which - smiling and laughing - she was inexpertly teaching Tasha to use.

Harry took a deep breath and started to walk over towards them. Out of the corner of his eye he saw Daniel, who must have been lingering by the side of the house, approach. Harry stopped and Daniel stood still in front of him staring at the grass.

"Do you have a moment?"

"Actually I'm swept off my feet."

"Oh."

"I'm joking. Jesus, I swear you used to have a sense of humour. It must still be buried in there somewhere. How's it going?"

"Fine," Daniel said. "Under the circumstances. I, you know…" His mouth opened and closed a couple of times. He sighed, then lifted his scarred face to the sky. "I miss Dad. Quite a lot. It's strange. I didn't see him for so many years, but now that he's gone…"

"I know exactly what you mean."

"Really?"

"Of course I do, Daniel. That's precisely how I feel."

Looking down, Daniel met his eyes for a moment. Then he looked at the grass again. "I was talking with Noy, last night," he said, slowly and delicately. "About Dad. I mentioned that I'd never told him that I loved him. Not since I was a child."

"I definitely didn't tell him enough, if that's any-"

"No," Daniel interrupted. "Please. You don't need to do that."

"Do what?"

"You don't need to comfort me. I only mention it because... You know... I realised that I never..."

"Daniel," Harry said, smiling and reaching up to put a hand on his brother's shoulder. "I love you."

"Do you?" Daniel said.

"Of course I do. There's a lot of things I want to do differently now. But being a good brother is right at the top of the list. We lost years together, and God knows we've been through some stuff. But we're still brothers, and I love you."

"I've done terrible things, you know. Really terrible things. I know that there was context to them. But I still did them. And now I can't sleep. I just lie there and think about them all. I think about the... the families. This one woman, back in Thailand. I had her husband killed, then I shot her myself. In cold blood, right there on the beach. And now her son will never..." Daniel squeezed his fists at his sides. His eyes were closed. "If I could take it all back now-"

"You can't," Harry said, his mother's words ringing in his ears. "You can only carry those lessons forward. I'd wager that the good you've done recently already vastly outweighs the bad."

"No," Daniel said. "We're going to carry on. Noy and I, I mean."

"How?"

"However we can. The Company might have been destroyed, but the Organisation is still just about alive. Once we've dealt with that... Noy says there will always be something we can do. And that that's a good thing."

"In this case, I suppose it is." Harry looked over as Tasha shouted with laughter again. "If you'll excuse me, I've got one of the most embarrassingly terrifying encounters of my life to attend to."

He was already starting to walk away when Daniel put a hand on his arm. "I love you too," he said, very quietly. "And Noy and I will come back. We both want to be a part of... you know."

"Actually, I don't know," Harry said, with a smile. "This is about to become one of the strangest families ever assembled. But being a part of it is definitely going to be interesting."

Harry clapped Daniel on the shoulder, then continued across the lawn. Noy saw him coming, said something to Tasha, and began walking towards him.

"He finally tell you?" she asked, pausing and frowning up at him.

"He did indeed. Thanks for making him."

"You're welcome."

"Noy."

"Hmm?"

"I'm so sorry about your family."

Noy's frown deepened. Then her eyebrows raised suddenly, and she looked quickly away and ran a hand across her face. "They always say that revenge doesn't bring people back. This is true. But I must say, it still feel really, really good. I'm proud of myself. Not only for that. For everything, you know? I never thought someone like me could do something like this."

Noy smiled at Harry, briefly and for the first time he could remember. Then she carried on towards the house.

Now only Tasha was left. She stood alone, wrapped up in a large, thick coat and trying to bounce the shuttlecock up and down on her racket.

"Want to play?" Tasha said, glancing over without suspicion or surprise as Harry approached despite the two of them never having had a conversation. Harry noted again the odd, fascinating inflection of her voice, caught somewhere between native English and her great-grandmother's eastern European accent.

"Sure, of course. But… in a moment," Harry said. He came to a halt in front of her, suddenly realising that he couldn't ever remember speaking as an adult to a child. He looked away so that Tasha couldn't see him, rolled his eyes at his own absurd terror, and turned back to her. He sank down to one knee in the grass so that their faces were level, and smiled at her.

"Can we have a little chat?"

"Okay."

"Do you know who I am?"

"Harry."

"Apart from that."

"You were mummy's friend."

"Yes. I definitely was. But… more than that."

"She loved you."

"Do you think so?"

"*Nooo*," Tasha said, turning back and forth and hugging the racket to her. "I *know* she did."

"Do you? How?"

"She told Nana. After all that crazy stuff in London."

The image of Tasha and Maria in the back of a ruined car, terrified for their lives and all of it partly his doing, flashed through Harry's mind. "That was a very, very bad night."

"It was scary," Tasha said, matter-of-factly. "But afterwards I heard Mum talking to Nana. And Nana had been really scared, obviously, and she wanted to know what happened, like why those men came to our flat and made us go with them. And Mum mentioned someone called Harry, that's you, but I think she did it by accident. Because then Nana asked who Harry was, and Mum had to explain, and then they had a big argument about that. They were speaking Ukrainian, I don't really understand it still, but Mum started crying and said that she loved this man called Harry. Really, really loved him, more than anybody in the world except me and Nana. More than anybody else since my Dad died, and that was *years* ago, before I was even born. Now I'm six. Why are you crying?"

"I'm not."

"Yes you are."

"Fine, I am, but it's not because I'm sad. Not only because of that, I mean."

"Nana says grown ups cry for lots of reasons. I think that's weird."

"It is weird, but she's right. Listen, Tasha. Could I hold your hand for a moment, please?"

"Okay."

Harry felt a foolish, momentary wonder at how small the girl's hand looked in his, and how beautifully smooth and free of injury and history it also looked in comparison. He made himself look up again and meet the girl's eye.

"Do you understand what happened to your Mum?"

"Not really. Nana just said she passed away, kind of went to sleep like people do in movies sometimes. I felt… I don't really understand…"

"That's okay," Harry said, squeezing Tasha's hand as softly as he could as he saw the girl's eyes starting to well. "You will know exactly what happened one day. I'll make sure of it. But you don't need to yet. All you need to know right now is that your mother was the bravest, strongest woman in the world."

"Really?"

"One hundred percent. Have you seen that big story on the news, about all the bad people getting caught and maybe going to prison?"

"Kind of."

"Well, that was your Mum. She changed the world. She… passed away so that she could save a lot of other people. She, ah…" Harry broke off, and swallowed. "She was a superhero, a heroine, like in the movies you watch, only she was real."

Whether because of his words or simply because of his tears, Tasha had begun to cry too. But she made no sound, only squeezed his hand tightly.

"I loved your Mum too, Tasha. Very, *very* much. She saved my life as well. We were planning to be together after we'd finished the work we were doing. Now it can't be…" Harry felt another lump in his throat, and coughed. "It can't be how we planned. But if it's okay with you, I'd really like to be around. To be your friend, I mean, but… I know I'm not your real Dad, but to look after you too. To be there for you, and just, you know… to help…"

Tasha came forward and hugged him, her arms barely extending halfway around his midriff. Harry felt the walls tumbling again and a sudden rush of emotion in his chest and closed his eyes as he put his arms around the girl and drew her to him.

Tasha used his sweatshirt to wipe her face hurriedly as she pulled away, and Harry laughed.

Then the sunlight caught her in a certain way, and suddenly all of the guilt and the regret and the self-castigation which had filled and dominated him, not only for the past fortnight but for all the years before, went away at once.

Perhaps it was all only for a moment, but Harry didn't care. Because he finally, truly, saw a path to the future. To happiness. To peace.

"What is it?" Tasha asked.

"Nothing," Harry said. "Only that you look so very much like Anna."

The End

ABOUT THE AUTHOR

Joe Halliday

Joe Halliday has ghost-written five acclaimed novels, and several novellas. He holds a Masters degree in Creative Writing, is a prolific writer of both fiction and non-fiction, and is a full-time professional copywriter. He is also an obsessive reader in a wide range of genres. Joe currently splits his time between the UK and Spain.

Find out more, and read Joe's latest writing for free, on JoeHalliday.com.

Printed in Great Britain
by Amazon